MAJ...
ROMANCE FICTION ROYALTY,
NEW YORK TIMES **BESTSELLING AUTHOR**

CHRISTINA DODD

"A MASTER ROMANTIC STORYTELLER."
Kristin Hannah

"SHE'S ONE OF MY ALL-TIME FAVORITES."
Teresa Medeiros

"TREAT YOURSELF TO A FABULOUS BOOK—
ANYTHING BY CHRISTINA DODD."
Jill Barnett

"DODD TRANSPORTS READERS INTO
ANOTHER ENTICING PLACE AND TIME."
Publishers Weekly

"CLASSICS NEVER GO OUT OF STYLE.
A LITTLE BLACK DRESS, A STRING OF PEARLS,
AND A CHRISTINA DODD ROMANCE."
Lisa Kleypas

By Christina Dodd

CHRISTINA DODD

The Barefoot Princess

AVON BOOKS
An Imprint of HarperCollinsPublishers

AVON BOOKS
An Imprint of HarperCollins*Publishers*
10 East 53rd Street
New York, New York 10022-5299

Copyright © 2006 by Christina Dodd
ISBN-13: 978-0-06-056117-8
ISBN-10: 0-06-056117-3
www.avonromance.com

First Avon Books paperback printing: February 2006

Avon Trademark Reg. U.S. Pat. Off. and in Other Countries, Marca Registrada, Hecho en U.S.A.
HarperCollins® is a registered trademark of HarperCollins Publishers Inc.

Printed in the U.S.A.

10 9 8 7 6 5 4

Prologue

*O*nce upon a time, in the small kingdom of Beaumontagne, there lived a young princess who decided that when she grew up, she would battle
dragons. Her two older sisters told her that only
princes battled dragons, but Princess Amy refused to
listen to the naysayers. She wasn't a girl like the others.
She loved to run and shout, to pretend a stick was a
sword and fight the suits of armor that lined the broad
marble corridors, to climb the aged oaks and tear her
silk skirts.

Unfortunately, the only dragon that presented itself
to Amy was her grandmother, a formidable old woman
with strong opinions on how a princess should behave.
Despite frequent attempts to vanquish Grandmamma,

Amy always found herself behaving as she ought . . . or being carried away, kicking and screaming, over a stolid footman's shoulder while her sisters wept and her father, the king, looked on and worried.

Amy hated her grandmamma the dragon and at night in her ruffled bed, she prayed that Grandmamma would die. Amy knew she was wicked, but she didn't care. She hated Grandmamma. Hated her, hated her, hated her.

Then one day Poppa sent the little princesses away. Gone were the fluttering flags to carry as Amy marched, gone were the long banisters that tempted a princess to slide, gone were the ponies and the nannies and the games. Amy knew it wasn't really Poppa who sent them away. It must be wicked old Grandmamma who was to blame, and blame her she did, for Grandmamma sent them to cold, dreary England—for their safety, she said. She separated Crown Princess Sorcha from Amy and her sister Clarice. She made Clarice and Amy stay at a boarding school where no one really cared if Amy fought dragons or behaved like a princess.

Then the news came, the most horrible news in the whole world. Poppa was dead, killed in the war, and Amy realized she was to blame. Somehow her wicked wish had skipped Grandmamma and taken Poppa's life. Somehow Amy had to make things right.

That was the year Amy was nine. That was the year she stopped pretending to battle dragons, and began to fight them for real.

Chapter 1

*I*f Jermyn Edmondson, the marquess of Northcliff, had known he was about to be kidnapped, he wouldn't have gone out on a walk.

Or maybe he would have. He needed some excitement in his life.

He stared fiercely toward the gray bank of fog creeping across the cresting green ocean and covering the isle of Summerwind. Far beneath his feet, the waves crashed in foamy malice against the rocks at the base of the cliff. The wind combed his hair and lifted his unbuttoned greatcoat like the wings of a black seabird. The salt stung his nostrils, and a faint beading of spray misted his face. Everything here in this corner of Devon was wild, fresh, and free—except for him.

He was bound here. And he was bored.

With disgust, he turned away from the vista with its constant, tedious, battering waves and limped toward the garden where spring crocuses had begun to poke their greenery up through the barren soil.

Yet he took no pleasure in the small glimpses of gold and purple that shown through winter's dull, brown blanket. His estate contained nothing to entertain a man of his interests. Only country balls enlivened the nights, peopled with bluff squires, giggling debutantes, and sly mamas on the hunt for a title for their daughters.

True, he had determined that the time had come for him to wed—indeed, he'd demanded Uncle Harrison submit a list of the current crop of debutantes and suggest a proper bride—but he would not take as his life's mate a girl who considered a hearty walk along a bucolic lane as entertainment.

So unless one could ride or sail—and the carriage accident two months ago he'd suffered had curtailed his activities sharply—the days were interminable, stretching endlessly, quietly, filled with long walks in the fresh air. And reading.

He glanced down at the book in his hand. My God, he was so sick of reading. It wasn't as if the London papers arrived with any regularity. He'd even begun to read in Latin, and he hadn't done that for thirteen years. Not since his father had died. Not since he'd left this place forever.

How he wished he'd stayed away!

It was pride that sent him dashing away from London. He hated being an invalid, and he hated more being the center of cloying attention as he recovered. When Uncle Harrison suggested Summerwind Abbey as a retreat, he had considered the idea had merit.

He knew better, now.

In the gazebo, he seated himself on a cane chair and rubbed his wretched thigh. He'd suffered a bad break in the accident, and that country physician he'd called to attend him two nights ago had told him, in his ignorant Devon accent, "The best medicine is time and exercise. Walk until yer leg is tired, but don't ye overdo! Walk where 'tis safe and flat. If ye slip and wrench that newly-mended bone, ye'll do yerself permanent harm."

Jermyn had dismissed the man with a snarl. It hadn't helped that, only the previous day, he'd taken the steep and winding path down the cliffs toward the beach—and fallen because of the weakness in his leg. He had scarcely been able to drag himself back up to the manor. It was that pain which had made him send for the doctor in the first place, and he was not appeased to hear he should stroll on his veranda like a dowager or a child.

Opening his book, he allowed himself to sink into the tale of *Tom Jones*, a tale told when England was green and warm, and youth was a joy to be savored.

The rollicking adventures penned by Fielding captured him against his will, and Jermyn started when someone said, "M'lord?"

A maidservant stood at the entrance, holding a glass on a tray, and at his consenting nod, she approached, the tray outstretched.

He noted three things. He'd never seen her before. Her blue gown was shabby and the silver cross around her neck was exceptionally fine. And she stared into his eyes without deference as she thrust the drink toward him.

He didn't immediately take it. Instead he noted the girl's fine-grained skin, so different from the tanned complexions of the local milkmaids. Her eyes were an unusual shade of green, like the sea thrashing under the influence of an oncoming storm. Her hair was black, upswept, and curled tendrils escaped from the ribbon that bound them. He'd wager she was not yet twenty, and pretty, so pretty he was surprised no farmer about had claimed her as his bride. Yet her expression was severe, almost austere.

Perhaps that explained her single state.

Without being given permission, she spoke. "M'lord, you must drink. I brought it all the way out here to you!"

Half annoyed, half amused, he said, "I didn't command it be brought."

"It's wine," she said.

She was a plucky wench, without the manners imbued in the least of his servants. Yet she was new. Perhaps she feared trouble if he didn't take the offering sent by the butler. "Very well. I'll accept it." Lifting the glass, he paused while she still stared, waiting anxiously for him to take a sip. In a crushing tone, he added, "That will be all."

She jumped as if startled by his presence, as if she had forgotten he was a real, living lord to be feared and obeyed. She cast him a glance, dropped a graceful curtsy, and backed away, her gaze still on the glass.

He cleared his throat.

She looked into his face, and in her eyes he thought he glimpsed a flash of bitter resentment.

Then, with a toss of her head, she hurried across the garden.

Interestingly enough, she didn't walk toward the manor, but toward the shore, and she moved with the confident stride of a lady who commanded all around her. Jermyn would have to speak to the butler about her. She needed to be taught to promptly return to her duties . . . and to treat her master with the respect due him.

When she was out of sight, he took a long drink, then sputtered at the flavor. Lifting the glass, he stared at the ruby color. The wine was bitter! How long had this been in his cellar?

Obviously the butler had grown lax in Jermyn's absence, hiring impertinent maids and serving inferior wines. Resolving to speak to him, Jermyn went back to his book.

And blinked at the words. The page was growing dim.

He looked up and blinked again. Ah, yes. The sun was setting and fog was encroaching on the land, bringing with it the gloom that seemed to brood endlessly over a Devon winter.

How odd that his boyhood memories of this place were so different. He remembered long days of sunshine, filled with walks accompanied by his father or romps with visiting friends. He remembered wild storms filled with the excitement of howling winds and crashing waves. He remembered the scent of spring flowers and the crushed grass beneath him as he rolled down the hill.

He shook his head. Such memories were evidently the fond recollections of a boyhood long vanished.

The bitter wine had stimulated his thirst, and reluctantly he took another swallow. The texture was almost gritty, the flavor foul, and with disgust he tossed the remnants into the rhododendrons around the gazebo.

He found himself sweating. Had a wave of heat struck the garden, like a sudden, early spring? Digging his handkerchief out of his pocket, he blotted his face, then shed his greatcoat in a graceless act that left it bunched beneath him on the chair.

Looking back at the open book, he discovered the letters moving erratically. The light was going faster than he had realized, or the words wouldn't behave so badly.

He tried to slap the book shut. The book flipped out of his suddenly clumsy fingers. His tongue grew large in his mouth. He lifted his head so he could stare across the garden, but the motion took a long time. The fog was creeping up from the ground, blurring his vision.

Or was it wine that made everything fuzzy?

The wine . . .

A startling conviction struck him. He staggered to his feet and stood swaying. *The wine had been poisoned.*

He was dying.

When his carriage had lost its wheel and he'd careened off the road between London and Brighton, he had thought he was going to die. But this . . . this was more insidious, more . . .

The floor wavered and rose defiantly beneath his feet. He toppled over, landing with a crash that reverberated the boards and made him distantly aware of the impact on his injured leg. "Help," he tried to shout. He heard people calling, running . . .

Aid was on its way.

High above him, a man's Devon-accented voice proclaimed, "It worked, Miss Rosabel. Worked fine."

Jermyn pried open his eyes. A huge pair of battered boots stood planted in front of his nose. With a mighty effort, he turned his head and looked past the thighs, past the belt, and far, far up toward the blunt, heavy face. A behemoth stood over him, a rough man with huge hands and a grim expression.

This wasn't help. This was danger.

What did the giant want?

Then Jermyn saw the girl standing beside the huge man. A pretty girl. A girl with a direct green gaze that seemed to scorch him down to his soul. She wore a blue, tattered gown. He'd seen her once before.

"He's looking at us," the giant's voice rumbled. "Why isn't he knocked fer kindlin'?"

"He probably didn't drink it all," the girl answered. "That's all right. He'll do as is. Wrap him up. Let's finish this before someone comes to check on him."

She was the servant who had brought him the drink. She had tricked him. She had poisoned him.

She pulled out a knife with a blade so bright and sharp he could see nothing but the point.

She was going to kill him . . .

Jermyn wanted to fight, but he couldn't lift his heavy

limbs. He tried to curse, but his mouth would not speak.

Taking a sheet of white paper from her bosom, she placed it on the table beside his book and affixed it to the flat surface with a swift, downward slash.

The giant shook out a white canvas shroud.

These people, these murderers were speaking, yet Jermyn could no longer pluck words from the gibberish of sound. His heart beat sluggishly. His blood slowed in his veins.

Death was approaching.

He closed his eyes one last time.

He had been murdered in his own garden.

Chapter 2

The next time Princess Amy Rosabel kidnapped an English nobleman, she intended to make sure he weighed less.

From a distance, Lord Northcliff hadn't appeared large or impressive, but up close he was disconcertingly muscular, and when she had served him his wine she had been able to tell he topped her by at least six inches.

Now, as she stood in the gazebo and stared down at his limp body, she whispered, "He's as big as a beached whale."

Pomeroy Nodder, as taciturn a man as Amy had ever met, said, "Not a whale, miss. No blubber. But he's a big un. Always was, even as a lad."

The setting sun peeked through the gathering wisps of fog, casting a golden light on His Lordship. His hair was a deep, rich red like burnished mahogany. His eyebrows were dark and slanted upward in devilish mockery. Even unconscious, Lord Northcliff managed to look scornful.

Fie on his scorn. For luck, she touched the silver cross of Beaumontagne that hung on a chain around her neck. He was in her power now, and she would make him pay for his treachery.

Pom grunted as he rolled Lord Northcliff into the sail. "Give me a hand, would ye, miss?"

Dropping to her knees, she helped wrap Lord Northcliff, and the effort made her sweat in a most unladylike manner. Her royal grandmamma would not approve of such improper perspiration—but then, her grandmamma was a thousand miles away in the kingdom of Beaumontagne in the Pyrenees Mountains, and with any luck, that was where she would stay. Just the thought of the forbidding old woman made Amy sweat even more.

As Pom hoisted Lord Northcliff onto his shoulder, she snatched Lord Northcliff's greatcoat off his chair. Lugging it after Pom, she followed as he carried His Heavy Lordship down the steep path to the shore.

The coat was hefty, and she hurried as she tried to keep up with Pom's long steps. He was a big man, a fisherman who made his living by lifting heavy nets filled with sardines, and even he was panting by the time their footsteps crunched through the gravel on the beach.

From the boat hidden in the thickening fog, Miss Victorine Sprott's fearful voice cried, "Who . . . who goes there?"

"It's us. We got him," Amy called. "We're bringing him aboard."

"What took you so long? I've been sitting here imagining dreadful things." The elderly woman sounded both relieved and fretful.

Amy steadied the boat while Pom stepped over the bow, then hurried to help lower Lord Northcliff onto the boards. "Everything went as planned," she assured Miss Victorine.

Miss Victorine had been in doubt about the whole scheme, and had needed reassurance every step of the way.

In truth, Amy found the execution of the plan to be more nerve-wracking than she had anticipated—and it was *her* plan.

"Gently. Set His Lordship down gently!" Miss Victorine commanded.

Amy's aching arms couldn't hold the weight any longer, and she dropped him the last few inches. Or perhaps it was more like a yard. Whatever the distance, she refused to be sorry, even when he roused from the depths of his unconsciousness to groan.

"Do be careful!" Miss Victorine rebuked. "He is our liege lord."

Amy rotated her shoulders. "A liege lord who has behaved abominably to his people."

"Not so dreadfully," Miss Victorine said.

"Abominably," Amy insisted.

"But our liege lord nevertheless." Miss Victorine's voice took on a anxious tone.

"Not mine," Amy said grimly.

Pom groaned as he straightened his back. "Sit on that coil o' rope, Miss Rosabel. We'd best get him back t' the isle afore he wakes, or we'll find out exactly how he shows his displeasure."

"The arrogant blackguard would probably upset the boat and drown us all." Placing the greatcoat onto the coil of rope, Amy seated herself for the two-mile trip.

"He's not daft," Miss Victorine said. "He won't drown *himself*. But he does have a dreadful temper. What if he had shot you? What if his servants caught you and shot you? What if—"

"Yet here we are, as planned," Amy reassured the aged gentlewoman. "All will be well, Miss Victorine, I vow it will. Don't lose your nerve now!"

Stepping out of the boat into the water, Pom pushed it off the beach. Leaping in, he expertly took up the oars. "We'll be home in a flit."

Home was the isle of Summerwind, another of Lord Northcliff's possessions. Another of Lord Northcliff's neglected duties.

The boat cut through the waves, then out into the open water. Amy listened to the slap of waves against the boat and Lord Northcliff's stentorian breathing. An escalating sense of urgency dogged her. She hoped Pom could find his way home, and quickly. It was too dreadful to think Lord Northcliff might awaken before she had him irrevocably bound. She had already been pinned by the direct gaze of his odd, light brown eyes, and she didn't relish any further experience. She thought him exceedingly like the tiger she'd seen as a child. Big, beautiful, wild, and dangerous, all teeth and cruelty, uncaring of the carnage left in his wake as he fed and played.

The sun had set and left only a fading, silvery light behind. The fog thickened around them. And something cool and soft touched her cheek.

She jumped and swatted at it—and caught Miss Victorine's hand.

Miss Victorine clutched Amy's fingers and whispered, "Lord Northcliff is so still. You don't suppose he's dead?"

"If His Lordship was dead, it would be no more than he deserved," Amy answered rather too loudly.

Miss Victorine gave one of her birdlike chirps of dismay.

"Lord Northcliff most certainly is not dead. Marcophilia doesn't kill one, it knocks one out," Amy said in a gentler voice.

"But Lord Northcliff is all wrapped up in that sail as if it were his shroud." Miss Victorine had been uneasy about Amy's plan from the beginning, and now that it was in motion, she was sure the noose swung close behind her neck.

"He's no good to us dead," Amy explained for perhaps the hundredth time. "We can only ransom him if he's alive. Besides—can't you hear him snoring?"

Miss Victorine giggled nervously. "Is that him? I

thought it was Pom huffing as he rowed." Lowering her voice as if someone could hear her, she asked, "Did you leave the letter?"

"I did." Amy thought with satisfaction of the sharp knife stabbed into her carefully worded ransom letter. She wondered when the servants would find it. She estimated it would take only a day to make its way into Mr. Harrison Edmondson's hands. And two more days for the money to make its way to the point of deposit—the crumbling castle on the isle of Summerwind.

Amy liked the irony of having the cash come there, to the ancient home of the proud Edmondson family. She liked even better the tunnels that combed the castle and made it possible for her to retrieve the notes without detection.

Waves caught the boat and lifted it onto the island, and as the boards scraped the sandy beach, Amy caught her breath. Almost there.

Pom leaped into the water and dragged the boat ashore, then stepped back. With Amy's help, he slung the canvas-wrapped body over his shoulder.

Miss Victorine whimpered as Lord Northcliff groaned again. "He sounds like he's in pain, the poor dear."

"Steady as she goes, Miss Sprott." The fisherman stepped surefootedly over to the bow of the boat and onto shore. "Secure me boat, please, Miss Rosabel," he said over his shoulder.

Amy leaped onto shore and, grabbing the bow, heaved the vessel above the tide line. As she assisted

Miss Victorine from the boat, the old woman said, "I do hope Lord Northcliff isn't angry with us."

Amy thought he was going to be more than angry. She thought he would be livid. A man of wealth and influence wouldn't take his helplessness with any amount of grace. And a man so obsessed with riches that he would steal an invention from an old woman would positively froth at the idea of being forced to give up a trifling part of his obscenely large fortune.

Amy grinned. Actually, not so trifling at all.

But she didn't say that to Miss Victorine. Instead she declared, "You must admit that there's justice to demanding a ransom for the return of the man who stole your idea in the first place."

"Yes. Yes, I know, dear, you're right. Quite right. But the Sprotts have lived in my house for generations, and always with the permission of the marquess of Northcliff. And it's not as if what we're doing is exactly legal—stealing Lord Northcliff, I mean."

Not exactly legal? A polite way of putting it. "The marquess is nothing but an overgrown bully who commands that we pay him rent on a poor, battered house the cows would be ashamed to call home."

"I rather like my house."

"The roof leaks."

"It has atmosphere."

"Miss Victorine, that's not atmosphere, that's rain."

Pom interrupted. "If you've secured the boat, Miss Rosabel, His Lordship isn't getting any lighter." He set off through the darkness toward their maligned cottage.

Miss Victorine walked after him.

Amy scooped the greatcoat into her arms and followed them along the path, onto the bare, grassy hills that made up the isle of Summerwind.

It was a pretty, bucolic island in the daylight, dotted with trees and cows. The village was set in a cove on the shore. Sprott Hall stood in a hollow surrounded by an apple orchard. And the crumbling castle, a brooding mass of tumbled gray stones, commanded the highest point on the island.

Sprott Hall had once been a handsome home constructed of white-painted plaster. During the daytime it was possible to admire the roses that climbed the trellis around the door—and see the faded green paint on the shutters. The thatching had fallen into disrepair, and two of the glass windows had been broken in a winter gale and were patched with nothing better than rags.

Miss Victorine had lived here her whole life, growing up and growing old in the same house, watching it deteriorate around her as her family died and Lord Northcliff paid no attention to maintaining his properties.

Yet the old woman was the heart of the village, a kind soul who had readily given Amy a home when she'd washed up on shore, barely conscious and half frozen. Although she had told Miss Victorine she recalled nothing of why she wore a seaman's uniform, that was a lie. She well remembered her dive over the edge of the ship when the captain and his crew had discovered their new cabin boy was actually a girl.

Men, Amy had concluded, were all swine, and it had

taken most of her year on the island before she grudgingly admitted that Pom was a kind man, and that a few of the other fishermen deserved accolades, too.

But it was Miss Victorine who had given Amy a lesson in graciousness and compassion—and sent her along this crooked path to justice.

Miss Victorine rushed to open the door. A large black cat coiled around her ankles, and she leaned over to pick him up. "Coal, my darling boy, how are you?"

He meowed and rubbed his head against her chin, then flung himself over her shoulder and hung there like a fur wrap.

Miss Victorine scratched his rump. "Make sure you don't bump His Lordship's head, Pom. We don't want to make him angry."

"Nay, ma'am, we wouldn't want to do that." Pom carried the sail-draped Lord Northcliff inside, and stood waiting while Amy discarded the greatcoat onto the floor and lit a lantern. The sitting room opened off the foyer, and a dark corridor led to the bedrooms. It was to the kitchen at the back that Amy made her way, followed closely by Pom and Miss Victorine. Pom bent to descend the steps to the wine cellar, the sail flapping against his thighs, Lord Northcliff unmoving.

In the small room carved out of the rock beneath the house, Amy and Miss Victorine had created a living area for His Lordship. Not so grand a living area as existed in Lord Northcliff's manor, but it would suffice for his needs for the three or four days he would remain here. In the small room was a bed, a table, a pitcher and basin, and a case full of dusty books. The cot had been placed under the high window where he could receive what light came in. Beneath it sat a chamber pot. A rocking chair was placed against the wall.

And bolted to the stone wall beside the bed was an iron manacle, rescued from Edmondson Castle.

Amy herself had ventured into the dungeons to get that manacle. She had frowned at the rust on the various implements of imprisonment. She had decided on this particular manacle, and a scrubbing with oil had proved her decision to be a good one. The manacle and the chain connected to it were not as good as she might have hoped, but—it had a key. A key that worked in the lock. Because heaven knew she didn't want to keep Northcliff longer than necessary.

The straw mattress crackled as Pom placed Lord Northcliff on the narrow, iron cot and unwrapped him from the canvas.

Amy handed Miss Victorine the lantern. Not without trepidation, Amy pressed her fingers to the vein in Lord Northcliff's throat. His heart beat strongly, and he gave off such a heat that she wondered if, on some unconscious level, he was aware of the indignity done to him and raged against it.

Hastily she pulled her hand back. "He's very much alive."

"Thank heavens!" Miss Victorine had insisted on dressing up to fetch Lord Northcliff back to her home, just as if he were a guest rather than a victim, and now she wore her finest purple cloak trimmed with a collar of aged ermine. The drooping, purring cat added an element of living elegance. She had styled her mass of white hair into a coiffure fashionable fifty years ago, and with Amy's expert help, she had dabbed rose on her wrinkled cheeks and faded lips. A velvet beauty patch adorned her upper lip, and her gray brows had been tweezed to a thin, arching line. Now she bustled about like a hostess caught unawares. She lit the stub of a cheap candle and added coal to the fire in the small iron stove.

Pom pulled off His Lordship's boots, leaving his white stockinged feet dangling off the edge of the bed.

Then, with careful precision, Amy placed the manacle around His Lordship's ankle and snapped it into place. The crack of metal against metal made her step away and rub the goose bumps that rose on her arms. "There," she said bracingly. "He can't free himself."

"Oh, dear." Miss Victorine stood with the candle tilted, the wax dripping on the floor. "Oh, dear."

Gathering the sail under his arm, Pom bowed to Miss Victorine. "I'll leave His Lordship t' ye, Miss Sprott. Call me if ye have need o' me."

Miss Victorine gathered her composure. She righted the sputtering candle and patted Pom's arm. "We won't call you. There's no reason for anyone to know what you've done here, and I promise we would die rather than betray you to His Lordship."

"I know, ma'am. I appreciate that." Pom clumped up the stairs to the backdoor.

Amy followed to let him out, and the wariness learned through years of poverty and deception made her inquire, "No one in the village knows what we've done here . . . do they?"

"Haven't a clue." Pom tipped his fisherman's hat, stepped out of the kitchen and disappeared into the gloom composed of fog and darkness.

What had he meant by that? Amy wondered. Did he mean the villagers hadn't a clue, or he didn't know if the villagers had a clue?

Yet she saw no use in worrying now. The deed was done, and the venture was so bold, so unusual, the surprise itself foretold success.

That was what she told herself. That was what she hoped.

Pom entered the pub and hung his hat on the rack beside the door. Turning, he saw every person looking at him eagerly. "It's done," he said.

A collective sigh wheezed through the air.

"Don't tease us, gent! Tell us the details." His wife stood with a bar rag in her hand. She tied her blond curls up in a pink ribbon, her blue eyes sparkled as if the sight of him gave her pleasure, and her handsome mouth was asmilin'.

Pom didn't understand why Mertle had chosen him, of all the fishermen in the village, to be her man, but he counted himself lucky to have her. He gave her the nod that meant he loved her, and added, "It went well."

Sitting at a table, he set his elbows on the surface and waited while she served him his dinner. He ate as if he was starving, which he always was. When he finished, he picked up the mug of ale and drank it dry.

Then he noticed everyone still stared at him as if expecting more of a report than he had given. Words came hard for him, so with some difficulty, he said, "His Lordship's chained in Miss Victorine's cellar. The ransom note's been left fer Mr. Harrison Edmondson."

"That bastard," Mertle said roundly. "Get on, gent!"

"Now we'll see what Lord Northcliff has t' say when he wakes up," Pom said.

"He won't be happy, I trow." Vicar Smith tapped his fingertips together.

The vicar was an elderly man with tufts of white hair on his head and great growths of gray hair over his eyes. He had a weak chin, a strong character, and a way of stating the obvious.

But Pom wasn't a learned man, and perhaps it needed to be said. "Nay," he agreed gravely. "That he won't."

"Will Miss Rosabel's plan work, do ye think?" Mertle asked.

Pom contemplated his wife. "Don't know why it shouldn't."

"Well, I can't approve." Mrs. Kitchen imagined herself to be a leader in the village, and she sniffed in disparagement. "It is shameful that ye've taken part in this drama. Shameful!"

The pub grew quiet under her rebuke.

Pom clearly saw the doubts that plagued the simple folk, and struggled to express why a plain fisherman like himself had helped with such an outrageous deed. "Miss Rosabel is right."

"About what?" Vicar Smith asked.

"Lord Northcliff owes us," Pom said. "He owes Miss Victorine."

"Why are we taking such a chance for *her?*" Mrs. Kitchen demanded.

Hands on her hips, Mertle swung away from Pom and advanced on Mrs. Kitchen. "Because she's helped every last un o' us at one time or another, and she's been around long enough that she's helped our parents, too. She's a good woman. The best. We'd be damned fer deserting her now."

Mrs. Kitchen tried to hold Mertle's gaze, but Pom knew from experience that no one could face his wife when she fixed him with that outraged stare. Mrs. Kitchen snapped her mouth shut and gazed down at her toes.

"We're doing His Lordship a favor." Mertle looked around at the tavern, challenging their doubts. "Aren't we, Pom?"

From the depths of his soul, Pom dragged a down-to-earth statement. "Aye. He'll learn. He needs t' realize he's done a bad thing."

"He's a lord," John said sourly. "Lords don't learn."

"We've got t' give him a chance." Pom hadn't put so many words together at one time in years. But he had to do so now. He recognized how important this was. "If we don't he'll keep on until he's sinned so much his black soul will drag him down to hell."

Chapter 3

*C*lutching Lord Northcliff's greatcoat, Amy carried it down the stairway.

This greatcoat was emblematic of everything that was wrong with Lord Northcliff. Sewn by a London tailor, it represented vanity incarnate. Made of the finest black wool, the greatcoat cost enough to have fed the village for a year. It was long and heavy, fashioned with a plethora of capes about the shoulders, each lengthier than the first, and . . . Amy dropped her head into its folds and took a lingering breath. Lord Northcliff's coat smelled of leather and tobacco, and she was transported back to the palace in Beaumontagne, to her seat on her father's knee. There as she burrowed in his jacket for sweets, she had felt safe, beloved, cherished.

Her heart warmed with unwilling fondness—but not for Lord Northcliff, she assured herself. For the memory of her father. Only . . . she hated to know that anything about Lord Northcliff reminded her of the affection that had celebrated her childhood.

As Amy set foot in the cellar, she held the coat at arm's length.

Miss Victorine stood petting Coal and sadly looking down at Lord Northcliff's limp body. "He was such a pleasant lad," she said.

"He's changed." Amy tossed the greatcoat onto the rocking chair. She couldn't wait to be rid of it, with its intoxicating scent and its precious weight.

"He used to coax one of the fishermen to row him over to the island." As she gazed through vague blue eyes at Lord Northcliff, Miss Victorine whispered, "He'd come to visit me and I'd serve him tea and my cream cakes, which he called the best in the world."

"As he should, since they are." With a grunt of effort, Amy pulled the blankets out from underneath Lord Northcliff and prepared to roll him between the sheets.

"He's a very handsome man, isn't he?" Miss Victorine asked in a wistful tone.

"How can you say that?" Amy didn't bother to glance at his face. "He has stolen our livelihood."

"Dear, stealing has nothing to do with the fact that he was a fine-looking lad who grew up to be a fine-looking lord." Miss Victorine's lace-gloved hands fluttered into the air, then descended to rest at her waist.

"Just because I'm too old to climb the ladder doesn't mean my mouth doesn't water when I gaze on the peaches."

Amy caught her breath on a choking laugh. Miss Victorine was an odd mixture of aged sauciness and old maid primness. She was quite severe with Amy's outspokenness, chiding her for any untoward remarks, yet she had lived alone for a very long time, and she believed that entitled her to say whatever she pleased. That candor was one of the reasons Amy found her so endearing.

In a reflective tone, Miss Victorine said, "His father was not at all handsome. It's a bit of a surprise to see young Jermyn looking like a darling angel."

Amy looked at the man lying on the bed.

A darling angel? What madness made Miss Victorine call the marquess a darling or an angel? He was neither; rather he was a spoiled lad who snatched what he wanted without a care for anything but his own desires.

Yet . . . yet Amy had to admit he did draw the female eye. His skin was toasted brown—from hunting, she supposed, or some other outdoor dilettante activity. He had a very nice nose, as noses went—strong and well-shaped. His lips were too big and soft, although perhaps that was because they had fallen open and a hearty snore issued from between them.

Miss Victorine giggled. "He sounds unharmed."

"He does, doesn't he?" For the first time since Lord Northcliff had burst into her life and ruined it with his perfidy, Amy wondered who he was and why he had done what he had done. "Did no one teach him anything of morals and responsibility?"

"His father did! He was a good man. A good lord." Wearily, Miss Victorine sank into the rocking chair and pulled Coal into her lap. The big cat curled himself up as tightly as he could, yet his front feet hung over onto the seat. "He was overly proud of his heritage, and taught his son to be proud also, but perhaps he was right. After all, the Edmondson family is one of the oldest in England. The original Edmondson was a Saxon lord who stood up to the Conqueror and declared his claim on Summerwind. The official legend says William I was so impressed with his bravery he gave him the island."

Sensing more to the story, Amy asked, "And the unofficial legend?"

"Says that the Saxon's wife had softened William's wrath in a bedtime tussle and won her husband the land."

Amy laughed aloud.

"I don't know, Amy." The chair creaked as Miss Victorine rocked, a troubled frown on her plump face. "Do you think we've done the right thing?"

Amy perched on the mattress beside Lord Northcliff's shoulder and took Miss Victorine's hand. Pressing it reassuringly, she said, "I truly do, but more important, we don't have a choice. We have no money. The villagers have no money. This Lord Northcliff is trying to run you out of your house—he says you owe him rent!—and the villagers off their lands, and your family has been here for over four hundred years, and their families have held their land for at least as long as the Edmondsons. With ten thousand pounds, we can go where we wish and leave money for the villagers, too."

"But even if we succeed I'm going to have to depart my dear island." Miss Victorine's hand trembled in Amy's.

"*When* we succeed," Amy said firmly. "I know we're going to have to find another home, and isn't it horrible that he's chasing us away? But we were going to have to leave anyway, and this way, with the money from the ransom, we'll be able to go somewhere we like and buy ourselves a nice new home, one that has no cracks to let the mice and the rain in."

"I'm too old to enjoy a new home." Miss Victorine's faded eyes were pleading.

"Wherever you go, I'll go and stay with you. I promise. We'll be happy." Amy hated to see Miss Victorine so miserable, and she burst out spitefully, "And who knows? Maybe someday Lord Northcliff will crash his carriage for good and all, and we'll be able to come back to Summerwind."

In horror, Miss Victorine snatched her hands away. "Don't wish for his death. It's bad luck!"

Coal stood up and glared at Amy.

Amy murmured an apology to Miss Victorine and rubbed Coal under his soft chin. But she didn't really regret her ill-wishes. When she thought of how Lord Northcliff was ruining the life of a poor, sweet, old lady, she wanted to shriek with frustration. She wanted to shake him until he saw sense. She wanted to . . . she wanted to arrange a carriage accident that would finish him off.

When she saw Miss Victorine trying to be brave and hide her misery, Amy burned with fury at the darling angel called Lord Northcliff.

Miss Victorine stared at the supine form behind Amy. "He lost his mother when he was seven, and he was raised without any feminine softening influence. That was why he used to come to me, I think. He liked to be petted and cosseted."

"Don't all men?" Amy asked tartly.

"I suppose." Miss Victorine sighed as if she were weary. "But some lads we want to pet, and some we want to slap."

Startled by the gentlewoman's vehemence, Amy asked, "Who do we want to slap?"

"Mr. Harrison Edmondson has never been a favorite of mine. He is Lord Northcliff's uncle, and I blame him for young Jermyn's indifference to his lands and his people. Harrison radiates cold, and his eyes are small and set closely together." Miss Victorine nodded sagely. "You know what that means."

Amy didn't have the foggiest idea, but she nodded back and stood. "You're exhausted. You should go to bed."

"I couldn't sleep! Not after this excitement." But Miss Victorine's eyelids drooped as she contemplated Lord Northcliff, and Coal's eyes drooped as he contemplated Miss Victorine. "His mother was an amazingly pretty woman. Dear Jermyn has his mother's coloring, and it looks even better on him."

It was true. His hair was a searing mahogany that made Amy's fingers itch to touch the curls and see if they burned. She did touch the slanted brows, so oddly dark, brushing them lightly with her fingertips. She checked to see if any soot came off, if he suffered from some peculiar desire for black brows, but it appeared nature had created that improbable combination of hair color and facial hair.

It was a curious thing to hold a vital man under her control. Odd and intoxicating. Musing aloud, she said, "I wonder if his body hair is red or black."

Miss Victorine gasped. "Amy! That is nothing that a proper young lady such as yourself should concern herself about."

Although Amy had tried to explain the life she'd led before she had made her way to the isle of Summerwind, Miss Victorine couldn't comprehend her background. Miss Victorine knew only that Amy was nineteen years old and had the manner of a princess—which she truly was, although Amy would never admit *that* to anyone here.

Yet the two of them had something in common—a wicked, mischievous streak, so Amy grinned at Miss Victorine. "Probably I shouldn't concern myself with his body hair; I do it to please you."

"Most certainly not." Miss Victorine sounded prim, but she scooted her chair closer. "I have never seen an unclad male form in my life, and I haven't suffered for the lack."

"By an extraordinary coincidence, I haven't seen an unclad male form in my life, either. I'd say it's time to remedy the situation." Tugging his shirt open, Amy peered down at his chest.

"We can't look at him when he's unconscious! It's . . . it's immoral." Miss Victorine fanned herself with her handkerchief.

Coal watched the white cotton as if contemplating how it would shred.

"Dear Miss Victorine, we abducted him from his own estate. I hardly think sneaking a peek at his chest compares." Letting his shirt drop back, Amy added, "Besides, we looked at his *face*."

"That's different." Miss Victorine leaned closer. "What color is it?"

"What color is what?" Amy teased.

"You know. The hair on his body."

Amy flashed her a grin. "Red."

"Appropriate," Miss Victorine said crisply.

"Why do you say that?"

"You're gazing upon the gateway to hell."

"I don't think I looked that far," Amy said reflectively. "Here, help me put him under the covers. I doubt if he wakes before morning."

"Mr. Edmondson!" Royd, the butler, stood in the doorway of the study at Harrison Edmondson's London home. "There's a messenger come from Summerwind in Devon, and he says it's urgent!"

Harrison Edmondson, Jermyn's uncle and his business manager, wondered if luck had done what planning and stealth could not. He doubted it; success had never felt so far away as in these last few weeks, and if he didn't bring matters to a satisfactory conclusion soon, he'd be the great-uncle of a bouncing baby boy who would be the heir to the whole grand and glorious Edmondson fortune.

As he remembered the list of possible brides he'd been ordered to submit to his arrogant twit of a nephew, his hands curled into claws.

Give him a pistol and he could do the job himself.

Hell, he didn't even need a pistol. He glanced toward the glass-front cabinet he kept in his office. Inside was a variety of interesting weapons—French poison rings, Italian daggers that popped out to surprise the victim, a sword hidden in a cane . . .

And when committing murder, no planning, no weapon could compete with an opportunity presented and seized.

He knew that. He had seized opportunity before.

The messenger crowded in behind Royd, splattered with mud, his chest heaving from his hard ride. With a tug of his forelock, he presented Harrison a stained, slashed missive. He gasped, "Footman found it . . . in the gazebo . . . affixed with a knife."

"My good man!" Royd remonstrated, a fearful eye trained on Harrison. "You can't burst into Mr. Edmondson's presence in such a manner!"

Harrison waved his butler to silence. In a soft, measured tone that promised retribution, he said, "If you can't keep him out, then I suppose he will burst in." Snatching the missive from the man's insistent hand, Harrison opened the crinkled sheet and read the carefully penned lines.

I hold the marquess of Northcliff captive. Leave ten thousand pounds in the old Northcliff's Castle on the isle of Summerwind, five days hence or your nephew dies.

Harrison gaped, disbelieving. It wasn't . . . it wasn't possible! Such a happenstance was amazing, impossible . . . more than he could stand.

Throwing back his head, he burst into wild laughter. At last, at long last, fate had played into his hands.

Chapter 4

*B*y degrees, Jermyn came to consciousness. He didn't particularly want to; he had just enjoyed the deepest sleep he'd had since he'd broken his leg. But his neck was kinked oddly and his mouth was open, dry, and pressed into the pillow. So although he fought waking, awareness came inevitably, filling his senses.

First he noticed how very much he liked the scent in his room, like clean linens overlaid with the odor of freshly turned earth. The sounds that came to his ears were rhythmic, a light clacking interspersed with a deep creaking. A warm weight rested against his side. He felt rested, really well, except . . . He frowned. What odd dreams he'd had, about bad wine and a boat and a beautiful girl with eyes the shade of poison—his eyes popped open. He sat up in bed.

No, not a bed. A cot. A narrow iron cot attached to the wall with bolts, with a thin feather mattress, thin sheets, and a shabby fur throw.

Beside him a huge black cat rumbled its displeasure, then settled more comfortably in the middle of the mattress.

A swift survey of his surroundings showed Jermyn a room with three small windows near the open beamed ceiling . . . a cellar. Gray light filtered through the glass, its feeble illumination allowing him to discern no more than still square shapes . . . furniture. A chest. A long table. Chairs. A small iron stove. He touched the wall beside his cot . . . rock. Cool, hard rock.

He still wore his clothes, although his cravat was gone and his boots were off. He wasn't wounded or hurt. So . . . "Where the hell am I?" he asked aloud.

"In Miss Victorine's cellar," a calm, female voice answered.

The clacking and the creaking ceased. He turned to look behind his head, and a womanly form rose from a rocking chair. With daunting efficiency, she lit a lantern and lifted it, hanging it on a hook on the ceiling. It illuminated his surroundings—a cellar the size of a bedroom, full of empty wine racks and old, broken furniture—but most important, it illuminated *her*, the girl with the poison-colored eyes.

She was handsome, with a thin figure and features so proud as to be disagreeable. The color of her mouth reminded him of cherries in the spring, but her expres-

sion was reminiscent of that of his first governess when
she had gazed on the small, dirty boy she had been
given to tutor. Something about this girl's air made
him very well aware of his dishevelment and more
than a little abashed that he'd slept in her presence.
Sleeping was vulnerability, and he didn't want to be
vulnerable in front of her. "Who, madam, are you? And
what am I doing here?"

"I'm your gaoler, and you're our prisoner." Her
matter-of-fact tone made the words all the more incon-
gruous.

"Absurd!"

At his vehement denial, the cat rumbled its displeasure and leaped toward the stairs.

Jermyn put his feet to the floor.

He heard a rattle.

Could it be . . . ? Was that . . . ? But no, that was impossible.

He moved again. Again heard the clank of metal
against metal.

A chain? Was that a chain? Did she dare . . . ? He extended his foot. He looked . . . and saw it.

He saw it, but he couldn't believe it. *He could not believe it.* "That is a manacle."

"So it is."

"Around my ankle." His chest constricted.

"You're a bright one." Her calm manner proved she
didn't even recognize her danger.

"Get . . . it . . . off." Chained! He growled with fury.

"No."

"Perhaps you didn't understand me, girl." He

looked at her from under lowered brows. "I'm the marquess of Northcliff, and I said to *get . . . it . . . off.*"

"And I don't care who you are, you're here and here you're going to stay."

A flame of pure blue rage seared all thought out of his mind. With the instinct of a caged beast, he let out a roar and leaped at her.

She jumped back, her face alive with shock.

His hands reached for her throat—and the chain jerked him off his feet. The stone floor met his outflung body with a thump that knocked the air out of his lungs. For a long, agonized moment he couldn't breathe. Then he could, and it was worse. Painful reprisal for his rage.

His leg, his stupid leg, felt as if he'd landed on hot pokers.

And all the time he lay there and gasped like a dying fish, that female stood and watched without offering sympathy or assistance. To him. To the marquess of Northcliff, the man whom dowagers and gentle ladies adored.

When at last he could lift his head, he asked, "What have you done?"

"What have I done?" She lifted a mocking brow. "Why, I've kidnapped the marquess of Northcliff."

"You dare admit to it?" Inch by painful inch, he dragged himself back onto the cot.

"Admitting to it is the least of my sins. I *did* it."

She was enjoying herself. He could see it in the saucy tilt of her lips, the jaunty lift of her brows. He couldn't comprehend that any woman would have the gall, the sheer unadulterated nerve to take him off his own property . . . He straightened. His eyes narrowed. "Wait a minute. There was a man."

"I hired him to lift you. He's gone now," she said swiftly. "You won't see him again."

"I don't believe you." Stretching out his leg, he rubbed the thigh, feeling the bone through material and muscle. It didn't feel broken, but he'd wrenched it again, and his pain was her fault. *Hers.* This insolent baggage. Speaking in the condescending tone she so richly deserved, he said, "No woman would come up with a plan like this, much less be able to execute it."

"I'm depending on that kind of thinking. Everyone will imagine you mad when you say a woman took you—if you even dare admit it." She inclined her head to him in mocking homage.

"Women don't have the ability to sustain a thought long enough to put such a plan in motion."

"Actually, you're right." She grinned, not at all offended. "It took two women."

"Miss Victorine," he remembered. "You said I was in Miss Victorine's cellar."

"That's right."

"Are you trying to tell me that Miss Victorine Sprott helped you kidnap me?" He well recalled Miss Victorine. When he was a lad, he used to come over with one of the fishermen, run up the walk to her stately old cottage, and she would serve him cakes and tea, then walk with him in the garden and tell him about the plants. Everything he knew about tending flowers he'd learned from Miss Victorine—and now she had *kidnapped* him? "Nonsense!"

"Not nonsense. If you think about it, there's a certain justice in her actions that you can appreciate."

He straightened. "What are you babbling about?"

"Please, I beg of you. Don't try to pretend ignorance. It does you little justice and will avail you nothing." The girl's contempt whipped at him.

In that moment, as he listened to her elocution, he realized what he should have realized before. She might dress like a servant, but she spoke like a lady. That was what had bothered him last night—at least, he hoped it was *last* night—at the gazebo.

She glanced up the stairs where the soft hush of a lady's skirt and the gentle patter of a lady's slippers could be heard. "I think that's Miss Victorine now with your breakfast. Are you hungry?"

"Do you expect me to sit here like a bloody fool and eat a meal?"

"You'll always be a bloody fool, there's nothing to be done about that, and I don't care if you starve to death." Moving to the bottom of the stairway, she took the tray from Miss Victorine's hands. "But right now you have to maintain a modicum of health or we won't get our money."

Until Miss Victorine walked into the circle of light cast by the lantern, he hadn't believed it possible she would take part in such a nefarious scheme.

She looked older, he saw. A lot older. Worry wrinkles cut deeply into her forehead and her soft hair had turned completely white. Her chubby cheeks sagged and her brown eyes looked tired. She no longer cared for her clothing; in fact, he thought he recognized the shabby dress she wore as one she'd worn when he'd visited as a boy. Her plump bosom and her stiff gait put him in mind of a puff pigeon, and he couldn't believe, he just couldn't believe . . .

With a thump, that dreadful young female put the tray down on the far end of the long table. The other end sat close to his cot, and she pushed the tray toward him until it was within his reach, but she remained far enough away that he couldn't grab her and shake her as she so richly deserved.

It had to be this wench who had influenced—no, blackmailed—Miss Victorine into doing this. Miss Victorine was a proper English lady. For heaven's sake, she was fond of him!

"Miss Victorine, you need to release me." He spoke slowly and loudly, fearing she had lost her hearing.

"No, dear boy, I can't do that. Not until we get our money. But I'm so glad to have you here and have a chance to talk with you once more." She definitely wasn't deaf, but she had obviously descended into senility, for she clasped her hands together and smiled fondly, as if she spoke exquisite sense.

"What money?" he asked.

"The ransom money. Now don't worry. We've already sent a message to your uncle Harrison, telling him that we'll kill you if he doesn't pay."

That contemptible girl perched one hip on the long, scarred, oak table and grinned at him.

He knew why. The expression on his face must have been priceless. "Kill me?" Jermyn could scarcely articulate his horror and disbelief. "You're going to kill me?"

"Of course not, dear!" As if he were the crazed one, Miss Victorine frowned reprovingly at him. "We won't have to go that far. I'm sure he'll send the funds right away and you'll be out of here in no time."

"You've kidnapped me. You've ransomed me." Jermyn counted the facts off on his fingers. "And you expect Uncle Harrison to pay for my safe return?"

"Yes, dear."

"That's outrageous!"

"We wouldn't have had to do it if you hadn't stolen my beading machine. Beaded lace is so popular now. Why, I'll wager you can't walk down a London street without seeing ladies carrying beaded reticules and beaded lace cuffs and beaded bodices."

"Yes, beaded lace is all the rage." The silly colorful glass beads caught on a man's buttons. Miss Mistlewit had shrieked in his ear when he jerked free of her embrace and miniature beads had scattered all over the garden path, and he'd been lucky to escape without being forced to propose to the lovely, silly debutante.

"Because I worked out a machine to make the lace and place the beads. It was my idea, my invention, and you took it." Miss Victorine clicked her tongue. "That was not well done. You have a fabulous fortune already, and the village is in need. If you're not going to care for them, surely you see that they should be allowed to do more than eke out a living." Her old voice quavered as she made her appeal, and her faded eyes peered at him reproachfully. "I hate to be stern, but I must tell you, your father would have never allowed such a shambles to occur."

"I have no idea what you're talking about," he said. She wasn't making any sense at all.

"Of course not." The girl stood up straight, and she had the gall to look disgusted. "You probably steal so many inventions you can't remember what you've done, and gloat when you think of a dear little lady living in a tumbled-down cottage with only gruel to eat unless her neighbors bring her a fish."

Damme, she was an insolent twit! He straightened up to shout—but although Miss Victorine's voice was as soft as ever, it held a snap that stopped the words in his throat.

"Now dears, you mustn't fight." She turned on the girl. "Amy, I will not have you parading my misfortunes as if I were a pitiful old woman. I am not. I have my own roof over my head, and that's more than most spinsters possess."

Amy—that miserable creature's name was Amy—said, "It's really his. He could toss you out in an instant, and as fast as it's disintegrating, that would be a blessing!"

"That's enough," Miss Victorine said with crushing certainty.

"Yes, ma'am." Amy subsided.

And as if he were eleven years old, Jermyn found himself gloating at the girl. He was half surprised he didn't stick out his tongue.

"As for you, young man—"

At Miss Victorine's tone, he snapped to attention.

"Eat your breakfast." In Miss Victorine's smile he saw an echo of the dear lady she used to be. "I made you my scones, and they're the best in England. Do you remember?"

"I do." Although he would have liked to arrogantly refuse, he hadn't had dinner the night before, and his stomach rumbled at the smells seeping toward him from the tray.

That girl, that Amy, knew it, too. She smiled in that catty smirking way and watched as he lifted the cover. "Yes, eat, my lord. I would hate to see you miss a meal."

"Amy!" Miss Victorine sounded as stern as a governess. "Mayhap it would be better if you went upstairs and rested. You've been up all night and you seem to be irritable."

It was clear Amy wanted to object, but she muttered, "Yes, ma'am." She shot him a poisoned glare that promised retribution if he tried anything.

And he knew just what to say to put her back up. "When you come back, bring me hot water and a razor. I need to shave."

She gave him a glare that would have made Queen Charlotte of England proud. "We've already discussed it. Once a day, you'll have a basin of water for shaving and bathing."

"How generous of you," he drawled sarcastically.

"It's more than most prisoners have, my lord." Then she ascended the stairs.

He found himself watching her, admiring the shape

of her backside. Best of all, he didn't need to be discreet about it. She didn't deserve sensitivity or any of the niceties owed a lady. She didn't deserve anything but a gaol and a rope tied into a noose.

He intended to make sure she got it.

"Isn't she a darling girl?" Miss Victorine clasped her hands at her bosom and watched with every evidence of affection as Amy disappeared. Seating herself in the rocking chair, she added, "She's foreign, you know."

"That explains a lot." He wrestled the heavy table toward him and without pride, dug into the eggs, the fruit compote, the fish pie. The scones were as delicious as Miss Victorine promised, as delicious as he remembered, and he ate three in a row. He picked up the knife to cut the sausage . . . he looked at the knife. It was old and thin from much whetting . . . and it was sharp. Very sharp, with a lovely point.

With a glance at the oblivious Miss Victorine, he slipped it up his sleeve.

"Yes, dear Amy came from a lovely country called Beaumontagne. It's very rugged there. The winters are dreadful, but the summers are glorious. The forests are absolutely deep and green, with evergreens and oaks and so many birds." Miss Victorine rocked and smiled, not at him, but at some crazed illusion in her mind.

"How do you know about this country?" Which Jermyn vaguely recalled from lessons that demanded he learn the location of every country in Europe.

"In my youth, I visited there. My father was quite the traveler, and after my brothers married and I . . .

well, when it was clear I would remain single, my father planned to take me to the great places of the world." She picked up a ball of twine and a small hand shuttle.

The shuttle was about the length of his palm, about the width of his finger, and was made of ivory worn thin from heavy use. On one end sat a sharp point that Jermyn remembered only too well, for when he was seven he stuck it in the skin between his thumb and finger. It had hurt like Hades and left a scar he still carried.

She shook out the tiny scrap of lace. "Only Father didn't make it very far. We were gone less than a year when he contracted a fever and died. That was a long time ago, but I lived in Beaumontagne for six months afterward, waiting for the winter to break so I could come home." Her gaze shifted to him, and for a lunatic she looked remarkably cogent. "Here I've been ever since. Do you know where Beaumontagne is, my lord?"

"I have an idea. It's in the Pyrenees on the border between Spain and France." It wasn't easy to eat with the knife in his sleeve, but he speared the sausage with his fork and ate bites off it. After all, why should he worry about manners? He had a *manacle* around his ankle.

"Your geography has not been as sadly neglected as I feared." Miss Victorine began the painstaking task of making beaded lace.

As his appetite was met, Jermyn watched her, remembering the sound of the point across the twine, the sight of her veined and spotted hands. Now her little finger crooked in at a painful angle and the skin looked thin and parched, but she still created her beadwork without looking at her efforts.

The thin stream of lace grew as slowly as ice melting.

"I warned your father you needed to know more than how to dance and which goblet to use." She smiled fondly at him.

Jermyn's education had been considerably broader than that, but he asked curiously, "Did you? And what did Father say?"

"He said if you knew your place in England, that was enough for any marquess of Northcliff." She shook her head in disillusionment. "If your father had one fault, it was an overabundance of pride."

"I would not say an overabundance," Jermyn said stiffly. His father had been proud, but gracious to his tenants. He knew every man's name who worked his estates, and personally oversaw the giving of gifts on Twelfth Night. Duties Uncle Harrison had taken over from Jermyn.

For the first time, Jermyn wondered what his father would say about that.

"I'm sorry. You miss him still," Miss Victorine said with an empathy that made Jermyn shift uncomfortably. "Please don't take my ramblings the wrong way. I feel as if I can talk with you about your father. I adored him. He was a great man. I miss him still, and it's a comfort for me to talk about him with someone else who loved him. Of course, you loved him like a son and I loved like a son . . . no." She frowned. "That's wrong. You loved him as a son should and I loved him as if he were my son. There!" She lifted her shuttle triumphantly. "I knew I could say it correctly."

"So you did." Jermyn tried to subdue a rush of affection. She was a dear old lady. He tried to remind himself that she'd help kidnap him, but that made no difference. The truth was, he, too, liked reminiscing about his father, and too few people were left who remembered him.

Jermyn supposed he could discuss Father with Uncle Harrison, but Uncle Harrison seemed interested in nothing more than figures on a page and profit from the estates.

That's what made this whole "steal the beading machine" so ludicrous. Uncle Harrison might not have the title, but he certainly comprehended the dignity that belonged to the marquess of Northcliff. He would never indulge in vulgar manufacturing.

"Perhaps if your mother hadn't left us so soon, your education would be more rounded." Miss Victorine seemed to be speaking to herself. "Andriana certainly had strong opinions on how you should be raised. Perhaps if your father had listened—"

"I'm sorry, Miss Victorine, I don't speak of my mother," Jermyn said gently and without a hint of the rage that, even after all these years, still possessed him. "Not even to you."

"But dear boy, it would be better if you did! I'll never forget how surprised we were when your father brought her back from Italy. She had such a charming accent, and she was so pretty and so kind." With a smile, Miss Victorine settled into her reminiscences. "She adored your father and she adored you. I've never seen a woman so in love with her husband!"

"Miss Victorine, please." Angry blood buzzed in his head.

"But I know you must have missed her. To keep such grief bottled up inside cannot be good for you." She sounded sincerely concerned.

He didn't care. "Not even to you," he repeated.

Hearing the creak of footsteps on the stairs, he realized he'd been saved in more ways than one. He pushed his fork off the edge of the table. It clanked as it hit the floor. He sighed pitifully. "Miss Victorine, with this manacle on my ankle, I can't reach that."

With a cluck of sympathy, Miss Victorine stood and moved toward him.

As Amy stepped into the cellar, he grabbed Miss Victorine and held her against him with the knife against her throat. With a direct and dreadful glare at Amy, he said, "Let me go or I'll kill her."

Chapter 5

"My lord!" Miss Victorine's frail voice quivered. "Dear boy . . ."

Against Jermyn's chest her body felt bony and fragile, and it trembled like that of a frightened bird in a
rough lad's grasp.

He didn't care. She'd betrayed him. The kind lady he
remembered didn't exist. She had been part of a plot to
kidnap him. She refused to release his manacle. Now she
would pay. And when he got loose, she would pay more.

But smoothly, as if she'd foreseen this very circum-
stance, that disdainful girl reached into the drawer and
pulled out a pistol. Her aim was perfectly steady as she
pointed it at him. "Let her go or I'll shoot you."

"I've never met a woman who'd have the guts to

shoot a man," he sneered. All the women he knew were too kind. Too gentle.

"I have the guts," the girl said. "Better yet, I *want* to shoot you."

That shook him. The words, and the tone, a kind of flat, plain aversion the like of which he'd never met in all of his privileged life.

What had he ever done to deserve this girl's contempt? And why did he even care? "Which part of me will you shoot?" he mocked. "All that's showing is my head—and you can't be that good with a gun."

"I am," the girl said. "On the count of three, I'll shoot. One . . ."

"You'd take the chance of hurting Miss Victorine?" he asked.

"I won't hurt her. Two . . ."

"Amy, please, let him go!" Miss Victorine begged. "He was such a sweet boy."

"Three." Amy's eyes narrowed, her finger began to squeeze the trigger.

And he released Miss Victorine, spinning her away from him and into a cabinet.

She landed with a thud and fell.

The pistol roared.

He dived to the floor.

A shot whistled past the place where his head had been.

Amy gave a sigh of relief. "Damn, that was close. Good thing you surrendered, my lord!"

"Don't swear, dear, it's not ladylike." And there on the floor, Miss Victorine burst into tears.

He felt surprisingly like bursting into tears himself. It didn't matter that he told himself Amy couldn't have hit him. He didn't believe himself. That sharp-eyed girl hated him, and until she replaced the gun in the cabinet, he didn't release his pent-up breath.

"Miss Victorine." Without sparing him another glance, Amy hurried to the old lady's side. "Are you all right? Did he hurt you?"

"No. No. Well, a little when he tossed me." Miss Victorine rubbed her shoulder. "But he didn't want me to get shot just because you wanted to blow him away."

"Blow me away?" What an odd phrase to come out of that gentle lady's mouth. He laughed shortly. He stood and dusted off his trousers, before placing the knife on the table.

And realized at once that his amusement did not sit well with Amy. She looked at him in disdain and distaste. "How does it feel to be such a big, bad aristocrat that you have to use this dear little lady as a shield?"

Actually, he was feeling a little ashamed of himself, but he wasn't about to tell this virago. "I pushed her aside when you shot at her."

"You shoved her out of the way when you realized I would shoot you," she answered hotly.

"That's not true." He couldn't believe how she misinterpreted his action. "Don't you have any respect for your betters?"

"I do. That's why I'm going to help her up the stairs and put her to bed with a cup of hot tea. You can just sit here and . . . and jingle your manacle!" With her arm around Miss Victorine, Amy started for the stairs.

"Now dear," he heard Miss Victorine admonishing, "he wouldn't have hurt me. He was always such a nice boy."

He sank down on the cot. When he was young, everyone said that, considering the circumstances, he *was* a nice lad.

He had loved coming over to call on Miss Victorine. He'd adored her cakes and the fuss she'd made over him and the scent of her lavender sachets. She had been a civilizing influence on a lad knocked flat by events he didn't understand and over which he had no control.

He didn't remember when or why he'd stopped his visits. It had been nothing more than part of growing up—discovering hunting and balls and women and cigars and forgetting the sea and the sky and the clouds and the earth. He'd seen them in a flash when Amy had raised her gun, pointed it at him, and said in a cool, strong voice, "*Three.*" He'd seen his whole life in his mind for the last time, or so he'd thought, and when he remembered that piercing moment of fear his hands shook.

He didn't know what the hell was going on here, but he didn't intend to die in this damned cellar at the hands of one crazed old woman and a young female steeped in bitter disdain. He bloody well was going to escape.

Sitting up, he went to work on the manacle.

In the best bedroom, Miss Victorine uttered no protest as Amy helped her out of her Sunday garments and into her worn flannel nightgown. She winced as she lifted her arms to let Amy drop the gown over her, and Amy could see that purpling bruises were rising from beneath Miss Victorine's fragile skin.

Hotly Amy wished that beast downstairs possessed a single moral, or showed a decent regret—or had his hands tied so she could pummel him until he repented of his ways, or was unconscious, or all of them.

Amy's fulminating silence must have indicated the direction of her thoughts. Or perhaps Miss Victorine understood Amy all too well, for she said, "Amy dear, do you remember when Pom brought you to me all wet and bedraggled?"

"Of course I do." With the tongs, Amy took a few red coals, put them into the bed warmer, and chased the chill from the thin sheets.

"I asked where you came from, and you turned your face away and wouldn't say a word. You refused to tell me about your country or your title or your poor lost sisters." Miss Victorine petted Amy's arm. "I feared you were deaf or mute. You were certainly starving."

"You gave me your dinner." Amy held up the warmed sheets and invitingly gestured Miss Victorine in.

"And the first words you spoke to me were, 'Aren't you afraid I'll kill you in your bed?'"

"I am eternally charming." Amy laughed at herself and at the absurdity of her current circumstances. "The marquess of Northcliff would agree."

"He doesn't know you yet, dear. Once he does, he'll be in love with you like the lads in the village." Miss Victorine sighed as she settled into the bed. "I felt so sorry for you, all alone in the world without a protector or anyone to care for you. I wanted to take you under my wing and keep you forever."

"You're the kindest lady in the whole wide world." Amy knew whereof she spoke. She had been out in the wide world since she turned twelve, most of the time with her sister Clarice, but for the last two years on her own. She'd seen terrible things, experienced cruelty and disdain, poverty and terror.

She had never met anyone as kind as Miss Victorine.

"In his way, Lord Northcliff is as lost as you were," Miss Victorine said in a sad little tone.

Amy refrained from snorting, but barely.

"It's true." Miss Victorine arranged the thin pillows behind her back. "When his mother left us Jermyn was only seven. Never had there been a more woebegone little boy. His father was a good man, but he took the loss of his wife badly. He shied away from affection, any affection, even affection for his son. He taught Jermyn his duty and how to be a man. No one cuddled Jermyn or kissed his scrapes or loved him."

Amy didn't understand why Miss Victorine thought that was so important. She couldn't remember her own mother, and if her royal grandmamma had cuddled her, she would have died of frostbite. But even without those services Miss Victorine deemed so vital, Amy had grown up without idiosyncrasies. Any perceived quirks in her nature were nothing more than the results of her determination in the face of adversity.

Yet Miss Victorine didn't insist on explaining further. Miss Victorine had a tendency to assume that people understood how necessary love was, even to despicable swine like Lord Northcliff . . . and lost souls like Amy.

Miss Victorine was alone in the world, without kith or kin or anyone nearby who was of her class or interests, yet through her kind and welcoming spirit, she had made herself the heart of the village and the conscience against which all living souls on Summerwind measured themselves. Without saying a word, she had shown Amy the value of family . . . and lately Amy had begun to wonder if her decision to leave her sister in Scotland and strike out on her own had been less the good sense she imagined at the time and more the result of adolescent rebellion.

Amy and Clarice had been lost to their family. Their father had died. Their sister had disappeared somewhere in England. Grandmamma was out of reach, they had no money, and they fled from one town to another, fitting in nowhere, afraid to settle anywhere. Most people saw the young princesses as vagrants and thieves. Women chased them with brooms and stones. Men leered and offered drinks and lodging, but demanded the most disgusting of services in return.

Yes, Miss Victorine had saved Amy in more ways than one. She'd saved Amy's life, and more than that, she'd saved Amy from the bitterest kind of hostility and cynicism.

Amy would do anything for Miss Victorine.

"All this excitement has worn me out." Miss Victorine smiled tremulously.

"I know. I'm sorry."

"Don't be sorry, dear! It's good for an old woman to have her routine shaken up occasionally. Gets the blood flowing. Makes the brain work." Miss Victorine tapped her forehead.

"I think your brain works just fine."

"Yes, Papa said I always was the smartest of the children." A satisfied smiled curved Miss Victorine's wrinkled lips. "But if you had known my brothers, you'd realize that was not a compliment."

Amy laughed as she knew Miss Victorine wished.

"I do like this room." Miss Victorine looked around, then closed her eyes with a smile.

Amy looked around, too. The thick curtains were faded from dark blue to a pale robin's egg. The flowers on the wallpaper were as faded as last summer's blossoms, and even the squares where the pictures had hung were faded. The white duvet cover had turned yellow and the down inside was nothing more than a thin fluff. The wooden floors were worn from generations of footsteps, and they kept a pan under the worst of the leaks.

But to Miss Victorine, this was home.

Amy's gaze moved to the sweet, plump face against the pillows. Miss Victorine had said it was good for her to be shaken up, to have her routine changed, but Amy didn't believe her.

Miss Victorine wanted—needed—to stay here in the house where she'd grown up, but when Amy had proposed her plan, Miss Victorine refused to hear of any variation that allowed her to remain out of sight and untainted by their transgression. If she was going to profit by the crime, she was going to take all the risks, and nothing Amy had said could change her mind.

So when they talked about what they would do with the ransom money, they discussed living in Italy in a villa, or a cottage in Greece or Spain. Someplace where Miss Victorine's bones would no longer ache in the cold, and oranges grew right outside their back door. And all the time Amy knew Miss Victorine wanted to stay here in her leaky cottage with its faded wallpaper and the neighbors she had known her whole life.

Amy didn't understand such a sentiment. Since she turned twelve, she had wandered the byways of England and Scotland. She couldn't comprehend the concept of home. She didn't dare try.

Tucking the blankets close around Miss Victorine's neck, Amy gave her a kiss on the forehead and left her to sleep.

Inside her bedchamber, Amy splashed cold water on her face to calm herself. She'd chosen the maid's quarters for its proximity to Miss Victorine; if ever Miss Victorine needed her, Amy wanted to be close. Not that Miss Victorine had needed anything; she was a spry old lady, not dotty with old age, but always eccentric.

The cold water did Amy no good.

That man had held a knife to Miss Victorine's neck! And while his cruelty and disregard for Miss Victorine's safety made her fume, it also brought into sharp focus the peril of her scheme. She held a dangerous man in the cellar, and one wrong step would send them plunging off a precipice. It was one thing to take a chance with her own life, another with dear, sweet Miss Victorine.

Making her way to the kitchen, she looked around. It was as shabby as the bedroom, with a wooden table cleaned so often with sand that it bowed in the middle, a huge fireplace that let in cold drafts in the winter, and thatching that was wearing thin in the corner. Yet Miss Victorine had made this a homey room; garlands of dried herbs and onions hung from the blackened rafters and pots of flowers bobbed in the windows.

Amy glared at the closed door to the cellar. She'd slammed it on the way out, but she would damned well go down those stairs in what her grandmamma would call a civilized manner. No matter how much his wonderfully handsome, totally ungracious lordship grated on her, she wouldn't give him the satisfaction of knowing he got under her skin.

Although perhaps with the shooting it was a little late for that.

Chapter 6

With great care, Amy opened the cellar door. With ladylike demeanor, she descended the stairs. And as her reward, she had the satisfaction of catching His Mighty Lordship sitting on the cot, his knee crooked sideways and his ankle pulled toward him, cursing at the manacle.

"I got it out of your own castle," she said.

Northcliff jumped like a lad caught at a mischief. "My . . . castle?" At once he realized what she meant. "Here on the island, you mean. The old ancestral pile."

"Yes." She strolled farther into the room. "I went down into the dungeons, crawled around in among the spider webs and the skeletons of your family's enemies—"

"Oh, come on." He straightened his leg. "There aren't any skeletons."

"No," she admitted.

"We had them removed years ago."

For one instant, she was shocked. So his family had been ruthless murderers!

Then she realized he was smirking. The big, pompous jackass was making a jest of her labors. "If I could have found two manacles that were in good shape, I'd have locked both your legs to the wall."

"Why stop there? Why not my hands, too?" He moved his leg to make the chain clink loudly. "Think of your satisfaction at the image of my starving, naked body chained to the cold stone—"

"Starving?" She cast a knowledgeable eye at the empty breakfast tray, then allowed her lips to curve into a sarcastic smile.

"You'd love a look at my naked body though, wouldn't you?" He fixed his gaze on her, and for one second she thought she saw a lick of golden flame in his light brown eyes. "Isn't that what this is all about?"

"I beg your pardon." She took a few steps closer to him—although she remained well out of range of his long arms. "What *are* you talking about?"

"I spurned you, didn't I?"

"What?" *What?* What was he going on about?

"You're a girl from my past, an insignificant debutante I ignored at some cotillion or another. I didn't dance with you." He stretched out on the cot, the epitome of idle relaxation. "Or I did, but I didn't talk to you. Or I forgot to offer you a lemonade, or—"

"I don't *believe* you." She tottered to the rocking chair and sank down. "Are you saying you think this whole kidnapping was done because you, the almighty marquess of Northcliff, treated me like a wallflower?"

"It seems unlikely I treated you like a wallflower. I have better taste than that." He cast a critical glance up and down her workaday gown, then focused on her face. "You're not in the common way, you must know that. With the proper gown and your hair swirled up in that style you women favor"—he twirled his fingers about his head—"you would be handsome. Perhaps even lovely."

She gripped the arms of the chair. Even his compliments sounded like insults! "We've never before met, my lord."

As if she had not spoken, he continued, "But I don't remember you, so I must have ignored you and hurt your feelings—"

"Damn!" Exploding out of the chair, she paced behind it, gripping the back hard enough to break the wood. His arrogance was amazing. Invulnerable! "Haven't you heard a single word I've said to you? Are you so conceited you can't conceive of a woman who isn't interested in you as a suitor?"

"It's not conceit when it's the truth." He sounded quite convinced.

She couldn't believe him. He imagined he was gold-plated. "I've told you the truth. We've kidnapped you as just retribution for your thievery and your neglect."

"I am not a thief." He spoke through his teeth, so at least he had enough honor left that he was insulted. "I did not steal anything from Miss Victorine, and even if I did, what difference would it make? A beading machine? Of what value is that?"

Oh, he was so ignorant. So smug. Amy wanted to put him in a factory and let him stand there for fourteen hours a day making lace while cotton flew threw the air so thick it choked the lungs. For just one day, she wanted him to work for a living.

Taking Miss Victorine's ball of twine and shuttle from the table, Amy dangled the tiny bit of beading and lace before him. "Ladies pay for beaded lace for their gowns and their reticules. The designs are intricate and difficult to learn. Do you know how long it takes to create an inch of beaded lace?"

"No, but I'm sure you're going to tell me." He couldn't have sounded more bored.

"Miss Victorine is a very accomplished, and it takes her two hours."

He pulled a long, scoffing face. "You exaggerate."

"Do I?" Amy was starting to have fun. "Let's see how quickly you can bead."

"I do not bead."

"Of course not. You're a man and a lord. You have better things to do. Ride, box, hunt, smoke, drink, dance . . ." She glanced around the cellar. "What are you doing now?"

His white teeth snapped together like a shackled dog's. "I can read . . . if you have a book."

"Oh, we have a book. We have several. They're old, well-read, and treasured. What we *don't* have is money for precious beeswax candles."

"Are you saying tonight I'll sit here in the dark?" He sat up, his feigned relaxation gone.

"I'm saying Miss Victorine will sacrifice her lamp to you rather than allow you to sit in the dark, but it's a dim, sputtering light at best, not at all what you're used to. That's why we bead. Once you learn, you can do it in bad light."

"How difficult can it be if you can do it in the dark?" He laughed with light contempt. "But of course. It's women's work. It's not difficult at all."

It was obvious he held her gender in disdain, and not the condescending disdain so many men displayed. His contempt was pointed and angry, and she pitied any woman he chose as his wife. "Don't be afraid, my lord. You needn't worry you'll make a fool of yourself." Amy shook the small piece of lace and beads again. "We'll start you out with the simplest design."

He ignored her with arrogant indifference, slithering back on the cot like a snake settling onto a warm rock. "Tell me the truth. Did I break your girlish heart?"

"My lord, I don't have a girlish heart to break." She cast a critical eye over his lounging figure. "And if I did, it would not break over one such as you. Bored, indolent, without honor or scruples—"

"So I take by your scorn you really weren't ever a debutante." He had never been so insulted in his life, and by this girl, this creature. . . . Who was she who dared imprison and disparage the marquess of North-cliff?

Without the key for the manacle or a weapon for enforcement of his will, he couldn't escape, so he bent his mind to discovering who this Amy creature truly was. If he discovered her weaknesses, he could escape. If she had no weaknesses, at least he would be entertained.

He lolled back on the cot, consciously cultivating the very picture of lazy decadence . . . because he enjoyed watching Miss Upright-and-Righteous get that sour-lemon look on her face. "Then who are you? Where are you from?"

"I'm Miss Amy Rosabel and I'm"—she hesitated, smiling slightly—"not from here."

"No. You're from Beaumontagne, I believe Miss Victorine said."

He had the satisfaction of seeing Amy's eyes widen in horror. "She told you that?"

"How else would I know?" Was she guilty because she had lied to Miss Victorine about her origins? Or was she appalled that he had discovered the truth? "You do have a trace of an accent, but I don't recognize it."

"What else did she tell you?" Amy leaned across the table at him. "*What else?*"

"Nothing else. Why?"

"For no reason." Amy leaned back. "I just thought—"

"You thought she had betrayed all your secrets." At the revelation, he almost purred with delight, and he experienced more delight when she betrayed herself with the smallest shake of the head. "Or . . . not all your secrets, but the one big one."

"I assure you, if I have a secret, it will do you no good to know of it." She dismissed him with a wave of her hand.

"Not while I'm chained, anyway. But it gives my mind a puzzle to work on. Let me think, what do I know about Beaumontagne?" He delved in his mind for every tidbit of information about a country he had previously dismissed as insignificant. "There was a revolution there about ten years ago. The king was killed in battle. The country has been recovered by the dowager queen, but she's so old, speculation exists she may be controlled by someone behind the scenes. A usurper of some kind."

Amy folded her arms over her stomach as she listened.

So he was giving her a gut ache. Good. "There were children, but they disappeared during the furor and are assumed dead so even if the queen is in charge, there's no one to inherit the throne." As he thought, he tapped his lips with his finger. "And I suppose you might be"—he watched her tense—"a refugee."

"I might be. Or I might be a wonderful actress who has turned my talents to imagining a past for myself that doesn't exist."

"Not an actress, I don't think. If you had been, I would have moved every obstacle to make you my mistress."

"You really are a swine." Her lips might sneer, yet still they promised sensual pleasure.

"And you *can't* have been one of my mistresses. I

would remember that." In fact, the whole of Amy sang to him like a siren luring a sailor onto the rocks.

He didn't like wanting her, but he was a pragmatist. If he had to be locked away, better to have a gaoler who moved with gratifying sensuality, whose downy skin courtesans would covet, whose eyes challenged and beckoned. In a meditative tone, he said, "Although you're not the kind of mistress I prefer. I prefer a woman of submission whose life is devoted to making me happy. Yet your green eyes are quite out of the ordinary. I fear I would not have been able to resist taking you."

Those green eyes narrowed dangerously.

"With the color and the exotic slant," he continued, "they're almost like a cat's."

Her hands curled into catlike claws. "Do you always catalog a woman's assets aloud to her?"

"Never." He poked at her with a verbal stick. "But I'm bored, indolent, without honor and scruples. Remember?"

When he threw her own words in her face, her eyes sparked and again he thought Lucretia Borgia must have had eyes that color. *The color of poison.*

This was a small retaliation for the humiliation of being chained, but he enjoyed himself excessively. "I suspect your hair, when unbound, is glorious."

As he knew would happen, she lifted her hands to cup the thick black braid she had wound in a chignon at the back of her head. With that simple movement, she exposed her figure, her vanity, and most important, a womanly instinct she could not subdue.

He took ruthless advantage of the view, and scrutinized her curves. The backside he had earlier admired was matched by a small, high bosom and a narrow waist. "You have a fine figure." Fortunately for his bored, unscrupulous self, she really did. "Although your gown is not at all the thing." And what an understatement that was.

The style of the gown could have been his grandmother's, with a gathered skirt, a bodice that was tight around her waist and up under her bosom, where it gathered it soft folds. The neckline was modest and made more modest by a draped shoulder scarf that hid even the hint of cleavage, and he found himself enmeshed in a flash of fantasy that involved his removing the scarf and sliding his hand inside the bodice . . . He caught himself and half smiled. Well, she *was* attractive and he *was* bored.

She suddenly realized that she posed for him—was it his smile?—for she dropped her hands to her side. "In what scenario of yours would I not be insulted to hear your judgment of my figure or my clothing?"

"As long as I remain here, I promise I'll tell you my opinion." His smile chilled. "It's the least I can do to reward your hospitality."

He could see she didn't like that—that he would dare to turn the tables on her and speak his mind.

One morning spent without seeing the sun, chained by his ankle, had given him a new appreciation for the prisoners in Newgate. And the idea of spending an entire day here, an evening, a week, alone in a dim cellar with nothing to do, made him want to claw his way through the walls or go on a rampage that broke every piece of furniture in this room. But trying to claw his way through the walls would do no more than offer this wretched Amy creature amusement, and he'd already lost his temper once today. That resulted in a painful testing of the damned manacle's strength when it jerked him off his feet. When he'd examined it, he'd seen a manacle that showed its age, but was stout enough to resist his every effort to knock it or saw it or pull it apart. He was definitely not going to test the health of his leg again. It still throbbed from the fall.

He wondered if she would get disgusted enough with him to let him go . . . but no, not this steely-eyed cat creature. Any woman who had imagined and executed so daring a scheme wouldn't give way over a few words.

Instead she cast an eye about the room. With a grunt, she lifted the edge of the long table and dragged it so that she could sit at the end opposite his cot and be out of his reach. "Did you think I'd be shocked by your mention of a mistress and run away?"

"No." He watched her lift the heavy weight and realized that for all her slight figure, she was strong. "You don't hide your face or gasp in horror."

"Every woman knows a man like you keeps a mistress." Satisfied with the placement of the table, she dusted her hands. "*Miss Victorine* knows you keep a mistress."

"But Miss Victorine would pretend she did not, and most certainly she wouldn't allow the word to pass her lips. She's a lady." He watched Amy closely to see how the insult affected her.

It appeared to affect her not at all. "So she is."

"You, on the other hand, may speak like a lady, but you haven't been protected from the realities of life. As I talk to you, I learn so much about you."

"What do you mean? Why should you care to learn about me?" She was disconcerted. Indignant.

He sat up slowly, allowing her to look him over, to contemplate how very much larger he was than she. "When I'm free and I capture you and send you to your hanging, I would like to know the type of female you are, so in the future I may avoid that female."

If the mention of hanging terrified her, if his gathering of forces impressed her, she hid it beneath a nonchalance that indicated confidence—or stupidity. And he feared it wasn't stupidity. "I can almost promise that you'll never meet another female like me."

"You imagine you're unique?" More and more fascinating. Most ladies he knew did everything in their power to look like everyone else, be like everyone else.

"I don't imagine anything. Imagination is a luxury I can't afford."

So. She was a pragmatist. A very young pragmatist. "I have an imagination. As I look at you, it's quite active."

"Imagining my hanging, my lord?"

"No. Imagining you as my mistress." He laughed aloud at the derision she displayed—and at the truthful, unguarded moment when her gaze flew to his and recognized the truth.

He was a man. She was a woman. They were alone together with no chaperone, talking of matters no ordinary gentleman and lady would discuss. No matter how much they disliked each other, the primal urge sparked between them—and he knew that with a little coddling, the spark could become a roaring blaze.

The question was—did she know? He couldn't tell. She wasn't an ordinary doxy, nor was she the typical servant, and certainly she wasn't a real lady. She eluded his analysis because he'd never had to work at understanding a woman.

From the first moment he'd stepped into society, ladies and opera singers alike had bent their wills to his. They took care not to bother him with their own desires, their own needs. If he needed quiet, they didn't chatter. If he wished for song, they played and warbled. Not once had he had to bother deciphering a woman's purpose, for her purpose was always the same—to please him.

Now an enigma stood before him, one who had already outfoxed him.

That would never do. He would beat her at her game. "As a rule," he drawled, "I don't take mistresses under the age of twenty. There's a marvelous enthusiasm but no finesse. No skill."

She didn't flinch at his brutal honesty. "I can imagine that would distract from your search for new forms of depravity."

"So while I can spin my fantasy whenever I wish, I'm afraid you wouldn't do for me."

Sarcasm dripped from her every word. "You're good at imagining, so pray imagine my heartbreak."

So. She wasn't yet twenty.

He was twenty-nine.

The need to outsmart this trifling adversary grew more imperative.

"The more I know you, the more I wonder who you are." He counted off her qualities on his fingers. "You have the accent of a lady. You dress like a peasant. You shoot like a marksman. You view the world cynically, yet you venerate Miss Victorine. Your face and body would be the envy of a young goddess, yet you sport an air of innocence. And that innocence hides a criminal mind and the cheek to pull off the most outrageous of felonies."

"So I'm Athena, the goddess of war."

"Definitely not Diana, the goddess of virginity."

As the last shot hit home, he saw Amy's mask slip. Blood rushed to her face. She bit her lip and looked toward the stairs as if only now realizing she could have—should have—left this whole discussion behind.

He laughed softly, triumphantly. "Or perhaps I'm mistaken. Perhaps you have more in common with Diana than I thought."

"Pray remember, sir, that Diana was also the goddess of the hunt." Amy leaned across the table, intent on making her point—but the blush still played across her cheeks. "She carried a bow and arrow, and she always bagged her quarry. Have a look at the bullet hole in the rock behind you and remember my skill and my cynicism. For we do know things about each other. I know that if you escape, you'll make sure I'm hung from a gibbet. You know that if I catch you escaping, I'll shoot you through the heart. Remember that as you cast longing glances toward the window." With a flourish, she picked up the breakfast tray and walked up the stairs.

Jermyn had learned something else about Amy.

She liked to have the last word.

Chapter 7

Who was she? Where was she from?

At the top of the stairs, in the kitchen, Amy stopped and clutched the silver cross that hung on a necklace around her neck. The necklace that united her with her country and her sisters.

Lost. All lost.

Who was she? Where was she from?

Northcliff demanded answers as if he had the right to know. That attitude Amy was used to facing. That attitude she always defied.

But never had she met a man who evinced the interest to subtly probe her mind and discover her secrets. She didn't like that. She didn't like him. She didn't trust him with his open talk about mistresses and his frank admission of fantasies.

About her!

Who was she? Where was she from?

She knew very well she was attractive. She'd known that since she was fourteen. A good number of the years she'd spent on the road with her sister Clarice had been spent transforming her through the use of cosmetics from a drab into a female worth a second look. But Clarice was the handsome daughter. She'd been the one who could charm every man and woman in any village and sell their products and keep them fed. It was Clarice everyone adored. Not Amy.

But to hear Lord Northcliff inform her he would have moved any obstacle to have her as his mistress . . .

He was jesting. Or a single day without indulging in debauchery had left him ready to be pleased by any female at hand.

But if that was true, what kind of lustful beast would two days create?

And why did she feel a warmth within her, a melting, a stretching of all that was instinctive and female?

Who was she? Where was she from?

Dear Lord. She hardly knew anymore.

Beaumontagne, twelve years ago

With a reckless glance behind her, seven-year-old Amy skidded across the marble floor in the royal antechamber. She flung open the door of the wardrobe. A tall, broad, ancient piece of fine furniture, it housed the king's ceremonial capes. In a desperate hurry yet equally desperate to keep quiet, she dived inside. The wood creaked beneath her, and she froze. Because if she didn't keep quiet . . .

Footsteps in the corridor.

The light, sharp sound of high heels accompanied by the tap of a cane.

Firm, heavy footsteps, several sets.

"That child is incorrigible." Grandmamma's voice. The Dowager Queen Claudia. Coming closer. Entering the room.

It was dark in here. It smelled of cedar. And Amy's heart beat so hard, she feared Grandmamma could hear the pounding.

With her long, skinny nose and uncanny accuracy, Grandmamma sniffed out Amy's larks. Would she somehow know Amy was there?

"Do you know what your youngest daughter has done now?" Grandmamma snapped.

"Has she once again slid down the grand banister and landed on our master of the horse?" Amy's father, King Raimund, sounded patient.

"No, sire." Sir Alerio whispered like a man who constantly worked with edgy beasts and took care never to startle them. "Princess Amy hasn't knocked me over for a fortnight."

Moving with great care among the velvet and silk and fur, Amy put her eye to the knothole in the wood. A cold rain streaked the windows. Footmen moved silently from one candle to another, lighting each one in a vain attempt to alleviate the dim grayness. The usual group of courtiers surrounded her father. Lord Octavio, the lord chamberlain. Sir

Alerio, the master of the horse. Lord Carsten, the castle steward. Lord Silas, the prime minister.

Except for Sir Alerio, Amy didn't like the courtiers. Sorcha said they were important, but Amy thought they were staid old men with droopy chins and droopy noses and no equanimity when faced with three active young princesses.

"I'm glad to hear that, Alerio." Poppa wasn't as tall as the other men, and he carried an impressive weight around his middle. His luxuriant mustache and sideburns gave his round face a jolly expression, and his purple cape provided a grand sense of royalty.

Amy loved her poppa. She loved him more than anyone else in the world, and right now, she wanted his arms around her. If only the others would go away. If only she could put her head against his shoulder and have him make her world right.

"So, Queen Claudia." Poppa removed his crown and placed it on the purple cushion Lord Carsten offered. The footman in charge of the crown whisked it away to the safe place, accompanied by two other footmen and Lord Carsten. "Has Amy again climbed the tree along the drive and dropped into the duchess's carriage?"

Faint chuckles erupted from the courtiers.

Grandmamma turned on them and frowned, and the chuckles became faint, apologetic coughs.

No one could confront Grandmamma's wrath with composure. She was gaunt and tall, with fierce blue eyes that pierced right through to Amy's sinful soul.

"When Amy dropped into that carriage, she made the duchess faint!" Grandmamma said.

The gentlemen of the antechamber clucked like a bunch of peevish old hens.

"But she did land exactly in the seat opposite the duchess, and you must admit that is no small feat," the king reminded her.

Besides, the duchess faints all the time. *Amy sat back on her heels in the stuffy wardrobe and nodded fiercely in the dark. That's why the duchess was so much fun to tease. The fainting, and the fact she was a widow who had designs on Poppa's hand in marriage. If she kept visiting the palace on flimsy pretexts, Amy would land right on her next time.*

"The duchess has such a delicate constitution, one is forced to wonder if she is entirely truthful about her reaction," *Poppa said gently.*

Amy barely caught back her shouted agreement.

"That is hardly the point," *Grandmamma said.*

Amy stuck out her lower lip.

"What did Amy do this time?" *Poppa asked.*

Amy was surprised to hear a note of weariness in her father's voice, almost as if he couldn't bear another crisis.

Was he tired of dealing with his troublesome daughter? With her?

"She blackened Prince Rainger's eye!"

The silence that followed was so full of portent, Amy leaned forward to put her eye to the knothole again—and accidentally bumped the door. With a click, the latch opened. The door swung open. Amy scurried to catch the edge with her fingers. The anteroom flashed before her gaze. Lord Octavio, Lord Alerio and Lord Silas stood with their backs to

*her, facing the king. Grandmamma paced away from the lit-
tle group, her cane tapping on the floor. Only Poppa could
see Amy. His gaze flashed toward the wardrobe, but he
didn't react.*

He seemed preoccupied with her crime.

"She blackened Prince Rainger's eye!" *Grandmamma repeated, as if the report was so dreadful it needed to be reiter-
ated.*

*Amy got the door closed with barely a sound. She leaned
back among the cloaks and calmed her racing heart. It was
stuffy in here, but so much better than the alternative—an
open door and exposure.*

*The silence drew out so long that Amy at last cautiously
looked out again.*

*Grandmamma's blue dress was without wrinkle. Her
white chignon rested in perfect order on her head. Her thin
lips pressed together as she considered her son.* "Do you understand, Raimund?"

"I believe I do. You're saying that my seven-year-old
daughter punched—I assume she punched?" *He looked to
Grandmamma for guidance.*

"What difference does it make?" *Grandmamma demanded. Then,* "Yes. Yes, she punched him."

"My seven-year-old daughter punched Prince Rainger—"

"My godson!"

*The courtiers backed away from the scene as if fearing
incineration.*

"Yes. I know who he is. Rainger is your godson and my
eldest daughter's betrothed. He is also sixteen years old, and
you're saying my seven-year-old daughter punched him in

the face hard enough to blacken his eye." King Raimund laughed briefly and rubbed his forehead with his fingers. "What a fighter she is!"

"I did not bring this to your attention so you could admire the child!" Grandmamma's voice did not rise with irritation. Rather it grew colder.

Amy huddled back in the wardrobe among the ermine trimmings. She shivered.

"No, of course you didn't. And I'm not admiring her." Poppa laughed again. Cackled, in fact. "I'm wondering what we should do to toughen up Prince Rainger."

"Toughen up . . . ! I never!"

Amy had never heard Grandmamma sputter before, and she rather enjoyed it.

Poppa got control of himself. Stopped laughing. "You have my word." Putting his arm around Grandmamma, he led her toward the door. "I'll take of the matter."

The gentlemen of the antechamber all nodded pontifically.

"But Raimund." Grandmamma's thin, penciled-in eyebrows winged skyward. "I've always taken care of disciplining the girls."

"You brought me this problem. Obviously you want me to handle this," Poppa said. "I'll take care of the matter."

Oh, no. Amy sat back in the wardrobe. Poppa was going to take care of the matter, that matter being her. He had never taken care of the matter before. Now Poppa was going to . . . oh, no.

The gentlemen of the antechamber waited until the footman had shut the tall door behind Grandmamma before they broke into speech. All of them. At the same time.

Amy couldn't understand a word, but she didn't care. She

was too busy rubbing her cheek against the silk lining of Poppa's Christmas cape and sniffing the scent of cigars on his clothes. She associated the scent with rare moments spent with a kindly father who had too many duties and too little time for his daughters. Now she was a matter to him.

Vaguely she heard Lord Octavio say, "Sire, did I detect a threat from the emissary from France?"

"I think you can safely say that was a threat." Poppa sighed.

"And another threat from the emissary from Spain?" Sir Alerio asked.

"We pay a steep price for living on the spine of the Pyrenees between two old foes," Poppa said.

Something about the tone of Poppa's voice made Amy edge forward and look into the room. "Yet sire, I don't think Spain or France are our primary opponents." Lord Silas's voice was high, almost feminine, but Amy knew Poppa listened to him more than anyone.

"No." The king allowed Sir Alerio to remove his cloak.

"The revolutionaries—" Lord Octavio said.

"Yes," Poppa agreed. "The revolutionaries."

"In Richarte and in Beaumontagne, too. The whole region has been subverted!" Lord Octavio said.

"We need to send Prince Rainger back to Richarte escorted by a large armed guard," Poppa instructed.

"Damn the French for setting Europe afire with revolution. Damn them for insinuating that old royalty should give way to new blood!" Lord Silas's drooping chin quivered with indignation.

Sir Alerio strode toward the wardrobe where Amy hid. In horror, she realized he was going to hang up the king's cloak. Now.

She scooted back among the other cloaks, back into the deepest corner, and huddled into a little ball, her head on her upraised knees.

In the antechamber, she heard the door open and shut, and Lord Carsten's voice said, "It was a bad time for the crops to fail."

"You're stating the obvious, Carsten!" Sir Alerio opened the wardrobe wide.

Light and air streamed in, but she peeked out to see if he spotted her.

"Someone has to," Carsten answered hotly.

Poppa overrode the incipient quarrel by raising his voice. "Put that away, Alerio, quickly, and get back here. I have instructions for you."

"As you wish, Your Highness." Sir Alerio hurriedly hung up the cloak and slammed the door hard enough to make Amy's ears ring.

She slithered into a relieved little mound.

"We need to purchase grain, as much as possible," Poppa said. "I'll go out and talk to the people and reassure them, but in the meantime, let me know if more riots break out."

"If there are more riots, Your Highness," Sir Alerio said, "you must consider sending your family away for—"

Poppa shushed him sharply.

Amy lifted her head. She scooted forward and looked out the knothole. She wanted to hear what Sir Alerio had to say. Sending your family away for . . . what? A few days? A vacation?

"You know what to do." Poppa waved the gentlemen away. "For now, I'd like to be alone."

The courtiers bowed and backed out of the antechamber. The massive door shut with barely a sound.

Poppa moved to the ancient throne and seated himself, and ruffled his brown hair. He did look tired, as if he'd suffered too many sleepless nights. She didn't understand. How could her father suddenly look so defeated?

Then his kindly voice said, "Amy, come here."

Her father was looking right at the wardrobe.

How had he known she was there?

"I used to hide there when my father was king," he answered quite as if she'd asked. "And you were lucky only I saw you when the door swung open."

Cautiously she pushed the door wide. She inched her foot out until it reached the floor. She craned her neck around to see Poppa watching her steadily, and she smiled with all her teeth. Her daddy loved her. She knew it. But he expected her to behave, not like a princess, but with kindness.

She had not been kind.

And she knew it.

And he knew it. He would be mad.

She inched toward him, one foot placed carefully after the other.

He said nothing.

She sneaked a glance at his face.

He didn't look mad. It was worse than that.

He looked disappointed.

"Your Highness? Poppa?" Her voice quivered.

"Come here, Amy." He even sounded disappointed.

Oh, no. She felt sick in the pit of her stomach. Daddy had always been her champion, but she had never been so bad before. Her walk across the antechamber seemed to take forever. When she stood right in front of the throne, she stared fixedly at the buckles below the knees of his formal breeches and waited for him to tell her to go cut a switch from the willow tree in the garden.

"All right, daughter." His hands came into view. He picked her up and sat her in his lap. "Tell me what happened."

He still loved her. Poppa still loved her. He smelled like tobacco and he was warm and kind. She buried her head in his chest and choked, "That stupid prince deserved what he got. He's a big old stupid . . . boy."

"I don't doubt that, but what specifically did he do this time?" Poppa didn't wrap his arm around her.

That was stupid old Rainger's fault, too.

"He said . . . he said . . ." Amy took a deep breath. "He said I killed my mother the queen." She held her breath, waiting for Poppa to deny it.

He said nothing.

"He said it's my fault she's dead and she must be sorry when she looks down from heaven and sees what a"—she could hardly get the words out—"a dirty, ill-mannered girl I am."

"Rainger is not someone to reproach a child for being dirty or ill-mannered." Poppa's voice had a snap to it. "When he was your age, he was both."

"He still is, and mean, too! He thinks just because he's the crown prince of Richarte and betrothed to Sorcha and older than any of us, that he's better, but he's not!"

"So since you've felt the pain he's caused in his cruelty,

and because you're smarter than he is, you won't want to emulate him."

Amy's little bubble of self-congratulation popped. Poppa wasn't on her side.

"Amy, let's not pretend that you've been an exemplary child today." He sounded very grave and very kingly. "Your grandmamma has good reason for wanting to have you disciplined, and so you shall be."

Amy never cried when she was disciplined, but she cried when she disappointed her father.

Now big fat tears worked their way out of her eyes and down her cheeks.

"Your grandmamma would tell you that you shouldn't lose your temper because you're a princess. I'm not your grandmamma."

"You're the king!"

"Yes, I'm the king, and I tell you you shouldn't lose your temper because you say hurtful things and wound other people's feelings."

She put her head on his shoulder and sniffled horribly. "I guess I shouldn't."

"And because if you attacked someone bigger than you and meaner than you—and there are many people like that in the world—he might seriously hurt you. I don't want that, and I would consider myself negligent if I didn't command you to never physically attack anyone again." He put his handkerchief to her nose. "Blow."

She did.

"Why are you crying?" he asked.

She didn't want to know, yet she had to find out the truth.

She had to, because she couldn't live with herself if she didn't. "Did I really kill Mama?"

"My dear daughter." Tilting her head back, he wiped her eyes and smiled into her face. "Your mother died when you were born, but you didn't kill her. She died because she loved you so much, she was willing to risk everything to have you."

No one had ever talked about her mother before. When she asked questions, her sisters got all weepy and her grandmamma had tightly folded her lips and told her to be quiet for once. Amy had never dreamed her beloved poppa would take her on his knee and tell her stories, but she had to interrupt. "She loved me? But Poppa, she never met me."

"Yes, she did. She held you cradled within her for nine months. You moved in her, she fed you with her body, and after she delivered you, she held you in her arms."

"Oh. It's a great honor that my mother the queen loved me so much." Amy's confidence rose. But when her father didn't reply right away, she faltered, "Isn't it?"

"Yes, it is. When someone loves you so much she will die so you might live, it is an honor—and a responsibility."

Amy wanted to groan. Not another responsibility!

But Poppa looked grave. So grave.

So she kept her voice small. She felt small. "I guess so. What do I have to do?"

"Live your life in a way that's worthy of that great offering. Be strong. Help those who are less fortunate. You're a very smart girl." He tapped her forehead. "Use that intelligence to make someone happy."

"Do you do that?"

"I did—with your mother. She and I loved each other so much we used our intelligence to make each other happy. We spoke without words." When Amy would have interrupted to ask what he meant, he put his finger on her lips. "We shared a soul. She still lives here"—he tapped his chest—"in my heart. I want that for you. For every one of my daughters."

"I can do that." She sat straighter on his lap. "I can use my intelligence. What else, Poppa?"

"Most important of all, be true to yourself."

"Okay." She hesitated, then asked, "How do I do that?"

"Listen to your heart. Follow your instincts. Believe in what they tell you, and do the right thing."

"Okay." Now she understood.

"Sometimes it's not easy being a princess." He hugged her.

"I know that. I have to wear nice gowns all the time and get my hair curled and wave to the poor children and learn deportment and never have fun riding the big horses—"

"That wasn't quite what I was going to say. I was going to say that it's not easy being a princess, but as long as you live in a way that honors your mother, you'll be a person I'm proud to call my daughter."

More responsibility! Now she had to live her life in a way that was worthy of her mama's sacrifice, and she had to become someone Poppa was proud to call his daughter. Still, she supposed she had escaped pretty easily . . .

Hadn't she? "What is my punishment?"

He studied her long face. "What does Grandmamma usually do?"

"Sometimes she sends me out to cut a switch off the willow tree and whips me with it."

"No. I won't do that," he said decisively.

"She makes me write stuff on my slate."

"Stuff?"

"Stuff like I will not kick Prince Rainger really hard in the knee."

Poppa sort of choked, then he cleared his throat and said decisively, "That's not fiendish enough. You know, don't you, that as king, I have access to devices of torture and war?"

Her eyes widened until they hurt. She nodded.

"But I'm your father." He put her on her feet before him. "I love you, and I don't want to permanently injure you or keep you in the dungeon for too long."

She swallowed. She braced herself.

He stood. He picked up his scepter. He drew himself up to his full kingly height, and made his pronouncement. "You will be nice to Rainger, to your sisters, and to your grandmamma—"

Amy caught her breath in dismay.

"—for three days."

"Oh, Poppa!" She put her palms together prayerfully. "Let me go cut a switch!"

"No," he said sternly. "You have to be nice for three days to your sisters, your grandmamma, and the prince."

"I could write a hundred sentences. A thousand sentences."

She thought she saw a glimmer of a smile.

"Be nice to your—"

"Sisters, Grandmamma and yucky ol' Rainger. I know." She dragged herself over to the tall, heavy door. With great effort, she tugged it open. She looked back at her father.

He still stood on the dais in front of the throne. He held the jeweled scepter. His hair curled over his forehead and *around his ears. His sideburns edged his jaw. He looked very kingly—and very patient.*

"All right, Poppa, I'll be nice." Before she snapped the door closed, she said, "But I won't like it."

Chapter 8

*O*utside, a sudden spring rain cast itself at the high windows. Wind rattled the casements. The small mound of coals in the stove smoldered, giving off enough heat to take the chill off the cellar. A tallow candle cast a feeble glow over the chessboard and a stench into the air. Miss Victorine did her handwork by the light of a tin lamp filled with oil, and it smelled, too.

Jermyn saw Amy strolling toward him, a seductive roll to her hips, discarding her clothing as she walked. She was smiling, teasing him as she stepped out of her petticoats and stood clad in her sheer chemise. Her nipples showed through the cream silk, puckered with desire for him—

Amy's disagreeable tone shredded his fantasy. "My lord, you have been staring at the chessboard for a full five minutes. Would you like me to make your move for you?"

He jumped like a lad with his fingers caught in the jam pot. The rickety chair beneath him groaned.

"Now, Amy, you must be patient with His Lordship," Miss Victorine chided. "He's spent the day manacled by his ankle and he's ready to snarl like a lion."

"More like a small, ill-tempered badger," Amy muttered.

Jermyn looked across the long length of the table at her. He sat on one end, she sat on the other. She wore a most contrary expression, and her eyes sparked with irritation.

She made it most difficult to indulge in a dream about her. He wished, just once, she'd give him something to work with—a flirtatious glance, a beckoning smile.

"Lord Northcliff will be better tomorrow when the ransom arrives and he can be set free," Miss Victorine said serenely.

"Tomorrow?" For one moment, he forgot about Amy and her stubborn refusal to cooperate with his whimsy. "Are you sure it will be tomorrow?"

"If your uncle follows directions, then the ransom will be delivered tomorrow and you'll be set free." Amy smiled at him with relish.

She liked holding him in her power. She liked having men jump at her command. She wasn't soft and sweet and pretty, the way he liked his women to be. She was clever. She was sharp-tongued. She was too

angular, with elbows that poked at her sleeves and
thin collarbones instead of plump shoulders. Her face
was handsome rather than pretty, and he would have
said she never smiled, except that she did.

She smiled when she gazed at Miss Victorine.

She might be—was!—misguided in her attempts to
extort money from him, but he couldn't doubt her sin-
cere affection for the older woman. Nor, unfortunately, could he doubt Miss Victorine's crushing
poverty.

He glanced at the plump figure in the rocking chair.
A yellowing cap topped Miss Victorine's white hair.
He recognized the shawl around her shoulders—he
had admired the pattern when he was a lad. Now half
the fringe was missing, giving it an oddly toothless appearance. She huddled within the wool's embrace as if
she were cold, yet when he demanded Amy add more
coals on the fire, Miss Victorine had waved her hand
before her face and claimed to be too warm. She moved
stiffly and he could see a bruise on her bare arm from
his rough handling, yet her gnarled fingers flew as she
created her beaded lace.

The beaded lace that grew as slowly as Amy claimed
it did.

Perhaps in one way at least, Amy was right. Somehow Uncle Harrison had signally failed when it came
to the care of Miss Victorine, and that led Jermyn to the
worry that he failed in other ways, too. Jermyn should
have kept a closer eye on the proceedings on his estate.
Perhaps, if Uncle Harrison had been truly negligent,

Jermyn could forgive Amy's unpleasantness . . . if not his imprisonment.

He gave her the kiss of peace, and slid his hand down her arm and up her skirt, and kissed her lips that smiled on him while she begged his forgiveness . . .

Blind with lust, he moved his knight.

"My lord, that was a careless move and I beg . . . oh!" Leaning over, she studied the board intently. "How very clever of you. I had not seen that stratagem before. Let me think how to counter it."

Clever? He had been clever? Perhaps the life of dissipation he led hadn't caused all his mind to atrophy.

He blinked.

From whence had that thought come?

He looked across the table. Did he even have to ask? After only one day, Amy had put ideas into his head. It had to be her influence. It couldn't be that all along, he'd been secretly aware he was shirking his duties.

"How will I be set free?" He hoped they had concocted a stupid plan. That would give him the chance to feel infinitely superior.

"After Miss Victorine and I are gone from here—" Amy began.

"You're running away?" A taunt softly spoken.

"Yes, rather than stay here and have you order that we be flayed alive, we are leaving." She challenged him with her sarcasm and her logic.

"I can't imagine he'd have us flayed alive, dear." Miss Victorine's forehead puckered. "That seems to have gone out of style with the rack. I believe Lord Northcliff would have to be satisfied with hanging us."

"True, my lord?" Amy laughed in his face.

Who was this shrew with her fine accent and her saucy mouth?

He bent his attention to the chessboard. With a dark glance and in a voice laden with innuendo, he challenged her. "It has occurred to me there are other ways to kill a woman."

Amy chewed at her lower lip and apprehensively stared at him as if not quite comprehending.

Was she truly so innocent? Or was this an act by an actress unparalleled in performance?

Certainly Miss Victorine, the perennial spinster, continued work as if undaunted, picking up her threads, stringing her tiny beads.

"Like . . . torture?" As if he were an odd, mysterious creature, Amy watched him from the corners of her eyes as she made her chess move.

"Some might call it torture." He laughed, a short, rough outburst. Yes, sitting here indulging in fantasies about an untutored, criminally minded female was certainly torture. "But you were telling me how I would be set free."

"Oh." Amy straightened. "You'll have no problem getting free and back where you belong. Your home is only across the channel."

"So I *am* on Summerwind." As the day had dragged on, he'd started to wonder. It was impossible to tell through the high windows, and this witch could have put him in any cellar anywhere and lied out of spite.

He moved his pawn.

"That you are." Amy moved her bishop. "The key to the manacle has already been placed in a drawer in your house. After we're away, we'll send a note to your uncle telling him where, and you'll be free as soon as he gets over here with it."

He pretended to scrutinize the board while surreptitiously studying her.

She wore most the spectacularly dreadful clothes he'd ever had the misfortune to view. He'd seen two gowns, which he suspected had originally been Miss Victorine's and remade to fit Amy's slender figure. The material had been turned by a seamstress with an excellent hand, yet the style was still old-fashioned to the extreme, and the colors had faded from blue to gray and from pink to white. The cloth drooped dispiritedly over petticoats that he supposed must be wool, or her stockings were, for he had twice caught Amy scratching the back of her leg with one lifted foot, and occasionally she shifted uncomfortably in her chair.

He should have been happy to know she wore a sort of hair shirt. Instead the thought of her wool petticoat led him to musings about what else she wore, which led to speculation that a woman so unfeminine would refuse to wear a corset, which led to the knowledge that beneath the petticoat she probably wore nothing at all, which led to the fact that while his mind scorned her for her surely masculine determination to right what she perceived as a wrong, his body recognized that she was, indeed, a female.

"Well?" Amy tapped her foot.

He shoved his queen into the path of Amy's oncoming piece.

"That was an excessively stupid move, my lord." Amy's displeasure was palpable. "Either you're a mediocre player or you're being gentlemanly and letting me win the game, and neither seems likely. Of what are you thinking?"

He was thinking very hard that if she was his he would clothe her in the finest silks and linens to protect that delicate skin . . . and that led back to vivid fantasies and such discomfort that he desperately longed for a wild ride across the island or a grand drinking spree with his friends or even a simple walk in the sun.

During the two months he'd been on his estate waiting for his leg to heal, he had suffered incredible boredom. He hadn't realized how lucky he was to eat well, to exercise as he wished and, most of all, to see the sun, the trees, the horizon. He was almost insane with the desire to be free—and of course for the scornful, contrary, righteous Amy.

When he was free, he would forget about her in another woman's arms . . . or perhaps he would find Amy and show her what happened to a female who dared to defy the marquess of Northcliff.

He tapped his fingers together and smiled.

He stripped off her ugly gown and cupped her breasts with his hands, examining the shape and color of her nipples. They were as soft and light as a peach . . . no, they were brown and puckered with desire for him . . .

"My lord, you look half asleep." Miss Victorine put her beading down on the table. "Shall we leave you?"

"Sleep at this hour? Absurd. It can't yet be nine o'clock!" In London, he had spent many nights carousing until the dawn.

"That may be true for you, but I am an old woman and need my sleep." Miss Victorine stood.

He stood also, a gesture of respect he found he didn't regret.

"I'll go with you." Amy hurried to Miss Victorine's side. "We'll leave Lord Northcliff the candle. He can read."

He glanced at the small pile of old books they'd brought him. He was familiar with all of them.

"No, no. I'll be fine and our guest should not be left alone. You two children stay here and finish your game." Without apparent fear, Miss Victorine came close and hugged him.

Amy lunged toward them, then when he returned Miss Victorine's embrace, she halted. She moved to the cabinet that housed her pistol, placed her hand on the drawer, and stared at him meaningfully.

He could scarcely contain his annoyance. He had learned his lesson this morning. Miss Victorine was fragile. He would never hurt her again.

Cupping her hands around his cheeks, she looked into his eyes. "It has been so good to have you as my guest again. Do come back soon . . ." She cast a guilty glance at Amy. "Oh, dear. I forgot. I won't be here, but I wish you won't be such a stranger to Summerwind.

The village and the farms would be glad of a visit from their liege lord."

Again he glanced at Amy. He saw exactly the sneer he expected. He knew her opinion of him. *Bored, indolent, without honor or scruples—*

"I'll do that, Miss Victorine." Leaning down, he brushed a kiss across her sagging cheek.

"Dear boy." Miss Victorine's voice quivered. "I have missed you." With a last hug, she took the lamp and departed.

The darkness hugged the small light of the candle, yet still he couldn't escape Amy's accusing stare. "Liege lord, indeed. You don't know how to be a liege lord."

"I am the marquess of Northcliff. We have been the liege lords of this area for five hundred years. My father passed down the knowledge necessary to be Northcliff." Yet he'd neglected his obligations, and her scorn stung. So he asked cruelly, "What did your father teach you? Or do you even know who he is?"

She advanced on him so fast, he thought for a moment he could actually get his hands on her. But she stopped a few, vital inches short. "My father *told* me to be true to myself, and do the right thing. He *showed* me the meaning of duty and sacrifice. I *learned* the lessons my father taught me. It's too bad you didn't do the same."

My God! She whipped him with her words, showed not an ounce of the respect due his position! "Is it better to be a gentlewoman who has fallen on bad times and allowed the bitterness of labor to poison you?"

"Is that your new theory about me?" She snorted. "I wonder what other nonsense you'll concoct to explain your imprisonment here?"

"There are a hundred things that could have made you who you are, but one thing remains inviolate. You are a *ridiculous* girl." He used a disdainful tone he hoped made clear he wished to call her other, less elegant invectives.

"Life is a *ridiculous* exercise performed by the bored, the hungry and the desperate. And I'm stuck with you." She glanced around. "I can't go upstairs yet. You're a dreadful chess player."

Stung, he replied, "Actually, I'm one of London's best." *When I'm not playing against a female. A female that makes my blood spring to the surface and hunger swim right beneath the skin.*

"London is a city of fools, then." Her gaze landed on Miss Victorine's handwork. "Beading would keep you entertained."

"No . . . it . . . wouldn't." He spoke through his teeth.

Picking up the small, complex piece, she shook it at him. "Come on, my lord. Think how satisfied you'd be to show that I'm wrong about anything."

"I am not a woman." But she was. He loved the way she wrapped her shawl over her bosom as if shielding herself from his gaze would protect her from his lust. Her action was futile and showed little experience with men—or perhaps too much.

"No, you're one of the bored."

She was damned right about that. He knew she was baiting him. He knew he shouldn't succumb to her gibes. Yet he was bored. And lustful. And desperate. "All right." He made his decision briskly. "Show me."

Amy looked startled, then suspicious.

"What?" He lifted spuriously innocent brows. "You've convinced me."

"You're being too pleasant."

"Some people actually call me a charming fellow."

"Debutantes." She imbued the word with scorn. "Am I right?"

"Yes."

"Don't believe them," she advised. "They're flattering you. They're after your ring on their finger."

That was what he believed, too, but she believed it in a different way. A disparaging way. One that plainly told him she couldn't imagine a moment when he was ever charming.

And he had the uncomfortable thought. Perhaps he *was* never charming. Certainly his father had never been charming.

Which was better than being like his mother: enchanting, inconsequential, fickle.

His mouth hardened. "Never mind. Go upstairs. I'm not a child. I don't need for you to entertain me."

"Fine." She stuffed the beadwork into her pocket. "I'm sure you're incapable of concentrating long enough to learn, anyway."

He took the two steps to his cot, the bloody chain rattling as he moved. He flung himself down. "Yes, because I am such an negligible, irresponsible, laughable fellow."

She hesitated, clearly not comprehending his mood.

"Take the candle." He dismissed her with a flick of his fingers.

With a flounce, she left him staring into the dark.

The next day, Pom stood in the sunny, bustling square in the village of Settersway on the first really fine day of spring. Unlike these mainland folk with their fine, colorful booths, Pom sold his fish out of a basket. He was a common sight here. He sold his fish every week at market and he knew the noise, the smells, the people . . . the pole by the well where scraps of paper flapped in the breeze. If a man had a mule for sale, there he placed the announcement. When the navy wanted to capture a deserter, there they placed the reward information. Sarrie Proctor had even advertised for a husband on that pole, and got herself a hard-working one, too. And the courting youth sometimes sealed their love letters and placed them on the pole for their sweethearts to find.

It was one such sealed letter that held Pom's attention. He'd seen a fine fellow step up to the pole, place the letter on a rusty nail, and leave. Pom was tall, taller than anyone else in the square, and he had spent an hour scanning the square, looking for suspicious men lingering in the shadows. Men who would capture the one who grabbed that letter and take him away.

He saw no one.

At last, satisfied that Mr. Harrison Edmondson hadn't sent a spy, Pom nodded to Vicar Smith.

Vicar Smith finished his conversation with Mrs. Fremont and strolled toward the center of the square. Toward the pole. He lingered, the wisps of his white hair ruffled by the wind, appearing to examine the booths with their wares, and at the moment when the ever-shifting crowd was at its height, he plunged into the center. For a tense moment, Pom lost sight of him. Then he emerged, walked to Mrs. Showater's booth hung with loaves of bread, and purchased a sweet bun. He headed for the booth selling the ale, ignoring the Gypsy fortune-teller as he passed.

Only Pom saw the letter transfer from Vicar Smith to his own Mertle, dressed up in bright rags with her skin dyed with walnut juice to a toasty brown.

She finished reading the palm of the giggling girl before her, no doubt promising wealth and a handsome husband. Standing, she tucked her coins in her purse, checked to make sure her kerchief and her scarves covered her blond curls, and started toward Pom. She winked at all the men she passed, read a few palms as they were thrust before her, and when she drew close to him she looked him over from head to toe. "Ye're a big one." She swayed her hips enticingly. "Does the rest o' ye match yer height?"

The women around them laughed, and Pom didn't have to pretend to be unnerved. He hated being the center of attention.

Mertle knew it, too, and grinned.

At the sight, Pom jumped.

Somehow, she'd blacked out one of her teeth. His wife was enjoying herself far too much.

Taking his hand, she cupped it in her own. She frowned, muttered, leaned in so that her scarves fell forward—and she placed the folded letter in his palm.

She pressed his fingers over it and drew back. To the crowd that had gathered, she announced, "He's married t' a blond witch who'll take my eyes out if I try a love spell on him."

One of the onlookers gasped. "How did she know that?"

"My destiny lies elsewhere," Mertle declared.

"So it does," Pom said. "Go on then and find it."

With another grin, Mertle walked from the square.

Vicar Smith had disappeared, too, but Pom made himself wait until he'd sold all his fish before he left. Then he hurried to the harbor to his boat, and as he untied it from its moorings, the vicar and his wife, now dressed in her usual garb, leaped in.

"Gents, did ye see anything?" Mertle asked.

"No one," Vicar Smith said.

"No one." Pom put his shoulders to the oars and took them out of the harbor.

"So Mr. Edmondson took Miss Rosabel's threats seriously. That's good." Vicar Smith coiled the rope on the bottom of the boat.

Pom shrugged.

"What's the matter?" Mertle rubbed his arm. "Everything went wonderfully well."

"Too wonderfully well." Pom scanned the horizon. "I've met Mr. Harrison Edmondson. A slimier, more sneaky coot I've never met."

"What are you saying?" Mertle scanned the horizon, too.

"That I don't like this," Pom said. "It was too easy."

Chapter 9

"We've got it! Miss Victorine, we've got it!" It was late afternoon when Amy ran into the cottage, the letter from Harrison Edmondson clutched tightly in her hand.

Pom followed at a slower pace.

Miss Victorine hurried out of the kitchen, an apron draped over her gown, her brown eyes sparkling, Coal on her heels. "Thank heavens! Now we can release His Lordship."

"Yes, more's the shame," Amy retorted, but she could scarcely contain her jubilation.

On hearing Amy's sentiment, Miss Victorine looked anxious. "Dear child, you can't say that you think it is right to imprison a young, healthy lord."

"It's done him good." Amy broke the seal.

"How can you say that?" Miss Victorine asked.

Amy scanned the words on the page. "He's, um, learning . . ." Her words petered out. ". . . patience."

"What's the matter, dear?" Miss Victorine's voice quivered.

Amy looked up. Miss Victorine and Pom were staring at her. She didn't know what to say. How to tell them.

"Might as well just speak it, miss." Pom stood there, stalwart as always but ill-able to withstand further financial hardship.

Miss Victorine was bent, fragile, still bruised from her tumble with Lord Northcliff.

Coal sat balanced on his rear, licking his stomach.

And Amy had dragged them into this.

"Mr. Harrison Edmondson declares he won't pay the ransom. He says . . . he says he's sorry, but we'll have to kill Lord Northcliff."

"I don't understand it. He must not believe we'll really kill him." Amy sat at the kitchen table and cradled her aching forehead in her palms.

Miss Victorine's forehead wrinkled in confusion. "Well . . . we won't."

"But he doesn't know that!" Amy wanted to be indignant. Instead she was flabbergasted. "He doesn't know we're two women with a desperate plan. As far as he's concerned, we're hardened criminals. We're murderers. Even if he pays the ransom, we could still kill Lord Northcliff!"

"We could never kill anyone."

"I don't know about that. As obnoxious as Lord Northcliff is . . ." At Miss Victorine's gasp, Amy relented. "All right, we couldn't kill him, either." Although when he lolled on the bed like some Roman god or snapped at her as if she were some village trull, she really thought murder seemed too good for him. "But Harrison Edmondson doesn't know that!"

"So ye keep saying." Pom stood at the door, his arms crossed over his massive chest. "Yet Mr. Edmondson is ever a treacherous swine. Perhaps he thinks ye'll kill his nephew and doesn't care."

Amy lifted her head and stared at Pom. The whole world had gone crazy, and Pom with it.

"Pom, what a dreadful thing to say!" Miss Victorine sounded shocked. "I do not like Harrison, either, but he's not a murderer."

"No, Miss Victorine. In that case, he would not be the murderer," Pom pointed out stoically. "If that's not the case, why wouldn't he send the payment?"

"We asked for too much." Miss Victorine thought about that, then nodded as if that satisfied her. "Poor man, he must be devastated at the thought of his nephew being put to death for lack of a few pounds."

"But he's rich! His factory is making thousands of yards of beaded lace!" Amy slapped the table. "With your design!"

"Dear, you don't understand finance," Miss Victorine said. "When an operation starts, it takes capital to pay for the machines and the building. That's probably where Harrison's money has gone."

"How do you know that?" Amy asked.

"My family hasn't always been impoverished." Miss Victorine nodded wisely.

"Neither has mine," Amy said, "but we've never had to handle our own money."

"You had a steward?" Miss Victorine's eyes lit up as they always did when she considered the romance of Amy's past. "Well, of course you did. And a lord chamberlain and a prime minister—"

From the cellar, a man's roar sounded. "Amy, I can hear you talking. If you're back, you can let me go!"

"Dear heavens." Amy was in despair. "What can we tell him?"

"We?" Miss Victorine widened her eyes artlessly.

"Yes, I suppose I deserve that." When Northcliff yelled again, Amy looked toward the stairs. "What do *I* tell him?"

"That we're going to release him anyway?" Miss Victorine suggested.

"Don't be silly. We can't give up now! He knows what we've done and without funds, we can't escape." Amy stood. "No. Let me handle matters." She started for the stairs.

"Miss. Ye might consider soothing the savage beast." Pom nodded toward the loaded tray Miss Victorine had assembled for Northcliff's tea.

"Why should I curry favor with that man? He's at our mercy." But Amy's defiance echoed emptily through the kitchen. Her feet dragged reluctantly as she walked to the teapot. She poured a cup, stirred in a teaspoon of sugar and a splash of cream. She placed half the buns on a separate plate for Miss Victorine and

Pom, and rearranged the ones remaining. She slipped Mr. Edmondson's letter under the plate.

The bellows of impatience from below were steadily increasing.

Picking up the tray, she moved carefully toward the stairs, wishing with all her might that she didn't have to face Lord Northcliff and try to explain what had happened.

Coal slipped down the stairs after her.

The bellows stopped as soon as the first step creaked beneath her weight. She felt Northcliff's gaze on her, intent on her every movement. She watched the full teacup, determined not to spill a drop. Determined not to look at him.

As she placed the tray on the far end of the table, he said, "What a lovely picture of domesticity you make. A mobcap and a white frilly apron would complete the illusion."

At his sarcastically drawled tone, her gaze flew to his.

He *knew*. Somehow, he knew.

She glanced toward the stairway.

"You're wondering if I can hear what goes on up there. I can't. But when you come down the stairs bearing a conciliatory tea tray and that expression"—his voice was rising—"I know something went wrong."

The cat slunk around the edges of the walls, keeping a wary eye on his humans.

Amy's spine stiffened. "But there's nothing you can do about it. You're our prisoner." Yet she pushed the tea tray toward him, staying well out of reach of his long arms.

"Yes, I am, and stinking sick of it, too." He had a gash on his chin, the mark of a razor wielded by his own inexpert hand. "When will I be released?"

"Have a bun. They were fresh baked this morning from Best's Bakery in Settersway."

"I don't want a bun." He spaced annoyance between the words. "I want out!"

"We can't do that yet." She perched on the arm of the chair, taking care to present a casual demeanor, as if she breathed without constriction. "At least drink your tea while it's hot."

He disregarded everything except what she wanted him to disregard. "Why can't you release me?"

"Because your uncle won't pay the ransom."

"What?"

The heat of his blast almost knocked her off the chair.

"Your uncle won't—"

"I *heard* you." He didn't so much stand as unfold to a towering height. "Do you expect me to believe that?"

"What reason would I have to lie?" Temper sizzled along her nerves—and the barest suggestion of excitement. For whatever disreputable reason, she liked having Northcliff chomp and roar. Seeing him possessed by anger made her heart skip in her chest. Made her skin tingle. This odd, shameful mood wasn't something she liked to admit, nor was it something she understood, but it lived in her and she lived in it. In him. "As big a boor as you have been, do you for a minute imagine I want to keep you here?"

"I imagine you've enjoyed this—holding a lord's

fate in your insignificant hands. Using me as a whipping boy for all the men who have treated you with disrespect and not accorded you the homage you presume you deserve." He paced to the end of his chain, his muscles flexing and stretching like a tiger's on the prowl. Like Coal's, who slid beneath one piece of furniture to the side of another, cautiously peering at them. "I don't know who you are, but Lady Disdain, this scheme of yours was always destined to fail."

"So do you believe the scheme is a failure? Or that I'm lying about the ransom so I can keep you here out of spite?" She offered the choice. "Because you can't have it both ways. Either your uncle is refusing to pay the ransom because he can't scrape the money together—"

"Absurd!"

"Or I'm playing a game that includes only you and me and a gloating pleasure at seeing you chained—"

"Do you deny it?"

"No, I don't deny it!" She came to her feet, too. "You deserve to be whipped, too, until you learn some manners, although I suppose it's too late for that. But if the latter is true, if I'm keeping you here to torment you, what's the end, my lord? When do I say, 'I'm done with this' and leave? Because in case it's escaped your attention, we've poured our last shillings into providing you with good meals."

"You call these good meals?" With a sweep of his arm, he cleared the tray. The china cup and saucer shattered as they hit the wall. The buns flew into the dirt. The letter fluttered to the floor.

Coal howled and raced upstairs.

At the shatter of porcelain, Amy saw red. "Although Miss Victorine could ill afford the white flour or the meat or the eggs, she bought the best for you."

"What would you have fed me? Gruel?"

"Gruel would have been more common fare here on the island."

"I am not a damned commoner!"

"You certainly are not. The common fisherfolk and farmers work. They create. They contribute. While you've abdicated every responsibility and become nothing more than a wart on the noble ass of England." She was shouting.

He was not. With each word, his voice grew softer and colder. "You are plain-spoken, girl. Ladies do not use such language, and they most certainly don't speak so to their betters."

"I would never speak so to my *betters*." Amy clenched her fists at her side and in her pique her eyes became the color of a tempest-swept ocean.

She was magnificent, and he wanted to take her and shake her. And kiss her. And take her. And show her the meaning of helplessness as she had shown him.

A broken cry from the bottom step distracted him.

"Children. Children!" Miss Victorine stood wringing her hands, her faded gaze darting from Northcliff to Amy to her broken treasures. "What are you doing? What have you done?"

"He's a selfish, conceited, arrogant jackass who deserves to starve—and as far as I'm concerned, he can crawl in the dirt after those buns and eat them in the dark and the cold. And I hope he chokes on them." In a rage, Amy stormed up the stairs.

Jermyn stared after her, furious that she had goaded him into a loss of temper.

Because he had nothing to do except read. Because he was bored. Because . . . because his hands itched to touch her. He'd seen much more beautiful women, danced with them, and if they were in the demimonde, slept with them. But he had never met a woman who challenged him as did Amy Rosabel. Her eyes flashed when she saw him, her sharp tongue ripped his character to shreds, yet the way she moved brought his heart to his throat . . . and brought other parts of his body to attention.

He could blame his incarceration for this madness, but he'd felt a stirring the first time he laid eyes on her . . . when she drugged him. Of course he had shrugged it off; a master didn't indulge himself with his maids. But discovering that she was not his servant had freed his desire, and meeting her challenges had captured his attention. When she was gone from his sight, he brooded about her. Who was she? Why was she so prickly? When she was with him and spitting defiance, she made him feel alive as he had never felt before. He was half mad with lust. Perhaps all mad to want a termagant like Amy. In fact, he was most certainly totally insane. "That woman brings out the worst in me."

"I know. The two of you . . ."

Jermyn started at the sound of Miss Victorine's quivering voice. He had almost forgotten she was there.

"I should never have let her come d . . . down alone. Not when it's such b . . . bad news."

Miss Victorine, he realized in horror, was crying and trying valiantly to hide the fact.

"She truly is a sweet girl, and you . . . you're a d . . . delightful boy, but the t . . . two of you are like oil and water."

"And somehow the oil keeps catching fire." He kept his tone prosaic as she trudged across the floor.

By painful inches, she lowered herself to the floor to kneel by the shards of her cup and plates. "Yes, yes, an apt simile, my lord." She touched the broken pieces as a mother would touch an injured child, gently, with bent and trembling fingers.

In the haze of his rage, a cool finger of guilt intruded. He remembered that most of the china on which he'd been served had been chipped, and that Miss Victorine handled it painful care, as if it needed to last the rest of her life. Or as if each piece carried generations of memory.

"Let me help you." He had enough chain to get that far.

When he stepped closer, she flinched.

And he recalled that he'd held a knife to her throat. He thrown her aside, too, with the best of intentions, but he'd seen the purpling bruises on the thin skin of her arms and seen how she hobbled.

"Please, my lord, let me pick up the pieces." She did so.

He watched her, his fingers limp. He'd never before thought of himself as a good-for-nothing, yet now he felt useless and helpless. When Amy said that, he'd rejected the idea with scorn. But now he wondered— when a man acted like a spoiled boy and blamed it on another—was he not in truth a spoiled boy?

Miss Victorine dragged the pewter tray toward her. She handed Jermyn the letter.

He glanced at it. Uncle Harrison's handwriting.

He put it in his pocket.

She picked up the buns and brushed the dirt off of hem. "I'll take these upstairs. I'll bring you down the clean ones, and pour you a new cup of tea."

And eat the dirty ones herself.

Leaning over, he swept two of them into his hands. "No. I'll eat them."

"No! Dear boy, you're the m . . . marquess of Northcliff." A big tear ran down Miss Victorine's face and plopped into the dirt. "You should be d . . . dining on beefsteak and strawberries, not dirty b . . . buns."

"The one thing I've enjoyed during my imprisonment is the chance to eat simple foods." He took a hearty bite and discovered he hadn't brushed off enough of the dirt. It ground between his teeth. Gamely he ignored the grit and tried for a little flattery. "I have missed your cooking, Miss Victorine."

She sniffed and dabbed at her eyes with her handkerchief. "I told her you were a nice boy. I *told* her."

He chewed and smiled with all the charm of which

he was capable. But it seemed Miss Victorine was not comforted and Jermyn realized his charm felt rusty, like a commodity he doled out too seldom.

"Miss Victorine."

She looked up, and in her eyes he saw no sign of madness or senility. But there was loneliness and a sadness so old and deep, he wondered that he hadn't recognized it before.

"Miss Victorine." With his hand under her arm, he helped her to her feet. "This evening you should bring your shuttle down and show me how to make beaded lace."

"You don't really care about making lace." The pieces of the broken cup caught her attention, and her lip trembled.

"Probably not, but I do care about your company. It's lonely down here, Miss Victorine, and it would seem I'm to be here for quite a few more days." He dragged the appeal from the depths of his shriveled, selfish heart. "Won't you spend your evenings with me?"

Miss Victorine perked up, then grew silent and sad again.

"What's wrong?" he asked.

In a soft, disappointed voice, she asked, "What about Amy?"

"She can come, too." And if it killed him, he would be polite.

For Miss Victorine's sake.

"So." Jermyn struggled with the tiny, palm-sized shuttle, miles of fine twine and dozens of tiny beads. His fingers were too big. Too clumsy. His rough skin snagged the thread. And if any one of his friends in London saw him sitting in the cellar with two women and a cat, doing handwork, they would laugh so hard he'd fear for the cleanliness of their linens. "What do you plan to do next?"

"About you, you mean?" Amy pointed at his beading. "You missed a stitch."

"No, I didn't."

"Yes, you did."

"Let me see." Miss Victorine placed her glasses on her nose, leaned close to the light, held the lace at arms' length, and squinted.

He grinned at her maneuverings. "Miss Victorine, you need new glasses."

"Yes, dear, that's probably true. There." She pointed. "Unravel to there and start again, and you'll be just right."

"See?" Amy muttered under her breath.

He grunted, unraveled, and started the painful process of making lace with tiny beads . . . again.

This evening the two of them were painfully civil, speaking in even tones, politely, and avoiding each other's gazes. It was easier for him if he didn't look at her; in that manner, he kept lust and fury in check.

"She can't afford new glasses," Amy said. "That's something she'll buy when we get the ransom."

"Uncle Harrison isn't going to pay the ransom." Jermyn could scarcely contain his irritation. "Remember?"

"Today I wrote another letter to Mr. Edmondson reducing the ransom." Amy smiled as if she were confident in her strategy. "He'll pay it now."

"You reduced the ransom?" Incredulously, he repeated, "You reduced the ransom?"

"That's what I said." Amy worked the beading quickly and efficiently. "Just hours ago, I delivered the letter to your home and left it where the butler would find it. I saw a messenger ride toward Mr. Edmondson's house—"

"You reduced the ransom? As if I were an unwanted *hat?* Or an old hunting dog? Or a stained handkerchief?"

"More like the old hunting dog than anything else," Amy said pertly.

He tensed, ready to snap back.

"Amy!" Miss Victorine reproved. "You promised!"

"Sorry," Amy muttered.

"Not a hat, my lord." Miss Victorine shifted the cat on her lap. "Nothing so inconsequential. We made a small adjustment in our demands so Harrison could collect the moneys."

"Uncle Harrison has no need to *collect* the moneys," Jermyn said scornfully. "I've allowed him to handle the family fortune."

"We believe he's invested it in factories and is short on cash," Amy said in that even tone that signified she had regained control.

"Ludicrous!" Jermyn answered.

"Then why didn't he pay your ransom?" Amy asked in a sweetly reasonable tone.

Jermyn didn't know the answer to that. He had read

the letter. He didn't understand Uncle Harrison's almost goading tone, or his glib refusal to give in to death threats.

Jermyn had begun to wonder if he understood anything.

"Never mind, my lord." Amy offered him false consolation. "In a mere three days, you'll be free."

Chapter 10

$\mathcal{H}$arrison Edmondson waved the messenger out of his office, then opened the second letter with trembling eagerness. He read the note, and his anticipatory glow was extinguished like a candle flame. "Why am I constantly surrounded by bunglers? Why is it so hard to commit one simple little murder?" He pulled out a new sheet of paper, uncorked his ink, and wrote an answer designed to infuriate his nephew's captors.

This time, they had better do the job they had promised they would do.

Amy scanned the sheet, then lowered it in despair. "He won't pay the ransom."

As if Pom had expected exactly this, he nodded. "Well. Got t' go t' the pub." He donned his hat and his damp wool coat. "Me wife's working there and I need me supper." He strode out of Miss Victorine's kitchen into an evening filled with a gray mist and lowering clouds.

Amy stared after him. He had accepted the news stoically, while she wanted to shriek and pound her fists on the table. What was Mr. Edmondson thinking? Never had Amy imagined such callous indifference to the fate of a man who was, in fact, a very important lord—and Mr. Edmondson's own nephew! "What are we going to do now?"

"Let His Lordship go." Miss Victorine sat at the well-scrubbed kitchen table, her hands folded in her lap. By all appearances, it seemed this refusal presented no surprise to Miss Victorine, either.

Nor, truth to tell, was Amy particularly astonished. The first time, she had been shocked and stunned. But she'd spent three days dreading this exact moment, and now she saw no recourse but to forge ahead. Far too loudly, she said, "We will not let Lord Northcliff go!" Then she moderated her tone. "We can't. We'll hang."

"He wouldn't hang me." Miss Victorine sounded very sure.

"He would hang me." Amy was equally sure.

Through the open cellar door, she heard Northcliff holler in a false reasonable tone, "Miss Amy, could I see you for a moment?"

"How does he do that?" Amy exploded. "Know that I'm up here and news has arrived?"

"He told me he can tell who's up here by the creaking of the floorboards." Miss Victorine stood, picked up Coal, cradled the big cat in her arms, and said, "It's time for our nap. Wake us when you're done." By that she meant that Amy had gotten them into this, and Amy was responsible for dealing with the unruly lord imprisoned in their cellar.

Amy supposed that was just. But she didn't like it. "I'll tell him." She slapped the letter down. "But I'm not carrying any crockery down with me this time."

"That is the best plan. I haven't a lot of china left." Miss Victorine limped toward her bedroom as if she hadn't a care in the world.

Amy stood. She shook the creases out of her skirt, and checked her bodice to make sure that the neckline remained high enough to hide all glimpse of cleavage from Northcliff.

Of course she wasn't indecent. This was one of Miss Victorine's old gowns, but even the most discreet bodice could gape and somehow show more than she intended. Picking up her shawl, she wrapped it around her shoulders and secured it at her waist. Over the last two days she'd developed these habits, for while she and Northcliff had exchanged no more of those improper conversations, and Northcliff had taken care to keep his licentious opinions to himself, she still felt . . . uncomfortable in his presence. Something about him made her . . . cautious.

Restless.

Sleepless.

Breathless.

He no longer spoke of his desire, but some stirring female intuition suspected he experienced it, and reluctantly she acknowledged that she felt odd, too. Uncomfortable. Sort of like she had indigestion. She frequently found herself glancing at him out of the corners of her eyes, and just as frequently found his gaze on her. When he spoke to her, the tone of his voice made her want to squirm and smirk like some flirtatious schoolgirl. It was all very awkward, and she hated feeling awkward. She hated feeling anything— toward him.

The first time she'd seen him, she'd wanted nothing more than to capture him, get the ransom, and depart with Miss Victorine. She hadn't thought about him at all except as a lousy, miserable creature and a means to an end.

Now it seemed she could do nothing except think of him.

She certainly couldn't get rid of him.

And when she did, she feared she would never forget him.

Life had been so simple before she met Jermyn Edmondson, the marquess of Northcliff.

Last time she had received a ransom refusal, she had descended into the cellar with trepidation.

This time she descended in defiance. Northcliff sat propped up on two pillows, pretending to read a book, but she knew, she *felt* his attention on her. She stopped at the other end of the long table and shook her finger at him. "Lord Northcliff! What kind of vexious nephew have you been that your uncle doesn't care whether you live or die?"

Northcliff looked up at her. She couldn't read what he was thinking in his expression or in his eyes. In fact, he seemed preternaturally calm. "Jermyn," he said.

"What?" What was he talking about?

"My name is Jermyn." He put the book down on the edge of the table. "And I have a great desire to have you call me by my name."

She hadn't expected that response, and the unexpected made her uneasy. He knew today was the day they would hear back from Mr. Edmondson. He should be demanding news of his release. Instead he wanted to chat?

She inched closer to him, staring and wondering if the long stretch of inactivity had taken its toll on his wits. "My lord, your name is of no interest to me."

"Really? That's odd, Lady Disdain, because *your* name is of great interest to me." He lounged against the blankets, his mahogany hair an attractive mess. "Might I know it?"

"You know my name." What was this new interest he showed in identifying her?

Had he somehow stumbled onto the secret of her past?

But no. That was impossible. He'd been hidden here for six days. He had no way to discover anything.

She glanced toward the stairs.

Unless Miss Victorine had spoken. But Miss Victorine had sworn she would be discreet, and Amy trusted her.

"Your real surname, please." He spoke crisply, a man who expected to be obeyed.

"No." Heavens, no.

"What do you fear?"

What did she fear? She feared returning to Beaumontagne to a life of stultifying propriety and a mismatched marriage. She feared an assassin's bullet. She feared having to leave Miss Victorine for her safety.

In an odd way, she feared Jermyn and his influence on her, because he made her want different things than she had ever wanted before. "My lord, I fear nothing." She smiled to cover the lie. "I have news about your release. May I continue?"

"Do." He waved a negligent hand. "Pray, do." He was chained to the bed in the basement of a cottage on the isle of Summerwind. His clothing was in shambles. His jaw, a jaunty, determined edifice, sported a scruffy beard. Yet he managed to exude a kind of noble command that overcame his crude surroundings and his ignoble situation. How did he do it?

And why was she impressed?

"Your uncle again has refused to pay the ransom."

"How could you have imagined that a silly girl like you could successfully blackmail the marquess of Edmondson or his agent?"

At his condescending tone, her hostility leaped to life. "My scheme is sound, it's you and your uncle who're twisted. And what do you mean, calling me a silly girl?"

"You *are* a silly girl. You don't understand the forces you've unleashed." He smiled with such confidence, she itched to slap his face. "Move a little closer and I'll show you."

Trust him to direct this quarrel toward the physical awareness that vibrated between them. "What a cad you are. You distrust women."

"Why would I distrust women?" He sneered like a man bred for sneering. "Perhaps because they kidnap and imprison me?"

She waved a dismissive hand. "*I* did that. I am not a typical well-bred English female, so to use me as an example is to avoid the question—and that makes the answer obvious. You don't like women."

"A man who uses females for companionship is a man who exposes himself to anguish."

"Anguish?" She didn't know what to make of his cool comment.

"Men and women are different. Women are careless, bright, and beautiful creatures created to break a man's heart. In a man's world, the sky is blue and a vow is eternal. In a woman's world—" He shook his head, and his sneer became a grimace, pained and directed—at himself. "I've never had a peek at a woman's world, so I don't know the color of the sky. But I do know that for a female, no vow is eternal."

"I don't understand." She did understand that they'd moved beyond the easy quarrel into something more. Something anguished. Something personal.

He leaned toward her. "When you were a child, did your mother tell you she loved you?"

"My mother died at my birth."

"Fortunate you." He relaxed back against the pillows.

Shocked, she said, "My lord, that is cruel."

"No, trust me, it's the truth. You don't realize how lucky you are, and that probably explains why you're so intelligent, daring, interesting—so different from the usual run of female."

"I'm not flattered."

"You should be. You may be wild and outspoken, but I know when you speak, no matter how much I hate it, you'll speak the truth. I watch you with Miss Victorine, and I know that when you give your loyalty, your loyalty is undying."

"I suppose." She inched away.

He sounded half mad, speaking feverishly and watching her with eyes that glowed golden with intensity.

"Do you know my mother used to take me on her knee and tell me that she loved me? She put me to bed every night with a story, and woke me every morning with a kiss. She made sure I was happy, protected, carefree."

"She sounds lovely." Although his tone told her a different story.

"She was. The most beautiful creature I've ever seen. The one woman my father ever loved. Some people called her a foreigner—she was Italian, from an impoverished family, a mad choice my father made on his grand tour, but she charmed everyone with her auburn hair and brown eyes and vibrant laugh. She was so kind, such a loving mother, so much in love with my father. All the other women wore subdued colors, but not my mother. She wore reds, beautiful rich hues that would have made any other woman look washed out and pale. She gave the most wonderful parties, and at one of them I heard some of the noble ladies gossiping. They said she rode a gelding too big and fast for her, that she flaunted herself. They said the way she dressed indicated a light mind and an immoral disposition. I was seven. I didn't understand what they meant, but I knew I didn't like their tone, so I ran into the drawing room and attacked them. I kicked one old besom right in the shin." Northcliff's intensity arched through space toward Amy like light made visible. "When I told my father what had happened, he laughed and kissed me on the top of the head."

"Good for you." She liked the idea of the childish Jermyn and his fevered defense of his mother.

"It was the last time I ever heard him laugh," Northcliff said flatly. "The last time he showed me anything but formal affection."

Somehow during this conversation the two of them had edged into something more than the razor-sharp repartee that had marked their moments together. Or had the change happened more slowly, over six days of enforced intimacy, over evenings spent in a ill-lit cellar reading, beading, talking?

What was it Miss Victorine had said about Lady Northcliff? *We lost her when Jermyn was seven.*

Yet faced with a hard-eyed lord, Amy suspected Miss Victorine had avoided awkward explanation and a painful memory. "My lord, what happened to your mother?"

"When I was seven years old, she ran away with our foreign agent."

"What?" Amy shook her head in bewilderment. "But you said she was kind and a loving mother and in love with your father."

"It would appear my childish affection misled me."

"I don't *believe* that. You *couldn't* have been so wrong."

"No? Yet she is gone." Northcliff's bored tone hid his pain, but he couldn't conceal the bleakness in his eyes. "In all my life I've never heard another word from her."

"I don't believe you!" She couldn't stand such an ending to the fairy tale of the beautiful, kind, devoted mother.

"My parents fought that day. I had never heard them raise their voices, but they did then. I couldn't understand them—I was outside the door—but Father was very angry, cold, and cutting, and Mama was passionate, fiery, arguing as if her very existence depended upon winning . . . the next thing I knew, she had taken her horse and ridden the road to the harbor." Northcliff recited the tale softly, not really understanding what had prompted him to reveal himself to Amy. Not that she wouldn't have heard the story if she remained here long enough—he was surprised she hadn't heard it yet—but to no one had he ever revealed his feelings. What was it about this girl that made him rattle on? "Our ship was there. Mama was seen speaking to our foreign agent. He boarded, taking her with him. They told the captain she would be disembarking before they sailed. But she never came home. She left me. She left my father. She never came home."

"I don't believe it," Amy repeated. "How could a

woman who loved her son and her husband leave
without a backward glance?"

"I've wondered that a thousand times. I have only
two possible answers. She didn't really love us." He
watched Lady Disdain closely as he offered his second
theory. "Or else all women are flighty and disloyal."

Amy didn't even stop to think. "That's stupid. Both
of your theories are stupid."

"What do you mean, stupid?"

Amy stood within the reach of his arms, daring him
to grab her, to shake her, to offer her violence. And he
was ready to do just that. In the six days since he'd been
taken, he had walked to the end of his chain countless
times. He had beaded two inches of lace. For the sake
of Miss Victorine, he had had civilized conversation
with this she-devil. He had even done the exercises the
doctor recommended—lifting his injured leg in the air,
turning his foot in circles, pressing it to his chest.

The damned leg felt better, but Jermyn was frantic.
He hadn't seen the sun in a week. Every day he had
been given hot water to shave and sponge off, but he
hadn't had a change of linen. He had given up on
wearing his cravat, and he knew his friends would be
horrified by his rumpled appearance.

"Look around you. Everywhere you look you'll see
women who love their husbands and their children so
fiercely they'll do anything to protect their family. To
condemn all women because of one lady's behavior is
stupid." Amy didn't mince her words, didn't bother to
use a conciliatory tone.

"So you're saying my mother *didn't* really love us."

Which he knew, but he didn't like having her rub his face in it.

He had been kept like an animal for a stupid scheme of revenge. And he was sick to death of being stuck here with little to do but occasionally when frustration got the better of good sense, pound on his manacle.

Amy frowned fiercely at him, obviously unconvinced. "Did your mother say anything the last time she saw you?"

"Say anything? What do you mean, say anything?" Why had he started this conversation with Amy? Why would she understand? She had proved her tactlessness again and again. "Of course she said something."

"Did she hold you against her, give you advice for the future, tell you that she loved you but she had to go?"

He knew exactly what his mother had said. After she was gone, he'd repeated her remarks over and over again, trying to squeeze some indication of warmth and loss from her words. "The last thing she said to me was, 'Darling boy, behave for Miss Geralyn until I get back.'" He mocked himself, his mother, and Amy. "Miss Geralyn was my nursemaid."

Amy stared at him blankly. "That's not the way a woman acts, especially not a woman who loves her son and is leaving him for the last time."

"Nevertheless, she did leave me."

"I'm telling you, your tale doesn't make sense. You were just a lad. You don't know all the details. And one thing is clear, my lord. If you're going to blame anyone for your current problems, you shouldn't blame your mother or me or any other female." The color rode high in her cheeks. Her green eyes sparkled with frustration.

"I shouldn't blame you? You abducted me!"

"Yes, but I would have released you by now. Please, my lord, blame your uncle, who won't pay your ransom. I've heard nothing but ill of him—and you—and it appears it's all true." Her bosom heaved under the influence of her aggravation. "Perhaps you should be more concerned about the rot in your character and that of your uncle than bemoaning my treachery."

Damn her. In her sentiments he heard the echo of days long gone.

At the same time, he observed the faint, erotic jiggle of her breasts with a need that brought his cock swelling against the buttons of his trousers. An opinionated, cheeky female in dreadful clothing gave him the cockstand of a lifetime while she, apparently innocent of any feeling for him, made aspersions about his worth. The situation could no longer be borne. "Where is Miss Victorine?"

"She's taking her nap."

"Good. Good." He placed his feet on the floor. Slowly he stood, rising to his full height closely against her, allowing her to feel his heat. His ire.

Her eyes widened.

He lunged.

She leaped away.

Too late. He caught her around the waist. Triumph roared through him.

The chain snapped to its full length. The manacle grabbed at his ankle. He fell. Twisted. Landed atop her on the cot. Beneath him, her breath whooshed out.

They were sideways—she had one foot on the floor, one on the bed, and he glimpsed a long expanse of stockinged calf and bare thigh. He had both feet on the floor and enough energy igniting in him to start a blaze.

For the first time in six days—no, six months, maybe six years—he was completely and vibrantly alive. He tussled with her, lifting her completely onto the mattress, using his weight to control her kicking feet and his elbow to block the strong punch to his head with her right fist. When he had her where he wanted her, with her head on the pillow and that softly curved body beneath him, he cradled her head in his hands. And kissed her.

Damn it, it was what he had wanted to do for six days. Hold her beneath him, master her struggles, and kiss her.

He pressed his lips to hers.

She bit at him, a hard nip that broke the skin and brought the taste of blood to his mouth.

Lifting his head, he smiled.

A full-bodied, vengeful smile that made her eyes widen, then narrow. "Let go, you—" She swung hard enough and with enough precision to slip under his guard and give a glancing blow to his cheek.

His head snapped sideways.

She shook her hand, flexed her fingers. "Damn it to hell, that hurt!"

She spoke like a lady, but swore like a sailor.

Who was she?

She wouldn't say. Yet before this affair ended, he would know.

He shifted them, bringing her whole body completely onto the cot, making sure his weight still trapped her.

She fought against him, of course. As much rage as he felt in being confined, she felt in being mastered. A drop of blood from his lip splashed onto her face. She jerked her head aside as if she could avoid the results of her actions.

"It's far too late for that," he told her.

And by God, she appeared to comprehend what he meant.

But she didn't believe him, and she wasn't resigned. She brought her claws into play, slashing at his face with vicious swipes that aimed right for his eyes.

He caught her hands. Stopped smiling. Stared down into her savage gaze and said, "You're exactly the woman I prayed I would never find—alive, unafraid, determined . . . untamable." He kissed her again, a hard pressure on her lips. "More trouble than I could ever imagine."

Chapter 11

"*D*amn you." Damn him! Amy should have been afraid that this caged beast, this being who at the same time bled and smiled, would rape her. Hurt her.

She wasn't afraid.

She comprehended Northcliff's rage.

All her life, she had felt rage like it, rage at the fate that had made her a princess in the first place, rage at the war that ripped her from her family and thrust her into the world, rage at Clarice for so long refusing to recognize that their royal life could never be recovered.

All the tumultuous emotion in Amy leaped to meet Northcliff's fury. They met and clashed like two storms, in violence and in yearning.

Amy pressed her thumbs hard against Northcliff's throat over his windpipe, cutting off his air.

With a gasp, he lifted his head. He stared down at her, silently demanding she let him go.

But he didn't grab her hands. He didn't overpower her.

And the mania to hold him off succumbed to the need to hold him.

Sliding her hands around his neck, she pulled him close and kissed him as boldly as he had kissed her.

His lips opened on hers, and he tasted of blood and frustration, rage and need. Everything about him found an echo in her. It was a response she'd never experienced before, the weight of a man's body on hers, and the fire of passion he ignited gave her skin a sensitivity that scorched her—and made him moan as if he felt the same burn. Her nipples grew taut and painful against the cotton of her chemise, and she pressed herself against him, trying to ease the ache.

He pushed his fingers into her hair, massaged her scalp, the shells of her ears.

She curled her nails into his skin, not hurting him, but keeping him in place as if he were trying to get away . . . when nothing was further from the truth. In fact, he slid his tongue into her mouth, over and over, and her own body beckoned, demanded she reciprocate. She sucked at the tip of his tongue, making a humming pleasure sound. She thrust her tongue into his mouth, too, needing to pierce him as he pierced her.

His large hand slid down her neck, down her chest,

and his palm cupped her clothed breast, holding the weight and testing her heat.

For one moment, pleasure thrummed through her veins.

Then shock blasted through her mind.

"Damn you!" She shoved at him, knocking his touch away.

He lifted his head, his lips damp from hers. He stared down at her, his eyes narrowed and hot. "You don't know anything about kissing." He made his pronouncement as if he had discerned everything about her past and her experience.

"I do, too!" She didn't, but he made it sound as if she were stupid. And she was, for remaining here, for kissing him . . . dear heavens, her skirt had ridden up and bared one thigh. Grabbing the hem, she struggled to make herself decent.

He caught her hand, halting her before she could cover herself. "No, you don't. You're a virgin." If anything, the heat in his gaze grew fiercer. "I've been kidnapped by a nineteen-year-old virgin who doesn't even know how to kiss."

His tone of self-disgust gave her pause and gave her direction. She knew what to say now. She didn't have to reveal herself. She could attack him. His weaknesses. She could save herself. Derisively, she said, "How mortifying for you, kidnapped by an old woman and a girl. The noble Lord Northcliff, drugged, imprisoned, kept for days in a cellar—and his own uncle won't even send the ransom to free him. And it's

your money he refuses to pay. Isn't it?" She projected
the kind of false compassion sure to infuriate him.

She succeeded.

He gripped her shoulders. "No woman has ever
made me angrier than you do. You speak to me without respect. You dare where no other woman would.
And sometimes I agree with you, that I should be mor-
tified to be tricked by a simple girl like you—and then
you do something as rampantly stupid as anything I
have ever done."

"What, my lord, would that be?"

He smiled down at her, his white teeth gleaming.
"You bait the trapped wolf while you're still in his
paws."

Her breath caught on the splinter of panic and desperation. He was right. She had been stupid.

She tried to slide out from under his weight and sit up.

He pressed her harder into the mattress, giving her
no quarter, holding her in place with his weight and
his strength.

She had to *think*. She couldn't fight her way free, so
she used her wits to slash at him. "What are you going
to do, my lord? Rape me? I can hardly believe your
grand ego would allow you to force a nineteen-year-
old virgin."

"You're not particularly alarmed yet, are you?" He
ran his thumb over the pulse at her throat. "You don't
know how to kiss. You don't know anything about
men. You can talk like a stevedore, yet you have had the
most sheltered upbringing of any girl I've ever met."

"Sheltered?" She laughed in a short and bitter burst. "My sister and I were thrown out of boarding school when I was nine because my father could no longer pay the price. I've wandered England ever since, homeless. Don't call me *sheltered*."

"Your sister must have done everything to protect you, then." His mouth replaced his thumb on her pulse. His lips moved against her skin. "Because you're a little idiot."

She doubled up her fist and smacked at his head.

Still he remained on top of her.

My wits. Use my wits. "So worse than being imprisoned by a nineteen-year-old virgin," she said, "you've been trapped by a little idiot."

He caught her wrists in one hand, smiled that lazy, intense, toothy smile at her again. "Yes. And you've been trapped by your own stupid victim."

He was still furious. He was much stronger.

Perhaps she *was* a little idiot.

He kissed her.

But not like last time. Last time had been two foes caught up in a struggle for . . . for something.

For dominance. Yes, that was it. For dominance.

This time she was struggling, but ineffectually, while he taught her a leisurely lesson about an emotion she didn't recognize . . . or want to.

She was still fuming, ready to fling blows and words, but he gathered her hands in a grip over her head. He trapped her legs in heavy wool petticoats and the gathers of her skirt. When she tried to slide sideways, he pushed his knee closer between her legs so that her movement spread them wider.

And where was she to go? The wall was on one side, he was on the other.

Worse than her helplessness was his calm. He seemed intent on her body, uninterested in her hostility. He slid his tongue in her ear, dampening it. Then he blew softly in the cavity, raising goose bumps on her skin. Taking her lower lip lightly between his teeth, he opened her mouth and kissed her . . . and this time their kiss wasn't war. It wasn't a lesson to be taught. It was mating.

He was male and she was female. He thrust and she received. The chill of goose bumps gave way to the warm slide of her thigh against his, to a softening deep within her. And still his tongue slid in and out of her mouth, creating an artistry of restlessness.

He slid his free hand beneath her neck, tilted her head back, and opened her body to whatever attentions he chose to bestow. His lips left hers to glide across the skin on her throat. He was almost caressing her with his lips, tasting her with his tongue.

Somehow he lulled her with his patience, with his unhurried pleasure in her.

He untied the scarf from over her bosom and untucked the ends from her bodice. Gradually he slid the cloth away from first one side, then the other.

The modest neckline and the expanse of creamy skin seemed to please him, and his gaze caressed the hidden mounds of her breasts. "Beautiful," he murmured. "The barest hint of provocation offered like a precious gift wrapped in faded muslin." He opened her bodice one button at a time, pausing between each one.

Each time she inhaled, his gaze grew more focused and she knew . . . she knew what he intended to do. But he held off, savoring the sight of her, tormenting her with expectations.

At last, when she was on the verge of shouting at him to let her go—or to hurry up and touch her—he lifted his hand and eased his fingertips beneath the fragile material of her chemise. He turned it back, baring her breast.

Her lids were suddenly too heavy to hold up, and as she softly sighed, her eyes closed.

Delicately he touched her, his fingertips summoning response from her bones, her blood, her soul.

His thumb circled her nipple, and it puckered tightly.

She hated that he anticipated her reactions, knew where to look, where to touch, what to say. He taught her eagerness . . .

Lowering his head, he pressed a kiss on the place he had touched.

In the silence between them, she heard her own rough breath.

The tip of his tongue made contact, branding her with warmth, then as the moisture cooled, with memory.

And she was relaxed, waited for next move.

When, like a shock of ice water, his hand touched her bare thigh.

Her eyes flew open. She jumped. She said, "Stop it, Northcliff!"

"No." His expression hadn't changed. He still looked lazily intent.

She simply hadn't realized what he was intent upon.

"You can't do this!" She kicked at him.

"I can." He subdued her with his leg and the weight of his body behind it.

"I'm going to scream."

"I don't think so." His palm slid up to her hip. "I don't think Miss Victorine could hear you to begin with, and I know you don't want her to rush down the stairs to rescue you. You don't want her to see you on the cot with me. She might realize you haven't been struggling as hard as you should."

"You're despicable." And he was right.

"I know. But although you're a virgin, I think you understand that you're safe as long as my trousers are firmly fastened."

"Yeah? So?" She didn't let him see her relief, only her enmity.

But he knew she needed the reassurance, for he said, "I'm not going to hurt you. I'm just going to show you exactly what it is you're in need of."

"What do you mean?" He was such a jackass! "The only thing I'm in need of is your ransom!"

He chuckled with real amusement. "And that proves how incredibly uninformed you are."

"I despise you."

"Almost as much as you want me."

He was a brash fellow with an overweening ego, fostered from too much money and power and—her breath caught as he stroked her lower belly—a very real charisma that made her weak and compliant when she should be fighting . . .

She locked gazes with him, mutely resisting what she couldn't physically repel. The silence between them was profound, fostered by the weight of the earth around them. His fingers combed through her curls at the top of her cleft, then between her legs, each contact teaching her to forget her innocence. The tension of waiting made her skin grown tight, as if it were shrinking with each hushed breath. Her heart pumped in little leaps of anticipation as she fought the need to escape as soon as possible. Now.

Yet his gaze constrained her. She felt as if she were falling into his mind, sensing all his frustration, his anger, his need.

Then he slipped his finger between her folds and along the soft inner skin.

She whimpered with desire, then bit her lower lip to hold back any more of those revealing sounds of pleasure.

But he'd heard her, for gold flamed in his brown eyes, revealing a satisfaction as great as hers.

Lightly his finger circled the entrance to her body.

She thought she would jump out of her skin in anticipation.

But his finger glided up, up to the sensitive, swollen nub. He caressed all around, not quite touching.

She tried to keep her gaze on his, but she had lost the ability to concentrate, and random thoughts swirled through her mind—that she had never seen so fierce an expression on a man's face, that she had never been so overwhelmed with pure sensation, that he was almost beautiful in his ruggedness, that she *wanted* with more intensity of emotion than she had ever imagined. He no longer restrained her with force, but invisible bonds of desire held her in place. Her knee lifted. Her hands clenched the pillow. Her body wanted more than he had given her, and she was in thrall to her body.

Then he touched her. A subtle, direct touch. And glory flashed through her. With an incoherent cry, she arched into his hand. He caressed her, increasing the pressure, maintaining a rhythm, forcing her to become a creature desperate for pleasure. And one mad thought stuck in her mind—*he was the only one who could give her fulfillment.*

He hugged her against his body, moving as if the same desperation that pervaded her also filled him. His heat warmed her. His need encouraged her. She wrapped her arms around him, binding him to her. His thigh replaced his hand, and she rode him, moving her hips to prolong the agony. To extend the bliss. He pressed against her. She pressed against him. Each sought pleasure with feverish desperation until they shuddered together, relieved—yet frustrated still.

Long seconds later—or was it years?—the waves of delight diminished. She drooped in his embrace, drawing in shuddering breaths, trying to return to the normal world . . . and all the while knowing the world would never be normal again.

Frustrated ardor rode Jermyn. He wanted to seize Amy. His body ached to mount her, enter her, relieve the pressure in his cock with a short, intense ride to satisfaction.

And he couldn't. He had promised.

He had promised for good reason. A man didn't take a virgin like a pillaging Viking, but my God! It took all his willpower to remain still.

Her eyes fluttered open, then shut, then open—and they focused on him.

He did not have the willpower to hide his triumph.

He saw the moment she realized what she had given him. What he had taken. Thought supplanted feminine satisfaction; Amy's usual hostility replaced her languid pliancy.

He smiled victoriously—and at once realized his mistake.

Resentment flared in her eyes. With both hands planted flat on his chest, she pushed, shoving him off the cot.

He hit the floor on his rear.

She scrambled over him and fled toward the stairway and up the steps.

Leaping to his feet, blasted by passion, he followed. His foot hit the bottom step before he realized the truth.

He halted. He stared at his feet.

The manacle around his ankle had broken.

He was free.

Chapter 12

*F*ree! Savage satisfaction coursed through Jermyn's veins. Free!

And he would have her. He could still catch her. He would capture Amy.

Primitive instinct sent him upward, his stockinged feet thumping on the boards.

It was that sound that brought him to his senses.

What he mad? He shouldn't be chasing after an aggravating, infuriating, galling, exasperating, vexing female. He could escape!

And the fact that he wavered showed how deeply this imprisonment had affected his mind.

He was free, and no one knew except him. He could go to the mainland and order the constable to take

Miss Victorine and Lady Disdain into custody . . . no. No, he found no satisfaction in that idea.

He could put on his boots, stomp upstairs, and frighten Miss Victorine and Lady Disdain enough that they'd never commit another crime.

But he remembered the huge man who had carried him away when they drugged him. At times during this interminable week, he'd heard a man's voice rumbling upstairs. He'd be lucky if Amy didn't hit him over the head—right now, she'd probably like to—and have the man drag Jermyn's unconscious body back down to the cot where they would affix another manacle.

Jermyn couldn't bear another six days without sun or fresh air. He had to get out of here.

Noiselessly he leaped back to his cot. He picked up the broken manacle. Small flakes of rust fell into his palm. Apparently, while its outer appearance was clean, the inner mechanism had rusted away . . . leaving him free. He thrust his feet into his boots. Donned his jacket and his greatcoat. Going to the aging cabinet that rested against the wall under the window, he performed a cautious test to see if it could hold his weight, then hefted himself onto it. He pried the window open—it had been sealed so long it squawked in protest—and peered out.

Spring-green grass thrust from the ground in clumps around the window. He pushed them aside, but he could see no one. It was safe to crawl out. Digging his toes into the rough rock of the wall, he hauled himself up by his elbows, through the narrow opening to freedom.

The air was cool and damp, swirling with the gray

mist that covered the setting sun. He rested his cheek on the grass and took the first fresh breaths he'd had in six days. His blood coursed strongly through his veins. He was free!

He couldn't wait to get home and set plans in motion to settle the score with Miss Amy.

No, wait. First he would have a bath. Then he would settle the score with Lady Disdain. Personally and very, very slowly.

Standing, he took another deep breath and, giving in to impulse, he beat his chest and laughed aloud. He had just escaped imprisonment . . . and he had just taken a woman from ignorance to ecstasy. He had never felt such triumph.

Miss Victorine's cottage stood on the hill overlooking the village and the sea. He knew if he followed the road, he could go to the pub and there find someone to row him back to the mainland.

Jermyn started toward the village. His leg felt good as he stretched out to stride with his normal gait.

He wondered if Miss Victorine would come down to check on him, and winced to realize she would. She would bring down his supper, discover he was gone, and be upset. Not because he had escaped; he'd heard Miss Victorine suggest he should be let go. No, she'd be upset because she enjoyed their evenings together. Every night she came down and made lace, listened as Amy read, or watched as the two younger people played chess. Miss Victorine reminisced about days gone past, told stories, and made Lady Disdain behave with courtesy. And she made him behave, too.

In truth, he had grown to like the evenings with Miss Victorine and Amy. They seemed . . . normal. Peaceful. As if he were part of a family, or living in a memory of his childhood before his mother had . . .

He jerked himself back to the present. He didn't care to think about *her*. His mother. The betrayer.

He entered the outskirts of the village. Light shone from none of the windows, and the mist and the encroaching night gave the line of cottages an air of desolation. At least . . . he hoped that was why they looked so unkempt. When he was a lad and he had visited, every home had been a place of pride. Now it seemed no one cared whether the whitewash peeled off the walls or the thatching needed repair. It was almost as if the village had been abandoned by those who loved it most.

He hunched his shoulders, thrust his hands in his pockets, and strode toward the pub.

That building had light enough, but the windows were covered with oiled cloth rather than glass. He could hear voices and the clink of pewter, and his mouth watered at the idea of good English ale from a country pub.

But he couldn't go in. The place hummed with voices; it sounded as if everyone in the village was within. Certainly Jermyn hoped so, for if that was true, Amy's thug was in there.

Jermyn leaned against the wall by the window. He would wait until some sturdy oarsman came out. Then he would be on his way across the channel to the mainland, to his home and bath.

He huddled into his coat and smiled into the mist. He enjoyed imagining the look on Lady Disdain's face when she got to the bottom step and saw the empty cot.

Of course, she might make an excuse not to come down tonight. He'd made her a happy woman and at the same time scared her out of her wits. She'd been as amazing as he had imagined, and when it came to Amy his imagination had been both fertile and diverse. But holding her in his arms had been almost as satisfying as dipping his wick in another woman's lamp, and that made him realize he couldn't have Amy hanged.

To do so would deny him his pleasures.

So tomorrow was going to turn out differently than anyone could imagine. Uncle Harrison would hear from his very displeased, very much alive nephew. Miss Victorine would get a stern talking-to from her lord. And Lady Disdain—

"Will they get any money out o' this kidnapping, do ye think?" A man's voice. A disturbingly familiar man's voice.

Jermyn's head snapped around. He moved closer to the window.

"I'm fearing fer the whole project." Another man's voice, also familiar.

"I told ye we shouldn't get involved." A woman's voice, lamenting and accusing.

"Ye're not involved." Another woman, her voice tart and snappish. "No one will accuse ye o' anything.

You'll not be punished at all—but remember this—if this had worked, ye'd have profited."

"I never asked fer money!" The first woman yelped like a kicked puppy.

"Yer cottage is as bad as any in the village. Do ye think we'd let it fall down around yer head? Ye'd have let us fix it fer ye, but don't ye worry. We'll not drag ye under int' our hash."

"Mertle!" Jermyn recognized the deep male voice. He'd heard it just this afternoon up in Miss Victorine's kitchen. Amy's thug. The tall man who'd helped with Jermyn's kidnapping. "Mrs. Kitchen doesn't deserve such a tongue-lashing."

"Well! I should hope not!" Mrs. Kitchen huffed.

Rather pointedly, Mertle said nothing.

"He hasn't always been this way." A different man's voice, yet somehow familiar. Deeper, with almost no accent and the slight quaver of age. "Do you remember, Pom, when you were lads together romping about, and you and His Lordship explored the cliff at Summerwind Abbey? The cliff above the ocean?"

As Jermyn strained to remember who this might be, the pub collectively started to chuckle.

"Ah, nay, ye don't have t' tell that story." It was the deep voice.

Pom. Jermyn remembered Pom from his childhood. They'd been the same age—and even then, Pom had been a big guy. A gentle lad, but three inches taller and already rowing out with his father after the fish.

Now, remembering that day Amy had drugged him,

Jermyn realized Pom wasn't big anymore. He was a giant.

Jermyn flexed his fists.

The older man continued, "The two of you started jumping off the cliff onto a rocky ledge not far below, and the old lord saw you and thought you'd both fallen to your deaths."

"When we crawled back up to the top, Lord North-cliff caught us by our jackets and exercised his good right arm on our backsides." Pom sounded pained, as if he remembered the lesson as clearly as did Jermyn.

The pub rocked with laughter. How could they know the way Father had looked, so pale and livid Jermyn had been frightened? And when Jermyn had tried to explain they had crawled all over the cliff and knew where to jump, Father had roared, "The wind and the waves are always crumbling the rock away, and I'll be damned if I let the ocean take you, too."

It was the only time Jermyn remembered hearing his father refer to the tragedy of his mother's disappearance, and the only time he showed the pain she caused him.

"Should there be trouble, I'll take responsibility for everything," the quavering old voice said. "If His Lordship hears that I led my sheep into rocky pastures, surely he'll—"

"Hang ye instead o' us?" Mertle's voice again. "We'll not stand by fer that, Vicar."

Ohh. Vicar Smith was the one who wanted to take responsibility.

"We're in this t'gether," Mertle said. "We did it t' help Miss Victorine, t' help ourselves, and t' right a great wrong—"

"And t' save His Lordship's soul." That deep male voice again.

Save my soul? Jermyn could scarcely believe the impertinence.

"Aye, Pom, that, too," Mertle agreed.

"I'd say we were trying to save Mr. Edmondson's soul, too, but I fear that's a lost cause," the vicar said wryly.

"Aye, and there's some o' us more concerned about His Lordship's soul than about Mr. Edmondson's." General laughter followed Mertle's pronouncement.

So they didn't like Uncle Harrison. After this week, Jermyn admitted to more than a slight niggle of unease about him, too.

"I've never heard o' a whole village being hanged, so I think we should trust t' God His Lordship will have mercy," she said in a forcedly cheerful tone.

Jermyn waited to hear someone agree that he would, indeed, have mercy.

Instead, Miss Kitchen said, "He's not like his father. He's like his mother, running away from tiresome duties he doesn't want t' perform. He won't have mercy. He won't even know what they do t' us."

When Jermyn slipped back into the cellar, the broken manacle still rested on the floor, his cot was still rumpled from his tussle with Amy, the stove still gave off its warmth, the chessboard was still set up awaiting a new game.

Nothing had changed. Miss Victorine and Amy hadn't realized he had escaped. The room looked exactly the same.

It was the world that looked different.

His *mother*.

Sitting in a chair, he removed his boots and thrust them, with their betraying wisps of grass and dirt, under the cot. Going to the cabinet, he wiped away all evidence of his escapade.

He hung his greatcoat over the chair, and reaching for one of the towels set out for his ablutions, he dried the mist from his hair.

He sat in the chair, and the gibe returned, relentless, distasteful.

He's like his mother, running away from tiresome duties he doesn't want to perform.

Standing, he paced across the room, then back again.

How dared that woman compare him to his mother? Why had everyone agreed? He was like his father. How could they not see that? He looked like Father. He rode like Father. He had the same pride in the Edmondson name and the Northcliff title.

But the villagers thought he was like his mother.

How could they say that?

With relentless logic, he answered his own question.

They didn't know who he looked like or what he took pride in. They hadn't laid eyes on him for eighteen years. All they knew was that he had neglected his duties.

He had. Not Uncle Harrison. *Jermyn* had. For Jermyn's father would have never allowed another to

assume the responsibilities of the marquess of Northcliff, no matter how closely connected he was. True,
Uncle Harrison had been handling the family fortune
when Father was alive, too, but Jermyn knew his father
had insisted on a quarterly accounting from his
brother. Father had personally employed a steward to
manage the estates, and that steward had reported to
him, not Uncle Harrison. Perhaps Father done so for a
reason. Perhaps he hadn't completely trusted Uncle
Harrison.

For good reason, if what Jermyn had heard tonight
was true. The villagers were destitute and so desperate they were willing to help Miss Victorine kidnap
him as a way of seizing control of their destiny. Now
they faced certain disaster—deportation, hanging, the
workhouse—stoically and together. Well, mostly together. Mrs. Kitchen had made her displeasure clear,
but she'd been the lone disgruntled voice.

As much as Jermyn hated to admit it, Lady Disdain
was right. He was a wart on the noble ass of England.

But he was *not* like his mother. He had wiped every
bit of that woman's treacherous influence out of his
mind and his heart.

He was like his father. He had strayed from the
proper path, but he would take the reins in his hands
starting now.

So how did he intend to start?

He would remove Uncle Harrison as his business
manager and find out exactly what he intended by not
sending the ransom.

He would visit each estate in turn, speak to the butler

and the housekeeper, to the villagers, to the farmers, and correct whatever problems had been neglected.

Before he left the cellar forever, he would seduce Amy . . . and he even knew how.

Amy walked toward him, smiling as she discarded her clothing . . .

"Jermyn, dear."

At the sound of Miss Victorine's voice at the top of the stairs, he jumped guiltily. Speedily he erased the full-formed fantasy from his mind. He did *not* want Miss Victorine to know what he was thinking—or what he was thinking with.

She came down the stairs carrying his dinner tray, Coal padding along on her heels.

He wanted to leap forward to help her, but he was bound by a broken manacle and a deception, and he had to satisfy himself with taking it from her when she reached him.

"Dear, I have bad news. Amy doesn't feel well tonight. I'm afraid you have only me to entertain you." Miss Victorine blinked at him as if awaiting an explosion of wrath.

Putting down the tray, he took her hands. "This is perfect. I've been wanting to spend some special time talking to you about the village."

"I would love that!" Miss Victorine beamed.

"And would it be possible for me to get paper and ink?"

Coal slid underneath the cot, and came out with a blade of grass between his teeth.

"The days alone down here are long. Tomorrow I'd

like to write down my thoughts." Elaborately casual, Jermyn leaned over and snatched the blade out of Coal's mouth.

"Of course, dear," Miss Victorine said. "I'll fetch you some paper and ink."

Equally casual, Coal sank his claws into Jermyn's hand.

Jermyn wrenched away. The long scratches oozed blood.

Coal smirked and licked his paw as if to rid himself of Jermyn's flesh.

That blasted cat had a lot in common with Lady Disdain.

Chapter 13

That night, Pom staggered as he left the pub. He waved as he went, his silent response to calls of "Good night, Pom!" "Good fishing, Pom!"

Everybody else in the village remained, even the fishermen who normally went out before dawn to fill their nets. But the others didn't see the sense in going out tomorrow. They figured they were going to hang soon, anyway. Might as well enjoy themselves tonight.

Pom didn't judge them harshly for such thinking. He understood it. He just didn't agree with it. Until his last breath, he had to keep trying to do the right thing. He only wished he was surer what that was.

"Ye'll be all right until I get done working, won't ye, Pom?"

He turned unsteadily to face the pub. Mertle stood in the lighted doorway, wiping her hands on her apron. With the light behind her, he couldn't see her expression, but he knew she was anxious.

"I've found me way home many a dark, foggy night, Mertle, me love. I'll find it again tonight."

"I know," she said softly.

He couldn't see her face, but he could see her silhouette and the slight thickening of her waist. "I'll be fine," he said softly. "We'll be fine."

"I know," she said again. "Good night then. I'll see ye in the morning."

He frowned. " 'Twill be a late night fer ye tonight. Ye sleep tomorrow. I can get meself breakfast and get off t' the sea."

"I'll fix yer breakfast and send ye off, then I'll go back t' bed." She sounded quite firm about that.

He knew why. Like every other fisherman's wife, she knew that any day could be the day the sea claimed her man. So no matter how late she worked at the pub and no matter how early he rose, she rose with him to kiss him good-bye and wish him God speed.

He couldn't change her mind. For her, it was the right thing, and he wouldn't deny her that. "Then good night, love."

"Good night, Pom." She turned back to the pub where men hollered her name and demanded their ale. "All right, me hearties. Here I am!" She shut the door behind her, leaving Pom in the pitch dark with the fog swirling around him.

Pom felt as lost as he never was on the endless,

boundless sea. He blamed his sad humor on the ale. It was unusual for him to drink too much. For one thing, it took too many pints to achieve the desired effect. For another, he always had to rise early in the morning to find the fish.

But for all his stoic encouragement to the villagers, Miss Victorine, and Amy, he couldn't escape the truth. They were doomed. Everyone in the village was doomed. His Mertle . . . his heart broke when he thought of his Mertle. They shared a secret, the two of them. In the fall, they would have a babe. That was why Mertle had encouraged him to help Miss Amy and Miss Victorine.

"Pom," she'd said, "we're starving most o' the winter, sitting here starving while our gracious lord steals the fish from our nets and the work from our hands. We've got t' do something fer this child, and Miss Amy's plan is a sound one. Ye think it is, ye know ye do. So let's not play it safe. Just once, let's take a chance t' make our lives better."

And Pom, desperately in love with his wife and urgently fearful for the survival of his unborn child, had agreed.

Now the plan had failed, so Pom drank too much and staggered off toward home.

That was why he never saw the attack coming. One minute he was passing the end of the pub, the next minute he was sprawled flat on his back in the grass on the side of the road, his jaw aching, a weight kneeling on his chest. A man, unseen in the darkness, held Pom's jacket in a crushing grip around his neck.

Gathering his wits, Pom braced himself to attack.

"You're lucky I don't kill you," his attacker said.

Pom couldn't see him, but he recognized that voice. Recognized the tone, the timbre, the aristocratic accent. He eased back onto the ground, his fists slack. No matter what the provocation, he wasn't going to hit Lord Northcliff.

Northcliff remained still, waiting for attack. Finally he said, "Well?"

"M'lord, 'tis good ye got free at last." Reflectively Pom said, "I thought ye would do it sooner." He heard the hitch in His Lordship's breathing.

"How did you know it was me?" His Lordship loosened his grip around Pom's collar.

"Ye're the only person right now who has reason t' want t' kill me. Can't say that I blame ye. 'Twas a dirty trick we pulled."

"That it was." Lord Northcliff took his knee out of Pom's chest, but he still leaned close.

Pom didn't make the mistake of thinking he could easily overcome him. The way Lord Northcliff held his body told Pom all too clearly that this was a man who wasn't afraid of a good row. Would like a good row. "I owe it t' ye t' let ye take a few licks at me."

"Let me?" Lord Northcliff chuckled with unexpected humor. "You know how to take the fun out of a fight."

"I can't hit ye. Ye're the lord."

"But you can abduct me?" When Pom began to explain, Lord Northcliff said, "No, don't tell me you want to save my soul, or I will be forced to hit you again and that's unfair. But I want you to do something."

"If I can, m'lord."

"I have a letter for my valet." Lord Northcliff reached into his own pocket, pulled out a sealed sheet of paper, and stuffed it in Pom's pocket. "Take it to him."

Easy for Lord Northcliff to say. He didn't understand that a fisherman couldn't walk into a great house and demand to speak with a swanky valet. But Pom didn't complain. He owed it to His Lordship to do as he wished.

"In the morning rather than fishing, go to the mainland to my estate. Biggers is an old cavalryman. He rides every morning at dawn. Catch him in the stables."

So maybe Lord Northcliff did understand about fishermen and fancy folk. "Should I wait fer a reply?" The ground was getting cold beneath Pom's back, but he didn't complain.

"No, but you'll row me over the following morning."

Pom's heart sank. He could explain no fish for one day, but how would he explain for two? And he and Mertle had no backup resources—they'd go hungry both nights. The child would go hungry both nights.

"I'll pay you for your services," Lord Northcliff continued.

"Ye will?" Pom couldn't keep the surprise from his voice.

"I will." His Lordship got off Pom. Taking his hand, he pulled him to his feet. "Do as I say and you'll not get hurt working for me." Without another word, he melted away into the night.

Pom smiled in silly pleasure. Perhaps their little kidnapping had gotten through to Lord Northcliff after all. He walked on, a little more steady after his contact with the cool grass and the chill earth. He wondered what the note said. He hoped it didn't tell him to bring the constable and arrest the whole village. If Pom could read . . . but he couldn't.

When he was little, he remembered learning the ABCs from Lady Northcliff. Her Ladyship had come over to the island every Thursday and taught the fishermen's children. She'd looked like an angel, her dark hair curling around her face and her kind brown eyes. He remembered learning his first words, and how proud of him she'd been. Then she was gone. Gone suddenly and ignominiously, and no one taught the children again.

No matter what people said, he would never understand what had happened to that lovely lady.

He turned up the little path to his house and caught the slightest whisper of a familiar scent. He sensed a movement and, on edge after his last encounter, he almost struck out.

Then a female voice whispered, "Pom? Is that you?"

"Miss Amy!" He put his hand to his pounding heart. "What are ye doing here at this hour? 'Tis gone ten o'clock!"

But he feared he knew what she was doing here. She knew His Lordship was free. She wanted Pom to recapture him.

Instead she said, "I need you to go to the mainland tomorrow for me."

"Tomorrow?" He swallowed. This was too peculiar. "Fer ye?"

"I want you to send this"—she shoved a small package tied in string into his hand—"through the post to Edinburgh, Scotland."

"Scotland." He furrowed his brow as he thought. "That's a long ways away, isn't it?"

"That it is," she said crisply. "It's imperative it goes tomorrow."

In the dark, he heard her fancy words and her noble accent more clearly. He mused, "When ye talk like that, so commanding and strong, I wonder who ye are and where ye came from." Because for all that she had come to the island wet, dirty, and half dead, he knew she hadn't escaped from the workhouse or the prisons.

She dragged in a long breath that sounded like a sob.

"Beg yer pardon, Miss Rosabel." He was covered in mortification. "I'm drunker than I realized if I said that out loud."

"No. It's all right." She gave a sniff, and he thought she must have rummaged for her handkerchief. "Someone on the island has to know what should be done with me if . . . if the worst comes to pass."

"Ye mean if no ransom is paid and we're taken fer our crimes." He wanted to say that right now he had greater faith in their survival than he had an hour ago, but he'd already said more words tonight than he did in a normal week.

"You won't be taken." In the dark, she groped for his hand. "No matter what happens, Pom, I want to tell you—I couldn't have done this without your assistance, and I will never betray you or your kindness."

"I know, miss." He pressed her cold, shaking fingers. "Maybe everything will come out fer the best after all."

"Maybe. But if the worst happens and I hang"—her voice grew stronger as she faced her fate—"I depend on you for two things. Try to protect Miss Victorine."

"Goes without saying, miss."

"And take this package." She handed him another package much like the first. "Send it to Edinburgh, too."

"What's in Edinburgh, miss?"

She waited so long to answer, he didn't think she would. Finally she said, "My sister. She lives not in Edinburgh, but in Scotland, and she'll see this. It's an ad that will run in the newspaper and tell her of my fate. I hadn't realized it before, but she is very dear to me. After all we went through together, I would have her know of my death—and my eternal affection."

Scotland, two years ago

"We're princesses. When it's safe for us to return home we'll eat wonderful foods, wear beautiful gowns, and be respected and loved by all." Twenty-two-year-old Clarice's hair dripped from the rain, her lips were blue from cold, but her face shone as she huddled in her wet cloak before the meager fire in the public room of a Scottish inn.

She really believed the litany she recited. As seventeen-year-old Amy saw it, that was the trouble. They had been gone from Beaumontagne for ten years, yet still Clarice really believed they would go back to the palace in Beaumontagne and resume their old lives.

Perhaps it was easier for Clarice to have faith in a handsome prince. She was beautiful: petite, blond, curvaceous, with a face that made men turn on the street to stare.

Amy knew she wasn't ugly, but when the two sisters stood together, no man noticed Amy. It wasn't a matter of contention for Amy—Clarice handled the attentions she drew with ease and tact, but sometimes things turned nasty.

Yesterday they had turned nasty. Amy's heart still pounded from their narrow escape, and she wanted to ride farther into Scotland.

The foul weather thwarted them.

She hoped it would thwart their pursuers, too.

"Sorcha will return, also." Clarice's teeth chattered, but she still spoke cheerfully—and softly. "We'll dance at elegant balls and be wed to handsome princes."

"If the choice in princes is as good as the choice in common men, it would be better to remain a spinster," Amy said crossly. The longer they were on the road being chased by magistrates and irate customers, the less Amy believed the tales Clarice spun. She handed Clarice one of the pieces of bread the innkeeper had placed on the table. "Here, eat this."

Clarice took a bite, then grimaced.

Amy held her piece down by the single candle the landlord had placed in the middle of the table. The bread was moldy, dotted with green specks, but the sisters were too hungry and too desperate to quibble.

Glancing around, Amy found a ladle and filled a bowl from the mutton stew bubbling in a pot hanging on the hook. "Do you remember what just happened back there? You repelled an English magistrate, stole his horse, and that's why we had to ride through one of the worst rainstorms in British history to cross into Scotland where we hope, please God, we'll be safe."

"Sh!" Clarice glanced around at the empty public room. "That dreadful magistrate was beating the horse."

Amy lowered her voice, too. "He was beating his wife, too, and if he catches up with us, he'll hang us."

"He won't catch us." Clarice's cloak steamed from the heat of the flames, wreathing her face, giving her an ethereal guise.

"You hope." Pulling her spoon from her belt, Amy took a ravenous bite. It was hot, greasy, and it tasted . . . off. As if it wasn't mutton, but some other meat about which she dared not inquire.

She hoped it didn't make them sick.

She knew it didn't matter. They had to eat.

In a vehement undertone, she said, "I am sick to death of the constant travel and the furtive half lies and the awful food. If we're not hanged, then we'll die of exposure."

Clarice turned stricken eyes on her. "I didn't know you felt that way."

"How could you not know?" How could Clarice be so dim-witted? Amy dropped a piece of bread into the stew and fed it to her sister.

"You've never said anything before."

"Yes, I have, you just don't listen to me." Maybe Amy hadn't really said what she thought, but she was in no mood to be fair. She suffered from that jittery sense, the one that she had developed in too many desperate flights from too many towns. She shoveled the food into her mouth, shoveled it into Clarice.

Where was the innkeeper? Why hadn't he returned from the kitchen?

"You think I'm your silly little sister who knows nothing." Amy pocketed the rest of the bread. "You think you have to shield me, but you can't. I have to go into towns on my own to set up your arrival with the creams. I know how to find a place of employment. I know how to live on my own. For heaven's sake, I'm seventeen years old, Clarice, the same age you were when we were thrown out of school!"

"Have I been too protective, Amy?" The rain had dried on Clarice's face, but now moisture slid down her cheeks. Hastily she wiped it away with her red, chapped fingers.

Amy felt a pang of guilt, but she swept it aside. "Yes. Why can't we pick out some perfectly pleasant town, stop there, and open a shop? You could sell creams, I could sew—"

"Because Grandmamma sent her messenger to warn us that assassins are after us."

"After five years, you think they're still after us?"

"Godfrey said that when it was safe to return to Beaumontagne, Grandmamma would put an advertisement in the English newspapers. According to the reports, Grandmamma is still alive and has gained control of the country."

"Probably scared the rebels to death," Amy muttered.

"Probably, but that's not the point. She wouldn't forget to call us back."

"No, not Grandmamma. She would never forget anything. So maybe she's not really in control."

"And maybe the assassins are still after us. Remember what happened in that inn after we left boarding school?" At the memory, a hard shudder wracked Clarice.

"Yes. Yes, of course I do." A fortnight into their flight, they woke to find a man in their dark room. He was huge, with bulky shoulders, and a cloth covered his features. The blade of his knife gleamed in the moonlight, and he advanced on them, waving it in slow circles. The girls had screamed. The innkeeper had burst in. The assassin had knocked him down as he ran out the door.

And when they explained to the innkeeper who they were and why they were being chased, he had growled, "Ye're trouble, the both of ye. Out ye go! And don't come back."

He'd thrown them out in the middle of the night. It had been a lesson in reality the girls never forgot, and the next day, they had spent some of their desperate coins on knives of their own. And in fact . . .

Where was the innkeeper? Where was his wife? Why hadn't they returned from the kitchen?

"But that was five years ago," Amy said. "We've been careful. Nothing's happened like it since. They're off our trail!"

"I can't take a chance. Not with your life or my own." Clarice glanced toward the door. "Where is that innkeeper?"

So she, also, was aware of the passage of time.

"They're taking an awfully long time," Amy said.

"If one of them goes out to the stable—" The princesses had groomed the young stallion themselves.

"If the hostler goes in and tells them what a magnificent creature Blaize is—"

The two sisters looked at each other in despair.

They heard the clomping of footsteps along the passage from the kitchen.

Amy snuffed the candle with her fingertips and tossed it aside. Picking up a heavy pewter candlestick, she put her back against the wall behind the door. She nodded at Clarice, who nodded back.

The door opened with a long squeak, hiding the room from Amy's gaze.

"There's one o' them, Bert. The other's probably upstairs stealing us blind."

Slowly Amy slid along the wall, taking care to remain silent and unobtrusive.

Their tall, bony landlady stepped into the room, wiping her hands on her apron.

Bert, slow, stout, ham-handed, followed his wife. "Nice horse," he said. "Where'd ye get it?"

"It was a present from my father." Smiling with all the charm in her considerable arsenal, Clarice advanced on him. "Isn't he beautiful?"

"Yer father!" The landlady snorted. "Like ye even know who he is."

Ignoring her, Clarice continued to walk slowly toward Bert. "It's such a foul night, Bert. I'm very glad for your kind hospitality."

Hypnotized by her smile, Bert reversed course and backed up—toward Amy.

In a soothing tone, Clarice continued, "You have no other guests and you did already take our coin—"

"We'll take the rest of yer purse before ye leave, too, for we're na keeping two o' the likes o' ye here. Right, Bert? Right?" The landlady turned to watch as Clarice herded Bert along.

The landlady's eyes widened when Amy stepped out of the shadows, candlestick raised.

The landlady squawked.

Amy brought the makeshift weapon down on Bert's head.

He dropped like a rock, thumping on the floor in a cloud of dust.

Scowling, Amy lifted the candlestick again and walked toward the landlady.

She fled, shrieking like a Beaumontagne windstorm.

Amy dropped her weapon on the table and dusted her fingertips. "With any luck, the hostler's in the stable and there's no one to hear her." Then, reconsidering, she picked up the candlestick again. "But we haven't had any luck lately, have we?"

Clarice knelt by the landlord and pressed her fingers to his neck. "He's alive."

"Good. That's one less crime I've committed," Amy said grimly.

"Why do they always have to be suspicious of us?" Clarice stood and pulled on her still damp gloves.

"Because we don't talk like them and we don't look like them." With jerky motions, Amy tied the dark hood over her sister's head to cover the bright strands. Donning her own gloves, she said, "Come on. We have our bellies full. Blaize has a willing spirit. We can ride farther tonight."

Chapter 14

"*A*my, dear Jermyn is asking for you." Miss Victorine came bustling up the stairs into the kitchen where Amy sat at the table, her hands cupping her forehead. "Do you feel well enough to go down?"

"No." *A little terse.* Lifting her head, she tried to smile. "That is—I'm afraid I'm still unwell and would hate to pass my illness on to him."

Miss Victorine's eyes got big. "I thought you said your illness was a female problem?"

"It is! That is, it was. But now I have a cough"—Amy hacked insincerely—"probably the result of spending too much time in a damp cellar."

"My cellar isn't damp, dear." Miss Victorine sounded huffy. "With the stove it's quite comfortable."

"Dusty," Amy offered.

"If you really believe it's disadvantageous to your health to go down, then in all honor we must free His Lordship or we will have his death on our hands."

"No!" Amy came to her feet. "No, no, no, we can't free him yet!" If they freed him, he could grab her and subject her to more of his kisses. Force them on her, make her accept a passion she didn't want to acknowledge.

Miss Victorine sighed softly. Putting her arm around Amy's shoulders, she hugged her and said, "Amy, you're not ill. You're avoiding Jermyn. I don't blame you. I know that it's unpleasant when we tell him he'll not be released—"

"*It's* unpleasant? *He's* unpleasant!"

"He can be cajoled."

"Why should I cajole him?" Amy expected Miss Victorine to mention Lord Northcliff's nobility.

Instead she said, "Because we kidnapped him and put him in my damp, dusty cellar." Playfully she pulled a strand Amy's hair. "Now go down and talk to the boy. Offer to read to him. You noticed that first day that he's very handsome. Perhaps you could flirt with him."

"Flirt?" Amy's gaze flew to Miss Victorine's in horror. "Oh, no. I can't flirt with him. He's . . . not to my taste."

"Really? I thought all those sidelong glances meant he was very much to your taste."

"You . . . you think that I indicated a liking . . . a preference . . . for His Lordship?" Had Amy unwittingly encouraged his attentions?

"A reluctant liking," Miss Victorine corrected.

"I don't want to like him." Amy thought she'd been a shrew, but what did she know about men? Maybe they liked shrews.

"No, of course you don't. But sometimes nature has other ideas."

With a fair imitation of her haughty grandmamma, Amy said, "Nature does not command me."

Miss Victorine sounded not at all like Amy's grandmother, but she still sounded implacable when she replied, "It does. Now go on down and see what he wants. It's not as if you have to remain there."

Amy stared at the dark hole leading down to the cellar, then grabbed Miss Victorine's arm. "Come with me."

"If you insist, but my knee..." Miss Victorine winced. "It's complaining with all the climbing up and down the stairs today. I did, after all, have to deliver his breakfast and his tea and his supper."

"Then of course, you must stay up here. You've done too much today already." Amy steeled herself to descend the stairway and face the man whom yesterday she had kissed.

Kissed! What a simple word to describe the panoramic pleasure he had shown her.

And she'd let him. That was the truth that haunted her. She had fought him, yes, but she'd fought him like a girl, not poking his eyes or slamming his throat. She hadn't wanted to hurt him—and how ridiculous that was. He hadn't hesitated to use his strength against her. Not that he'd hurt her; quite the opposite. He'd forced pleasure on her and showed her things about herself she had never imagined. She couldn't imagine looking him in the eye.

Worse, she couldn't look at herself in the mirror.

For the first time in the year Amy had lived here, Miss Victorine examined her critically. "You need some color." She pinched Amy's cheeks.

With her first flare of indignation at Miss Victorine, Amy flounced away. But before she descended the stairs, she turned back. "You never told me about his mother."

"I did, too." Miss Victorine puffed up like an offended partridge. "I said we lost her."

"She wasn't *lost*. She abandoned her family. At least that's what *he* told me."

"It looked that way. She left and was never seen again. But I never believed it." Miss Victorine seemed to drift away. "Never believed it. She was sweet and lovely. She was kind to me. She loved her boy and she loved His Lordship." Abruptly Miss Victorine returned to the present. "Lady Northcliff couldn't have walked away from them."

"Exactly what I said, but he—"

"Imagine, if you will, what it was like for that little boy to have people believe his mother was light-minded and immoral." Miss Victorine cupped Amy's cheek. "He heard adults gossiping most cruelly. They forbade their children to play with him because his mother's dissipation must have been passed on to him. The children taunted him, said how awful he must be that his mother ran away from him."

Amy's stomach sank. "I may have said something similar."

"Oh, Amy." Miss Victorine's hand fell away. "I love you most dearly, but you have a fault which you should mend. You speak too hastily and with too much candor."

"Honesty is a good trait."

"Not when it's used to wound. Now bite your lips to bring color to them, too, and go to see my dear Jermyn."

As Amy walked down the stairs, she did as she was told and pressed her teeth into her lips. She was embarrassed at herself, but she wanted Lord Northcliff to look at her and long to be loose of his chain.

At the same time she mocked herself; never in her life had she been so . . . silly. It was as if his kiss had stolen her stolid good sense and left her a breathless, silly girl concerned with nothing but a man's approval.

When she stepped into the cellar, he was straightening his cot. That startled her; she had never seen him do anything that looked vaguely like a chore. He must be deathly bored. Holding the fur throw before him, he bowed slightly. "Miss Amy, if you would be seated, we have to talk."

Courtesy. He showed her courtesy.

Why? "Talk about what?" About their kiss? She didn't want to talk about that.

"If you would be seated," he repeated.

She sidled over to her usual chair at the table and sat.

He sat across from her, the fur throw tossed carelessly on the table. "I need clothes," he said.

Clothes. He wanted discuss his clothes. How deflating.

Not that she wanted to talk about their kiss, but she had thought it would be on his mind—although if it wasn't on his mind, it certainly wasn't on hers.

"I've worn the same garments for six—or is it seven?—long days now." His shirt and waistcoat looked as if he'd tried to straighten them, but with little success. "At the rate your plan is progressing, I could very well wear them for another six."

"I'm sure your uncle will be able to pay the ransom this time." She was sure of no such thing.

From the way Northcliff's teeth snapped together, it was clear he doubted he would soon be freed. "Nevertheless, I need clean clothes, and clean clothes are available to me in my bedroom on the mainland a mere five miles from here. All I need is someone to fetch them." He bent his gaze on her. "Since I find myself unable to discuss the particulars of my linens with Miss Victorine, that someone would be you."

"You want me to sneak into your bedchamber at Summerwind Abbey and steal your clothes?"

"*Brava*, Lady Disdain. You understand completely." He pulled a folded sheet of paper out of his pocket. "I've written a list of my needs."

"Your needs?" She could scarcely believe his gall. "How do you propose I get into your home without being noticed?"

"You've proved to have an analytical and criminal mind and the ability to put any plan into motion. I have complete faith that, if you had to, you could steal the silver out from under my butler's nose as he was cleaning it."

"Are you flattering me or insulting me?"

"I leave that for you to decide." He shook out the list. "Now listen carefully. My linens are in the chest in the bedchamber—not the sitting room, but in the bedchamber—facing the foot of the bed. I want two clean shirts, two clean pairs of drawers, clean hose . . ."

As she listened to him recite, she swallowed. She supposed she could manage to walk into Summer-wind Abbey without being stopped. As long as she behaved as if she belonged there, she was unlikely to be stopped, and if she was, there were three hundred servants and three hundred different tasks for a maid in a great house.

Sorting through his linens was an entirely different proposition. She knew nothing at all about a man's undergarments, and the chances of bringing back the right clothes seemed remote. She could ask him, but his answer would involve—possibly—disbelief or amusement and—definitely—an embarrassing explanation. Better to nod and pretend she could do the task he had set her.

"—and that's all," he finished. "I've drawn a map to my bedchamber and a listing of the times my valet is likely to be about. I'd suggest you avoid him. If he catches you up to your elbows in my underwear, he's likely to be testy and unwilling to listen to any tale you try to tell him. He is quite intelligent and very fond of me—"

"Why?"

"—and I imagine my disappearance has caused him some disquietude." Northcliff held out the paper for her to take.

"Put it on the table and slide it toward me," she said.

"I thought we'd progressed further than that." He did as he was told.

She picked up the sheet, spread it out, and pretended to study the map.

"Of course, that was before yesterday when we kissed."

She set her teeth and looked up at him. "Don't worry, my lord. I've forgotten it."

"Have you? Good for you. For myself, the heat of that kiss is burned into my memory so that in dotage when all else about my life has vanished from my mind, I will still remember the heat of your lips against mine." In the flash of a second, the matter-of-fact aristocrat in need of clothing disappeared, leaving the primitive man stalking the woman he would take as his mate.

And he hadn't moved an inch.

Why had Miss Victorine pinched Amy's cheeks? She didn't need more color. She felt the blood rush to dye her face and she could scarcely look at Northcliff with any equanimity. "Please, my lord, I don't wish to—"

"Nonsense. Of course you do, Amy, and you want to with me."

She flashed him a glance that scalded and abhorred.

"I know. You don't like me. But think about it from my point of view. You've made a fool of me. You've kidnapped me, imprisoned me, made me feel guilty, made me doubt my uncle and business manager—all very uncomfortable for me, I assure you." Northcliff was a very tactile man. As he stared at her, he stroked the old fur throw, and she found herself watching his fingers as they combed the long brown coat. They stroked and stroked again, and all the while his gaze caressed Amy's hair so fondly, warmth enveloped her like the throw. Like his body. "I should despise you. Instead I want you. It's all I think about, and the only thing that comforts me is knowing that having me is all you think about, too."

"That's not true." The hypnotic motion kept her seated, trapping her to hear his slow, deep, seductive voice.

"Perhaps not. I have nothing to do down here except think. You have duties to occupy your mind." His hand stopped. He leaned forward. "But Amy, I know women. I know that in the dark of the night when dreams slide under the doorsill as relentlessly as fog from the sea, you dream of me."

Aghast at his insight, she denied it. "No!"

"You act as if you have a choice in the matter. You don't. I don't. Some odd quirk in our natures unites us in desire." He sat in his chair, still as a lion waiting for its prey to step within reach. "Do you know that when you rise in the morning, I hear your footsteps over my head? I imagine you slipping out of a worn nightgown, your body gleaming pale and sweet, and donning one of your ghastly gowns. At night the floorboards creak as you ready yourself for bed, and I imagine you undressing. And all night long, every time you turn over in your virgin bed, I hear you. You have me imprisoned, but I am watching you."

Yet his words wove a spell around her. She couldn't move, could scarcely breathe, and desperate mortification slid easily into heady anticipation. Some remnant of good sense, or maybe it was just a virgin's natural reluctance, kept her sane enough to say, "I'd release you if I dared, and then we'd be done with this."

His deep chuckle caught her by surprise. "You are an innocent. We'll never be done with *this*, as you call it. We'll carry it with us our whole lives. Do you know how desperately I want you?"

Eyes wide, she shook her head.

"If you took off my manacle right now, I'd remain here in this dark, small cellar to make love to you."

She had come to associate his scent with the earthiness of the cellar. "We can't. I can't."

He said nothing, but his eyes were eloquent with a knowledge she longed to tap and a passion she longed to know.

"There's too much difference in our stations. When you are freed, you'll try to find me and punish me—"

"That's true," he conceded. "But you won't die of my punishment, sweeting. You'll beg for more. I promise, I will make you beg."

When he looked at her, his brown eyes golden with flame, when he spoke to her, his voice slipping along her nerves like black velvet, she wanted to push him onto the cot, unbutton her gown, and discover if he could fulfill his promise. "Impossible."

She spoke more to herself than to him, but he answered her anyway. "It's not impossible. Think about it, Amy. Never again will you have a chance like this. I'm manacled to the bed. When the house is quiet and even the cat is asleep, you could come down the stairs and make love to me."

"Don't be ridiculous. You would never let me—"

"But I would. I'd let you take the lead, explore me as you liked, show me what gives you pleasure. I would kiss you anywhere you instructed—on your lips, on your breasts, on your—"

"My lord, please!"

"—shoulders. Really, Amy, what did you think I was going to say?" His eyes twinkled with the kind of wicked amusement that would have made him attractive . . . if she was interested in insensitive, dishonest, dissipated aristocrats. "Consider, Amy, how sweet it would be to know that you had me under your control and if you chose to leave me frustrated and wanting, you could go without a backward glance."

"If you grabbed me as you did yesterday and pressed me into the mattress, I wouldn't be able to control you."

"Yesterday I lost my temper. I won't apologize because I'm not sorry—I already told you how I feel about that kiss. But I swear on my honor—and Amy, although you doubt it, I do have honor—that I won't force you again. Not while in this cellar."

With her palm, she rubbed the tabletop, over and over, the smooth grain of the wood slipping beneath her touch. He offered her the devil's deal—and she was tempted. So tempted.

Because what he said was true. In the daytime, thoughts of him invaded her mind, taking over sensible thoughts and average feelings. Worse was the night. She dreamed of him, constantly and in color, sometimes fighting, sometimes crooning, always menacing, always demanding, always enticing.

Like now. How did he know she had told herself, *If I was in control, then maybe . . .* How had she betrayed herself?

With a start, she came back to the cellar to find herself staring at the amused and knowing expression on Northcliff's face.

Had she betrayed herself?

Of course. He knew her—or perhaps it would be smarter to say he knew women—far too well.

Leaping to her feet, she started for the steps.

"Amy," he called.

She turned back to him. "What?"

"You forgot the list."

Of course she had. He had distracted her.

She walked back and picked it up.

"There's something I didn't put on the list," he said.

"It doesn't matter. I'll be lucky to get up to your bedchamber, take these items, and leave without being caught."

"But this is very important." His deep voice snagged her unwilling attention. "When a woman makes love to a man for the first time, it's best if she uses oil to ease the way."

Amy froze, her gaze on his.

"Also, it's best if she protects herself from unwanted pregnancy."

"God, yes!" How could she have even have considered the enticement he offered and not thought of the obvious?

"In the top drawer of my bedside table, there's a small box. It contains everything we need to make our night pleasurable. If you have to, leave everything else behind, but bring that box."

She snorted as if in derision—but it was a weak snort. She walked toward the steps again.

"Amy."

She turned back to him. "What?"

"Did you notice I didn't ask for a nightshirt?"

She glanced at the list in her hand and wondered why he told her that.

Then she knew why.

He had just told her he slept nude.

Every night in the cellar right beneath her bedchamber, his naked body remained at the ready to welcome her. Now that she knew it, she could never escape the image . . . or the temptation.

Chapter 15

"𝒥 cannot take that jacket to wear. It's too different from the one I was wearing."

"And that you ruined." Biggers and Jermyn stood in his shadowy wardrobe off his bedroom and argued about the garb Jermyn would take back on his return to his prison. Jermyn insisted the clothes be essentially the same.

Biggers, a usually reasonable man, lectured on the necessity of variety.

"The ladies aren't stupid. They'll notice I've changed." Jermyn chose a jacket that matched the original in color and cut. "I'll return with this one."

"They can't be too intelligent. You escaped days ago and they haven't noticed," Biggers argued.

"I would presume that once I set my mind to keeping them in the dark, I would be equal to the challenge." Grimly aware he was repeating Amy's words almost verbatim, Jermyn said, "However, please recall that a nineteen-year-old girl and an old woman did plan, and succeeded in, the kidnapping of the marquess of Northcliff. You might choose to consider them simple, but I like to believe that the people who outwitted me are more than half-wits."

"I see, m'lord. Of course you're correct, m'lord. Exceptionally intelligent women, m'lord." Biggers in no way indicated amusement. He was the perfect valet: upright, punctilious, always ahead of the styles, able to shave Jermyn's chin without a nick and iron his cravats to a snowy crisp. He was also tall, thin and perpetually forty-three. He had been with Jermyn for twelve years and never revealed his history, yet he was well-spoken and shrewd in ways that implied his past had been far more perilous than his present. "I've sent a request to your solicitor to come with the books for the Edmondsons' business."

"And you told him—"

"That your uncle made the request. He has no idea who Mr. Edmondson has writing his letters, and believe me, m'lord, he's too frightened of your uncle to question any order."

"Good. Now I need you to scrutinize the servants. Almost all of them have been here for years, and if my uncle is corrupt, it only follows that he could have wooed their loyalty away from me and to himself by whatever means—bribes, I suppose."

"Or blackmail," Biggers said.

That hadn't occurred to Jermyn.

"I'll subtlty question the servants and ascertain which ones keep their allegiance to you." With great delicacy, Biggers asked, "So with the events of the recent weeks, is it safe to say we no longer place our trust in your uncle?"

"It is safe to say that."

"And in fact, it's no accident that you've suffered so many calamities?"

"That's right." Jermyn rubbed his thigh where the bone had broken.

"Then, m'lord, I would feel safer if you were to carry this with you." Biggers rolled up his sleeve and showed Jermyn the thin leather strapped there. From the sheath, he pulled a small knife with a shining blade.

Yes, Biggers definitely hid some kind of disreputable past. The blade and its cleverly hidden sheath proved it.

Jermyn accepted the knife, touched the sharp point, and smiled. "Very good."

"When you disappeared, I took the liberty of confiscating a firearm from your father's collection of dueling pistols." Biggers produced a gun from his pocket. "Please, m'lord, this is a fine piece. Take it, too."

Jermyn examined the pistol. With its distinctive ivory handle, the beautiful decoration on the barrel, and the initials J. E. on the bottom of the stock, it might have been nothing more than a toy. But his father collected only the best, and Jermyn hadn't a doubt this pistol would shoot straight and true. He took it and the powder and shot Biggers offered.

Right now, Jermyn felt he could trust only Biggers, the people on Summerwind . . . and his eternally candid Lady Disdain.

And while he didn't doubt she would try to obtain the clothes, she couldn't bathe for him. "When will my bath be ready?"

"It takes time, m'lord, to heat the water, and may I point out it took a fair bit of explaining as to why I wanted a bath delivered to your chambers in the middle of the day when you were gone." Biggers chose another jacket. "How about this one for your evening meal?"

Jermyn laughed and began again to explain his circumstances when he heard a click, and the door to his bedroom suite opened.

Biggers prepared to step out and see who dared enter without knocking, but a caution honed by kidnapping and imprisonment made Jermyn place a restraining hand on his servant's shoulder.

Biggers's eyes lit up as he realized that this unauthorized entrance could mean intrigue.

Bold as brass, a dark-haired serving girl strolled past their line of sight.

Softly Biggers sighed in exasperation.

But although her face was turned away, the insouciance with which she walked, the straight line of her back, the ugly, old-fashioned gown warned Jermyn . . . it was Amy.

Grabbing Biggers, Jermyn pushed him against the wall and signaled for silence.

Biggers nodded, eyes wide with interest.

She walked toward the bureau, moving out of view.

The two men sidled around to watch her.

She examined the bedchamber first. She tugged at the bed curtains, rubbed her hand over the polished footboard, and went to the window that looked out onto the balcony and from there, out to sea.

She was satisfying her curiosity about Jermyn, and Jermyn found himself delighted in her interest.

Then she opened the top drawer of his dresser. She removed a soft white shirt. She shut that drawer and opened the next. She removed a cravat. She shut that and opened the next . . . stockings and underwear joined the growing pile.

Jermyn's breath stilled. He watched intently. So far, she had followed his instructions. Now he waited to see if she would follow his last, insistent direction.

In the top drawer of my bedside table, there's a small box. It contains everything we need to make our night pleasurable . . . leave everything else behind, but bring that box.

He bent his will on her. *Amy, get the wooden box. Get it.* If thoughts had power, then his directive would surely be followed.

She gathered the clothes, wrapped them in a piece of brown paper and tied them like a package with a string. She thrust the package into a large cloth bag that hung by her belt and started toward the sitting room.

In frustration, Jermyn wanted to stick his fist through the wall.

Why couldn't the girl just once do as she was told?

At the doorway, she hesitated.

Jermyn's heart lifted. *Do it*, he mentally urged. *Get it.*

She glanced toward the bedside table, then away. Jermyn could almost see the tug-of-war between her good sense and her yearning.

Had he baited the trap with enough desire? Had he played the meek, willing male with enough sincerity?

With a soft "Blast!" she hurried to the bedside table. Opening the drawer, she pulled out the wooden box and stared at it as if it were a striking snake. With a glance around her, she placed it on the table and raised the lid. She lifted the small, gilt-and-blue bottle. Pulling the stopper, she sniffed.

Jermyn preferred a combination of bayberry and spice, and he held his breath as he scrutinized her face, waiting for her reaction.

If she didn't savor the scent, he had no doubt she would put it back.

But for a mere second, she closed her eyes. Pleasure placed a faint smile on her lips.

She liked it.

And he hoped she associated the scent with him, with the day she'd kidnapped him. That would be sweet justice indeed.

Briskly she stoppered the bottle, replaced it in the box and slid the box in her pocket.

Together the two men watched as she left the bedroom. Jermyn heard a click as the outer door closed. Guardedly he walked out, surveyed the sitting room.

Empty.

Turning to the bewildered Biggers, Jermyn said, "Quickly, man. I need that bath!"

A new moon shown through Amy's bedroom window, faintly illuminating the minuscule chamber, her narrow bed, and the sparse furniture. She'd never felt claustrophobic here before, but tonight she did. It seemed that if she only dared seize the chance, Northcliff would teach her to soar independent of the pedantic reaches of gravity.

Sliding her arm beneath her pillow, Amy stared at the dark square box on the table.

Grandmamma, Poppa, and her sisters had worried that Amy was wild and foolish, but to Amy it had seemed the things about which they worried—manners, daring, a decided lack of interest in the quiet arts—held no importance.

But maybe Grandmamma was right. Maybe Amy's propensity toward running fast, dancing joyously, and singing loudly were indicators of a wild character.

Amy tossed in her bed, then froze as she heard Northcliff's voice in her head. *Do you know that when you rise in the morning, I hear your footsteps over my head? I imagine you slipping out of a worn nightgown, your body gleaming pale and sweet, and donning one of your ghastly gowns. At night, the floorboards creak as you ready yourself for bed, and I imagine you undressing. And all night long, every time you turn over in your virgin bed, I hear you. You have me imprisoned, but I am watching you.*

A shiver ran up her spine at the memory of Northcliff's words, but it wasn't fear. It was desire. She wanted to rise from her bed and go to him. She wanted to see him. Not just his face or the expanse of his chest, but all of him. Because while he said he had been imagining her, she had also been imagining him.

In a motion so slow and cautious her ancient straw-stuffed mattress made no noise, Amy sat up and wrapped her arms around her knees. Northcliff was awake below. She knew it; she could feel his unswerving attention, the waves of his will beckoning her to him.

It shouldn't matter what he demanded.

It didn't—except that that was what she wanted, too. She had fought stronger, more determined foes than Northcliff, but Northcliff had adopted a strategy she couldn't resist. He had enlisted her own body.

It was chilly in her bedroom, but she was hot. She worked hard all day cleaning Miss Victorine's house, mending the roof and the walls, tending the garden. She should be relaxed and fast asleep, but her fantasies kept her tense and awake. Certainly her mind would not rest. Again and again she visited every word he'd ever spoken to her, the sensations he'd created when he kissed her, the color of his eyes and the resolute way he turned his head. Everything about him was jumbled up in one huge ball of snarled emotions and she didn't know how to untangle them.

She glanced at the box again.

She wanted to sing, to dance, to soar . . . to experience joy once more. And she thought Northcliff could give her joy. Bring her fulfillment.

He was chained—by his ankle, and by his promise. That tiny niggle of insecurity she still experienced could be dealt with . . .

She called herself Princess Nobody. Northcliff called her Lady Disdain. Yet she was only Amy, taking on a cruel world in a hopeless fight and losing the battle.

Tonight she had the chance to seize a moment for herself. Never again would she have such a opportunity.

As she sat up, the mattress crinkled and the bed frame groaned. She didn't care.

Lifting hands to the chain around her neck, she removed the silver cross that marked her as a princess of Beaumontagne. She hung it on the bedpost, painstakingly placing it so the ornate design of the rose of Beaumontagne hid its face against the wood.

She stood. The floorboards squeaked. She didn't care about that, either. He would know she was coming to him. As he waited, let him suffer.

She lit the stub of her candle. She picked up the box. She tiptoed down the corridor. Miss Victorine was snoring peacefully, and Amy sighed with relief. She shielded the flame as she passed Miss Victorine's bedchamber, watched her half-opened door, took extra care to be quiet . . . and her bare foot came in contact with a large, furry, solid object.

She gasped in fright. She stumbled. Her bare feet struck the boards in an uneven rhythm. The candle swayed wildly.

Coal yowled and raced into the kitchen.

Amy caught herself. She righted the candle before it

dripped. Stopping, she listened, her breath tight with anxiety.

Miss Victorine's snoring halted. She snorted, coughed . . . the bed squeaked as she turned over . . . silence followed, a horrible silence during which Amy imagined Miss Victorine staring at the light. She waited to hear her call out.

Then Miss Victorine started snoring again, more lightly.

Amy ran lightly after the cat and glared at him, that malevolent, tattle-tale black cat.

He glared back, his fur fluffy, offended as only a feline can be. He settled on his haunches before the fireplace where the red coals still gleamed, judging her as she tiptoed across the cool floorboards to the cellar door. "I don't care what you think," she told him. "I'm going down there."

But she hesitated for one long moment at the top of the stairs.

If she answered Northcliff's call, she'd never be the same.

Chapter 16

ermyn rose on his elbow and stared at the still, small light at the top of the stairs. Amy had to come down. She couldn't change her mind now. If she did, then be damned to this manacle and be damned to this farce. He would rise from his bed and fetch her back here—and all his promised restraint would have vanished.

Still she didn't move.

It seemed to him that the air grew warm, humid and scented with stress. He tensed, prepared to fling off the covers and go get her.

After minutes so long they felt like hours, she took the first step.

His body tightened. She was doing as he wished, yet still he fought his instincts. *Go to her. Possess her. Make her your own.* He knew that would never work with Amy. She had to be the one to make the moves. She had to imagine she held him in her power.

Later would be soon enough for her to discover otherwise.

She descended the stairs barefooted, clad only in a nightgown so sheer he could see right through it. The way she held the candle out to her side ensured a good view . . . a magnificent view. She held the box in the other hand, and she gazed at him without a flutter of shyness.

Of course not. Once she made her decision, his Lady Disdain would fling herself into the adventure.

Blood surged in his veins at the realization. She had come to him. She had come without fear. Soon she would take him . . .

She walked up to him, stood over him, looked down with a smile.

"I didn't know if you'd find the nerve to come," he said.

"I knew if I didn't, I'd regret it all my life."

No other woman would be so frank with him—or with herself.

He'd been at a disadvantage with this confident virgin. With a more experienced woman, he could promise bliss and she would know what he meant. A woman familiar with the pleasures of the flesh understood what a skilled man could achieve with his kisses and his body.

Instead, he had drawn Amy down here with only words and promises, and the smoky suggestion of the ecstasy their two beings offered.

He showed her his hands palm up. "I have no hidden weapons this time."

She laughed, a throaty little chuckle, and her gaze wandered down his form beneath the covers. "You lie."

Every muscle in his body was taut. His cock and balls ached in what seemed like an eternal, unquenchable erection. He couldn't have imagined he could laugh. But he did. He laughed back at her. Her bawdy sense of humor combined with that chaste body gave him a sense of wonder.

Had there ever been a woman like this one?

She placed the candle and the box on the table. Without an ounce of hesitation, she pulled her nightgown off over her head.

Abruptly his laughter died and he swallowed. Amy clothed in a ghastly gown made his heart thunder. Amy clad in nothing at all made a mockery of all the silks, the satins, the furs of the couturiers. Her shoulders were strong, her arms sculpted with muscle. Her breasts were still new, set high on her chest and tilted proudly, with a rosy aureole that made his mouth water. He could see every rib, her waist was too narrow and her belly concave, but her hips were rounded, made for the cup of a man's hand, and that was where Jermyn placed his. The hair between her legs was sparse, dark and curly, barely shielding her private parts from his gaze. He could see glimpses of the lips that he had touched, the lips that protected her womanhood.

He wanted to touch her again right now. Only his promise deterred him.

She must have realized what he was thinking, for her smile took on a Mona Lisa quality.

Placing one knee on the mattress, she leaned over him. Her breasts moved closer, almost within reach of his lips. Her thighs were parted and he could see between them, and it seemed as if he could see within her, into the soft, velvet heat that would sear them together.

Then she caught him off-guard.

Taking the corner of the blanket, she peeled it back, revealing his chest, his stomach, his groin, his legs. As he'd promised, he wore nothing—and she looked on him. As thoroughly as he had examined her, she now examined him.

Her face remained expressionless, but her eyes . . . how her eyes glinted! Like a child's on Twelfth Night as she opened her best toy.

Touching the still-red scarring on his thigh, she said, "That hurt. Is it tender?"

"It's bearable."

"So I won't hurt you?"

"You won't hurt me." Just with the torture of her touch.

Her fingers slid up over his hipbone, across his stomach, and into the hair on his chest. She pressed her palm there; he felt his heart thumping beneath the pressure.

She tilted her head as if she could hear his anticipation. "Do you want me so much?"

He recognized the question for what it was. A young woman exulting in her power.

Yet he held power, too. Gently he slid his hand from her hip to the inside of her thigh and up. Unerringly he found the entrance to her body.

She jumped. Her green eyes widened.

As he knew she would be, she was damp and needy. For the first time, he pushed his finger inside her.

Outside she was silk and satin. Inside she was fire and pleasure. "I want you as much as you want me. Apart we're two people who speak and walk and see— ordinary, mundane. Together we're glory and flame, a conflagration of spirits. I've never wanted a woman like I want you, but I promise—in all your life, I'm the only lover you'll ever have. The only man you'll ever want." He moved his finger slowly in and out. "You should flee while you can."

She watched him, her eyes half shut. "I'll take my chances."

"Then come and explore me." He allowed his hand to fall away. "I promise, this new country awaits your conquest."

He lay flat on his back, a new country indeed, composed of valley and ridges—and one high peak for her to climb. But she didn't have to tackle it now. First, there were other places to visit.

After all, he had nowhere he *could* go. "You're mine to do with as I wish." She laughed, because of course she didn't for a moment believe he couldn't grab her and roll her beneath him, but it was heady to know he remained chained on her command.

He was like a feast and she didn't know what to

sample first. His skin was tan all over, a legacy from his Italian mother. His body hair was sparse, a lighter, brighter red than the hair on his head, and beautifully soft and curling. His chest and arms swelled with muscle; when he was free, he did more than sit and read.

"Do you ride?" She ran her finger along the line of his shoulder. "Do you box?"

"And fence."

Muscle corded his belly, and rising from the thatch of hair at his groin was a most magnificent display of masculine vigor. She understood why he said they would need oil to place *that* within her; the width, the length amazed her . . . her outstretched hand trembled as she caressed him, making a leisurely exploration of the map of veins and silky smooth skin. Beneath her touch, his member swelled further, rising to nestle her palm. "Magic," she whispered.

He smiled, swift and implacable.

Finally she lowered her body against his. First her nipples touched, rubbing into the hair on his chest. Then her hips rested against his, and for the first time she felt the heat of his manhood against her. At last she rested on him fully, and the paradise of contact with his entire body made her whimper with pleasure. "You're so warm." More than that, he was so alive. In the meeting of their two bodies, she could almost experience the dynamic rhythm of his heart, the strong workings of his lungs, the power of his muscles. She unfolded herself on him, rubbing against him like a cat, and he groaned as if she had hurt him.

A glance at his face proved that his pain mixed with rapture to form a new sensation, one that kept him bound to the bed as surely as the manacle.

She kissed the hollow of his throat, savoring the clean taste of his skin. His chin was smooth against her lips; he'd used the razor today.

"How did you know"—she nipped at his lips—"I would come down to you tonight?"

"You'd have to be a fool not to, and you're no fool."

She laughed again, a throaty chuckle. "You're a confident chap."

"It's one of my charms." He stretched beneath her, a long, slow motion that carried her to another level of intimacy. He challenged her with his glance. "One of my *many* charms."

In response, she bit his shoulder.

He caught her head in his hands. He brought her lips to his and kissed her with appetite and passion. A different kind of intimacy, warm and wet, one she had experienced before. One she had imagined repeating. With a sigh, she slid her arms around his shoulders and kissed him back.

He moved beneath her, then dropped the covers over them, giving refuge to the heat their two bodies created. She relaxed against him even more, savoring the deepening unity between them.

With the fingers of both hands, he counted down the vertebrae of her spine until he reached her bottom, then he cupped her cheeks, her thighs, and spread her legs around his hips. She broke the kiss and looked down at him. "For a man who claims to be helpless, you have a way of making your wishes known."

"I have so many wishes and you've made so many come true, I barely know where to start."

The sensible part of her, the part that planned a kidnapping and carried it out, scoffed at his smooth flattery. But the soft part of her, the feminine part, wanted to moan in wonder. Who would have thought that the condescending Lord Northcliff hid a poet's soul?

Bringing her knees under her, she opened herself over him, experiencing the intimate pressure of his erection against her dampness.

He groaned, rippling his hips again when he wanted to do nothing so much as to thrust. Thrust hard, thrust deep, thrust fast until he was satisfied. But Amy would find no satisfaction in a fast race and a speedy finish. So gently he rolled her onto her back, taking care to keep his place between her thighs.

She started to raise up, to complain.

Ingeniously he made the chain clink against the stone wall.

At the sound, Amy's dawning consternation faded and she relaxed onto the mattress. She smiled up into his face. "What do you want to do now?"

In response, he kissed her elegant throat, her pale shoulder, the high globe of her breast. Lifting his head, he said, "I want to taste you."

Her eyelids drooped, and languidly she wrapped her arms around him. "I think you should do whatever you want."

He didn't laugh aloud, although he very much wanted to. He had gentled the wild creature, and now he had his reward. Catching her nipple in his mouth, he circled it with his tongue, light sweeps that propelled her toward arousal. Gradually he used greater eagerness, suckling until she squirmed beneath him. Lifting his head, he blew lightly on her nipple and watched as it puckered, a small, sweet raspberry of desire. Her hands clenched against his back, and her smile had been replaced with an expression of concentration. He was moving her to a place she'd never visited before, a place where bliss reigned and reckless young virgins writhed in his arms.

He subjected her other nipple to the same treatment and listened with relish to the faint moan she couldn't suppress. He kissed his way down the taut line of her belly, sliding beneath the covers into the darkness where the candlelight didn't reach.

He knew the moment she realized what he intended, for her fingers became claws holding lightly in his skin. "No. Northcliff, no."

"I serve at the pleasure of my Lady Disdain." But he didn't give up his position. Instead he caressed her inner thighs with long, downward strokes, and kissed the delicate pocket where her leg joined her hip. He used every technique he'd ever learned to seduce her, for every lovemaking had been only a preparation for this one. "I'm going to show you heaven. You're not afraid, are you?"

"No!"

He smiled. If he could just challenge her, she was easy to manage.

"But I don't believe you've found heaven under the covers." Her voice sounded stronger, more logical.

Logic was the last thing he wanted from her now so, sliding his hands under her thighs, he lifted them, spread them, opening her to his touch and his taste.

She flinched, tried to fight him, but he crooned, "No, darling, this is my paradise. Let me help you find yours."

She was open to him and before she could protest again, he kissed her. The warm, clean scent of woman rose into his head like heady perfume; he wanted to shout his delight. Instead he took her womanhood into his mouth and sucked delicately.

Her nails tightened into his skin, but she was no longer trying to push him away. Now, instinctively she tried to hold him. Her faint, sipping sighs and restive, erratic motions quickly changed to the marvelous sounds of amazed euphoria.

He moved down to the opening of her body and circled it with his tongue. He tasted her excitement, excitement that grew as he fondled her, thrusting his tongue into her at first slowly, then more quickly until he mimed the driving rhythm of sex.

She trembled, fighting against the first surge of orgasm, and his balls tightened in response. Revelation flashed through him; her untutored virgin reaction created an echo in him. He had no control and if he didn't get inside her *now* . . .

Surging up from under the blankets, he braced his hands beside her shoulders and positioned himself to enter her. He shook with the effort of restraining himself. He wanted to bury his cock inside. He urgently needed to possess her.

Taking a deep, restrictive breath, he watched her face as he slipped inside the first inch. At once her passage spasmed around him.

Sweet heaven above! She was coming. She was coming! Her moisture surged around him, sucking him in, welcoming him in the most basic way a woman can welcome a man.

With her head thrown back, her eyes closed, her fists twisted in the pillow beside her head, she was the picture of newfound ecstasy.

An ecstasy that found its counterpoint in him. Sweat gathered on his brow as he pressed with his hips. Her virgin body pressed back, wrapping him closely even while new waves of orgasm shook her. The bliss of being inside her drove him on.

He needed to get as close as he could to Amy.

He needed to possess Amy.

He needed to be one with Amy.

No other woman would do. Only Amy.

Her maidenhead blocked his advance, and he bared his teeth that anything, even her body's defense, opposed him. He surged forward, a swift attack against the barrier, and as he broke through, she gave a brief and bitter scream. Her eyes opened wide; tears gathered in the corners of her eyes and dropped onto the pillow.

Abruptly pain had recalled her to this place, to her actions, to him. She saw him, the man she had taken as her lover, and fierce pride possessed her as surely as did he. Clamping her legs around his legs, she pushed her hands against his shoulders, shoving him onto his side. "Let *me*." Her demand was no feminine plea, but an order from a woman accustomed to command.

He laughed, a low chuckle of mirth and frustration. He was halfway to paradise and *now* she recovered enough to demand sovereignty?

But he yielded. Of course he yielded, helping her scoot around so he lay flat on his back and she straddled him, sitting up, her breasts thrust proudly forward, strands of her hair brushing her chest.

He'd never experienced such an explosion of feminine heat and greed. Inside her, his cock grew harder, longer, expanding as his need grew ever more lawless.

Lawless . . .

Realization burst upon him. He'd forgotten the oil to ease his way, but more important, he'd forgotten the French sheath, the one that guarded against pregnancy. Unless he pulled out now, there was a chance that he would be a father . . . and Amy would be a mother.

And he didn't care.

When they were finished making love this time, he wouldn't be satisfied. With her sarcasm, her swift wit, her vibrating desire, Amy branded him.

Pull out? Hell, no, he wouldn't pull out. When they were done tonight, he would do a branding of his own. In every way possible, he would put his mark on Amy.

Before too much longer, she would know what it was to be his woman.

Putting his hands on her hips, he writhed with a very real agony as she used him to impale herself. Then he allowed her to set the pace, to soar within the limits of her body, to torment him with inept and magnificent lovemaking.

And as his seed burst from him, a bare fragment of a thought clamored in his body.

She's mine. And I will never let her go.

Chapter 17

*M*iss Victorine read the letter over Amy's shoulder, and sighed heavily. "I feel guilty."

"Guilty?" Amy greedily read Mr. Edmondson's newest rejection, then lifted her gaze to Miss Victorine's. "Why?"

"I've come to enjoy Jermyn's company so much that I was actually hoping Mr. Edmondson would refuse the ransom." Miss Victorine examined Amy's face. "Is that what you were thinking, too?"

"No, that can't work. If Mr. Edmondson doesn't pay the ransom, we'll be stuck here forever with Lord Northcliff in the cellar." The idea didn't fill Amy with dismay—and that made her realize what Miss Victorine meant. Despite Mr. Edmondson's insulting prose, the letter lifted Amy's spirits. With this *no*, she could plan another evening with Jermyn . . . and another night spent in his arms. Last night had been . . . so wild, so free, the kind of excitement she'd imagined her whole life. But she'd never been able to achieve that on her own. It had taken ardor and skill and daring.

It had taken Jermyn.

"Of course, you're right. I just wanted to mention that I feel guilty about . . . enjoying Jermyn's company so much." Miss Victorine went to the hooks by the door and donned her bonnet and shawl. "I'm going down to the village while you tell His Lordship."

"Oh, I'm not going to tell him now." Amy glanced uneasily at the cellar. "He's not yelling, so he's probably sleeping."

"He's been sleeping a lot in the daytime lately." Miss Victorine glanced at the cellar, too. "I hope he's not sickening with something."

"I'm sure he's not." If he was exhausted today, Amy knew why.

"You look peaked yourself." Miss Victorine patted Amy on the arm. "Perhaps you should take a nap."

Amy blushed. That Miss Victorine had noticed! "Yes. Yes, I'll do that."

"I heard you wandering the corridor last night. Perhaps you'll sleep more quietly tonight." Miss Victorine smiled sweetly. So sweetly. And she departed, leaving Amy staring in shock.

She sank into a chair. Did Miss Victorine know . . . ?

The idea didn't bear thinking about. She couldn't bear for Miss Victorine to think badly of her. She hated that everything for which she had fought seemed to be in peril, that her schemes had proved to be a dismal failure, that Jermyn despised his mother for acts which haunted Amy, and that that malicious cat had woken Miss Victorine.

Yet it was the thoughts of Jermyn's possession, of last night's pure pleasure which distracted Amy from the worries which buzzed like wasps through her mind and—

A sound blasted through the house.

Amy jumped. Fear leaped into her throat.

A detonation. A gunshot.

She knew it. Those difficult days on the road had taught her to recognize the blast of a pistol.

The gunfire came from—*dear God, it came from the cellar.*

"Jermyn!" She ran for the stairway, down the first two steps. A man, a stranger dressed in black, leaped up the stairs toward her.

He knocked her aside, slamming her into the wall.

She didn't notice the bruises. Didn't try to chase him. "Jermyn!" She scrambled down the stairs into the cellar's dim light. From the floor above her, she dimly heard the thumping of men's boots. A scuffle. A thump.

She didn't care. Flame-tipped feathers flew in the air like burning snowflakes. Smoking blankets mounded Jermyn's shape. She gagged at the stench of sulfur and burning wool. Gagged as the icy fingers of terror closed her throat.

He was dead. Jermyn was dead.

As the covers burst into flame, she yelled, "No!" Her

heart pounded, not with the heat of passion, but with the rush of blood chilled by dread. She leaped, ripped the blankets off the cot, expecting, fearing to see blood and broken flesh.

More blankets. The pillows. Blackened, burning . . . but no Jermyn.

In the turbulence of the moment, she didn't understand.

She stomped out the flames. Stood gasping, shaking, wide-eyed, staring at the cot as if she could see the answer there.

Jermyn wasn't here.

But where . . . ? How . . . ?

Above, she heard a man's running boots as they struck the floorboards in the kitchen. She ran for the drawer, for her pistol—and Jermyn appeared at the top of the stairs.

For a second, a splendid, glorious second, joy crashed through her. He was alive. Thank God, he was alive!

He saw her. He stopped. He closed his eyes as if he were relieved.

Then the truth blasted her joy to crumbs.

He was alive—and he was free.

The swine!

"Are you all right?" he asked.

She shook her head, speechless with shock.

Jermyn glanced at the wisps of smoke still rising from the blankets. He focused on her blackened hands and face.

As he watched her, her whole body began to tremble.

The manacle was off. And he wasn't gone. He was still here which meant that sometime, somehow, he'd freed himself and ever since, he'd been playing her for a fool.

"Are you burned?" he asked.

"I believe I have been burned. Yes. Yes, I'm sure I have been."

"By the flames?"

"No." She whispered, "How long? How long have you . . . ?"

His gaze grew more intense. "Since the first time I kissed you."

The tremor grew. In her life, she had been cheated, harried, chased, condemned. But never had she felt so betrayed. She'd made love to him, imagining that she held him in her power, and instead . . . instead he'd been laughing at her.

The iciness of her fear turned to blistering humiliation.

"Amy. Upstairs, I knocked out the shooter." Jermyn paused as if giving her a moment to come to grips with her newborn reality. "I need you to help me tie him up."

She stared at Jermyn, her eyes so wide they ached.

She wanted to kill him. She wanted to murder him. She wanted to slaughter him more than she ever had wanted that before—and only ten days ago she'd shot at him and would have killed him if he hadn't ducked. Her ire that day was nothing to the wrath that burned her up now.

"Amy. I need help." His voice held a whiplash that jerked her to attention.

She *couldn't* kill him. That would be foolish. More foolish than all of her previous acts during this last, long fortnight.

She *could* find out who had tried to kill him—and why.

Meticulously she walked to the stairs and started up, each movement almost painful in its precision.

He moved to one side to let her pass.

She stopped. "No. You first." She didn't want him to touch her. And he would. She could see that in the spark and anger in his eyes.

How dared *he* be angry?

He waited. She waited. Silently they fought, a stand-off between two strong-willed people.

Abruptly he gave in, going up the stairs and into the kitchen.

She didn't know why he'd surrendered. She didn't care. All that mattered was that he had and she could move forward, go up and face the consequences of months of scheming and plotting turned to ashes in a single moment with a single gunshot. Still in a turmoil of rage and grief, she followed.

In the kitchen, the door hung open. The table rested on its side, one fragile leg broken off. The vase was shattered, the unconscious man was half inside, half out, in an odd crumpled mass that indicated a collision and a struggle.

"I need rope." Kneeling beside him, Jermyn rolled him over onto his stomach.

Amy laughed sourly and went after one of Miss Victorine's fichus. Long and narrow, made of thin cotton and created to wrap around a woman's shoulders and tie at her bosom, it would have to do. She handed it to Jermyn, careful not to allow his finger to touch hers.

Winding it into a narrow binding, Jermyn used it to tie the man's hands tightly behind him. Rolling him onto his back, Jermyn looked up at Amy. "Do you know him?"

The fellow had brown hair, pockmarked skin, and a narrow face with a receding chin. A bruise swelled his temple and purpled his eye. He wore cheap clothes that didn't quite fit him, a brown muffler around his neck and a knee-length black cloak enveloping his shoulders. Grime ringed his neck and ears.

He looked like a thousand other villains she'd met, and she shook her head. "I've never seen him before."

"Neither have I."

Now, Jermyn . . . Jermyn she had met before, but in the open space of the kitchen, he looked different to her: taller, bulkier, in control of the situation.

Because *she* was no longer in control.

Looking down at her hands, she saw the black that covered her fingers. Her futile effort to save Jermyn's unthreatened life had left her smelling like burning wool and feathers. Going to the washbasin, she ruthlessly used to the soap, scrubbing at her nails, wetting the towel and using it on her cheeks.

The balance of power had shifted. She didn't like it. Everything in her rebelled against it. But as so often in her life, she had to face the implacable truth. She had no power here. Another human being dominated her, and her wishes were as nothing.

When she returned, her skin scoured to a painful purity, Jermyn was rifling through the weasel's pockets. He pulled out a grubby handkerchief and a pouch with a few pence. Those he tossed aside, his contempt for the coins showing Amy only too clearly the gulf between them. He found the second pistol in an inside waistcoat pocket, and if Amy hadn't been watching him closely, she wouldn't have noticed his start. He examined the ivory handle, the decorated steel barrel, and even looked at the bottom of the stock. Its gleaming surfaces were at odds with its foul owner. "This is a fine piece." Jermyn sounded odd, like a man who'd had his worse suspicions confirmed. "And it's loaded."

They both knew why. If the first shot had failed, Weasel-face planned to use the second.

Painstakingly Jermyn placed the pistol in his coat pocket.

Amy eyed Weasel-face closely. He had gained consciousness: he watched them from beneath his pocked eyelids. He looked like nothing more than an Edinburgh pinch purse—yet he owned two pistols and he'd made his way here. He was no ordinary scoundrel.

As if to confirm her conclusion, Jermyn pulled a stout polished walnut stick from a pocket hidden beside Weasel-face's thigh.

"Give me his cloak," Amy said.

He hadn't fought when they took his weapons, but now the villain sprang to life, struggling against his bonds.

Jermyn let him test the knots. In a conversational tone, he said to Amy, "My father taught me to sail. By the time I was eight, I could tie a fine knot, one that tightens as a man fights against it."

"So I see." Amy stayed against the wall, well out of the way of Weasel-face's thrashing form. In all the times she and Clarice had been in desperate predicaments, she had many times wished to be elsewhere, but never so much as now.

When the fellow was satisfied he wasn't getting free, he gave up and glared at them.

With a smile that looked like a prelude to a snarl, Jermyn pulled a knife, a small, wicked-looking blade that Amy had never seen before. He cut the cloak's fastenings, pulled the length of it out from underneath the man, and handed it to Amy.

She ran her fingers along the hem and found what she expected. As she ripped open the stitching, one by one twelve gold guineas dropped into her hands.

"A man of means. How unexpected." Jermyn examined the fellow again. "One wonders where he got the money." Again Jermyn smiled that toothy, threatening smile. He rubbed his fist into his palm.

The man's gaze shifted warily to watch as if he had personal acquaintance with Jermyn's fist.

She knew how he felt. Jermyn had knocked her sideways, too, although not with his fist. No, for her the pain came in different ways, in blows to her pride and her heart.

"Where, my evil-smelling friend, did you get the blunt?" Jermyn asked.

Amy saw a flash of panic, then the man gave a pitiful moan and collapsed back into unconsciousness. But one eye remained slightly open and far too cognizant of the surroundings.

Her mouth twisted wryly.

Unexpectedly Jermyn's gaze caught hers. The gold flames lit his brown eyes in a determined blaze. The mouth she'd so recently kissed was a firm line, the chin she'd admired was squared and stern. He was no longer her companion of the long evenings, her restrained lover of last night. He was the marquess of Northcliff. Not a man, but a master.

Clearly he considered himself *her* master.

Well, why wouldn't he? She had foolishly claimed him—but he wasn't available to be claimed. He was the marquess of Northcliff. And while a princess of Beaumontagne could kick dirt in his face, and a woman who had him in chains could feel confident she called the shots, she was now merely Miss Amy Rosabel. Miss Amy Rosabel who had abducted him, imprisoned him, chained him, and seduced him. Now he was free. He was the master. She was not even English. She was a foreigner, without family, a criminal. If he wished, he could order her death. If she took her life into her own hands and appealed to the Beaumontagnian Embassy, he could refuse to send the message.

For why should he believe she was a princess? Her grandmother would tell her that a real princess would never be deceived by so obvious a ruse as Jermyn's.

Amy could tolerate wet and cold, pain and hunger. She couldn't bear to wait for trouble. She might as well hurry things along.

Picking up the pitcher, she dashed the water in the man's face, and on Jermyn, too . . . right into his lap.

Jermyn sucked in his breath. His irate gaze flew to hers and he half-rose, menace brought to life.

The man on the floor shouted, " 'Ere, what'd ye do that fer?"

With a last look at Amy that promised retribution, Jermyn knelt beside him again. He grabbed his shirt and lifted Weasel-face so he was nose to nose with the wet, furious marquess. "Who sent you?" Jermyn demanded.

"What?" The guy pretended to be barely conscious.

Jermyn slammed him against the floor, then lifted him again and shook him like a terrier with a rat. "Don't pretend with me. Who sent you?"

The villain's head wobbled on his neck. "I don't know."

"You should have taken the opportunity to answer me." Jermyn's lips peeled back from his white teeth and his fingers squeezed the guy's throat until his feet flailed and his eyes bulged.

The violence of the scene shook Amy.

No, Jermyn's violence shook Amy. She'd never seen him as anything but an annoyed-with-her, too-attractive-to-resist nobleman. Somehow, somewhere, he had become more: a lord born to command and capable of enforcing his will with whatever means necessary. Somehow, he'd hidden his true self from her.

She watched him throttle Weasel-face until she couldn't stand it anymore. Rushing forward, she grasped his wrist and protested, "Jermyn!"

He relaxed his grip. Gathering the ends of the guy's

muffler in each hand, he waited until Weasel-face caught his breath. "I want to kill you. The lady says no. Your life is hanging in the balance. Now—who sent you?"

"I don't know," the guy rasped. "I swear—"

Jermyn twisted the scarf.

The guy struggled frantically, kicking, gagging and choking.

Jermyn held him down with his knee in his gut.

In her travels through England, she'd witnessed beatings and hangings. Never had ruthlessness shocked her—until now. She'd thought Jermyn a dilettante, a worthless nobleman, not this cool-eyed purveyor of justice.

He must have seen her flinch, for he looked across at her. "When I heard the shot, I thought you were dead."

He seemed to think that explained everything.

Perhaps it did. When she heard that shot, she had thought Jermyn was dead, too—and the memory of that moment still had the power to twist her stomach into knots of terror.

She didn't want to feel so much for Jermyn.

"So should I feel mercy for the beggar?" Jermyn asked her.

"I think you'd better find out why he's here and how he found you before you kill him," she answered steadily.

Jermyn dropped the ends of the scarf.

Weasel-face fell backward, gasping for breath like a beached fish.

Jermyn began, "This time, if you don't answer my questions, I'll make you sorry."

It took Weasel-face several attempts before he could speak, and his voice rasped wretchedly, but he managed a sneer as he said, "Ye'll take me t' the constable?"

"Good God, man, no! Don't be ridiculous. No, I was going to say—the next time you refuse to speak, I'll take you to one of our cliffs and throw you off. The rocks will break your every bone, the tide will take your body out, and the sea monsters will feast on your flesh." Jermyn's upper-crust accent contrasted with the crude cruelty of his words.

Weasel's ruddy face turned pale, and he spoke fast, as if he couldn't wait to get the words out. "I got a job. I gets 'em all if they're lookin' fer the best."

"The best what?" Jermyn asked.

"Assassin. Do ye know what that means?" Weasel-face was quite serious. "I shoots people, see? Fer money."

Amy had known what he was going to say—after all, what other explanation could there be? Yet at his words, she withered. How had her plot come to this?

"Go on." Jermyn was impassive.

"This swell cove tells me t' go t' Settersway and follow this letter. 'E said no matter what, I was t' keep track o' the letter, and that would lead me t' another swell cove who was in prison. I was t' kill 'im any way I liked and when I came back wi' proof, I'd get another twelve guineas."

"A most generous reward for the job," Jermyn said.

"I'm the best," Weasel repeated. "I followed the letter—didn't like the crossing, I can tell ye, never been in a boat before and the bastard who rowed laughed

when I puked—and followed it up t' this house. Looked
in the windows, saw the women in the kitchen, saw *ye*
in the cellar with a chain on ye and figured ye was me
man. Figured if ye were chained ye weren't goin' anywhere, so I went down t' the pub and 'ad me a meal.
Guess that's when ye left, heh?"

"Yes."

"When I saw the ol' lady walkin' down the street, I
figured that was me chance. I slipped into the cellar
and shot ye—only ye weren't there."

"No."

"So ye weren't really chained?"

"No."

"Damn. That Mr. Edmondson was so sure ye could
be offed wi' no trouble."

The name fell with a thud into the conversation.
Amy felt the blood drain from her face.

"Ye know 'im, do ye?" Weasel was watching them
both. " 'E's a scary one, yer Mr. Edmondson. Gave me
the money wi'out a single squawk at the price. Then 'e
told me if I failed, 'e would 'unt me down and rip out
me guts and flay me alive and 'ang me from the highest gibbet as a lesson fer 'is servants that failed 'im. I
thought it might 'ave been bluff, but the butler turned
green while Mr. Edmondson was talkin' and afterward
'e told me I'd better do the job and no' get caught
'cause Mr. Edmondson kept 'is promises."

"It seems I've been mistaken about my uncle's character." Jermyn looked across at Amy. "Go get Pom. I'm
sending this fellow to my valet. Biggers will know
what to do with him."

"Pom will be out fishing," she answered.

"No, he won't. Pom now works for me."

"Of course." Amy tasted the bitterness of betrayal. Pom knew Jermyn was free, and he'd said nothing. He hadn't warned her. He'd let her make a fool of herself.

No, that wasn't fair. He hadn't had anything to do with her making a fool of herself. She'd done that all on her own.

With a nod, she started out the door.

"Amy, wait." Jermyn's voice brought her to a halt, and in his tone she heard a note of warning. "Don't run away. I would catch you."

"Don't worry." The sourness of her dilemma bled into her tone. "I wouldn't go without Miss Victorine and she . . . won't leave. I was foolish to imagine otherwise."

It did nothing for Jermyn's self-esteem to know that it was her love for an old lady that bound Amy here. But it was a guarantee that let him conclude his business here before he solved the riddle of Amy.

When he knew she was out of earshot, he picked up the long stout walnut stick and slapped it against his palm. He leaned over the still figure on the floor. "Say, friend, tell me the truth. Were you supposed to kill everyone in the cottage?"

"Nay, I was supposed t' get in, do the job, and get out, and let the people who 'eld ye get 'anged fer murder."

Chapter 18

Wax candles lit Miss Victorine's kitchen with a steady light. A full bucket of coal burned in her stove, chasing the evening's chill from the thick walls, warming Jermyn all the way through for the first time in ten days. Pom had hastily repaired the table and now Miss Victorine, Amy, Pom, and Mertle sat among the remains of an excellent meal culled from the contents of Jermyn's pantry at Summerwind Abbey via Biggers's intercession.

Miss Victorine was frankly pleased to have Jermyn out of her cellar. "Dear boy, what are you going to do?" she asked.

Jermyn paced from one end of the room to the

other, dominating the room. He used his height, his title, his largesse to remind everyone that he held their fates in his hand, and he did it deliberately, directing intimidation at Amy without subtlety. "I'm going to go home. I'm going to take up my life as if nothing interrupted it."

Amy was intelligent; he knew she understood. But she didn't understand why; she couldn't imagine what he intended. If she could, he wagered she would run as far and as fast as she could.

"I'm giving a party to celebrate my thirtieth birthday." He slid a glance at Amy. "And to celebrate other events. I'll invite my friends *and* my uncle."

Amy wasn't sulking, but she'd eaten very little and she had never once looked him in the eyes. She wore her ugliest clothing like a suit of armor, and faint circles ringed her eyes.

Well, of course they did. She'd been awake most of the night . . . with him.

Pom considered his lord, then touched his wife's hand.

As if Mertle knew what he wanted to say, she asked, "What will that accomplish, m'lord?"

"My uncle wants to kill me," Jermyn said. "I've decided that the next time he tries, there should be witnesses."

Amy considered, then nodded. "You'll trick him. That works."

He found himself pleased that she was of the same mind.

"But dear boy, how will you explain your escape from the kidnappers?" Obviously it never occurred to Miss Victorine to fear his vengeance.

She was right, the dear old thing. He wouldn't harm a hair on *her* head. "I'll tell him I got away." Jermyn didn't think his uncle would have the nerve to publicly doubt him.

Amy frowned.

"You don't agree, Lady Disdain?" Jermyn asked.

"Yes, you can tell him you got away." For the first time this evening, Amy lifted her gaze to his. Her eyes were sharp and engrossed. "But first, write him a frantic letter asking that he send the ransom because you're afraid for your life."

"For what purpose?" Mertle asked. "We've proved he isn't going t' send the ransom."

"Because that makes it so much better when Lord Northcliff announces he's escaped, then immediately asks to borrow money." Amy wore a contented half smile.

"What? Why would I do that? It's all my money." Pointedly Jermyn added, "A great deal of money."

For someone who was destitute, Amy showed a breathtaking indifference. "*All* your own money? Your uncle has no money of his own?"

"He received a small inheritance when my father died, but yes, the money is all mine."

"Is there any reason you can imagine why he's trying to kill you right *now*?" she asked.

"None that I know of." He stared directly at her, using information to make her pay attention to him. "But Uncle Harrison is my manager. He has had complete control over my fortune."

"Perhaps he's lost your fortune," she said cheerfully.

"If he has, I'll regain it." While at Oxford, Jermyn's friend Mr. Fred Engledew had come to grief with a moneylender, and one of their many rescue plans had included buying and selling stock for a profit. Jermyn had shown a remarkable instinct for the activity, one he'd dabbled in since on a regular basis. "I think it more likely he's done something so despicable it will reach the newspapers soon."

"Or he ran into trouble and sold one of your entailed estates and next time you go to visit, someone else will be living in your house." Amy was positively luminous with amusement.

"Amy, what a dreadful idea!" Miss Victorine shook her head admonishingly.

"Oh, come, it has great potential as a farce," Amy said.

Jermyn supposed he would allow her the small pleasure of teasing him. After all, tonight he would take his own pleasures. "I consider it most likely to be something to do with my thirtieth birthday."

"Ohhh. Yes, very clever, my lord." Amy stood and started clearing the dishes from the table. "That does seem likely."

Mertle shook her head admonishingly, pressed Amy back into her seat, and did the work of cleaning up.

To Jermyn, it was clear that Amy wanted to be busy. She knew that somehow, Jermyn intended to have his revenge, and she would have no say in her fate. The waiting was killing her—and Jermyn was pleased to see her suffer.

"Does your uncle pay your expenses?" she asked.

"He takes care of the accounts for my estates. I receive a large amount every year for my own use. I certainly have never needed more."

"Excellent. Ask for more." Amy deliberated on her plan. "We'll start a rumor about your gaming—that's easily done—and once he hears that you've been gambling to excess and that you've asked for an advance, he'll think you're the one who arranged your own abduction to extort money from him."

She surprised a chuckle from Pom, a giggle from Mertle, and a gasp from Miss Victorine. "My dear girl, you have the most extraordinary mind."

Jermyn agreed. Any woman who could think up a plan for his kidnapping and recognize how to counter his uncle's villainy had an extraordinary mind. Someday he intended to discover how she came to have it. But—"The fortune is not his," Jermyn insisted.

"It sounds as if he would like it to be," Amy retorted.

Pom pressed his wife's hand again. "Is he yer heir, m'lord?" she asked.

"Yes." Jermyn was brief and irritated. Not irritated that they'd asked, but irritated that he'd been oblivious to what seemed so obvious now. His uncle wanted to kill him. And knowing Uncle Harrison, he cared not a fig for the title, the land, or the respect. He focused on only money. He could quote the price of every piece of fruit, of every piece of clothing, of every horse bought and every carriage sold. One of the reasons Jermyn had paid so little heed to his uncle in recent years was his incredible vulgarity.

"He always was a dreadful boy," Miss Victorine said. "I remember how he used to egg you on to do the most daring things."

"Like what?" Amy asked.

"To sail into a storm, to climb the cliffs, to hunt alone in Scotland, and to break the wildest horse. I used to get so upset when I heard about it!" Miss Victorine was upset now, wringing her hands and looking anxious.

Amy took her hands and stroked them.

"Yes, he did." As a young man, Jermyn had done all those things, taking chances while thinking his uncle was a decent chap for encouraging him to do things most guardians refused. "What a fool I was."

Amy's gaze flashed toward him.

"You don't need to agree," he said.

"Not at all." She sounded brusque and cool. "I was thinking that we had that in common."

"I did not set out to make a fool of you," he said crisply.

"No, you set out to have your way. Making a fool of me was an added windfall." Her chest rose and fell with agitation, and two spots of color burned in her cheeks.

He placed his hands on the table, leaned across until he was close, so close she was forced to look him in the eyes. "You're not going to forgive me, are you?"

"Never."

"A week ago, I felt the same way about you, but you convinced me otherwise." He got closer until they were nose to nose. "I'll have to see if I can do the same with you."

She held his gaze as the rosy blush in her cheeks expanded to cover her whole face. She understood the threat. She comprehended the promise. Still she whispered, "Never."

He smiled. "We'll see." Standing, his hands on his hips, he stared at Amy.

Everyone else was staring at *them*.

Amy glanced around, and misery wrenched the words from her. "I wish I could run out to the road and start another journey, one that would take me miles and days from here."

He offered no pity at all. "If you were crafty, you could."

"I can't leave Miss Victorine."

And that gave him more satisfaction than anything else she could have said. She wasn't like his mother. Despite her troubles, Amy remained here out of loyalty to a woman to whom she wasn't even related. Once she was bound to him by loyalty and affection—and he never doubted he could generate those emotions within her—she would be his forever.

It was time to put his plan into motion. "Pom and Mertle will stay here with you, Miss Victorine, until I'm satisfied that you're safe from any other assassins my uncle might have sent."

Pom and Mertle nodded.

"Where will Amy stay?" Miss Victorine asked.

"With me." Jermyn's two words fell softly into the silence of the kitchen.

"No." Miss Victorine shook her head decisively, and for a soft, sweet female she looked remarkably stern. "I'm very fond of you, dear, but you're not keeping an unmarried young lady who lives under my protection as your mistress."

"That was never my intention," he said. "Rather, I'll follow in my father's footsteps and take an inappropriate foreign girl . . . as my wife."

"Pardon me?" Amy bobbed up out of her chair like a cork. "Are you talking about *me*? I'm not marrying *you*."

"Dear boy, unless you have a special license, the vicar would have to call the banns for four weeks first." Miss Victorine's forehead crinkled. "Unless—"

"Exactly." Jermyn took Amy's wrist and with a bow, kissed the pale skin over the blue vein.

She jerked free, but not before he felt her pulse racing. "What do you mean?" Her gaze traveled from one face to the other.

"The wedding arch," Mertle said.

"Why, the wedding arch is so pagan, and it hasn't been used for years," Miss Victorine chirped like a plump, cheery pigeon. "Do you suppose it still works?"

"Oh, it works," Mertle said.

"What wedding arch?" Amy demanded belligerently.

"It's an old tradition on the island," Jermyn told her. "Down by the beach past the village stands a rock arch wide enough for a man and a woman to walk through. When they do, they're wed for a year."

"Or until they have a ceremony in the church," Miss Victorine reminded him firmly.

"Or until they have a ceremony in the church," he agreed.

"Or until the first child is expected," Pom said.

Miss Victorine tittered.

Amy sounded absolutely aghast. "The first child?"

"Come, Amy, I'll show you." Catching her wrist again, Jermyn dragged her toward the door. She set her heels, but he caught her other hand, and her heels slid along the floor.

"I won't walk through the wedding arch with you," she said.

"The arch is traditionally used by grooms with reluctant brides, for the arch is tall enough for a man with his woman on his shoulder." He overpowered her. He knew damned good and well that was the only way he'd win this fight, and besides, he rather enjoyed it. He had turned the tables on the vixen. Now she danced to his tune.

"Oh, no." Amy fell back and twisted her arm, trying to get free. "Oh, no—"

As they reached the door, he bent and put his shoulder in her stomach. As if she were a sack of potatoes, he swung her up and over.

Amy shrieked and gave his back a good hard thump.

He dropped her down until her rear sat uppermost on his shoulder and her head dangled almost to his trousers, and kept walking.

"Miss Victorine!" she shouted.

"I'll come as fast as I can, dears!" Miss Victorine called from the doorway.

"Shame on you for appealing to an old lady for res-

cue." Jermyn grinned as he strode toward the village.
The night was cool and clear, the stars twinkled in the
black sky, a half moon lit the road at his feet.

"My lord, I won't be wed in such a way." Amy
thumped him again.

He grunted. "I didn't ask you if you would be wed. I
told you that I would wed you."

With a wave in their direction, Mertle ran past them
headed straight for the pub.

"I'm not one of your peasants to be used for a year
and then discarded." Amy clutched his waistcoat in
her fists.

"I don't think you're a peasant at all." They reached
the outskirts of the village and people began to pour
out of the pub. "I think you're a nobleman's bastard
daughter or an educated lady who ran into difficult
times or a dispossessed princess—"

"*What?*"

"And we're using this method rather than going to
the church because I can't wait four weeks for the
banns to be called nor even a week to obtain a special
license. Miss Victorine won't let me take you any other
way, and I will have you in my bed this night."

Her fists pulled at the thin material of his shirt in
frustration. "Since when does the mighty marquess of
Northcliff care what Miss Victorine Sprott has to say
about his actions?"

"The marquess of Northcliff has been brought low
and made humble by the revelations of the past ten
days. Only one thing has kept me from a total collapse
of pride—you and your seduction most gentle."

She hated his tone. It sent a shiver up her spine and made her want to wrap her arms around his waist instead of pounding on him and clawing at him. Better to tell him the truth right now and save her pride than to succumb to infatuation. "I'll tell you who I am. Since I was twelve I've traveled the roads and byways of England as a peddler. I ran a scam with my sister, selling face creams and cosmetics to poor, delusional women who want to imagine they can be beautiful. I've rubbed elbows with thieves and beggars."

He halted.

She must have said the right thing at last. She had convinced him. He would go away and leave her alone . . .

Carefully he slid her off his shoulder and stood her on her feet in the grass beside the path leading to the beach. He supported her until she regained her balance, and when he looked down at her, his shoulders blocked the sky. "Did your tough act frighten away those thieves and beggars?" he asked.

"What do you mean?" The villagers followed them like children after the Pied Piper.

"If you were as dissipated as you claim, you wouldn't have marked me with your virginity."

Maybe his other women could deal with such remarks. Maybe other women wouldn't mind if the whole village heard him. Amy glared and shouted, "Shut your muzzle!"

"Then you stop trying to convince me you're something you're not." He lifted her again, into his arms. The rocks slid under his boots as he descended the slope toward the beach. "You're a lady. I don't know how. I don't know why. But with every well-articulated word and every fastidious instinct, you prove to me that your past has been a sheltered one."

"It has not!"

"At least part of the time." His heels sank deeply into the sand.

The breeze from the sea was brisk and steady, tugging at her hair and raising goose bumps on her arms. She could hear the excited murmur of voices behind them. Her every sense sparkled, yet reality lagged one step behind. Nothing in the last few weeks, not even last night, had prepared her for this. *Marriage.* With the marquess of Northcliff. With the man she'd taken as a lover. It wasn't possible.

"There it is." He stopped and made his announcement as if she would be delighted. "Since pagan times, the people of Summerwind have walked—or been carried—through that arch to be married. I won't be the first Edmondson to use it to legalize my union."

On the rocky outcropping that framed the beach stood a stone arch, taller than Jermyn, wide enough for two to walk through. The arch itself was shaped like two heads, one taller, one shorter. That had to be the reason the absurd marriage superstition had developed. Yet she could see the stars through the opening, twinkling like merry eyes, and she uncovered a bit of superstition in her own soul. "I can't marry you."

He started walking again. The man was like steel lace: complicated, difficult to handle, and strong. Strong in his body, strong in his mind.

"I'm not who you think I am." As a last-ditch defense, she told the truth. All the truth. "I'm one of the exiled princesses from Beaumontagne."

He slowed. "Are you?" He didn't question her, didn't scoff at her. Instead he seemed to weigh the possibility—and find some satisfaction in it.

"Really. I am." She gritted her teeth and admitted, "I have a duty to marry for my country."

Now he smiled, a glint of white teeth in the pale moonlight. "Are you trying to convince me that *you* would wed a prince chosen for you?"

"Well . . . well, I have to!" she sputtered.

Even in the darkness she could see the twinkle in his eyes.

How did he know about Grandmamma? Why did he appear to believe that she was a princess but not that she would do as she was bid?

When had he gotten to know Amy so well?

Looking over his shoulder, she saw a line of people silhouetted on the rocks against the stars. The villagers. She saw a large lump of a man pushing his way toward the front, saw a head bobbing by his shoulder, realized that Pom had carried Miss Victorine from her cottage so she, too, could be here. Amy wanted to yell for help, but they weren't here to help her. They were here to bear witness to their lord's marriage.

She faced forward; the wedding arch loomed above them. Jermyn stepped out of the sand. Steadily he climbed the rocks. The arch rose higher and closer. She stared, hypnotized, seeing her fate coming inexorably toward her. Toward them.

As the arch loomed above them, she grabbed a handful of his hair. "My lord, don't do this. You'll regret this for the rest of your life."

Throwing back his head, he laughed a full-bodied, joyful laugh. "My dear Princess Disdain, I would regret this for the rest of my life if I didn't."

Chapter 19

"*H*ow could you believe me when I said I was a princess?" Amy struggled against the rope that bound her wrists. "What kind of fool believes such a tale?"

"This kind of fool." Jermyn sat opposite her in the boat, wielding the oars. Pom sat behind him, wielding another pair. "The kind of fool who trusts his uncle to handle his affairs without supervision because he's too arrogant to imagine anyone would cheat him and certainly never would try to kill him. You've taught me lessons with a heavy hand, and I'm grateful. I'm alive because of you."

Too swiftly the boat moved across the sea, taking her away from Summerwind and toward the kind of life she dreaded. Toward Jermyn's estate and Summer-wind Abbey. It wasn't yet midnight, still clear, still cool, yet it seemed as if her life had been chopped in half. One moment she'd been an independent woman, free of all entanglement, the next she'd been carried beneath an arch and pronounced a wife by the village vicar.

By the vicar, for heaven's sake! How was it possible that a sweetly spoken, mild-mannered, elderly Church of England vicar could authenticate a marriage based on a pagan rite?

"You're learned, you're intelligent, you seize life by the horns and shake it until it gives you what you want. You show a vast indifference to the condition of your garments." With a laugh in his voice, Jermyn said, "You'll be the despair of Biggers."

"As if I care what your valet thinks!" She couldn't see Pom, but she heard a snort and she thought he must be having the time of his life.

"There's that, too."

In the starlight and moonlight, she could only faintly see Jermyn, but she could definitely discern the flash of his teeth. He was enjoying himself. The cad!

He continued, "You don't give a farthing what anyone thinks of you. You have the courage to speak honestly. No, more than that, you consider blunt speaking to be your right. You've raised tactlessness to an art."

Like a petulant child, she snapped back, "So have you."

"Yes, but I'm a man and everyone knows men are great hairy beasts scarcely tamed by civilization." He sounded quite cheerful about his failings. "I know of only one other woman who has even some of your attributes, and Lady Valéry is an elderly duchess, so convinced of her superiority that she doesn't require the usual methods to show the world her importance. Her Grace is wealthy, she's privileged, she's lived a long life blessed with husbands and lovers, she's traveled the world . . . when you're as old as she is, I imagine you'll be just like her."

Amy opened her mouth to retort.

He interrupted her summarily. "Except for the husbands and lovers. I'm *not* leaving you alone."

He made it sound like a threat. He'd put her down in the boat to help Pom push off the beach, and just because she leaped free and started running, he'd tackled her and tied her wrists. She'd be spitting sand for a week.

"Most of all, you don't wait for anyone else to take action." Jermyn had the impudence to sound admiring. "You saw an injustice and you moved to correct it."

"Without success!" He'd used his handkerchief under the rope to protect her from chafing and he'd taken care to tie the knots firmly yet without cutting off her circulation.

"Yet you tried and if my uncle hadn't already been trying to kill me, you'd have succeeded. You're my inspiration."

"Inspiration?" She didn't want to be an inspiration. She wanted to be free. "To do what?"

"To take you and wed you before you could regroup and flee."

So she was a victim of her own audacity! Grandmamma would call that justice.

Grandmamma would also sit in icy judgment of this marriage. "You might think that we're married," Amy said with false confidence. "But in Beaumontagne, no member of the royal family is married unless both are members of our state church."

"And what is your state church called?"

"The Church of the Mountain." She tugged at the rope again. The handkerchief slipped, but the knots remained firm. "We lived isolated for too many years to be subjects of the Roman Catholic Church, and our archbishop always officiates at the royal weddings."

"So we'll have three weddings," Jermyn announced coolly.

"Three?" With every minute that passed, her life spun more summarily into a whirlwind of madness— and Jermyn stood at its center.

"One under the arch, one in the Church of England, and one in the Church of the Mountain. I hope you don't mind waiting on the ceremony in Beaumontagne. We're going to be busy for the next few months trapping my uncle as he tries to kill me."

"But I'm not a member of the Church of England, and you're not a member of the Church of the Mountain."

"You'd be surprised the dispensations that can be obtained when deed is already done—and, of course, the proper price is paid."

"So I don't have a choice."

"No, of course not. It was a courtesy query, nothing more."

Why had she imagined he was attractive? He was absolutely the biggest, most complete and utter jackass she'd ever had the bad fortune to meet.

"Why do we have to go to Summerwind Abbey tonight? Why couldn't we have waited until I at least combed the sand out of my hair?" She heard the whine in her own voice and realized she'd been reduced to petulance. With any luck at all, she'd become a nag and make Jermyn a dreadful wife.

"Didn't I tell you? We're not going to Summerwind Abbey. We're going to the honeymoon cottage Biggers prepared for us on the estate."

"You know you didn't tell me, and how did you know to have Biggers prepare a honeymoon cottage?"

"Because last night, when I made you mine—"

"Shush. You didn't!"

"All right. Last night when you made me yours—"

She definitely heard Pom snort.

"I decided it would be a permanent possession involving every kind of vow and binding known to man." Jermyn's teeth flashed in the moonlight. "Including apparently, rope."

The cliffs of Jermyn's estate loomed higher and closer.

"That's why I left Miss Victorine's cottage this morning. Because I wanted Pom to take a message to Biggers. I wouldn't have abandoned you if I'd known there was trouble brewing." Jermyn brought in the oars. Leaning forward, he clasped her fingers. "Believe me, I'm not going to lose you now."

* * *

With great ceremony, Jermyn lifted Amy into his arms and carried her across the threshold of the large cottage. He kicked the door shut behind him—and for the first time since her pagan wedding, she found herself speechless.

So this was what a fortune could buy. Tall white wax tapers, lit so recently droplets hadn't yet formed to run down the sides. Fresh flowers arranged in procelain vases, filling the air with the scent of spring. A fire blazing in the fireplace. A magnificent Oriental rug of cream and gold and blue. A sumptuous cold repast laid on a white linen tablecloth, and two gleaming wood chairs pulled close for intimate conversation. Billowy gold curtains over the windows. And in the corner, the covers turned down on a wide bed where more billowy gold curtains could be pulled to form a love nest for two. All in a gardener's cottage.

If Amy had an ounce of romance in her soul, she would be sighing with gratification. Instead, she said acerbically, "All that's missing is the love poem."

Jermyn deposited her in a chair by the table. "I'll order a pen and ink for you."

How neatly he turned the tables on her! Holding up her wrists, she said, "Untie me."

"Not yet, my love. I need to speak to Biggers—"

Jermyn was leaving her alone? She subdued her leap of anticipation.

"—and I'm afraid I can't trust you to remain here." Reaching under the table, he brought out a coil of rope.

Frozen with shock, she stared. *This could not be good.* Stepping behind her, he looped the rope around her and the chair. The rope settled at her waist, holding her arms in place, her back against the wood.

Too late, she sprang into action, kicking and fighting.

For all the notice he paid, she might have been an actress performing on cue. He tied a knot behind her, caught her ankle, looped the rope around her leg and the leg of the chair, caught her other ankle, and performed the same service.

With a few flicks of the wrist, he had subdued her.

The knots, of course, were secure.

"Do you think you tied me well enough?" she asked sarcastically.

"I know." His voice rang with fake empathy. "For a ordinary woman, I would call this excessive restraint—but you, my princess, are no ordinary woman." He dropped a kiss on her cheek. "Biggers is waiting. I promise I'll be gone only a moment."

He walked out into the night.

She stared venomously at the closed door.

She should have waited to make her break.

She should have realized that, after she put a manacle on his ankle, he would enjoy restraining her.

She should have seen that pistol on the bed stand sooner . . . quickly she surveyed her surroundings and mapped her route. Across the wooden floor, across the rug, to the bed. She could do it. She knew she could.

Fixing her gaze on the ivory handle, she pressed her feet to the floor and pushed. The chair moved. Just a little, but it moved. Encouraged, she pushed again. And again. The legs squalled as they slid across the polished wood. She was moving backwards, but by pressing on one foot more than the other she aimed herself at the bed stand. Halfway there, she paused to catch her breath—and thought she heard a noise outside.

With renewed desperation, she flung herself into reaching her goal. The legs of the chair struck the rug, sinking into the nap and holding her prisoner.

There was no way around.

So she jumped. Small jumps that lifted the chair and set it down, lifted the chair and set it down. Her calves ached, her shoulders hurt, the weight of the chair grew greater with every motion. She crept by painful inches across the floor and at last found herself by the bed stand.

Less than a foot away, the pistol gleamed in the candlelight, its barrel oiled and set with ornate scrolls, the ivory handle beautifully pristine.

But she couldn't reach it.

She looked down at her hands. They were bound by a tan rope, covered by a white handkerchief. Extricating herself would still be a stretch, but if she got free she had a chance.

She tested both hands. Her left was incrementally more lax. She tried to lengthen her hand, make it thinner. Then without a care for her skin, she pulled. The handkerchief slipped with her, right until she reached the wide point where her thumb connected to her hand.

There all movement stopped. She struggled for a moment, then stopped. She tucked her thumb into her palm. Taking a breath, she tried again. The bones, the ligaments, the muscles screamed in agony.

But her hand skidded an inch. Then another.

Then her fingers were free.

She reached for the gun.

Jermyn had spent most of his adult life in London, and he had forgotten how ungodly dark the countryside could be. The moon had slipped below the horizon, and the gardens at the far corner of his estate were lush with budding trees and towering shrubs. Even the starlight couldn't reach here. Yet the faint light from the curtained cottage windows beckoned him, and he never let it out of his sight.

Still, he didn't need to see Biggers to find out the information he needed. "You're sure Walter isn't suspicious?" he asked.

"My lord, since your kidnapping he's been almost comically lax about his duties as the butler. Also, he drinks and lately he's been dipping into the brandy your father set down. Clearly Walter believes you're gone and won't return." Biggers's tone made it obvious what he thought of such behavior. "Fortunately I believe he's the only one your uncle has subverted. I've taken the housekeeper into my confidence—a remarkable woman—and she helped me arrange your bower."

"Then we'll be safe hidden in the cottage." That was Jermyn's concern—that he could lose himself in Amy without danger to either of them, for he recognized the danger that stalked him would now also stalk her.

She faced peril unafraid.

His duty was to care for her.

"Yes, but you'll not be unprotected," Biggers assured him. "You have the knife I gave you?"

"Yes."

"And the pistol."

"At my side."

"And I placed another pistol beside the bed."

Jermyn's heart leaped in horror. "Loaded?"

"Yes, my lord, of course."

Within the instant, Jermyn absorbed the information, turned and ran. He stumbled across the gravel paths, sprinting toward the cottage where Amy was alone—with a loaded pistol.

Of course, she was bound. He'd tied the knots himself. He knew they were firm . . .

But her hands. He hadn't checked the knots on her hands. And that handkerchief could be used to help free her . . .

He burst through the door.

Amy and the chair were at the bedside table. Her left hand was unbound—and she held the pistol.

"Amy." He held up his hands. "Don't do this."

"If you don't untie me, I'll shoot you." Her green eyes were cool. Her voice was calm. Her hand was steady.

The black eye of the pistol pointed right at his heart.

"My lord, what . . . ?" Biggers stood in the door. "Dear God in heaven!"

Satisfaction sizzled through Amy's form. "This is better." She kept the gun leveled at Jermyn. "Biggers, if you don't untie me, I'll kill him."

"Biggers, leave us." Jermyn took a measured step toward her. "And shut the door behind you."

"Please. My lord. My lady." Biggers wrung his hands. "Don't do this."

"Biggers, do as I tell you." She shot a menacing glance at Biggers, but kept her attention on Jermyn. "Untie me."

"Go on, Biggers," Jermyn said. "Go back to the house. Either she'll kill me and be tied here when you come back with breakfast, or she won't and we'll be in the bed. In either case, you're not responsible."

"Biggers, you *will* be responsible if he dies." Amy sounded composed and instructional.

Biggers squared his shoulders. "But my lady, while at any other time I'm yours to instruct, in the bedchamber I serve my lord's will." With a bow to them both, Biggers left.

Amy's fierce gaze met Jermyn's. "Do you remember what I told you in the cellar before I shot at you? I said I would really like to kill you. What do you think now after you've humiliated me in front of the entire village, forced me to wed you, and tied me up like an animal?"

"I'll call the score even"—he stalked toward her, knowing that with her aim, she'd shoot him right through the heart—"when I win."

"You—" Her finger tightened on the trigger.

He prepared to hurl himself aside.

And he saw it. Inside the blackness of the gun's eye. A faint wisp of white.

Someone had stuffed the barrel. When she shot, the gun would misfire. She would be killed.

He flung himself at her, shouting, "No!"

Like an obedient wife, she threw the gun aside—without pulling the trigger. It smacked the wall hard, then clattered across the floor.

He caught her in his arms, chair and all. "You little fool!" His hands trembled as he stroked her face, then took her shoulders and gave her a small shake. "You might have been killed."

"*I* might have been killed?" Her voice sounded raspy. Her eyes looked unfocused. "I was going to kill *you*."

"Yes, and if you had fired, the gun would have exploded in your hand. My God." He pressed his lips to her forehead. His heart pounded in his chest. "My God." The words were a prayer of thankfulness. "My God."

He loved her. He loved Amy the Disdainful, Amy the vengeful, Amy the princess. He loved her in all her guises—and she had almost killed them both.

"It's time you learned to love life." Pulling the sharp little knife from the sheath in his sleeve, he used it to cut her clothes away. "And I'm the man who's going to teach you."

Chapter 20

*J*ermyn pulled a knife out of a leather sheath bound to his arm. The blade slashed toward her. And she didn't even flinch.

Why would she? He might as well kill her. She had lost her will to . . . to execute a man who deserved death.

No matter how much she wanted to, she couldn't kill Jermyn.

"I'm sorry to do this to you"—the knife slashed through the neckline of her gown—"but I've hated this costume since the first day I saw it on you and this gives me great satisfaction."

And she really truly wanted *to kill him.* Never mind that this afternoon when she'd heard the gunshot, she had thought she was going to die of anguish, fury, and guilt. Within a few seconds, she'd discovered his deceit, and her whole outlook had changed. She'd been ready—no, anxious—to murder him.

He slashed her sleeves open, then taking the rent material in his fists, he yanked. The thin old cloth ripped as easily as paper.

Then, by God, he'd compounded his sins by marrying her. Tonight, if she could have just pulled the trigger, in one shot she would rid the world of the most deceitful bastard who ever lived.

Instead she'd thrown the gun aside. Because she couldn't . . . she couldn't bear to live in this world without him.

Dear heavens, she didn't *love* him, did she?

The dress was gone, cut and torn until it was a mere memory. He grinned savagely as he looked down at the shreds. "I have never enjoyed anything as much as I enjoyed destroying that awful gown." Then he looked up at her, tied to the chair, still in shock at her own timidity. His gaze wandered over her clad only in an ancient chemise, stockings and sturdy shoes, but instead of the leap of passion she expected—that she still, to her shame, wanted—she saw the flare of fury.

"I leave you alone. I have to tie your legs and arms, and still you try to kill me." He paced away from her. Ran his fingers through his hair. Paced back. "Do I have to tie you to my side? Do I have to fear every moment, every day, that you'll leave me?"

She didn't know what to say. If she had the chance, would she disappear?

"No, because you don't want to leave Miss Victorine." He mocked her earlier words. "I'm not going to do anything to Miss Victorine. I'm going to make things better for her. I'm going to make things better for the whole damned village, but in the meantime"— he gestured widely—"I'm married to a woman who longs to travel the open road." Catching the end of the rope, he untied the knot and freed one foot, then the other. He unwound it from around her waist and her arms. He tossed it aside.

Was he going to force a choice on her?

Slowly she stood. She extended her arms.

"I can't take this kind of suspense. Decide now." He untied the ropes around her wrists. "Walk out the door. In a year you'll be free of any entanglements with me. Or stay and be my wife. My real wife. Make your choice."

She looked down at the loosened ropes still wrapped around her, then up at him.

He wore an expression of fierce indifference, but she knew better. This proud man, this noble marquess, had made up his mind he wished to marry her without knowing who she was or what she'd done. She would guess the decision was his first impetuous gesture since the day his mother had disappeared.

Amy couldn't fool herself. For him to go so contrary to his own nature, he must feel an overwhelming emotion for her. Maybe it was only passion, but she didn't make the mistake of dismissing his desire—or her own—as insignificant. It overwhelmed her, too, consuming her thoughts, her feelings, and possibly . . . her soul.

Was he the man her father had spoken of? She and Jermyn shared so many other things—the loss of their parents, a mistrust of the world, a fierce loyalty to their friends and a deep hatred for injustice—did they also share a soul?

In her life she'd had little time to think about falling in love, but when she did she had imagined that she would *know* when her soul mate appeared.

Instead she was married to a man who tricked her, forced her, tied her, and she didn't know whether to follow her instincts and run, or follow her feelings and stay.

She stood on a precipice, and a step in either direction could mean disaster.

So without knowing what she would do, she shook off the ropes. Blindly she reached out and touched Jermyn's arm. She felt the steely strength and the tense anticipation—and driven by an impetuousness she barely recognized, she whispered, "I'll stay."

Fire blazed golden in his eyes, the kind of fire that could consumer her. "Good."

He sounded calm, but he held her tightly against him, melding the two of them together with heat and passion. Leaning over her, he kissed her. Everything about this kiss felt different. Different from the kisses he'd forced on her when he'd grabbed her and pulled her on the cot. Different from the ones she'd pressed on him when she'd gone to him to make love to him. And she realized—this was the first time they'd been standing. This time she was very aware how tall he was and even more aware of the narrow span of her waist between his large hands, his strength, his supremacy.

Sliding his hand into her hair, he tilted her backward. Off-balance and totally in his power, she clutched at his shoulders. He opened her lips with his with a certainty that didn't wait for permission or even acquiescence, but moved on her, filled her, occupied her as if she were a city and he its conqueror. The taste of him, the scent of him, the intensity of him, filled her until nothing was left except to give him what he wanted as long as he wanted.

Picking her up, he laid her on the sheets. The linen, cool and sweet-scented, brought her eyes open. He stood over the bed, hands on his hips. His brown eyes held not a hint of gold, and his face was unsmiling. He was waiting for her, waiting for . . . what?

For her to look at him, really look at him, see his strength, his power and know the deal she had made.

In a measured motion, she slipped her hand into her dark hair, spreading it across the white pillow. Giving him a slumberous smile, she untied the ribbon at the neck of her chemise and with a finger slowly but surely slid the thin material off one shoulder.

The gold flame blazed instantly to life in his eyes. Color scalded his skin. He yanked off his shirt. Unbuttoned his pants and dropped them, revealing the taut muscles of his belly, the bunching muscles of his thighs, and an erection that thrust upward in aggressive need.

Alarm shot through her, and she half rose on one elbow.

But he placed one knee on the mattress and the weight made her roll toward him. Catching her firmly under the thighs, he pulled her around so she was open to him. Vulnerable to him. Her gown slithered up, and the white light of tall tapers showed him . . . everything.

She felt awkward and shy as he looked at her, scrutinized her, his eyes intense and dangerous. "You're beautiful. Beautiful everywhere."

The anticipation that gripped her made her heart pound. Each breath ached as she drew it in, as if her lungs no longer had the capacity to perform. The space between her legs ached, grew damp, and she wanted to lift herself to him, thrust herself on him.

Yet he had scarcely touched her.

He leaned forward, put his hands on either side of her head. "I need you now."

She didn't recognize her own voice as she replied, "Please. Now."

Sliding one arm under her hips, he lifted her up to him. He fit their bodies together, and alarm shot through her as she acknowledged his size and heat.

Last time had been so different—she had been in charge, or thought so, and he'd allowed her delusion. This time he dominated her. On purpose, to impress on her his power? Or because he had no choice? She didn't know. Didn't care. For as he pressed himself inside her, as her body yielded and enveloped him, she yielded, too. He needed this assurance and she gave it to him because she had no choice. Everything that was feminine in her acquiesced to everything that was masculine in him, and she melted around him.

And he looked . . . he looked as fierce as an eagle who held her in his claws as he soared through the heavens. His hips moved in slow increments, in and out, deepening the invasion each time. She tried to meet him, to bring him closer faster, but still he held her hips and controlled the pace.

The intensifying impact of his flesh inside her brought soft incoherent cries to her lips. He was taking over her body, making her nipples tighten, her thoughts scatter. In all the world, there were only she and he and the passion that possessed her. Possessed them.

When his cock pressed against the back of her womb, the contact made her heels dig into the mattress, and brought him to a stop. For a long moment, he held himself still, staring at her dishevelment. Then slowly he pulled out, all the way out.

"Jermyn, please!" She wanted so desperately to make him hurry, to take what she needed.

But he mocked her. "Please what? Please . . . this?" He slid back inside. Again he touched her all the way inside.

"Faster," she said through lips that felt frozen. "Please, Jermyn."

"Like this." His hips thrust harder, more quickly, making her writhe with the pleasure of his possession.

"Yes." She struggled, trying to free herself, trying to *move.* "Oh, Jermyn, let me—"

"No!" He lowered himself on her, pushing her into the mattress, holding her down with his weight. "Tonight you're *mine.* Tonight I make love to *you.*"

But at the contact of their bodies, his flesh caught fire. He drove into her, propelled by need, by heat, by a desire so new and yet so ancient they were united with every man, every woman for all time. They danced the dance of the gods, reaching with a frenzy for fulfillment.

She moaned. She wrapped her legs tightly around his hips. She clutched at his back, holding him close and knowing it could never be close enough.

The climax when it struck blinded her to every scent, every sight, every sound. All she knew was his cock inside her, compelling her to reach for a height she'd never imagined. This was the man she'd been made for. This was the moment she'd been born to experience—a moment that grew in intensity until she thought she would die of a delight too intense to survive.

And when he joined her—when his thrusts grew faster, his manhood swelled inside her, he groaned as if in violent agony—her orgasm gained more strength. Her womb received his seed, absorbed his ferocity, took and gave with equal strength.

Together they were one.

When he finished, he collapsed on top of her, sweaty, heavy, and beautiful. She smoothed his hair off his forehead with trembling hands and tried to understand how this was possible. How two people who had never seen each other two weeks ago could fight their way to such a madness of joy.

"Don't," he said hoarsely.

"Don't what?"

"Don't try to figure it out. Until you understand with your soul, there's no use trying."

Her soul? What did he know about her *soul?* How dare he speak about her soul like some worshipful poet, like some reckless lover?

He was neither of those things. He was the marquess of Northcliff and she would be wise to remember that . . . and to forget that somewhere in this world, her soul mate existed.

Somewhere in this world . . . perhaps closer than she thought.

Lifting his weight off her, he supported himself on his elbows and looked down at her. "Woman, you drive me mad. I've never been in so great a hurry. I never got my boots off."

"Really?" She was charmed. "But you never put your feet on the bed, either."

"I'd better take them off now, for I intend to—and not get out for a very long time." He watched her keenly. "You promised you would stay with me."

She shifted beneath him, overcome with wariness. "For a year. I promised I'd stay for a year, the length prescribed by our pagan wedding." She thought she saw a flash of something in his eyes. Could it be disappointment? "Then . . . then we'll see if I should stay forever."

For a long moment, he was silent. Then—"All right." He slid from within her. Sitting up, he pulled off his boots and flung them, one after the other, against the wall.

She flinched at the violence of the gesture. Pulling her legs together in sudden, misplaced modesty, she covered herself with the sheet.

But his voice was calm and even when he said, "I know you, Princess Disdain. I know you'll keep your promise." He looked at her again, his gaze pinning her to the bed. "For at least one year."

Chapter 21

*H*arrison Edmondson stared at the letter in frustration.

11 May 1810

Mon Cher Uncle,

*You must help me in my hour of need. My abductors
are cruel men who whisper at night of their desire to
murder me, and when I hear them my blood runs cold!
They speak of torture, of cutting off my head—*

"No great loss there," Harrison muttered.

—of putting me in a weighted bag and sinking me in the sea, there to die a most horrible death! If you don't pay them soon, you'll lose your only and beloved nephew, the one remaining Edmondson other than yourself! Only through the cleverest of ruses and the kindness of their downtrodden maid was I able to sneak this plea out to you! I beg of you, come to my aid with a swift infusion of cash! I know it must be difficult to raise the gold required, but please, uncle, for my continued good health, it must be done!

> *Your most loving and faithful nephew,*
> *Jermyn Edmondson*
> *The most honorable and noble marquess of Northcliff*

"Melodramatic little pustule." Harrison threw the letter aside. Now in addition to being plagued by inept kidnappers and a missing assassin, Jermyn his almighty snot-nosed marquess was annoying him, too. The puny swine imagined his dear old uncle Harrison, the one who tended his estate and his fortune with no thanks from Jermyn, would come to his rescue. "Not likely," Harrison whispered. Picking up the letter, he examined it again.

Yes, that was Jermyn's writing, all stately noble loops and sharp corners. Harrison recognized it from the infrequent communications Jermyn sent. The ones that demanded the yearly accounting be sent to him at one of his lofty estates. He never actually asked for the books, which made Harrison's industrial activities all the easier, but bugger! how Harrison hated making money for someone else. And if something wasn't done within the next month, all his activities of the past ten years would be revealed, and he doubted that Jermyn would be grateful.

He doubted it very highly.

There was something to be said for a silence broken only by the calls of seagulls, the crash of the waves on the rocks far below, and the faint whisper of the salty breeze. Nothing could match the sheer perfection of a moment gazing upon the gray cloud draped in wisps over the distant island of Summerwind and beyond that, a faint sweet promise of blue sky. A fishing vessel skittered over the swells, and in her deepest senses Amy felt the earth cradling her as it welcomed the rush of the ocean's tide.

In the five days that she'd spent alone with Jermyn in the cottage, a spring rain had fallen every day, Biggers had brought them their meals, and they'd spent the time inside in the bed, barely speaking, yet making promises with their bodies.

Today for the first time the sun shone, drawing them out with a rug and a basket to picnic on the cliffs.

"This precise spot is where I stood and looked out to sea on the day that you kidnapped me. The fog was coming in, everything was gray and dull . . . I had nothing to do, nowhere to go, and I wished to be anywhere but here." He spoke softly, not breaking the peace but enhancing it with the slow, precisely chosen syllables. "Little did I know my life would change so drastically . . . so marvelously."

"You weren't saying *that* two weeks ago." Contentedly domestic, she packed their meal away in the basket.

They sat on the rug in the midst of the spring green grass and budding spring flowers, he clad in his most informal wear, which in Amy's opinion was not informal at all, and she wearing one of Miss Victorine's old gowns. They made an odd couple.

Amy imagined that would never change.

"Pragmatic as always. Do you see that wing of Summerwind Abbey?"

She looked down the cliffs to the solid arm of the manor that stood poised on the cliffs. "It looks precarious."

"Since the manor was built two hundred years ago, the ocean has cut back the cliffs, bringing the house closer to the edge." He waved at the large windows and beautiful white stone balcony that looked out onto the ocean. "That's the master's bedchamber, remember? You've been there collecting my underwear."

"That's right. You're the swine who sent me on a fool's errand when you could have gone yourself." She observed his expression. "You did go yourself!"

"I saw you there," he admitted.

"Did I call you a swine?" Remembering the drama with which she sneaked into Summerwind Abbey, she didn't know whether to laugh or shout. "Louse, rather!"

"Yes, but you must forgive me. Being a louse is my nature."

"It certainly is." But she couldn't rouse herself to heat. Apparently, sex applied often and with vigor made her as placid as a breeding mare. The thought should have upset her . . . but she was too serene.

What an ever-widening circle!

Jermyn's arm curved around her shoulders and he drew her into him, opening his coat so that she could rest against his chest.

She went gladly, absorbing his warmth and giving back her happiness. "Your home is very beautiful, especially the gardens."

"So your year will be spent pleasantly." Jermyn whispered in a low, deep voice, as if every word was a love word.

"Very pleasantly." Amy rubbed his thigh to hide her anxiousness. "Although I was wondering when I can go back and visit Miss Victorine?"

"Whenever you wish. It's a swift voyage."

"I miss her." Amy needed to talk to Miss Victorine about the situation with Jermyn. For all Miss Victorine's vagueness, she understood human nature and she would tell Amy what to think of the devil's bargain between them. A year together, then a thoughtful assessment and perhaps a wedding . . . when Jermyn took off the ropes, Amy had thought she could be happy with a temporary bond. Now she didn't know if she had been quite wise.

Jermyn seemed pleased with their pact. Seemingly without a care, he prattled on about the island, telling her, "Pom has set a great many plans into motion on the island. He's hired men to repair the cottages, beginning with Miss Victorine's."

"Is she happy with the changes?"

"I understand she's fussing about having a stove in her bedroom, but once it's installed and she's warm, she'll like it. Pom ordered a huge load of coal to be delivered and distributed to the villagers, and Mertle has gone to market and bought bolts of cloth for the women. Oh, and in honor of my thirtieth birthday and my wedding, I've ordered a whole beef to be sent over, as well as bread and cheese and barrels of ale."

"You are so sweet." And every day, Amy became more of a fool for him. More convinced he *was* the other half of her soul.

"As you so plainly told me, I'm responsible for letting the village fall into such desperate straits." He tilted her back to look into her face, concealed from him by her old-fashioned, wide-brimmed hat. He licked his thumb, then softly ran it over her lower lip. His gaze rested on the gleam of moisture, and at once the need to be kissed drove all thought from her mind.

He knew too well how to create desire in her. It was frightening, how desperately she wanted him. And when they were done making love, she wanted him again.

With well-feigned impatience, he asked, "Don't you recognize a man who's urgently trying to impress his woman with his good deeds?"

"No, is that what you're doing?"

"Most definitely." He did kiss her, but only a swift brush of the lips, a tease that made her want for more. "Although I suspect it had lost its impact since I had to point it out."

"Not at all. I'm overcome with gladness at your generosity." She meant every word.

"Good." Then he sat her up, his arm still around her.

She drowsed against him in that state between waking and sleeping, balanced in that single moment between one point in her life and the next. Last week the weight of the world sat on her shoulders. Next week she would assume new duties. But now all was peaceful.

"When I was a child," Jermyn said, "sometimes I could just stop playing and throw myself on my stomach on the grass and stare out to sea."

"I used to stop playing, throw myself on my stomach and stare up at the mountains."

"Do you miss it? Your home?"

A gust of wind blew in from the sea, then died, like a nudge to banish serenity. She never talked about Beaumontagne. Not to anyone. The memories were banished to a secluded place in her mind, surrounded by walls that kept the anguish in and the loneliness out.

But she ought to share a little bit of her past with him. For all that he'd lived a life of privilege, he'd suffered his traumas and perhaps he would understand. She really thought he would understand. "I used to miss Beaumontagne. When I first went to school, I'd cry at night when no one could hear me. Then Poppa died and Grandmamma stopped sending our tuition. The headmistress threw my sister and me out into the streets and I was too frightened and confused to think about Beaumontagne anymore."

"What did you do?"

"I told you. We sold creams. We promised beauty." She smiled crookedly up at him. "We did what two women alone in the world do—we wandered, and we survived."

"My blood runs cold at the thought of you left alone to travel the roads. Why didn't you stop somewhere? Make a home of some kind? There must have been someplace that would welcome you."

She drew away from Jermyn's arm, wrapped her hands around her knees and stared out to sea. "Grandmamma's personal courtier found us and told us we were marked for assassination."

Jermyn's face went from blankness to amazement.

"So although I wanted to stay somewhere, Clarice said no. I knew she was right, but I hated the constant deception, the fear . . . and we were looking for Sorcha, too. I felt—I think we both felt—that if we could just find our oldest sister, we would have won an important battle. So we kept moving."

Jermyn's eyes narrowed on her.

After all his freely-given trust, did he not believe her now? While she and Clarice traveled together, heartless suspicion had paved every road. Yet so easily, she had grown used to Jermyn and the credence he placed in her promises and her words. She didn't want to lose that. She didn't want to lose him. Yet she didn't know what else to do except tell the truth. "Godfrey said Grandmamma would place advertisements in the paper when it was safe for us to come back. Her Majesty always does as she says, and she hasn't yet placed the advertisements."

"I'm sorry, but this tale your grandmother's courier told you sounds absurd. No innocent young ladies should be subjected to such an ordeal!"

A telling relief swept Amy. It wasn't her he didn't believe, but Godfrey.

Jermyn continued, "She knew you were in England alone with no means of support. She sounds like a strong woman, and a strong woman wouldn't have sent a message, she would have sent protection. You could have been killed—should have been killed—a hundred times over. If this Godfrey was truly your grandmother's servant, he would never have left your side."

"You're right. It does sound stupid." She swallowed, and admitted, "And my grandmother is many things, but stupid is not one of them."

Why hadn't Amy realized this before?

Because she'd been twelve when they'd been thrown from the school. She'd had a child's skewed perceptions of what was right and wrong. As she grew, the mere act of survival had occupied her mind while at the same time, she pushed the hurt of abandonment and her father's death into the depths of her mind. Had she and Clarice avoided Beaumontagne when in fact they should have returned? That would be a bitter irony indeed, one that left her feeling tearful and silly.

"Do you trust this man?" Jermyn asked. "This Godfrey? For if you don't trust the messenger, you can't trust the message."

"I don't know the truth about Godfrey, Jermyn." Her voice wobbled. "I was a child."

"You're *still* a child." Deftly he turned the subject as he nudged her trembling chin. "Only nineteen!"

His compassion dug at her pride, and she answered, "I might have been a fool about Godfrey, but I assure you, Jermyn, I have experience enough for ten lifetimes."

"And you're prickly about being young."

She was amusing him.

"More than ever, I feel as if I've robbed the cradle."

But she knew how to puncture his mirth. "You are very old," she agreed demurely.

He pushed her backward onto the grass.

She laughed and fought him.

Within minutes he had her arms trapped over her head, and he kissed her while the world whirled around them. "I win!" he said against her lips.

"Only because you used brute force."

"It's better than drugs in a glass of wine," he retorted.

"You would think so, since you hold the brute force."

He grinned down at her. "But I did win."

"Yes, yes, you won." She dismissed his boasting as if it were of no consequence. "Are you ever going to forget that stupid manacle?"

"No, I think I'll be bringing it up at inconvenient moments for the rest of our lives."

At his ill-thought-out words, they both froze, their eyes wide with shock. *The rest of their lives?*

Their gazes shifted away from each other.

Her mind worked feverishly. Did he mean it? Did he plan that they would be together forever?

Sitting up, he offered her his hand and pulled her

up. As if nothing important had happened, he said, "Britain has diplomatic ties with Beaumontagne. I believe they're cordial. With your permission, I'll have discreet inquiries made in London."

Her rush of excitement surprised her. In all those long years with Clarice, Amy had given up on ever again seeing Beaumontagne. Now with swift kindness, Jermyn offered her her home. "I would like that." Belated caution made her add, "If we can not tell them why we're asking."

"We can do that. No one will question my interest. There are advantages to being a marquess." He grinned. "Besides, I'm getting good at deception. My uncle has by now received the letter I wrote him the day after we married, begging him for the ransom before the villainous kidnappers most cruelly kill me."

"Lovely."

"Today I'll write another letter declaring that I escaped, that I'm throwing a party to celebrate my thirtieth birthday and he's invited, and that I wish an advance on my allowance."

"Delightful."

"And when we return to the manor, I'll give Walter a commendation for his loyalty and industry during my absence."

"Why?" She couldn't believe Jermyn would praise his treacherous butler.

"Biggers says it's best that we appear imperceptive of wrongdoing on his part. That we don't want Uncle Harrison to have to buy or threaten another one of my servants into his service."

"All right." She stuck out her lower lip. "But I don't like it."

"Don't worry." The gold disappeared from his eyes and they became bitter brown and flat. "When this is over, Walter will discover a different world—the one in Newgate Prison."

"On one occasion, my sister and I saw the inside of a prison." A memory she didn't relish. "Walter won't like that at all."

"My dear girl! Prison? How? Why?"

"I've told you. We were peddlers promising youth and happiness to anyone who used them. We sold good creams, but they couldn't live up to that guarantee. That was why Clarice and I fought. I wanted to give up on the dream of returning to Beaumontagne, stay in one place and make the best of our lives. She was like a mother hen, keeping me safe, holding up Beaumontagne as our shining goal when I had given up on ever returning . . . How odd that, with your help, I may go back." An abrupt thought caught her attention, and she whipped around to stare at Jermyn. "Do you realize how much our lives are in tune? You may be the one to take me home, and I may be the one to change your mind about your mother's guilt."

His face grew still. "Why are you still thinking of that? Forget her. If you want to make me happy, forget her."

"I can't. Especially not here on your estate where her presence demands the truth be told."

"It was told. There's no possible reason that would justify her abandonment of her husband and child."

"It seems impossible that a lady you loved so much

would leave you." Amy rubbed her knuckles under his rigid chin. "Miss Victorine doesn't believe it."

He moved his head away. "Miss Victorine is a lovely lady who thinks the best of everyone."

"Not everyone. Not Harrison Edmondson. She's old, Jermyn, but she's not senile. She remembers the events of twenty-three years ago with the clarity of someone who was not personally affected by them. You were just a boy. Just as I don't know if Godfrey can truly be trusted, you don't really know what happened to your mother."

Rising, he walked to the edge of the cliff, then returned. "I know she never came back. And why do you even care about my mother?"

"Because you care."

"You feel so strongly about this. There must be some other reason." He stared down at her, demanding that she delve in her mind and tell him the truth.

And although she thought she had told him the whole truth, she slowly admitted, "I never had a mother. And my father sent me away. For my own good, he said. Then he marched off to war . . . and died leading his troops. He flung himself into the breach to triumph over the rebels. His death signaled the beginning of the end for the revolt. His sacrifice saved Beaumontagne from anarchy." Bitterly she added, "Or so I hear."

Jermyn knelt before her. "I'm sure that's what happened."

"When I'm being rational, when I'm not feeling like an abandoned child, then I'm sure that's what happened, too." Yet so much of her life had been marred by injustice, she sometimes wailed in absurd despair. "I can't bear to imagine a parent so kind, so loving as to invoke the devotion of a child, who walks away without a backward glance. I want to remember Poppa as being there until he couldn't be. Until death took him away."

"Death didn't take my mother."

She pounced on that. "Are you sure?"

His eyes narrowed on her, seeing only her, listening with seeming intentness.

"No one in the whole world has seen her since she left you," she said.

"The world is a big place."

"But not so big that a lady and her English-speaking lover can hide without detection." Amy saw that Jermyn was at least listening. Right now, that was all she could ask. "Has anyone talked about her since you were a child?"

"Only Uncle Harrison, and he said he was surprised she hadn't left sooner. That she was a flighty foreigner and—" Jermyn stopped, abruptly aware and defensive.

"If you don't trust the messenger, you can't trust the message." Jermyn had said that about Grandmamma's courtier, and only now did Amy realize how true it was.

Tonight she would write directly to Clarice, inform her where she was, give a tactful rendition of the pagan wedding ceremony, ask all the questions she longed to know, and most important, she would tell Clarice that she doubted Godfrey. She'd say Jermyn was going to speak to the Beaumontagne Embassy and find out the truth about Grandmamma, about the assassins, and about Beaumontagne itself. And she hoped Clarice would approve.

"It doesn't matter whether I trust Uncle Harrison and what he said about my mother. The truth doesn't matter, because the fact is—she's gone. Your father died in battle, an honorable death. We lost them both. But we're not our parents. Perhaps my father failed my mother in some way. I know that was the question that tormented him."

"The poor man!" Amy's heart bled for the late marquess. "Did he tell you that?"

"Once. Only once. But I don't believe he failed her. My father was a conscientious lord, and he loved her. He raised me to be like him and take responsibility for what was mine. I had simply forgotten his teaching—until you so forcibly reminded me." Jermyn took her fingers and lifted them to his lips. "You're good for me."

Sometimes families argue. That doesn't mean that they should separate. But she couldn't say it, for hadn't she done exactly that? Left Clarice in Scotland rather than insist they work things out?

And Jermyn wore a still expression, the sort that hid an anguish deeper than the sea. So to lift his spirits, she said in a saucy tone, "I always say chaining a man is a good way to deal with his stubbornness."

"Do you?" His hands tightened. "I always say a smart wife knows when it's time to stop talking and kiss her husband."

He was challenging her to change the topic. To get his way.

She relished a challenge. Her sisters knew it. Rainger knew it. They'd been able to tease her into dragging them around the castle grounds in their little carriage, and walking the parapet three stories up over the courtyard. They'd all been thrashed for that, and Grandmamma, for all her age, had a strong arm and an unerring sense of justice.

Amy had seen lovers in villages and manors, and they always looked besotted. How hard could it be to kiss a man silly?

Pushing him flat on the grass, she applied her lips to his. The brim of her hat enclosed them in a dim world of his breath and her breath, his smile and her persuasion. Soft, warm, damp, his mouth opened under hers and she pursued his tongue with hers. The slow slide, the gentle touches, the heat of his body under hers; they worked like narcotics to turn her into a woman who found adventure within the confines of one man's arms. It was a voyage she loved making. It was a voyage she loved taking him on.

With conscious coquetry, she pressed her breasts into his chest, reminding him how much he loved to caress her nipples. She massaged his shoulders, then with one hand sliding down his body, she found his erection and stroked it. The material of his trousers strained as their kiss deepened and changed from challenge to passion. Impulsive, irresistible, infinite passion.

They rolled over and over, bodies driven together by

weight and need. The scent of crushed grass rose, heady and warm, and they kissed with mindless passion until they bumped into something . . .

Something that gave her a hard kick. A man's cultured voice snarled, "How many times have I told you servants that you are not to use the gardens of Summerwind Abbey as your own private den of vice?" Amy found herself lifted off Jermyn by her collar.

The voice belonged to a tall man with a long, thin chin to match his long, thin nose and blue eyes set close together in peevish displeasure. "Girl, you'll not roll around in the grass like a wanton while *I'm* butler at Summerwind Abbey, and you there—" The man looked down. He must have recognized Jermyn, for his voice rose like a little girl's. "My lord! I didn't realize . . . I didn't know . . . please forgive my insolence . . ." The hand holding her gown shook with a distinct tremor.

Gazing down at Jermyn, Amy knew why. He looked like a man who'd been interrupted in the middle of coitus. He looked like a man who could kill.

Slowly he rose to his feet: taller than his butler, younger than his butler, and absolutely furious. "Walter, I would suggest you take your hand away from my—"

Wife. She could see the word hovering on the tip of Jermyn's tongue, and ruthlessly she interrupted. "Jermyn, you should commend Walter for his vigilance in watching over his staff and their virtue."

"What?" Jermyn glared at her with red-rimmed, incensed eyes.

She glared back meaningfully.

His fury retreated enough to allow good sense to

reign. "Oh. Yes. Of course I should. Still"—Jermyn plucked his butler's hand from the back of Amy's gown—"it would be best if Walter removed his hand from my fiancée."

"Your . . . fiancée . . . my lord, I never imagined . . . is that why you went missing?" Walter blanched until Amy felt almost sorry for him. Almost. "I mean, my lord, we've been worried about you, especially Biggers . . . and I, of course, I was terrified for your safety."

"As you should have been. I had been kidnapped. I'm sure you arranged a desperate search, but you can call it off now. I'm home." Jermyn leaned into Walter's face. "To stay." He leaned back. "Now perhaps you'll go and ask Mrs. Valentine to prepare a room for my dearest Princess Disdain."

"Princess . . . ?" Walter's gaze darted over Amy's miserable garb.

"Disdain," Jermyn said again, and they watched as Walter backed away, bowing, then turned and hurried toward the house.

"So much for our idyll." Jermyn looked to the sky, then out toward the island. The breeze lifted his hair off his forehead and tossed it around his face. "But it's probably safer in the manor. There's a storm brewing, a big one." Taking her hand, he said, "Come on. I'll take you home."

Chapter 22

*I*n the cottage, later that afternoon, Biggers took one look at Amy in her clean, pressed and absolutely dreadful leftover from Miss Victorine's wardrobe, and his expression of horrified disbelief made Jermyn want to guffaw. But he held back his amusement while Biggers stammered, "If . . . if I might be so bold, Lady Northcliff . . . the carriage will be here soon to take you to Summerwind Abbey. The servants are anxiously anticipating meeting their new mistress. I dare say they'll expect a little more than your usual . . . That is, your style is your own, unusual and versatile, but at this, the first formal presentation at your lord's country seat, you might wish to freshen the . . ." His hands quivered in the air as he tried to think of a tactful way to criticize Amy's attire.

Obviously, he failed, and his voice died away.

"Biggers, you'll want to leave off calling me Lady Northcliff." She sounded absolutely unruffled and her expression was no more than slightly interested. "Especially since Walter believes I'm Jermyn's *future* wife."

"Quite right, my lady. I believe I hear the carriage now." Biggers cleared his throat and looked relieved.

"Biggers, you'll stay behind and return the cottage to its previous state." Jermyn helped Amy into her short, shabby cloak. He thought she looked lovely with her dark hair piled atop her head, her bonnet, now slightly crushed, perched atop her head, and her beautiful skin rosy from his lovemaking. "It's imperative that no one know we were here this week or our tale of being engaged to be married will be ruined."

She glanced over her shoulder at him. "So until the wedding ceremony in your chapel, we'll be chaste?"

Her smile flirted and taunted, and he marveled at how quickly Amy had learned to entice. "There is an advantage with living in a building that was once an abbey."

"What is that, Jermyn?" She pulled on her tattered gloves.

Biggers moaned softly.

"The place is riddled with secret passages," Jermyn told her.

"But my lord! You're not suggesting you'll visit my bedchamber for a tryst?" She fluttered her lashes and tried to look shocked.

With a straight face, he replied, "Absolutely not!

You've already proved your skill at sneaking into my bedchamber, so I thought you would come to mine." She burst into laughter, a full-bodied peal of merriment. Taking his arm, she scolded, "Layabout!"

"Only with you, my bride. Only with you."

At the door she halted. "Give me a minute, please." Turning back, she stared at their honeymoon cottage, allowing her gaze to touch the stone fireplace where last night the flames had rollicked, the curtained bed where they'd explored each other, slept and woke to explore again, the drooping bouquet of flowers she'd gathered and put on the table. He heard her breath catch, saw her expression of aching melancholy.

She liked the simplicity of this place. It suited her, and he wondered, not for the first time, how she would adapt to the role of mistress to a great country estate.

Turning back, she walked with him into the bright sunshine.

The crest of the marquess of Northcliff graced the pristine white side of the open carriage. Inside, the wood trim gleamed and the black leather shone. The spirited team of chestnuts pranced as they waited, and the coachman and footman wore powdered wigs and a formal blue livery.

Jermyn was bringing his bride—or, some thought, his future bride—to his home, and he well knew the show he should make and the judgments that would be made based on that display.

"Milton is my loyal coachman," Jermyn told Amy. Loyal, yes, and he'd been hurt even more than Jermyn during the accident that had broken Jermyn's leg.

When the carriage had rolled, Milton had taken a blow to the head which had rendered him unconscious for three days. He really shouldn't be working yet, but Jermyn had needed him and Milton wouldn't hear of anyone else taking his place.

Before Amy, Jermyn would have taken Milton's loyalty for granted; now he planned a thank you in a sum large enough to enable Milton's son to become a solicitor. "And Bill is my own footman. You can trust these lads with your life." If anything went wrong with their plan for Uncle Harrison, she would need to know her allies.

Bill set the steps for Amy to climb inside, but she lingered on the ground, letting them get a good look at her. "Milton, Bill, thank you for taking such good care of his lordship for me."

"M'lady." Bill bowed.

"Miss Rosabel." Milton tipped his hat.

She took Jermyn's hand and stepped into the carriage. When Jermyn settled himself beside her, she said, "No one knows what to call me. We need to decide on the proper form, and heaven knows your elaborate English etiquette must have something to cover this occasion."

"Did you not have forms of etiquette in Beaumontagne?"

"Indeed, but English high society has a barrage of rules, and I'll never remember all of them." She looked disgusted that she even had to try.

"We are a self-important bunch, aren't we?" As Milton set the horses in motion, Jermyn leaned back and wrapped his arm around Amy's shoulders. He hated to leave the cottage almost as much as she did. Even as they left, he made plans to return—and be alone with Amy once more. "I think we should call you 'princess' or rather—Your Highness."

"A little ostentatious, don't you think?" She inclined her head toward Milton and raised questioning brows.

"But it's true, and you should be accorded the respect due royalty."

"Exiled royalty is nothing but an embarrassment. No, my lord, I prefer 'Miss Rosalyn.' "

"As you wish, my dear." He was well-aware of his servants' listening ears, and he knew that although both were loyal to him, that wouldn't discourage them from spreading gossip—gossip which this time he wished to spread. Satisfied that his intention had been a success, he pointed out to her the sights of the estate: the gardens, the paths, the ancient oaks and rimming the estate, the cliffs that dropped off to the restless sea. She asked about the history of the area, and he kept up a light chatter.

Yet the air felt still and stale with the scent of salty ocean and old shipwrecks. The horses whinnied unhappily as if sensing nature's gathering wrath, and Milton utilized all his skill to handle them.

Jermyn scanned the sky and a shiver ran down his spine as if someone had walked on his grave. The leading clouds had a thin, stretched, ragged appearance, followed by bulbous puffs sagging across the blue. On the horizon, like an ominous hand, a dark line rose with the speed of a runaway horse.

Jermyn had seen his share of storms, but never a storm like this.

Amy had grown up far away and seemed mercifully unaware. In a teasing tone, she said, "I don't know why you marquesses of Northcliff call this Summerwind. The wind blew all winter, too." The breeze picked up, plucking tendrils of her hair from beneath her bonnet and tossed them in circles.

"Year-round-wind takes too long to say." As the road meandered toward the house, it skirted close to the sea. The waves gnashed at the rocks, growing wilder under the impetus of the gathering gale. "We're almost there. Around this next bend, you'll have your first view of the house. Or rather—the view of the house the guests are supposed to see."

She leaned forward as the horses took the corner.

"Summerwind Abbey is a great rabbit hutch of a place." He scanned the building, looking it over as he always did when he approached. "A little medieval, mainly Tudor and Stuart, with one wing of Georgian sticking out like a sore toe. Architecturally, it's hideous."

"And you love it," she said shrewdly.

"Yes. I admit I do. For a long time, I didn't allow myself to remember that, but all those hours I spent alone with just a manacle reminded me of what was important in my life." Picking up her hand, he kissed the fingers. "And what is important in my life, I offer to you."

"Thank you." But her gaze slipped away from his, then rose, then slipped away again.

He thought . . . he hoped she wanted to ask *For how long?* Then he would say *For as long as you like.*

But the silence between them grew until she giggled

and said, "You really owe me a lot for locking you up. It's improved your character immensely."

She didn't giggle well. It wasn't in her character and it showed him only too clearly the fight he had ahead to keep her with him. He smiled as she wished him to do and said, "I'll give you what's coming to you. Don't worry about that."

She grinned at him, obviously relieved that their conversation had returned to safe waters.

The carriage pulled up to the front steps. The servants were lined up in order of rank with Walter and the housekeeper at the front and the scullery maid at the back.

"Here we go." Jermyn patted Amy's hand. "There's no need to be nervous. Walter's a louse that needs to be wiped out, but the rest of the servants will be delighted to meet their future lady."

As the footman set the steps, she flashed Jermyn an ironic glance. "Nervous? I'm not nervous. Resigned would be a better word."

He didn't understand what she meant until he descended and offered her his hand. Then he saw it.

The mantle of royalty settled on her shoulders. Her lips curved gently. She stepped gracefully from the carriage and thanked him in a warm, throaty voice. She placed her hand on his arm and allowed him to lead her to the head of the line, repeating each name as he introduced her. She engaged each servant in a glance that expressed personal concern and interest. Yes, she wore clothes so old and worn as to be threadbare, but it wasn't her gown that they noticed. It was her manner;

this woman, Jermyn realized, had made many an arrival at stately homes and palaces, arrivals in which she was the center of attention. She'd learned how to make anyone she met respect her.

He had believed her when she told him she was a princess; it was the only reasonable explanation for her education, her manner and her pride.

But he hadn't seen her in action before. He hadn't had the proof ram him in the gut.

Like his mother, his wife was foreign, but unlike his mother, Amy was born to rule. And although he tried to shake the thought away, it shadowed this bright moment of triumph.

If duty called, an English lord could scarcely hold a Beaumontagne princess.

15 May 1810

Mon Cher Uncle,

Glorious news! I have escaped the clutches of the evil villains who abducted me for their own gains and am now free! I know you rejoice with me and will attend as a guest at the house party I am throwing to celebrate my thirtieth birthday! Which, by the by, is going to cost more than I had anticipated. The invitations to all the right people, the necessary expense of food and drink, and of course the salaries of the increased staff. Therefore, kindest, dearest uncle, I ~~request demand~~ require an advance on my yearly allowance. As much as the fortune can afford right now, please.

Perhaps you have heard tales of my losses in gambling; however, let me assure you those are rumors of the most vile sort, a mere tempest in a teapot, and absolutely untrue. In addition, I am sure I will recover the moneys without having to use Summerwind Abbey as a stake. Please assign my allowance to my account at once. I look forward to seeing you the tenth of June for the festivities, and rest assured that as my only surviving relative, you'll be treated with the highest honors.

> *Your most loving and faithful nephew,*
> *Jermyn Edmondson*
> *The most honorable and noble marquess of Northcliff*

Harrison Edmondson burst into laughter. It rang through the emptiness of his office.

Outside the door, his footman cringed and covered his ears.

Harrison rubbed his hands together. Why, the little pustule had a brain after all! Who would have thought it? All was clear now.

Northcliff had arranged his own kidnapping because he needed money. Very clever in the general run of things, for certainly most uncles would be fond enough to send the ransom.

Harrison frowned. Why wasn't Northcliff screaming his silly little head off that his *cher uncle* hadn't sent the ransom?

Harrison's face cleared. Because Northcliff didn't know enough about his cash holdings to realize he could have ten thousand pounds immediately, and much, much more when the factories and estates were tapped.

He frowned again. But as Northcliff reminded him, his thirtieth birthday was rapidly approaching and nothing had been accomplished in the way of eliminating him. None of the people he had hired to kill the little pustule had succeeded—not the assassin, not the carriage driver, not the butler who stuffed the barrels of Northcliff's gun collection. This incompetence proved one axiom was true.

If you want something done right, do it yourself.

Harrison called his valet and ordered his bags packed for a house party at Summerwind Abbey. Then, thankful for his unusual hobby, he chose a variety of weapons to use on his nephew . . . whenever opportunity presented itself.

Chapter 23

"*A*fter much thought, I realized the reason why I'm so compelled by Lord Northcliff." Alfonsine, countess of Cuvier, sat like a fat, satisfied cat in the middle of the drawing room in Summerwind Abbey and in an amused tone said, "It comes to one thing. I want to climb his highest peak."

The ladies surrounding her—Miss Hilaire Kent, Lady Pheobe Breit, and Her Grace, the duchess of Seymour—trilled with laughter.

Amy smiled enigmatically and kept walking.

The two gentlemen who accompanied her, Lord Howland Langford and his brother Manning Langford, earl of Kenley, turned shocked eyes on the four ladies as they passed.

"I'm brokenhearted over his choice of bride." Broken hearted? Ha! Lady Alfonsine sounded spiteful. "A girl of whom no one has ever heard who claims she's a princess! Really!"

"Absurd!" Miss Kent said.

Of course the ladies had seen Amy strolling through the foyer toward the door and had dipped their forked tongues in venom.

"Living with him before the wedding and claiming to be an orphan." Lady Pheobe lowered her voice, but not so much that Amy missed a word. "His servants say they stay in bedchambers in different wings, but you know how undependably servants report the tittle-tattle."

"One would think after the scandal with his mother he'd see the error in stooping low to take a mate," Miss Kent said.

"Exactly," Lady Alfonsine said. "But this proves bad breeding will out!"

Turning on her heel, Amy stalked back toward the drawing room, eyes narrowed, claws out.

Kenley caught her elbow and used her momentum to turn her like a fulcrum. "Don't pay attention to them." He was a fussy man with impeccable taste and a clear preference for his own gender when choosing a mate and the opposite when choosing a friend. "Those women are jealous."

She tugged at her arm. "I don't care if they're jealous, but they're not going to talk about Jermyn or his mother that way."

"What are you going to do?" Kenley asked. "Knock their heads together?"

"Do you think I can't?" She looked sideways at him. He hastily withdrew his hand.

But he was right. She shouldn't make a scene here, today. She didn't want the guests gossiping about her behavior. Rather, she wanted all the attention focused on the dreadful murder of her dear fiancé . . . which would happen very soon. So she kept walking toward the outdoors where an elegant luncheon was spread in the gazebo in the heart of the gardens. It was Jermyn's birthday luncheon, to be followed by a tragic and well-witnessed accident this evening and an elegant ball tonight.

The footman opened the wide doors and she stepped out onto the steps at the front of the house. Jermyn and Amy had moved into the manor house just in time, for the storm raged for three days, ripping trees from the earth, lashing rain at the windows, propelling giant waves toward the land to thrash at the cliffs and chew at the rocks. It had been an awesome display of nature, one that had sent the gardeners scurrying to clean up the flower beds, cut down the fallen trees and rake up the shredded leaves. Yet today no one would ever suspect the destruction wrought by the tempest; the estate was pristine, the sun shone from a clear blue sky and the marqess of Northcliff might have ordered this day specifically for his melodrama.

"Kenley, you're jealous that Northcliff is now unavailable, too." Lord Howland said mildly.

"Yes, but I don't parade my grief in front of Lord Northcliff's fiancée, for pity's sake!" Kenley sounded shocked, then added slyly, "Although, my dear Princess Disdain, if you would allow me to advise you on how to dress we could knock those witches to their metaphorical knees."

Amy grinned at the two brothers, so different and yet so kind. Jermyn had introduced them as his best friends and requested they care for her while he was arranging matters elsewhere. "But I don't care how I dress, and I don't care if I knock the witches to their knees, metaphorical or otherwise, and I most certainly don't care if Lady Alfonsine wants to climb my lord. Or you, either, Kenley. Neither of you has the stamina."

Kenley pressed his handkerchief to his trembling mouth. "Princess Disdain! How shocking!"

But she thought he was chortling.

And Lord Howland roared with laughter. "You're not shocked, Kenley. You're piqued that you didn't think of such a rejoinder!"

"True. Yet I do believe there is nothing more breath-taking than a woman so much in love she can't be made jealous."

Amy turned her head sharply to glare at him. "So much in love—what do you mean?"

Both brothers chuckled as if she'd made a witticism. *Did she act like a woman in love?*

Then Kenley sighed hugely. "Nevertheless, my offer stands. With your style and my wisdom, I could make you the most fashionable female in the *ton*."

How did a woman in love act?

She didn't want to talk about what was all the rage. She wanted to ask why he said she was in love. She wasn't in *love*. She had simply agreed to remain with Jermyn for the length of their year. Then they would decide if they should wed in a church ceremony . . . it meant nothing that they had yet to use the preventative against pregnancy and that the appearance of a child made the pagan ceremony permanent. If asked, she would say she still had no idea how she did feel about him . . . if he was her soul mate. She didn't know why she couldn't shoot him.

And even more important, she had no idea how he felt about her.

Except that he'd done everything to make her a part of his society, including giving her a bedchamber separated by the whole breadth of Summerwind Abbey from his. Of course, the rooms were connected by a secret passage, one which Jermyn trod every night, but no one knew that, apparently not even the servants.

"I've got Biggers and some French maid he hired working with all their hearts on my gown," she said in as casual a tone as she could produce. "I suspect they're both very good, but Kenley, you have to understand—I won't wear scratchy lace, I won't wear a train that I'm constantly tripping on, and I won't bear a neckline that I can't dance in for fear I'll flop out at the top."

Lord Howland laughed again, great hoots of amusement.

Kenley stopped walking and covered his eyes with his hand. "Flop out? *Flop out?* We do not use such a term in regards to your trim figure, my lady. And surely it wouldn't hurt you to just once avail yourself of Northcliff's vast resources."

"Northcliff has done nothing but spoil me since the day we met." Which the guests had been informed was last month while she visited Miss Victorine Sprott on the isle of Summerwind—which was as much of the truth as anyone needed to know, Jermyn said.

"Do you at least have something grand to wear for the ball celebrating Northcliff's birthday?" Kenley asked.

"The gown is very grand," she promised.

"Tell me about it," he urged.

"I don't know. I think it's pink." She tried to remember, but lately she'd been fitted for so many gowns. "Or blue."

"Pink or blue," Kenley soundlessly mouthed the words.

He seemed so distressed, she decided to give him something to make him happy. "I remember now. It's pink."

In a pleading tone, he said, "You're the style now. You're the newest thing. You're handsome, you captured the heart of the elusive Lord Northcliff, and it's rumored that you are a princess. Northcliff has even given you a marvelous nickname—Princess Disdain. All of the other ladies envy you that. But such fame is fleeting." Kenley earnestly knit his brow. "How do you expect to *stay* the thing if you don't *exert* yourself?"

"She'll stay the thing precisely because she doesn't give a spin. *I* think she's charming as she is." Lord Howland smiled as they approached the gazebo where the afternoon repast had been laid out.

"So she is." Kenley bowed to her in graceful homage.

"You're a dear man," she said. Then Jermyn looked up from his conversation with the elderly Lady Hamilton, and Amy no longer gave a hang about Kenley or Howland or any of the guests gathered in bright, chattering clumps. She saw only Jermyn, his strong figure, his gleaming auburn hair, his soft lips which so deftly brought her delight night after night . . .

Jermyn gave only the slightest of nods to her, then looked back at Lady Hamilton, giving her all his attention.

And like an idiot, Amy's heart twittered. He was so *nice*, taking care that a old woman isolated by her encroaching deafness.

Long tables were spread with white tablecloths, loaded with food and drink. Uniformed footmen circulated with champagne. Ladies in bright spring gowns and handsome gentlemen drifted along the paths admiring the flowers that had been so recently transplanted from the conservatory. Only a few shattered stumps stood as mute witness to the virulent attack of the ocean storm, and the beauty of the scene made Amy's heart catch.

When had she grown to love this place so much?

Again her gaze rested on Jermyn.

When she had learned to love him. It wasn't the place, it was the man who belonged with this place. Dear God, Kenley and Howland were right. She was hip-deep in love for Jermyn, the marquess of Northcliff.

Did he . . . did he love her, too?

"Princess Disdain, do you know everyone here?" Kenley asked.

She tore her gaze from Jermyn and stared absently at Kenley. "Huh?"

"Do you know all the guests?" he repeated.

She looked them over. "I've been introduced to most of them."

And she didn't care a farthing for any of them. All she cared about was Jermyn. Did he love her? She thought perhaps he did. He loved her body, of that she was positive. Yet in addition, he acted quite fond. He believed her no matter how absurd the tale she told, and she freely admitted her tales were extraordinary, although true.

But did that mean he loved her? She didn't know. The problem was—she didn't know how to recognize love. She knew sisterly love, or fatherly love, but not this kind. Not the kind that battered her soul as surely as the storm had battered the cliffs.

"Do you remember their names?" Lord Howland asked.

"What?" Why was Howland interrupting her thoughts?

"Do you remember the guests' names?" he repeated slowly and patiently.

"Of course. Remembering names is an art learned by every princess." And perfected by years on the road when knowing a name could mean the difference between a swat with the broom or a meal kindly given.

Kenley's eyes sparked with interest. "So you're really a princess?"

"As surely as I'm a peddler." She smirked at Kenley's crestfallen expression. If he only knew the truth!

She had no time to further examine her emotions for Jermyn. The time for the play had begun. But later tonight when the drama had been completed and the villain vanquished, she would talk to Jermyn. She would tell him straight-out that she loved him. Then she'd ask if he loved her, and hold him while she waited for the answer, and—

"Northcliff wanted us to introduce you to any unknowns," Kenley said peevishly. "How may we perform our sworn duty if you won't pay attention?"

She shook off the feeling of anticipation and concentrated on the task at hand. "I don't know those two gentlemen standing off to the side. There, by the table with the bowl of iced punch."

Lord Howland squinted through the sunshine at the two well-dressed older men with the serious faces. "I can't see that far. Dreadful vision, you know. Kenley?"

"I never thought I'd see those two outside of London! Mr. Irving Livingstone and Oscar Ingram, earl of Stoke," Kenley said.

"Really? I wonder what brings them out?" Turning to Amy, Lord Howland explained, "They were close friends of Jermyn's father. I think during his reign here they used to visit, but it seems they've hardly left White's since. I'm surprised Northcliff thought to invite them."

"I don't think he did." In fact, Amy knew very well Jermyn had not, for she'd studied the guest list to familiarize herself with the names and those two hadn't been on it.

Kenley's voice developed a cooing note. "And look at that gentleman. He looks mean and tough—and handsome!—not at all the sort to frequent a *ton* party."

"Where?" Amy asked.

"There by the stump of that big tree."

She spotted him right away.

He was watching her.

Of course a great many people were. She was Jermyn's fiancée, and as such, important.

But the way this fellow watched her was different. He *was* handsome, he *did* look mean and tough, and he studied her as if she were his to approve. And when he had made his decision, he nodded at her as if sending her a message.

But she didn't understand what it was, or why he thought he had the right to send it.

"Well!" Kenley said in tones of despair. "You seem to have made another conquest. Do you know him?"

"Not at all," she answered. But she had trouble taking her gaze from him. Something about him did seem familiar . . .

"Here comes Lord Northcliff," Kenley said.

Promptly Amy forgot the stranger. She forgot Kenley, Howland, the wretched lot of the guests. Jermyn was striding toward her, his auburn hair shining with sunlight, his brown eyes smiling, his clothing impeccable, and he was hers. All hers.

"Have you noticed that whenever his Princess Disdain is around, Northcliff has eyes for no one else?" Lord Howland inquired.

"You don't have to rub it in," Kenley said sadly. Then as Jermyn came within earshot, he waved his gloved hand. "Ah, Lord Northcliff, how well you look this afternoon!"

"Thank you. I feel well indeed." Taking Amy's hand, he held it in both of his. "As long as my princess is nigh."

Amy blushed. Jermyn had a way of looking at her and making her feel . . . warm, wanton, alive. As if all they needed was a moment alone and he would give her passion such as she'd never experienced.

Moreover, it was true. The two of them had only to be together alone for the merest moment and they were in each other's arms, discovering new ways of desire.

Now he stripped off one glove and placed a kiss on the back of her fingers, then in her palm.

"Oh, piffle," Kenley said in disgust.

Lord Howland clapped his brother on the shoulder. "Win some, lose some," he said. "The trick is not to wager on a fixed game."

"Thank you for your lofty advice, Lord Social Graces." Kenley stalked toward the tables.

Lord Howland nodded toward the path behind them. "Northcliff, is that chap a friend of yours? He looks quite unique and, if I may be so bold, rather out of place."

Amy turned to watch another strange gentleman approach. He was of average height, about fifty years old and twelve stone. The bags under his eyes drooped, his cheeks drooped, his neck drooped, his earlobes drooped. He had a long body and short legs, with a jolly belly that thrust at his blue waistcoat and brown jacket and drooped over his brown plaid trousers. As if he never walked out of doors, he picked his way through the graveled paths, lifting his blue tasseled boots high.

"Ah. Yes." Jermyn watched Amy with amusement. "That's my uncle, Mr. Harrison Edmondson."

She had expected a villain. Instead, she saw a basset hound—morose, but friendly.

"Oh, my!" She started forward. "I should greet him."

"Let me walk with you." Jermyn caught her hand and placed it on his arm.

"Of course. I forgot. You have to introduce me," she said in disgust. The house party had begun only yesterday. She'd met people like Kenley and Howland whom she liked, people like Alfonsine, countess of Cuvier, whom she despised. But while she found the dozens of guests to be friendly or not friendly, entertaining or dreadful bores—in other words, normal human beings—the constant barrage of rigid British courtesy stifled her so much she found herself fighting a constant fatigue.

Yet Jermyn insisted on admiring her: loudly, publicly, and constantly. He had decided his fiancée would be a success. Since apparently she was the first female in whom he'd ever taken a public interest, his guests followed his lead . . . although she was not so foolish as to imagine they did so gladly. Certainly the ladies in the drawing room had proved that.

Uncle Harrison's eyes sparked with interest as she approached. Obviously, he'd heard the rumors about her.

"Uncle Harrison, I have news which will no doubt bring you great joy." Jermyn heartily shook his uncle's hand. "This is my fiancée, Princess Amy of Beaumontagne."

Amy glanced at Jermyn in surprise. They'd agreed to let the rumors about her title swirl through society; she because she dreaded a return to the elaborate courtesies due a princess, he because the mystery would give her a greater cachet and ease her traverse through English society. Yet for his uncle, Jermyn introduced her with all honors . . . and she wondered why.

Harrison's avuncular display of surprise and pleasure almost convinced Amy that he was innocent of any wrongdoing. "Princess Amy of Beaumontagne!" He bowed with all the etiquette of her father's oldest courtier. "It's an honor to meet you. And my boy!" He pumped Jermyn's hand. "Congratulations on finding the perfect bride. I envy you no end."

Amy heard no ring of falseness. Where was the Uncle Harrison she expected: oily-tongued, murderous, and deceitful?

"It's good to meet Jermyn's only relative." She gave Jermyn a wide-eyed, adoring look. "He's such a wonderful man, and I can't wait to hear all the stories about his childhood."

"He was a wild lad, I can tell you that. Always getting his cuffs filthy as he ran about stirring up trouble." Harrison cast a roguish glance at Jermyn. "Especially after his mother . . . left us."

Jermyn's smile disappeared.

Ah. There he was—Uncle Harrison, the villain she expected. "Yes, I can see that without a mother's guidance, young Jermyn would run wild," she said cheerfully.

Harrison's face fell further, its drapes and folds looking like a cook's first attempt at egg soufflé.

She continued to chat, drawing the attention away from Jermyn. "When I lost my home and my father, I became rebellious myself. I was the despair of my sister, and when I left her, I know she must have worried."

"You mean when you lost her," Jermyn corrected.

"No, when I left her—" For the first time, Amy realized what Jermyn had thought. He had thought that her sister was dead. "I wanted to travel alone, so I left her two years ago in Scotland."

"Left her?" Jermyn's voice grew quiet. His eyes grew bleak. "No. She's your sister. Your family. You wouldn't have left her."

Perhaps Amy should mention the letter she'd sent three weeks ago . . . but not now. Now when the hard line of his chin radiated cruelty and she shivered at the cold that radiated off of him. Yet she wouldn't lie to him. Between them, only the truth would do. "But I did leave her."

Jermyn stared at Amy, at her earnest upturned face, at the supple body which inevitably moved him to desire, at the shining perfection he'd grown to worship—and he saw the first cracks in the pedestal he'd placed beneath her feet.

"Excuse us, Uncle." Taking her arm, Jermyn led her away from the party.

He spoke to the guests as they walked, smiling, nodding, accepting birthday congratulations, keeping up the façade of the proud marquess. All his life, he'd cultivated that veneer, for it kept the laughter about his mother's abandonment at bay. When he'd decided to take an exiled princess for his bride, he'd known there would be more laughter, but he hadn't cared. For the first time, the face he presented to the world had represented his real feelings: happy, excited, superior.

Now . . . now a savage sense of betrayal carried him along. This woman, this *princess*, had abandoned her sister? In the wilds of Scotland? She'd walked away from a member of her family?

She'd walked away as surely as his mother had walked away from him. Without a backward glance. Without a moment of guilt. He'd been making assumptions about Amy . . . were any of them true, or had he been living in a fool's paradise?

Although Amy squirmed, he marched her along with him toward the cliffs. Toward the place where they'd sat and stared out to sea and she'd duped him into confessing his past, his fears . . . "My God. What an idiot I've been!"

"Jermyn, listen to me, it's not what you think." She used a reasonable tone on him, a tone that grated on his nerves.

"Wait until we're completely away from the party." He made no effort to hide his cutting contempt, and he kept his fingers wrapped tightly around her elbow.

She didn't listen to him. Of course not. "You think I abandoned Clarice like you think your mother abandoned you, but it's not true."

"Wait," he said again. He couldn't bear it if any of the guests heard this . . . this muddle that he'd made of his life.

"Clarice and I disagreed about what we should do with ourselves." Amy sounded so heartfelt.

He moved her along more quickly. They got to the edge of the cliff. He let go of her gladly, not wanting to touch her for fear she'd contaminate him.

Amy continued, "I tried to make Clarice listen, but she is my elder sister. She thought I was still a child. She insisted we do as she thought best."

But as badly as he wanted nothing to do with Amy, he just as much wanted to hurt her for betraying Clarice. Clarice? Hell, for betraying him. For betraying his stupid dreams of a woman who felt loyalty where loyalty was due and returned love in full measure. Grabbing her shoulders, he asked, "Where is she now? What is she doing? Does she miss you every day? Does she feel guilty because she chased you away? Is she starving and in pain and you aren't there for her?" He could see that she resented his questioning.

Too bad.

"I didn't abandon my sister!" she said. "She was safe in that household and she was a powerful woman, a force to be reckoned with! And I saw the way Lord Hepburn looked at her. I thought he was in love and I was right. She married him. She's a countess. She's going to have a baby!"

"You write her?" At least that was something.

"Yes, I—"

"So you know about her marriage and her child through her letters? You keep them? You can show them to me?"

Amy's eyes sparked, and the color changed to the green of poison. She looked like she had the first time he'd met her: hostile and bitter. "I don't have letters. We have kept in contact through advertisements, just like I hoped to do with my grandmother."

"Damn you! You won't even send a note to your sister?" Another hope dashed. Amy wouldn't allow even so feeble a connection as the written word. All those years he'd hoped for a letter from his mother . . . had Clarice hoped, too? "What's Clarice going to do to you from Scotland?"

"I don't know." Amy crossed her arms over her chest, shutting herself away from him. "Possibly nothing, but I'm a princess, Jermyn. Until Clarice knows that I'm married, she'll want me to live the bright dream of being a princess in Beaumontagne. So I didn't write because I know the price of royalty."

"Your father paid that price."

She caught her breath.

Jermyn knew he'd been brutal. He didn't care.

Her voice rose. "Yes, and if called to battle, I'll gladly fight. But I won't sacrifice myself on the altar of an arranged marriage and that's where princesses are sacrificed."

"Excuses."

"I'm not making excuses. I'm explaining myself, although why I'm bothering when you can't tell the difference is beyond me."

"You don't even feel guilt." He didn't try to temper his disgust.

"Of course I feel guilt. I've had experiences that made me grow up since I left Clarice two years ago, not the least of which is the past two months." She waved at his house where tonight they would put on their play. "But I'm not ready to fling myself off the cliff about it."

"You don't dare go to your grandmother. You don't know where your oldest sister is. And yet you abandoned your last scrap of family you have left." He drew away from Amy as if she were diseased. She was like his mother. He'd married a woman like his mother. "Even if you keep your promise to remain with me for a year, I'll wonder if you intend to leave as soon as soon as the time is over."

"No. Yes. I don't know." She wrung her hands. "What do you want?"

"I don't want *that*."

"I'll keep my promise!" she shouted.

He lowered his voice. "Don't. I don't want you. Not a flighty woman like you."

"A flighty woman like me?" She had the gall to betray astonishment. "Are you telling me to leave?"

"Exactly." Better to have her go now than to wait for the morning when he woke and found her gone.

"What about our plan for tonight? You . . . you need me."

"Anyone can play your part. I'll send Biggers to Uncle Harrison—he'll perform well."

"But I want to know how this would end." She stepped toward him, urgent, beautiful . . . toxic. "You're condemning me for a sin I haven't yet committed! And I . . . I . . ."

"You what?" He lashed at her with his tone.

"I love you."

The waves crashed against the base of the cliff. The seagulls wheeled overhead. The breeze carried the tendrils of her hair around the sweetness of her face.

And he laughed. Laughed at the words he had hoped most to hear. Laughed while his heart cracked. "What an amazingly convenient moment you've picked to confess that."

"But I didn't know it before." She gripped his arm. "I just discovered it a few minutes ago in the garden. Kenley and Howland told me it was so, but I didn't believe them. Then when I saw you talking to that old woman, I felt such a tide of—"

"Manure rising in you?"

She gasped as if he'd slapped her. Her eyes filled with tears. "Jermyn . . ." she faltered.

He couldn't stand to see her cry. He wanted to wrap her in his arms and soothe her pain, tell her he didn't mean it, tell her that he loved her, too. But he knew better. He'd learned his lesson many years ago, and he'd learned it well. He had only temporarily forgotten it. "Pack," he said. "Leave now. Take whatever you want. Go to Beaumontagne or wherever you wish, but don't stay here to break my heart. You said I was stupid to distrust all women because of my mother, and I had begun to believe you." He walked away. "I'm not so stupid after all."

Chapter 24

*L*ivid, Amy stared as Jermyn stalked away in high dudgeon, a stiff, proud figure. Yes, the marquess of Northcliff had returned.

Turning, she wiped her cheeks on her sleeve and stalked in the opposite direction.

Beside her, a deep voice spoke. "Where are you going?"

She glanced at the man who had so smoothly joined her. He was the gentleman Kenley had swooned over, the dark-haired, hard-eyed fellow in the dark suit. The one who looked vaguely familiar—not that she cared right now, not when she viewed him through a red haze of fury.

"I'm going to the house," she said.

"To pack, I hope."

"Yes, how did you know?" She stopped and turned on him, snapping like an angry dog. "I'm going to leave here, leave Jermyn and his ridiculous prejudices and his stupid opinions and his superior attitude."

"But you're a princess. He's not superior to you." The fellow said the right things, just the sort of stuff she wanted to hear.

"Someone should tell him that. I'm going to go back to Beaumontagne and take my position as a princess and use my authority to have Jermyn beheaded." She drew her finger across her throat.

"That seems a little greater punishment than he deserves for . . . whatever he's done." The stranger sounded amused.

"You wouldn't say that if you knew." She started walking again, her arms straight, her fists clenched at her side, but she turned toward the cliffs. "All right. I'll have him manacled to the wall in the dungeon for years while every day I'll go down and taunt him with his helplessness."

"That is more reasonable."

"*Then* I'll have him beheaded."

"Why?" The stranger sounded patient.

"Because any man who judges my actions harshly deserves torture and imprisonment and . . ." Her steps slowed.

His mother had abandoned him, and he decided that Amy had abandoned her sister.

Well, she had, but not really. "I'm not going to abandon him because I'm *flighty*. I'm not *flighty*." Dreadful word!

"I hope not." The stranger sounded rather grave, and he watched her as if the matter was of exceeding interest to him.

"And I'm not abandoning him, I'm leaving."

"A sensible decision."

"Exactly. I'm making a sensible decision to leave where I'm not welcome." She speeded up again, taking a turn toward the cottage where she and Jermyn had spent their honeymoon.

"This is not the way to the house where you can pack," the stranger pointed out.

"What?" she asked absently.

She was not flighty! Leaving Clarice had been the result of years and years of frustration and the need to show her older sister that she was a responsible adult who could survive on her own.

She slowed again.

Softly she said, "I do now realize I should have tried harder to talk to Clarice about our plans instead of sulking like a child." And running away.

Amy had been in trouble when she met Miss Victorine. She had been almost raped, and close to death from exposure and starvation. She would never tell Clarice that because she knew very well that even now Clarice would take responsibility for Amy's suffering—and it wasn't Clarice's fault. It was Amy's. She had imagined she could wander England alone on her own when in fact it had taken the sisters' combined wit and experience to survive the rigors of homelessness. Amy had been arrogant and impetuous, and she'd paid the price.

Clarice had been her sister and companion for years, and Amy hadn't wanted to admit it, but she missed her. She'd come to realize what she'd lost, and she wanted to see her sister.

Both her sisters, Sorcha as well as Clarice. She even missed that grand old dragon herself, Grandmamma. Jermyn was right. She wanted her family back again . . . and she would not take the chance of losing Jermyn as she had lost the others. As she had lost her dearest poppa.

Slowly she lowered herself onto a bench outside the cottage. She wanted to leave Summerwind Abbey right now, but a heaviness of the limbs kept her in place. She was tired. The quarrel must have drained her, for she felt almost faint. She wanted to be alone to collect herself.

Yet uninvited, the stranger sat with her.

"Oh, go away." She was surprised to hear the peevish tone in her voice.

He didn't go away. "Amy, do you know who I am?"

"Should I?" She didn't care about *him*. Why should she care about him?

"I'm Prince Rainger."

For all the sense that made, he might have been speaking a foreign language, one she couldn't easily comprehend. She turned her gaze on him and stared unseeingly.

His black hair was tossed in studied carelessness about his face—a face that was not gaunt, but worn by life and distilled into strength. His eyes were brown, rimmed by dark lashes and guarded. So guarded. Yet in their depths she saw the remnants of a lad she'd once known, and slowly she realized the truth. "Of course. I should have recognized you. But you've . . . changed." He'd been such a spoiled boy, and now he was the kind of man who caused women to swoon and men to walk warily.

"Seven years in a dungeon will do that." He scrutinized her as she absorbed that information. "Queen Claudia wants you to return."

Queen Claudia . . . Grandmamma. "Is she well?" Amy asked eagerly.

"Very well, the last time I saw her. I believe she's indestructible."

"I expect so. I hope so. And . . . have you seen my sisters?"

He smiled. "Princess Clarice has already scorned me as a suitor."

"She's married."

"She wasn't when she scorned me." His mouth turned up in the corner as if he were painfully amused. "Then she sent me on a wild goose chase—after you. She made sure you had time to get away, and that piece of deviousness I hadn't expected of her."

Amy absorbed the truth. Clarice had given Amy the chance she desired. The chance to make her own destiny. And hadn't she done a marvelous job of it?

The world whirled around her. She put her hand to her forehead.

"Are you all right?"

"Yes, I'm just tired."

"Are you?" He stared at her searchingly. "And feeling ill?"

"I'm fine!" Just because she'd known him since she was in the cradle, he had no right to interfere so outrageously. And she wasn't overreacting, either! "Have you seen Sorcha?"

"No. I haven't."

"I miss her." Amy's eyes filled with tears. "For all that I haven't seen her in ten years, I still miss her."

"She is your sister." He extended his handkerchief to her.

Amy took it and blew her nose. Hard. Why had this wave of nostalgia ripped over her? It had to be because of that louse, Jermyn. He'd resurrected all the pain of separation and left her stripped of pride and alone. She couldn't wait to leave him. She would leave him *right now*. She stood. "How did you trace me, Rainger?"

"When Lord Northcliff sent a query to the Beaumontagne Embassy about what was happening in the country, I managed to, er, intercept the message and I followed up on my own." He stood also, and extended his hand. "Go with me to Beaumontagne now. I'll take you to your grandmother and there you'll be safe."

She stared at his palm. Looked at him. And was stricken by a dreadful revelation. "I can't leave. I swore I'd stay with Jermyn for a year."

"You're a princess."

"And as such, I am bound by my vows." She started walking back to the party. Then turned back to him. "Isn't that right, Rainger?"

Reluctantly he nodded, then watched her walk away. In a soft voice, he said, "I'm bound by my vow of revenge, too, Princess, but I think you may have thwarted my plans in a most permanent way."

She returned to the path that led to the gazebo and walked toward the party. As she met the guests, they either stared at her or their eyes slid away, and everyone turned to watch Jermyn's reaction when he saw her.

Clearly, the guests who an hour ago had been so pleasant knew that she and Jermyn had quarreled. They'd seen Jermyn return without her. They thought the engagement was over.

She glanced at Harrison Edmondson. His gloating satisfaction sent a chill through her.

Of course. She couldn't go to Jermyn now. She couldn't explain, plead, make him see sense. They had carefully planned the scene for this evening, but this— this was better, more convincing, seemingly real because it was real.

And what did a few hours more matter? She would talk to Jermyn tonight after all the drama was over. Even if he didn't want to talk to her, she would make him listen. She wasn't going to lose someone else to her own misplaced pride. She knew the cost of that. She had paid that price, at least.

Dropping her head in well-acted mortification, she turned and dragged herself back to the house.

Tonight Harrison Edmondson would get his comeuppance.

Tonight he would kill his nephew while all the world watched.

* * *

The gown was pink satin with puffed sleeves and, despite Amy's bold pronouncement, had a neckline so low she feared she would indeed flop out. Her black hair had been cut with fashionable bangs and dressed by her maid with a tall pink feather. Her white gloves reached over her elbows and fastened with a long row of real pearl buttons that drove Amy insane with their fussy show. She sat straight-backed in her bedchamber.

Biggers hadn't come to approve her ball gown and that, more than anything, proved Jermyn had washed his hands of her. Biggers had been an interfering fusspot about His Lordship's fiancée, but he'd left her and her maid alone to prepare for the grand occasion of Jermyn's birthday ball.

Amy glanced at the clock on the mantel. Ten more minutes until six o'clock. The sun still rode high in the sky, providing plenty of light for their dramatic piece. The audience would soon be in place. The ticking of the pendulum marked the moments of her life, and Amy waited, tense with her anticipation for her cue.

"It's time, miss," her maid said.

Squaring her shoulders, Amy stood and moved toward the door. Purposely she and Jermyn had planned that Harrison Edmondson's room be within easy walking distance of hers and that she should go to him at exactly six o'clock. She had memorized the route, and she made her way through the corridors now frequented only by maids hurrying with ironed gowns in their arms and valets with polished boots. At Harrison's door she stopped, took a deep breath, and rapped hard with her knuckles. Then she slumped and tried to look small and dejected.

Harrison's valet answered, clearly annoyed at being interrupted while he prepared his master. "What is it—" His eyes widened as he recognized Amy. "Miss! Your Ladyship! Your Highness!"

In a small voice, Amy begged, "Please, could I speak to Mr. Edmondson? It's imperative."

"Of . . . course. I . . . yes, that is . . . if you would wait here." The valet hurried away.

She watched him, idly thinking he looked nothing like any valet she'd ever seen. Rather, he looked like a fighter who made his living with his fists. Perhaps that explained why Mr. Edmondson's clothing was so very peculiar.

She could hear a low, hurried discussion inside, and as she waited she concentrated on how much she missed her sisters, on her father's death and Jermyn's fury with her. By the time Harrison appeared in the doorway, shrugging into his coat, she had worked up a despondent expression and a sheen of tears.

"Miss . . . Your Highness." Harrison's perpetually hangdog appearance was accentuated by the fashionable garb that fit him so ill, and by the confused pucker between his brows. "Is there some assistance I can show you?"

The valet adjusted Harrison's coat and observed them out of the corners of his eyes.

"Would it be possible for you to walk with me a little?

I have questions . . . that is, concerns with which I hope you might help me." Amy twisted her handkerchief in her hands and managed a fair imitation of misery.

"As you wish, Your Highness. At your service." To his valet, he said, "Merrill, keep an eye on things. On *all* of the things we talked about."

Which she thought was an odd command, but she didn't have time to worry about it now. Instead she started toward the other wing of the house. Toward Jermyn's bedchamber. In a soft, trembling voice, she said, "I fear you may have heard that Jermyn and I had a disagreement this afternoon."

"Yes. Such a shame when young love comes to grief." Mr. Edmondson glanced at her. "You did come to grief, didn't you?"

"It was just a lovers' tiff, really. I didn't know he would get so upset, so angry with me. So I sent him a note and I got a vile answer. Vile!" She waved the letter she had filched from Jermyn's desk, one in his handwriting . . . but to his steward on another estate. "So I was bold. Wanton even, but oh, Mr. Edmondson, don't think badly of me. I love him so!" Pressing her handkerchief to her lips, she made small sobbing noises and watched Harrison from the corners of her eyes.

"There, there." He flapped one hand in her direction and looked around for assistance.

At once she stopped sobbing. She didn't want him getting assistance. She needed to talk to him on her own.

Grabbing his hand, she pressed it in hers. "All I want is your nephew's love. I live to support him in every way possible. When I have the good fortune to be his wife, I will care for his health and never let him risk himself in any careless endeavor. More than anything—I beg of you, don't think badly of me for being so reckless—more than anything, I want to bear his children and continue the Edmondson line."

The sagging lines of Harrison's face grew rigid with his rejection of the idea.

And Amy realized that with the mention of heirs, she had captured his attention in a way Jermyn had never imagined.

"I know what that must mean to you, to know that your beloved nephew's children will continue this noble line, but Jermyn is . . ." She turned away, her shoulders shaking as if she were crying. "You will think me licentious, but I went to his bedchamber to beg his pardon."

"Did you?" Harrison no longer sounded sympathetic. He sounded sharp.

"He wouldn't listen to me. He . . . he had been drinking, and he was so angry. Destructive. He threw things. He was walking on the railing on his balcony, threatening to throw himself off. Are you familiar with that room, Mr. Edmondson?"

"Yes. Yes, I am." Harrison's voice was eager now.

She turned on him in magnificent despair. "The balcony hangs over the cliffs."

"If he jumps, he will fall to his death and the ocean will wash him away," Harrison said.

"His valet couldn't convince him to come down. He wouldn't listen to me—indeed, when I spoke to him, he seemed even more suicidal. Please, Mr. Edmondson, you're his uncle. He'll listen to you. You can convince him to live for the sake of his future children!"

"My dear princess, I'll go to him at once." Harrison's eyes gleamed. "I'm sure I can dissuade him from this deadly behavior. Just leave him to me."

"Oh, thank you, Mr. Edmondson. I knew you'd do everything you could for my dearest, sweetest Jermyn." She watched with sharp contentment as Harrison hurried away.

Biggers, hidden from view, now stepped out from around the corner and stared at her in openmouthed amazement. "That was magnificent, Your Highness."

"Wasn't it?"

"I thought you were leaving."

"Oh, no. I'm not leaving." She bent a eloquent gaze on him. "Not now, not at the end of the year, not ever. Better gather an audience, Biggers. The last act of the play is about to begin."

"Come, come," Biggers called as he waved the guests into the seats placed in the garden. "We should take our places and conceal ourselves so that we may surprise His Lordship in the proper manner."

The chairs were set behind shrubs and behind trees, and most of the guests seated themselves without grumbling.

But Lord Smith-Kline complained, "B'God, Biggers, it seems we could have waited in the ballroom to offer our good wishes for Lord Northcliff's thirtieth birthday."

"But he would be expecting it there." Amy batted her eyes and tried to look like the biggest featherbrain ever to walk the earth. "So this venue makes sense."

"To whom?"

"It makes this party a real surprise," she said. "And I do love a real surprise, don't you?"

"Oh, I suppose." With her fall from grace this afternoon, Lord Smith-Kline no longer felt the need to exert himself in being polite. "Hey, you there! Footman! Bring me a light for my cigar."

Kenley sidled over beside Amy and seated himself. "This setting *is* rather eccentric, Your Highness."

"Trust me, Kenley. You'll enjoy every moment of this." She allowed a fillip of mischief to color her smile.

"Really?" Kenley looked up at the balcony clearly lit by the westering sun. "What do you have arranged?"

"Wait and see." She stood and put her finger to her lips. "Only please. Let's be quiet."

The first blast of shouting from inside the master's chamber caught everyone by surprise.

She sank into her seat, satisfied that their plan was proceeding as they had hoped.

"Damn you, Harrison, how dare you interfere with me?" It was Jermyn's voice, slurred, furious and revoltingly arrogant. "I'm the marquess of Northcliff, the head of the family, the youngest surviving member of a noble line. I'll marry who I please."

Mr. Edmondson was quieter and also hidden from sight. "I would merely like to point out that the female with whom you've involved yourself came to my bed-chamber tonight."

Kenley turned to Amy in horror.

Everyone turned to Amy in horror.

"You didn't?" Kenley whispered.

"Please." She made an incredulous moue at him, then at the fashionable group. "No woman has ever stooped so low."

The *ton* nodded in a single accord. They must truly despise Harrison to agree so unanimously.

"Tonight?" Jermyn sounded sharp and quite sober.

"Yes, tonight," Mr. Edmondson said.

Amy tensed as she waited for Jermyn to proclaim he'd sent her away.

Instead he laughed unsteadily. "Tonight you saw her. I should have known you'd say that."

"Question the servants," Harrison said. "I assure you it's true. But after her disgraceful lack of respect for you and your authority this afternoon, she should be nothing to you."

"But I love her." Jermyn's voice took on a broken-hearted tone. "Have you ever loved a woman, Uncle? It's the most beautiful thing in the world. I would for-give her anything just for the pleasure of her company. You didn't really let her into your room, did you?" Jermyn staggered into view on the balcony: sham-bling, disheveled, with his hair standing on end. He wore his black cape which he tossed about with many a grand flourish. A scarlet scarf hung loose around his neck, and he waved a pistol.

Below him everyone gasped and a few hid more securely behind their trees.

"Because if you did," Jermyn took careful aim inside, "I'll have to shoot you right now."

"Go ahead." Harrison remained hidden in the shadows of the room, but Amy knew why he sounded so blithe about the prospect of being killed.

All the barrels of all the firearms in Summerwind Abbey had been stuffed, and although Jermyn had had them cleaned, Harrison didn't know that, and hoped Jermyn would fire and end his own life.

Instead Jermyn extended the pistol butt-first toward his uncle. "No, I can't shoot you. You shoot me."

Harrison sighed in such patent disgust Amy thought he had lost what little respect he had for his intoxicated nephew. "I'm not going to shoot you. Not with that pistol. Pay attention to what I'm saying. Your fiancée came to my bedchamber, but I rejected her. This demonstrates how unfit you are to care for yourself."

"I'm not unfit. I can do whatever I want."

"I was told you were trying to walk the parapet. In your condition, that's ridiculous and impossible." Harrison's contempt whipped at Jermyn.

"Ridiculous and impossible, huh? Well, I walked it earlier this afternoon right before I drank that third bottle of brandy."

"Only three bottles? You can't hold your liquor. Here, drink this and show me what you can do." Harrison walked into view. He pressed a bottle of brandy into Jermyn's hand.

Amy watched with satisfaction as the guests carefully shifted to better watch the drama. None of the company could tear their fascinated gazes from the scene above, and no one made a sound.

With a foolishly resolute expression on his face, Jermyn vaulted onto the railing. Tilting back his head, he took a long pull from the bottle, then walked lightly from one end of the parapet to the other.

Two of the women gasped. Their escorts hushed them. The audience was enthralled.

With a formal, courtly bow at his uncle, Jermyn said, "I have wonderful balance. No matter how deep in my cups I get, I never fall."

"It only takes once." Mr. Edmondson gave an peculiar cackle.

Jermyn waved one leg in the air and looked down at his uncle. "I don't know what you mean, but see, Uncle? I am perfectly capable of walking, and while way up here with the breeze blowing off the sea, I've made a decision. I'm going to wed Princess Amy and raise a dozen children to be my heirs. And Uncle, I'm sorry to say this, but Mr. Irving Livingstone and Oscar Ingram, earl of Stoke, showed me the lost codicil in my father's will which requires me on my thirtieth birthday to take over the administration of my own fortune—"

Amy sat forward. She knew nothing of this.

"—and henceforth, I have no need of your services."

"Nephew," Harrison interrupted as he picked up a chair, "you're not going to eliminate me."

"Did you hide the codicil from me so I never heard about it?" Jermyn's tone had changed, become sober and intense.

"I did."

"What makes you think you can change my father's will and get away with it?"

"This." Raising the chair, Harrison smashed it across Jermyn's knees.

Jermyn flew into the air as if he had jumped—which Amy knew he had. With a loud, long, dramatic shriek and a great fluttering of his black cape, he disappeared over the edge of the cliff.

Amy watched Harrison lean over the railing, evil glee on his face.

A moment of stunned silence hovered over the immobile audience. Then as one, they shouted. They screamed. They rose to their feet.

Harrison saw them. He jolted backward. His sagging features convulsed as he heard the horrified outcry. He ran inside the master's bedchamber then, chased by Biggers and a large footman, he ran back out onto the balcony.

Amy smiled at his terror.

"Your Highness, have you lost your mind to smile at such a time?" Kenley was shaking. He couldn't hide his revulsion. "Your fiancé is *gone*."

"It's not what you think," she assured him.

Then a female shriek from the edge of the cliff caught her attention. "Oh, dear God," Miss Kent cried, "I can see his body."

"Whose body?" Amy asked.

"You don't know what you're doing, do you?" Kenley spoke in a pleading tone. "You don't realize what's happened?"

"There's no body." Jermyn had said he'd leap onto a shelf of rock and climb into the sea cave to hide. "You'll see."

But the laments grew louder.

Lord Howland looked over the edge of the cliff, clapped his hand over his mouth, and ran away.

Lady Alfonsine looked over the edge of the cliff, turned away, and burst into what looked like genuine tears.

Amy refused to be alarmed. "There might be something down there, but certainly not a body," she assured Kenley again. Ludicrous, really, the way people saw what they expected to see. She walked to the edge of the cliff. She looked down.

On a ledge thirty feet below, she saw a dark shape. It did look like a body, but that was impossible. Except . . . except black material, like the cloth of Jermyn's cape, covered the figure and fluttered in the wind. And a lock of auburn hair sticking out from the hood caught the late sunlight . . .

"Jermyn?" she called down. It was a ruse. He should have told her first. "Jermyn, this isn't funny."

No one answered from below.

Her breath hurt her chest. She scanned the cliffs, looking for him. Louder, much louder, she shouted, "Jermyn, you promised this wasn't dangerous."

Vaguely she heard Kenley say, "She's gone mad with grief."

Someone took her shoulders and tried to lead her away.

She jerked herself free and leaned over the edge again. "Jermyn, answer me *now!*"

Jermyn didn't appear.

She sank to her knees in the grass. She saw a flash of scarlet below the black cape. A scarlet as bright as the scarf Jermyn wore.

Jermyn . . . That body below was *Jermyn*.

She rose slowly off her knees. She couldn't believe it. This wasn't possible. Jermyn had promised, he had *promised* this wasn't dangerous. He'd said he was familiar with every inch of the cliff. He'd said he'd done this trick before and it was foolproof.

But who was the fool now? The man who'd gone over the edge? Or the woman he'd left alone to mourn?

Why hadn't she known that she should go to him right away, make up their fight, take the opportunity to make love?

Now she would never see him again. Never see him in this life. Never see him in the sunshine, in the candlelight, touch him in love, breathe in his scent, be with him . . .

"May God damn your soul to hell, Harrison Edmondson!" She lifted her fist to the balcony.

The women around her gasped at the language.

The men milled about, helpless in the face of her fury and grief.

And everyone moved aside as she stalked toward the house. Toward Harrison Edmondson. Toward revenge.

She didn't see Lord Smith-Kline get out his telescope and focus on the form below. She didn't hear him announce, "That's not Northcliff. That's a woman down there—and she's been there for a long, long time."

Chapter 25

*H*arrison Edmondson marched along the corridors of Summerwind Abbey, hearing the sounds of lamentation from the crowd outside fade as his little escort led him farther into the main part of the house.

With Walter on one side of him, a hulking young footman on the other side, Biggers at his back, and Merrill roaming the halls, he considered his odds of escape good. Not great, for every snob in the whole bloody *ton* had seen him knock the little pustule Jermyn off the railing. But he knew that if he waited on a trial he'd hang, so when opportunity presented itself, he would make a dash.

And as they rounded the corner, opportunity appeared. Behind him a door opened. Someone stepped out.

"Who . . . ?" Biggers began.

Harrison turned in time to see Merrill bring a bat down on Biggers's head. Biggers twirled and went down, unconscious and bleeding at the temple.

"Good man." Harrison nodded at his valet. Merrill was turning out to be worth the hiring.

The youthful footman gawped at the valet, at Biggers, lying facedown on the carpet, and at Walter, who gestured at him and snarled, "Get out!"

The youngster's eyes grew wide, and he scuttled away.

"I've sent to the stable for a horse, Mr. Edmondson," Walter said.

Harrison snorted. He hadn't ridden a horse for ten years. "I want my coach."

"So many coaches have arrived that I can't get yours out of the carriage house." Walter broke into a sweat. He knew damned good and well if Harrison went down, he'd take Walter with him.

It was good to have motivated allies.

"Then give me one of the others." When Walter tried to object, Harrison exploded with impatience. "For God's sake, man, tell them I forced you." He started toward the master's study, and over his shoulder said, "They'll believe it when they see Biggers's body. Merrill, go with him and make sure that my wishes are done. I'll meet you both at the servants' entrance in twenty minutes." He didn't wait to see them go to do his bidding. Instead he walked briskly toward the master's study.

He needed money to get to port and buy passage to India in suitable splendor. There he'd hidden a good portion of the Edmondson fortune in his own name. He liked to be prepared; he'd always known something like this could happen. Just not so . . . publicly.

He set his teeth. He'd always thought he could get away with anything. He'd despised men who got caught committing their crimes. Yet here he was, running like a dog.

The drapes in the master's study were tightly drawn. The shouting from the servants and the guests was almost undetectable in here. Harrison stood quietly, allowing his eyes to adjust to the dim light. He remembered this room well. Nothing about it had ever changed. The carpet was thick, the furniture heavy, and everything was arranged to impress any unfortunate fool called to report to the marquess of Northcliff.

In Harrison's youth, his father had sat behind the great desk and expressed his disgust with his sly younger son.

Then when Father died, Harrison's brother had taken his place and dispensed obligation with a shovel and reward with an eyedropper. Once Lady Andriana had disappeared, even those small rewards had ceased.

But Harrison had spent plenty of time in the study alone in the dark sniffing out its secrets, and he knew them well. Going to the desk, he opened its locked drawer with his private key. He riffled through the contents, and when his hand touched the stack of bound bills, he easily recognized the feel of money—and this was a lot of money. The pile created an unsightly lump in his pocket, but he was willing to bear the discomfort.

Going to the portrait of the third marquess, he took the painting off the wall, set it on the floor, and smiled to see the metallic gleam of the wall safe. He turned back the corner of the old, softly tinted Oriental rug, picked up the key, and fitted it in the safe's lock. He reached into the dark depths . . .

And he heard a sound behind him.

He whipped around, fists up.

No one. He scanned the room. There was no one here. Everything looked exactly the same. "Come out!" he said sharply.

No response. The room settled into silence. He let out his pent-up breath. He was jumpy, that was all. This whole ordeal had upset him, and no wonder. It wasn't every day he killed not one, but two men.

Well. At least he hoped he had killed Biggers. The interfering fool deserved death.

But look. There on the desk. He hadn't noticed it before. A pistol gleamed in the faint light that shone through the crack in the curtains. His own pistol!

Merrill must have placed it there. But when?

Again he scanned the room, but *no one* was there.

"Stupid," he muttered, not knowing whether he spoke to his imagination or everyone else in the world. Nervousness must be making him imagine threats where none existed.

Again he reached into the safe. He found the bag

right away, heavy with coins. Pulling it out, he weighed it in his hand.

Gold guineas, of course, the marquess of Northcliff would have nothing else, and lots of them.

Perfect.

He stuffed his pockets until they sagged under the weight. He felt satisfaction as his waistcoat hung heavy against his belly and for the first time since the unfortunate incident, his spirits rose. He was going to get away with this.

Then someone, some witless bastard who hid behind the drapes, flung them wide. Sunshine streamed in. Harrison blinked in sudden blindness and leaped for the desk. He groped for the pistol.

A man stood silhouetted against the light. It looked like . . .

"Jermyn?" It wasn't possible. After the fall he'd taken, he had to be dead.

But the little pustule answered, "Yes, Uncle," and stepped into the room.

Harrison aimed the gun.

"Are you sure you want to shoot me?" Jermyn asked in an interested tone. "You've already knocked me off the parapet and over the cliff. This seems a little excessive—and I guarantee the noise will bring the guests and servants running."

"How the hell did you live?" Harrison's finger twitched with the need to fire.

"When one goes over the cliff, one needs only some padding and to know where to land. Unfortunately for me, the storm ripped some of the cliff away and I got a few bruises." Jermyn's face came into focus as he prowled toward the desk.

Harrison saw a long scratch marking his cheek, but he looked remarkably, disgustingly healthy.

Defeat stared Harrison in the face. God knew, between his father, his brother, and Andriana, he'd seen defeat enough times before. But he never thought to see it staring at him through Jermyn's eyes. All that was left was to parlay his rout into something besides a gibbet.

"Can we make a deal, nephew?" He thought he could depend on Jermyn's word. The boy had the same silly ideas about honor as his father.

"It depends on what you do with that gun," Jermyn answered. "Keep in mind, Walter has been detained, your valet is dead—"

"Dead?" That was a shock.

"He tried to resist me, and he is quite dead."

If that was true, then his nephew was quite capable of defending himself, for Merrill had a way with fists and every other weapon.

"The guests are streaming back to the house, and last but not least, *I* have every reason to be incredibly angry at you." Jermyn smiled as he paced, a young, vital, vibrant and handsome man who Harrison hated with more virulence than even he had hated his own brother.

"I suppose that you do." Slowly Harrison lowered the pistol—but he didn't take his finger off the trigger. At this moment, the bullet inside was his only bargaining chip.

"Not for the reasons you imagine. Not because you

fell into my trap and tried to kill me in full view of all my guests. I can't be angry about that, can I?"

"You outsmarted me, nephew." A little flattery couldn't hurt. Harrison wouldn't make it out the door, much less off the estate. Not unless Jermyn allowed him to go.

"No, you should know that the waves ripped into the base of the cliff. Some of the caves collapsed. One of them in particular, Uncle." For a moment, Jermyn halted and looked directly at Harrison. "When I jumped, the ledge I was aiming for crumpled. I barely caught myself on the rock. While I was dangling there, I noticed . . . that a cave below had opened up. The roof was gone. Most of the stones were gone. The only thing left was—"

"Andriana," Harrison blurted. "You found Andriana."

There it was. The betrayal. Jermyn recognized it at once. Uncle Harrison knew exactly what Jermyn had found on the cliff. Satisfied with his uncle's guilt, Jermyn started pacing again. "Yes. I found my mother's body." The pistol weighed down his belt, but Jermyn couldn't grab it, pull it out and aim it before his uncle shot. Instead he counted on the surprise of the short, sharp knife he held hidden in his palm. "She's only a skeleton, her scarlet gown hidden by a man's black cloak."

Cunning intelligence replaced the blank shock in Harrison's eyes. "Then how do you know it's her?"

"Strands of her hair are still connected to her skull— and as you recall, dear Uncle, the mahogany color is the same as mine." Jermyn circled the desk, stepping lightly. He never kept still, pacing, turning, watching Harrison.

"Tsk, tsk." Harrison managed a fair imitation of sympathy. "If this is true, then I extend my sincerest sympathies, but why are you telling *me?*"

"Because before you pushed me you told me I only had to fall once. That is the comment of a man who knows." Jermyn had come up from the cliff by the narrow path, determined to confront his uncle and get the whole story, but he wasn't stupid. He wasn't going to die here. This afternoon he had lost his temper and sent away the only woman who mattered to him. No, he wasn't going to die here. He was going to live long enough to ride after Amy, find her, and tell her she had been right all along.

Whatever sins, if any, Amy had committed against her sister were more than balanced by his lack of faith in his mother. If Amy would forgive him, he'd promise to make her happy for the rest of her life. He'd beg. He'd plead. He'd grovel, because his life was worthless without her.

"That statement would never stand up in court. You know it's true." Harrison said.

"It's *your* cloak, uncle. Your best wool cloak. I recognize it. I remember that when Mama disappeared, you had 'lost' yours. I remember how odd I thought it that a grown man should lose his cloak and think the matter worth discussing when I had lost my mother and couldn't bring her back." Those moments, all those moments of the time following his mother's loss were etched in Jermyn's mind by agony. Jermyn recalled his father's stoic grief, his own childish bewilderment. "Why did you kill her? What did it profit you?"

"Profit?" Harrison laughed harshly. "That was exactly it. Andriana was so beautiful, so gracious . . . so *damned* smart."

Jermyn observed the cold gleam of malice in Harrison's eyes and felt the warmth of the thin, sharp blade in his palm. He had practiced with this knife. He was fast and he was deadly. But first he had to *know* . . .

"She came from peasant stock. She read people so well it was almost eerie. And she read me. You see, I was keeping your father's books and helping myself to a little bit of the fortune. Not much, really, and I'm an Edmondson. I'm due for more than crumbs from the table."

Remembering his father's generosity, Jermyn asked sarcastically, "Were you getting only crumbs from the table?"

"I was *taking* half the profits from the foreign interests. I told your father the business was failing, but it wasn't." In a voice laden with wistful memory, Harrison said, "That was a grand time."

"Except that my mother knew what you were doing." Jermyn strode to the far end of the room. He circled the book stand. He returned and started off again, keeping Harrison off-balance, making him pay close attention to Jermyn's movement and too little to his words.

"She thought the money should all be reserved for her and her brat. For *you*. But when she told your father that she suspected me, he fought with her."

"I remember that fight." It was the last time Jermyn had heard his mother's voice. Strong and angry, she'd scolded his father while Jermyn listened in the corridor outside the closed door.

"So Andriana went off to port to interview the foreign agent and when she got the proof she needed, she came riding back, so lofty, a filthy peasant girl on crusade." Harrison shook his head in disbelief. "She tried so hard to be noble. She came to warn me to stop stealing from the estates or she'd make your father listen. She *warned* me—and when she turned her back on me, I hit her as hard as I could on the back of the head."

Jermyn stood stoic under the lash of words, but inside he ached with anguish and shook with fury. All this time he'd cursed his mother, and she had died brutally, painfully, for an act of honesty and kindness.

And he . . . he had chased Amy away for reasons he didn't now understand.

Harrison continued, "I wrapped her in my cloak and pushed her off the cliff. But she didn't go all the way into the sea. I could still see her. So I crept down that tiny path and shoved her body into one of the caves. That was better than the ocean, because usually the sea gives up her dead." Harrison watched Jermyn as if hoping to see a crack in his façade.

His mother. His poor mother, killed and tossed aside like rubbish. "But the ocean betrayed you anyway. It brought the storm. The storm opened the cave for me to find her." Remembering the storm that had ripped apart his estate, Jermyn could almost believe his mother had directed its fury. "Uncle, it's a bad thing to be at outs with the elements."

"Are you trying to spook me? I don't believe the elements are supernatural. I don't believe in ghosts and I don't believe in fate. The sea rages and roars without consciousness, your mother has never haunted me, and I've never had to pay in like coin for anything I did." Harrison might have lowered the pistol, but still he held it. He held it too tightly and the tiny veins etched his corpulent cheeks with red. Jermyn could see that his uncle was close to one of the few careless moments of his life. Only a fool would shoot Jermyn, but Harrison wanted to. He wanted to so badly.

"You're my only living relative, Uncle Harrison. We're obliged to treat each other fairly," Jermyn said with measured reason.

"Are we?"

"I shall probably have to let you go."

"I don't believe that." But Harrison's killer grip on the gun loosened.

"You'll have to go into exile, of course." Jermyn picked up an Italian glass vase and tossed it in the air as he paced against the back wall, hoping the ornate wallpaper would distort Harrison's aim. "But surely a man of your intentions and experience has a place where you're prepared to flee in case of emergency."

"Yes. Yes, you should let me go. I've been, on the whole, very good to you. The fortune has grown. I've tended it as if it were my own."

"So you have." Amazing how Harrison made himself sound virtuous when in fact he'd tended the money so lovingly because he *planned* to make it his own. "You took control of the family fortune when my father died. What I didn't realize is that after my mother's death, my father no longer trusted you with the family fortune. Mr. Livingstone and Lord Stoke told me that."

"Those worms."

"So I surmise when you got control of it again, you took every precaution to assure yourself an ample income no matter what the circumstances."

"After Andriana's death, I fixed the books, gave all the money back. Your father never knew *anything*, so why did he change his mind about me?" Harrison answered his own question. "It was guilt for driving Andriana away. Or maybe he thought she was right after all. Until the day he died, he never let me alone with the fortune again." Frustration burst from him in a spray of saliva. "Now history repeats itself. You get entangled with some pretty thing, that Princess Amy, and you get clever. She was in on it, wasn't she? She sent me to your room on purpose."

"Uncle, I don't understand you." That was the part Amy was supposed to play, that of messenger to Harrison, but Jermyn had ordered her away just that afternoon.

"She came and got me, told me a pretty story about how you'd fought and she'd gone to your room and you were drinking—"

In shock and in joy, Jermyn dropped the vase. It shattered at his feet, a spray of cobalt shards that shot across the room and glittered in the carpet.

Harrison jumped. He lifted the pistol and pointed it

at Jermyn. "What the hell's the matter with you? Are you crazy? That was worth over a thirty-seven pounds when it was bought twenty years ago."

Jermyn paid no heed. Was it possible? Amy? Amy had stayed to do as she had promised? But that would mean . . . that would mean she always kept her word regardless of the provocation. That she was more in a woman than Jermyn had ever hoped to meet, much less to have. That Jermyn was wrong, that he would have to grovel to win her back and that he would do gladly, for she was the only woman for him. She was his wife, and he loved her.

He lifted the knife, determined to end the stand-off with Harrison and go to her, when the study door flew open. It banged against the wall.

Amy stormed into the study.

She failed to notice Jermyn, posed against the back wall, but her slender figure was the sweetest thing Jermyn had ever seen. His heart lifted. So it was true. She *hadn't* broken her promise.

With her gaze fixed on Harrison, Amy marched toward the desk, her back straight, her fists clenched. "You miserable little man."

Jermyn's pleasure shattered as surely as the glass vase. Fear and horror took its place.

She was walking into the path of a bullet.

"I'm so glad you've arrived." A satisfied smile curved Harrison's mouth, and he glanced from her to Jermyn. "I'm going to use you to escape."

"What do you mean?" Amy demanded. "You're not

going to escape. I've made sure of that. I've taken the precaution of setting a guard."

Jermyn sprinted toward Amy.

"Nephew, look!" Harrison pointed the gun at her. "When I shoot your pretty little fiancée—not kill her, just wound her, you understand—you'll be so busy trying to staunch the bleeding, I'll have a wonderful chance to get away. So—"

Amy half turned. Saw Jermyn. Her face lit up in wonder and joy.

Jermyn lobbed the small knife at Harrison. He caught Amy around the waist. He threw the two of them to the floor.

But he was too late. He knew he was too late.

He heard the deafening roar of the gunshot, heard the high-pitched scream.

And he tasted ashes and fear.

Chapter 26

*Y*ou're alive. You're alive! Amy tried to speak, but they'd hit the floor hard.

She didn't care. Jermyn was alive!

And running his hands all over her.

"Where are you hit? Amy, where did the bullet hit you?"

The panic in his voice brought her eyes open. She gasped, "Nowhere. I'm fine."

"Are you sure?" Still he moved her arms, her legs, slid his palms over her looking for a wound.

"I'm fine," she repeated. She struggled up on one elbow, grasped his shoulder. "You?"

"I'm . . . going to be all right." He touched her face, a somber glow in his eyes. "Now that you're here."

"Then we've got to get out of here." Mr. Edmondson had shot the pistol. She'd heard it. *Did he have another?* She tried to struggle to her feet.

Jermyn held her still. Looking toward the desk, he listened, then said, "Yes, we need to get out of here."

She heard it, too. From behind the desk, she heard a thrashing, a choking sound.

Jermyn rose. He glanced behind the desk, then turned away. "Come on." He helped Amy to her feet. "You don't want to see."

She heard the cough that signaled the onset of death. And the flailing behind the desk ceased.

Somehow, Mr. Edmondson had been killed.

She recognized the scent of blood and death. Recognized it from the brutal days of her past.

The room whirled slowly. She saw a slash of light as a man pushed the curtains aside and stepped out from the window seat. She saw servants and guests crowding the doorway. She heard a woman shriek, "Oh, thank heavens, Lord Northcliff, you're alive!" Amy reached out to lean on something, but her hand groped thin air. Black veils and red spots crowded her vision—and she fainted.

"Dear God, no!" Jermyn caught her before she hit the floor. "Amy. Amy!"

She lolled in his arms, limp and lifeless, her face colorless, her hair dragging back her head.

The crowd gasped and murmured.

A strange man caught her drooping head and tucked it up on Jermyn's shoulder. "She's all right."

"How would you know?" Jermyn asked fiercely. She looked so . . . lifeless.

"I've seen cases like this before."

Jermyn heard the edge of humor in the fellow's voice, and looked at him sharply. Black hair, strong form, good clothes, good breeding, but tough in a way Jermyn identified and respected. He'd seen him earlier today walking with Amy.

Somehow, this man was a threat. "Are you a doctor?" Jermyn asked sharply.

"No."

"Then get me one—now." He strode toward the door, Amy's limp body cradled in his arms.

The servants fell back, but the aristocrats crowded forward, wanting a look, murmuring, jostling for position, calling his name. Then, viewing the expression on his face, they moved aside. He heard them close in behind him. Behind him, he heard the stranger's voice coolly ordering up a doctor—and a mortician for the body behind the desk.

Then Jermyn forgot about the stranger. Forgot about everything but the woman in his arms.

Amy had collapsed. She remained too still. Never had he imagined that the vital, vibrant woman he loved could be so quiet, so silent. Not even in the face of death.

Jermyn moved swiftly up the long stairway to her bedchamber. His blade had stuck in Harrison's shoulder, but that hadn't killed him. It was the pistol that had backfired—a gruesome irony not lost on Jermyn.

But how, when he'd had all the pistols cleaned, had this one escaped to find its way here, now?

Looking down at the woman in his arms, he realized that he didn't care—as long as she was all right.

As he approached her bedchamber, he found himself once again suddenly and smoothly joined by the stranger. "What do you want?" Jermyn demanded.

"I want to make sure she's well." The fellow walked like someone who believed he had the right to know Amy's condition.

"She wasn't hit with the bullet." Jermyn hoped that was assurance enough.

"Of course not." The stranger spoke with the slightest breath of an accent. "That was never an issue. I stuffed the barrel and I placed the pistol on the desk for your uncle to find."

The sheer nerve of the stranger took Jermyn's breath away. He stopped. Cradling Amy close to his chest, he turned and faced him. "Who are you?"

The stranger bowed. "I'm Amy's prince."

Amy woke in her bed when someone put a dripping wet cloth on her forehead. Goaded and annoyed, she threw it off, flinging it hard across the room.

She heard it smack against something, and a strange voice, a man's voice, cursed in a language she hadn't heard in years.

She didn't care. In tones of acute exasperation, she demanded, "Do you *have* to get me all wet and sloppy?" She wiped water off her face. Opening her eyes, she saw Jermyn leaning over her, his auburn hair glowing in the candlelight, his eyes golden and intent.

At once the events of the day crashed into her mind. Her fight with Jermyn, the farce on the balcony,

Jermyn's plunge off the cliff, Mr. Edmondson's death . . . and overshadowing it all, her joy that Jermyn was alive. He was here, he was alive, and he was hers. He would always be hers.

"Are you all right?" He sat on her bed with her. "You fainted. You scared me half— I thought you had died."

"It wasn't a dream. You're really alive." For the ex-cruciating thirty minutes it had taken her to locate Mr. Edmondson, she had believed that she'd helped kill her love. Instead he was here, breathing, talking . . . be-ing. She stroked the stubborn jut of his chin, the bones of his cheek. Bringing his face down to hers, she kissed him. "I'm the happiest woman in the world."

"Exactly as it should be." He brushed her damp hair back from her face. "Do you feel better now?"

She glanced around her curtained bed in confusion. Why was she here? What had happened? "Your uncle . . . ?"

"Don't think about it," Jermyn quickly said. "The body's been taken away."

"Good. May he find peace wherever he is." Her words were more grudging than they should have been.

"I don't think it's peace he'll find. Not where he's go-ing. When I thought he'd killed you—" Jermyn put his forehead against hers and closed his eyes, and for one long moment, the two of them breathed each other's breath. Then he lifted his head. "He killed my mother, too, and she"—regret and sorrow colored his brown eyes—"she lies in state in the main drawing room."

"Your mother?" Amy was bewildered.

"The body on the cliffs was—"

"Your mother?" Amy struggled to sit up.

Jermyn shoved pillows under her shoulders.

He was trying to care for her as a convalescent—and doing a terrible job. Yet she enjoyed his attention. "Tell me everything."

When he was done, she pressed his hand in hers, for while he'd gained the sweet memory of his mother, he had also just lost her. For the first time in twenty-three years, he knew for sure she was dead and his grief was new again.

He cleared his throat. "Also, Biggers is in bed with a large lump on his head and a larger headache. The guests could leave, but they refuse for fear of missing another morsel of juicy gossip. And"—he moved back so she could look out into the room—"Prince Rainger is impatiently awaiting a report on your health."

Rainger moved into sight. He held a still dripping rag, and a wet spot stained his black jacket.

Ah, it was he she'd hit when she flung the cloth. Extending her hand, she allowed him to kiss it, and for a moment, reflected on how easily the habits of being a princess returned.

He didn't release her hand. Instead he lightly squeezed her fingers, looked into her eyes, and said, "Princess, I want you to tell me everything, no matter how inconsequential, about where Sorcha may have gone."

She blinked at his abrupt demand. "Good evening to you, too, Your Highness."

He frowned at her reprimand. In an imposing tone, he said, "I don't have time for pleasantries. Fate is nipping at my heels."

"That could be said of all of us," she said crisply. She knew how to play the royal role as well as he.

His gaze ran around the expensive room, at the glowing candles, the rich materials, the leaping fire. "I spent seven years in a dungeon so deep and dark I had only rats for companions. I ate gruel once a day. I was beaten on the whims of the man who stole my country. My friends, the men who had supported me, lived and died there. We communicated by tapping on the walls, and I escaped because we dug a tunnel with our fingernails and our spoons. I'm only one of two who lived." He moved closer without seeming to take a step.

She wanted to back away, but the horror of his story held her transfixed.

"I owe those men my life," he said. "I owe them to take back my kingdom from the bastard who rules it now. As soon as you help me, I'll leave this place. I'm racing to save our two countries—*and I need Sorcha to do that.*"

Did she believe him? Yes, he had the look of a man driven to seize destiny by the throat. But did she dare trust him? "I don't *know* anything."

"Then tell me what you suspect—and don't, I beg you, give me false information." He fixed his intense, driven gaze on her. "When I asked where you might be, Clarice sent me on a wild goose chase, but I assure you, the longer Sorcha is alone the more danger she's in."

"So there *are* assassins after us?" Was this the threat Amy and Clarice had feared?

"Yes." Rainger thoughtfully considered her. "But who told you?"

"Godfrey, Grandmamma's courtier, seven years ago."

"There was no threat to you then," he said in clipped tones.

Amy exchanged a look with Jermyn.

"So we suspected," Jermyn said.

"But since I escaped from my prison, I've been hunted." Yet Rainger didn't act like prey. He behaved like a hunter. "Now I must find Sorcha and take her home. She's the crown princess. She's my fiancée. I need to wed her. We need to produce children and create a dynasty."

"Have you thought she might not want to do that?" Amy asked.

"Have you thought that she is a princess and should do her duty? That one of you must do her duty?" In a softer tone, Rainger countered, "Have you thought that becoming the queen might be exactly what she wants?"

Amy remembered Sorcha as a soft, sweet, obedient older sister. Would marriage to this man fire her to steel or melt her like tallow?

Rainger touched the silver cross of Beaumontagne which hung on a chain around her neck. "In any case, helping me will save her life."

"Amy, you have no choice," Jermyn said. "You'll have to trust to Sorcha to decide what she wants and tell the prince. If she's anything like you, he'll not have an easy courtship."

She grinned at him. "Why, my lord, whatever do you mean?"

Jermyn planted his fists on the mattress and leaned toward her, a lascivious smile on his face.

Rainger cleared his throat.

Jermyn straightened and crossed his arms like a guard protecting his mistress.

"All right, listen to me, Rainger." She took a deep breath. "I know nothing for sure. Nothing. But Clarice and I discussed where Sorcha might be, and we thought an abbey seemed the most likely place Grandmamma would stash her. Sorcha's the crown princess, and while it was important for us to be safe, for her it was imperative. But there aren't many abbeys in England, they're far apart, and to reach them is difficult. We started searching in the south and moved north. When we reached the Scottish border, we asked if there were any abbeys in the country. They said no, and treated us like vipers. But I left on a ship from Edinburgh. One of the seamen was from the Highlands, and he said he'd heard that in a hidden vale on an island off the coast was a small abbey called Monnmouth. Perhaps you can find it." Leaning forward, she met Rainger's gaze and touched his hand. "I beg of you, if you find her, save her life. If you find her, let me know."

"I will." He stood, bowed over her hand, and kissed her fingers. "Farewell for now, Princess Amy."

"Farewell, Prince Rainger. Godspeed."

At the door, Rainger turned. A smile slashed his

grim face. "And congratulations to you both on the forthcoming child."

He left the two of them staring after him.

Amy's hand clenched a handful of Jermyn's shirt. "Does he think that I'm—"

"Are you?" Jermyn hadn't realized it before, but now that Rainger had spoken the words, Jermyn remembered her pallor during their fight today, her faint at Harrison's death. It had to be true. Amy was pregnant with his child.

But Amy denied it. "No, of course not! That would be so quick." She placed her hand on her flat belly. "It doesn't happen that suddenly, does it?"

He nuzzled her cheek and grinned. "You are an innocent."

She counted on her fingers. "I've not had my courses since that night in Miss Victorine's basement, but . . ."

When her voice faded, he prompted her. "And you fainted today. Do you faint often?"

"I've never fainted before, but . . . and I was so tired today, but . . ."

He shook with the onset of blessed laughter. Thank God. She was going to have his child. "When you fainted, you scared me past good sense."

"That's obviously not too difficult," she said tartly. She watched him, perplexed, as he laughed.

"A baby. We're going to have a baby." He was exhilarated . . . and she didn't look pleased at all. He sobered. "What's the matter? Did this come too soon? Would you rather have waited?"

"No, but don't you realize what this means?" Her voice faded. "Our marriage is legal. Binding. Eternal."

Now was the time to tell her the truth. "I never intended otherwise."

Still she watched him, a question in her troubled eyes.

Gently but inexorably, he said, "I'm sorry if you wished to be free, but once you placed that manacle around my ankle, I was bound to you."

Sitting up, she tucked her knees under her chin and stared at him with her sea green eyes. "Today, you told me to leave."

Time for confession. "I was . . . angry. I was . . . afraid. I carried you through the wedding arch . . . because I loved you." He felt so uncomfortable. He could scarcely force the words past his throat. "And you didn't love me back."

"You loved me?" How could she look startled when everyone on the isle of Summerwind and in Summerwind Abbey knew the truth? "But you didn't tell me!"

"I didn't know if *you* loved *me.*"

"You tied me up and I still couldn't shoot you. What do you think?"

Her absolute disgust with herself made him laugh, then sober. "I had to force a promise from you to stay. I'm only a dim-witted man, but I know what promises extracted under duress are worth."

"*I* don't make promises unless I intend to keep them."

"I know that now. I knew it then." He hated exposing his sniveling soul . . . but why not? She already knew the truth, and she loved him anyway. "But the old fears don't easily die, and I feared that someday you would walk away from me. It seemed safer to tell you to go than to wait to lose you."

"No. Once I shut the manacle around your ankle, I couldn't walk away from you." A slow smile lifted one side of her mouth, and she repeated his words back to him. "I was bound to you."

"That's right. That chain does tug both ways." His smile faded, and he grew solemn, so solemn she grew alarmed. From his pocket, he pulled a small carved wooden box. "I have something for you."

Her heart thumped hard, then settled into a rapid skipping.

From the box he extracted a ring: gold, simple in design, with an emerald so warm and green, she could have fallen into its depths. It was perfect, the kind of ring that made her think of vows and forever.

"As soon as you kissed me and the manacle was broken, I wrote a letter to my jeweler in London and told him exactly what I wanted." Kneeling beside her on the bed, Jermyn took her hand.

She never cried, but she *must* be pregnant, for at his words, at his gesture, at his tender expression, tears once again filled her eyes.

In a voice so deep and earnest he thrilled her and shook her to her core, he asked, "I've been waiting for it to arrive so that I could ask you—will you marry me?"

"Only"—she struggled to speak without sobbing—"only if the marriage is forever."

"I swear with all my heart." He slid the ring on her finger.

She wiped the tears off her cheeks. She turned her

hand from side to side, letting the emerald sparkle in the candlelight. "But I don't have anything for you."

He laughed and hugged her. "You're giving me the best present in the world. You're giving me a child."

"That's true." An idea struck her, and with mischief and with love, she said, "And tomorrow, I will present you with your manacle as a reminder that *I* know how to bind a man to my side."

"It's broken," he reminded her.

"I'll get you a new one—and this one will not break." She grinned. "And that's another promise I will keep."

Epilogue

The harvest moon rose huge and orange in the clear sky over the isle of Summerwind. The moonlight bathed the hills and the village, lit sparks on the ocean and illuminated the feast laid out on rough plank tables on the hill above the village. It shown on the faces of the older villagers as they groaned and patted their bellies and on the younger villagers as they danced to the fiddles and drums before the enormous bonfire. Red sparks snapped skyward, and the scent of wood smoke and roasting oxen drifted on the breeze.

Jermyn leaped onto the platform where the humble quartet played. The music sputtered to a halt. Vicar Smith shouted for silence. The villagers stopped dancing, stopped talking, and cheered to see their lord and the provider of their feast standing before them.

Jermyn lifted his mug to Mertle, to Vicar Smith, to Mrs. Kitchen and John, and finally to Amy and Miss Victorine, seated together at the banquet table.

He shouted, "Six months ago on a blustery spring day a girl with poison-colored eyes served me a brew that knocked me unconscious."

The villagers cheered, lifted their own mugs filled with ale, and toasted their lord.

"And since I awoke with a manacle around my ankle, nothing has been the same."

Once again, the villagers cheered, lifted their own mugs filled with ale, and toasted their lord.

Amy grinned to see Jermyn weaving a little. The ale was pungent and he had been drinking since late afternoon—drinking, dancing with her and every other woman in the village, singing in a tuneful baritone, and playing games. *Rough* games. He'd been soundly trounced in the rowing races, beaten everyone except Pom in the wrestling matches, and almost dropped the massive pagan stone on his foot during the boulder throw. Now he was stripped down to his shirt and pants. He was almost indistinguishable from the other villagers. Dirt and grass stains streaked his shirt and his face, and from the expressions of adoration sent his way, Amy knew he'd redeemed the neglect of too many years.

He continued, "Because of that brew, I was soon to wear a much heavier restraining device—a wedding ring."

"Ooooh." The amused villagers craned their necks to look at her.

"We can walk backward through the wedding arch," she shouted back.

The villagers nudged each other.

"Explain that to our son," he answered.

Gently Miss Victorine rubbed the growing mound of Amy's belly. For the first three months of his existence, the baby had made its presence known with a wrenching fatigue, a daily morning sickness, and a sudden increase in the size of her waist. Now she felt the baby shift under the weight of Miss Victorine's hand, and she smiled to see Miss Victorine's surprise.

Miss Victorine smiled back. The elderly lady's increasing frailty had been countered by better meals, Mertle's daily care and a respected position at Jermyn and Amy's wedding—their second wedding—in the chapel at Summerwind Abbey five months ago. Now the dear lady pushed the drooping crown of yellow chrysanthemums further up on her forehead, and Amy's throat closed with sentimental tears to see how she glowed.

"You—everyone here—knew that Miss Victorine and my Princess Disdain had imprisoned me in their cellar. None of you did anything to help me." Jermyn managed to look stern—for about half a minute. Then he grinned. "Thank you so much. Without your severity, I would surely be dead of my uncle's evil machinations."

"Here, here!" Vicar Smith called. Everyone turned and stared at him, and he said impatiently, "That's the right spirit, to recognize that we saved his life."

"Exactly so." Jermyn again grew sober. "My imprisonment taught me a great many things about myself that I didn't enjoy learning. In the past I've been irresponsible, lazy, and foolish, imagining that because of the tragedy in my past, I deserved to be all those things and worse. But while I was held in the cellar, I learned a different way to think. In the way Miss Victorine always placed my comfort ahead of her own, I learned graciousness. With Princess Amy's constant and kind praise—"

Even Amy laughed at that.

"—I learned I had stolen from the very people who helped raise me. And from the hours spent alone, I learned that accomplishing something, even a small task, can fill a dark hour. Most of all"—he took a deep breath—"I learned to doubt what I'd always believed, that my mother had betrayed her family. I had no concrete reason to doubt my conviction, yet as I grew to know people of principle, I recalled my mother's kindness, her generosity, and her love. My mother's body now lies next to my father in the Northcliff plot on this island, and I thank you, all of you"—his gaze sliced toward Amy—"for helping me discover the truth."

The women wiped tears off their cheeks to see their lord so earnest and grave.

Lady Northcliff's funeral had been a solemn occasion, attended by the greatest aristocrats and the most humble of fishermen. All of them told Jermyn that they had never believed ill of his mother, that they always suspected foul play.

Jermyn pretended to believe them. It did no good to do otherwise.

Amy had remained at Jermyn's side every moment, holding his hand, sharing his grief in a way no one else could.

Because for her, the funeral for Jermyn's mother had been the chance to formally mourn her father. The black crepe, the mournful songs, the lowering coffin— they were symbols of love and of death, and she cried for Lady Northcliff and for King Raimund in equal parts, washing away bitterness with her tears.

Harrison Edmondson's funeral had been much smaller and attended by only his friends—that was, no one.

Now Jermyn's voice swelled. "Most of all, I thank Princess Amy, my Princess Disdain, for teaching me how to have faith in an old dream. She taught me what it means to love forever. Thank you, Amy. Thank you, my love."

Amy smiled a wobbly smile—and realized with horror she was crying. Not little ladylike sobs, either, but big gulping uncontrollable gasps of sentiment. It happened all the time now because *apparently* carrying a baby made a woman *act* like a baby. But to see Jermyn without the cynical mask he'd first worn, to hear him declare in front of everyone that he loved her and that she was responsible for his happiness, and to know that he had given her what she needed, too, a home, a passion, and a soul mate . . . well, maybe that was worth sobbing about.

The villagers chuckled and nudged each other. Miss Victorine hugged Amy and offered her handkerchief.

Jermyn watched with an odd, crooked smile when at last Amy fought back the last of her tears and raised her head.

"Finally," he said, "I want to show the proof that I learned my lessons and will never forget them." Reaching into his pocket, he pulled out a small piece of handwork and lifted it so that the moonlight stuck a thin, flat, ragged, rounded circle of pale twine lace and tiny blue beads. He dangled it before them, his expression expectant.

The women broke into a round of applause.

The men looked puzzled.

"It's a collar," Jermyn told them helpfully.

Amy stifled a grin. The lace collar was too small for her or him, oddly shaped and out-of-round. But Jermyn looked so proud of himself, and he brought it to her. Kneeling before her, he offered it, and even in the moonlight she could see his eyes shining. "It's for the baby. For her christening."

Ragged, oddly shaped, out-of-round . . . made with his own hands in odd moments, in private hours, at times she'd imagined he was out riding. The collar would rest around the baby's neck at the most important moment of her first year, solid proof that her father loved her . . . and loved her mother. As Amy accepted the collar, her chin trembled. "Thank you. It's beautiful. It's just . . ." She stared into Jermyn's eyes, so overcome with tenderness for this tall, broad, magnificent man she could scarcely speak. "Thank you."

Taking her hand, he kissed her fingers. "You're so beautiful."

"That's right." She sniffed, fighting back the constant surges of emotion that sent her hurtling to a vale of tears. Happy tears, but still tears. "I am, and you're lucky to have me. Now go on." She shoved at his shoulders. "Get me some of Miss Victorine's plum cake before it's all gone."

He grinned and stared into her eyes. He knew that later, she would *show* him how she felt about him.

She watched him walk away, and without looking at Miss Victorine, she asked, "Did you hear me go downstairs that night?"

"Dear?" Miss Victorine did an admirable imitation of a confused old woman. "Downstairs where? When? Whatever do you mean?"

"Um-hm." Amy shot her a lethal glance and caught her smiling without an ounce of confusion on her face. "And did you deliberately encourage me to kidnap him knowing full well he was irresistible?"

"Now, dear, you know when you get the bit between your teeth there's no stopping you. No one, certainly not me, could have imagined that Harrison would refuse to pay the ransom and leave Jermyn in our care for days. And don't you think that *irresistible* is a very strong term?"

"No, and you didn't answer my question."

"Oh, dear." Miss Victorine gazed toward the table loaded with cakes and pies, and shook her head. "That's too bad. It appears my plum cake is already gone."

Jermyn was making his way back, empty-handed, and Amy experienced a profound irritation because not only did she like Miss Victorine's plum cake, right now she *needed* a piece of Miss Victorine's plum cake. When Jermyn stopped to talk to Mrs. Kitchen, Amy pushed herself away from the table and stood up. "I feel as if someone has been manipulating me for months."

"I feel as if *manipulate* is an exaggeration, dear," Miss Victorine said.

"Oh, really." Amy pulled a disbelieving face. "Just last month Jermyn heard of a spa reputed to bring health and an easy birth to pregnant women. I thought that sounded stupid and superstitious, so he managed to get me to there without me suspecting a thing. Without ever mentioning the name of the place!"

Mertle stood up with her and helped Miss Victorine to her feet. "Yer Ladyship, we'll see if we can find ye a piece of plum cake hiding in the crowd." She looked down at herself, hugely swollen with child. "Two pieces."

"Three," Miss Victorine said.

Amy strolled along the tables, her gaze darting from place to place, looking for the elusive plum cake. "I sometimes wonder if I'll ever do anything of my own free will again."

"I understand how ye must feel." Mertle watched the men with narrowed eyes as if she was sure one of them hid the treasured cake. "Especially when ye realize how neatly his lordship maneuvered ye into marrying him and thinking ye could leave in a year."

Amy's feet suddenly tangled beneath her. She stumbled to a halt. "What do you mean?"

"Did m'lord neglect t' tell ye?" Mertle smiled saucily. "The marriages performed under the wedding arch always last."

"Why?" Amy suspected she wasn't going to like this.

Vicar Smith stood close, and he must have agreed for he frowned at Mertle. "Woman, you talk too much."

Mertle ignored him. "Because the wives are always with child by the end the year. 'Tis said that years ago, long before that rock was a wedding arch, the pagans worshipped it because it gave fertility." She smoothed her hand over her bulging belly. "Pom and I got this babe by walking beneath the arch."

"That rat." Amy watched Jermyn as he made his way through the crowd toward her, shaking hands as he came. He'd carried her through the wedding arch, but he'd acted as if it was possible to dissolve their union if they weren't compatible. And all the time he'd known . . .

He walked up and tried to sneak his arm around her.

"You manipulative, conniving, deceitful rat." She smacked him.

Jermyn looked around for an explanation.

"Mertle told her about the wedding arch," Vicar Smith explained.

"Oh." Jermyn viewed Amy's stubbornly outthrust chin and smiled with all his charm. "But darling, that's superstition. You said you don't believe in superstition." He tried to sneak his arm around her again.

She smacked him again. "The wedding arch is superstition, yet you declared we were married after we passed under it, so it would appear *you* believe in the superstition."

"Hm." He stroked his chin. "You have me there."

Miss Victorine patted her hand. "My dear girl, is it not more flattering to think that he cared enough to coax you, yet was never willing to take the chance of losing you?"

"Miss Victorine, whose side are you on?" Amy asked.

"Yours, dear. I want you to be happy." As happy as Miss Victorine looked now.

Jermyn glanced over Amy's head toward the harbor. His eyes widened, and his vibrant aura of anticipation blossomed into something different. Something solid and satisfied. "Ah. Here comes your wedding gift now."

Miss Victorine turned to look. So did Mertle. As if they saw the signal, the band stopped in the middle of a lively dance tune, and changed to a slower, more sentimental melody. The villagers drifted toward them, drawn by the promise of a spectacle.

Amy tried to look, too, but Jermyn caught her and covered her eyes. "Not yet," he said.

"What is it?" Everyone was behaving with such keen expectation. What could it be?

He didn't answer. He turned her around to face the harbor, keeping her eyes covered, and slowly walked her forward.

"Why can't you tell me?" She shuffled along.

"Because then it wouldn't be a surprise."

"I don't like surprises." She suspected she sounded surly.

In direct contrast, Jermyn sounded sprightly. "Don't worry, it doesn't matter if I carry you through the wedding arch again, you're already pregnant. Almost there. Almost there." He stopped her, held her still. "All right. Now look."

He removed his hands, and she looked.

They stood at the crest of the hill overlooking the harbor. Pom towered above and behind the two people who walked up the road toward her. The man was a stranger—no, not a stranger, but almost a stranger: tall, broad, dark, with a hooked nose.

But the woman: petite, blond, carrying a baby . . . she walked steadily, her gaze fixed on Amy, her smile irrepressible.

Amy blinked. She stared. It was impossible, yet . . . recognition and belief arrived in a rush. "Clarice!" She ran. She screamed. "Clarice!"

Clarice handed the baby to the stranger and raced toward Amy.

The sisters met. Clarice's arms enclosed Amy. Amy's arms enclosed Clarice. Amy laughed and cried. Clarice laughed and cried. They drew back, looked at each other in the light of the big moon.

Amy saw the beloved, familiar, beautiful features. "Oh, Clarice. I've missed you," she choked. "So much."

"I've wondered every day where you were, what you were doing. I prayed you were safe." With trembling fingers, Clarice stroked Amy's hair.

"I shouldn't have left you. That was wrong of me. I'm sorry." The apology came easily, more easily than Amy could ever have imagined. "But you taught me well. I was never in trouble. I'm fine."

Clarice smiled through her tears. "You are! I know." She laid her palm on Amy's belly. "And now this!"

"I did get in a *little* trouble," Amy admitted.

The others gathered close. Everyone chuckled.

Turning to Jermyn, Amy fiercely hugged him. "You've made me so happy."

"It's fair that I should return your kindness," he said in her ear, and for one precious moment of connection, he held her tightly. Then, arm in arm, they faced the others.

A flurry of introductions ensued. Clarice exclaimed over Jermyn, charming him without effort. Amy remembered the man at her sister's side—Robert MacKenzie, earl of Hepburn. Her sister's husband, the father of her baby, and a man who in Scotland had frankly frightened Amy. But holding the sleeping baby made him almost . . . approachable.

"The day I got your letter, I was so happy. I would have come at once, but . . ." Clarice gestured toward the baby.

"Oh, let me see!" Amy peered into the little face, smoothed her hand over the fuzzy head. "How beautiful. Is it a . . . boy? A girl?"

"Her name is Sorcha." Clarice's voice was heavy with sadness.

Amy glanced up. "Have you heard from her? Have you heard from our sister?"

Clarice shook her head. "Nothing."

"Prince Rainger found me," Amy said. "I told him that we thought she was in an abbey."

"Robert looked throughout the Highlands, trying to find her." Clarice took the baby into her arms and cradled her as if the weight of the small, warm body brought her comfort.

"I found nothing," Robert's voice reflected his frustration. "If there is an island abbey, it's well hidden."

"He said"—Amy's voice wavered—"Rainger said her life was in danger."

"If that's true, Rainger is the man who will protect her." Jermyn sounded absolutely confident.

Robert nodded.

Amy and Clarice drew comfort from the men's conviction.

"Come up to my cottage and have your reunion." Miss Victorine put an arm around each of the sisters and led them forward. "I made an extra plum cake just for you."

Four weeks later, Prince Rainger of Richarte stood outside an abbey in the isolated outer island of the Scottish Highlands. He stared up at the lichen-covered stone walls, observed its formidable gate and the tiny, high-set windows. Smiling grimly, he tied a handkerchief over his head and one eye, and prepared to kidnap his bride.

Welcome to the world of
New York Times bestseller

"Christina Dodd keeps getting better and better!"
New York Times bestselling author Debbie Macomber

"Nobody writes historical romance better."
New York Times bestselling author Kristin Hannah

"Christina Dodd is everything I'm looking for
in an author—sexy and witty, daring and
delightful. She's one of my all-time favorites!"
New York Times bestselling author Teresa Medeiros

"Sheer enjoyment."
USA Today bestselling author Jill Marie Landis

"Treat yourself to a fabulous book—
anything by Christina Dodd."
New York Times bestselling author Jill Barnett

"Classics never go out of style. A little black dress,
a string of pearls and a Christina Dodd romance."
New York Times bestselling author Lisa Kleypas

**Don't miss a moment of the passion and
laughter Christina Dodd brings to life
in all of her treasured series. . . .**

The Lost Princesses

Once upon a time three young princesses—Sorcha, Clarice, and Amy—were sent away to different homes where they would be safe from war, but were lost. Their only hope is that Prince Rainger, Sorcha's betrothed, who has traveled to England in search of them, will succeed.

Meet Clarice in
Some Enchanted Evening

Meet Amy in
The Barefoot Princess

And look out for Sorcha's story available soon!

The Governess Brides

Rules of Surrender

Determined to make her fortune and gain control of her life, Lady Charlotte Dalrumple helps found the Distinguished Academy of Governesses and agrees to take on the agency's first, most onerous commission . . .

Rules of Engagement

Lord Kerrich's position in Queen Victoria's court is imperiled by his rakish reputation, so he attempts a desperate ruse. He hires Miss Pamela Lockhart to find him an orphan to adopt and give the patina of respectability. However, he quickly discovers himself loving the irrepressible child—and seducing her beautiful, wary governess.

Rules of Attraction

Hannah Setterington has decided to retire from governessing, become a paid companion to an elderly lady in the country, and lead a more restful life. But when she arrives at the rustic manse, the place seems awfully gloomy. And all the servants are most improperly whispering about the master. His strange moodiness . . . his coldness . . . and the rumor that he killed his wife. But when Hannah sees the man in question, she instantly knows that he has not killed his wife. How? She *is* his wife.

In My Wildest Dreams

Gently bred Celeste had only one dream: to capture the heart of Ellery Throckmorton. But what chance did a gardener's daughter have of charming one of the wealthiest gentlemen in England? Sent away to be trained as a governess, Celeste returns home refined, educated, and sophisticated. A captivating combination for both Ellery *and* his brother, John . . .

Lost in Your Arms

Enid MacLean is finally living a peaceful life when she receives word that an explosion has injured the husband she hoped she'd never have to see again. Reluctantly, she agrees to do her duty but, except for his distinctive green eyes, the man she nurses back to health is not the man she remembers. From the depths of his amnesia, he reaches out for the woman he believes is his wife, tempting her with ardent words and a reckless passion she finds unable to resist. The last time, marriage cost her her happiness. This time, love could cost her more.

My Favorite Bride

Governess Samantha Pendregast arrives at the grand estate of Silvermere to take charge of six rebellious girls, and at once sees that the children aren't the only ones who need to be tamed. She wants her new employer, the dashing Colonel William Gregory, to spend more time with his daughters . . . and, if she's truly honest, with her as well. And while William is more than happy to satisfy her desire, allowing herself to fall for him would mean risking a secret she dares not reveal. . . .

My Fair Temptress

Learn how to flirt in ten lessons or less!

Miss Caroline Ritter, accomplished flirt, acknowledged beauty, and ruined gentlewoman, offers lessons to any rich, noble lord too inept to attract a wife. Send your request to the Distinguished Academy of Governesses. Please, absolutely no devastatingly attractive men with hidden agendas . . .

Switching Places

Scandalous Again

While playing cards with a mysterious blackguard, Lord Magnus lost everything—his fortune and his estates. Luckily, his opponent offered him a deal. He would put up the estates and fortune against the lord's daughter Madeline's hand in marriage. Unluckily, Lord Magnus lost, and now Madeline is to be married within the fortnight. It's up to Madeline's formerly jilted fiancé to help her family out of the mess her father has made, and remind her what true love feels like.

One Kiss From You

Eleanor de Lacy must have been mad to agree to exchange identities with her stronger-willed cousin. She would never convince Remington Knight of the folly of this union—especially since the man seemed so determined for it to take place. Worse still, she finds Remington dazzlingly attractive and she's charmed by his attempts to seduce her, even though he believes she is already his. But if he ever learns of Eleanor's deception, this daring rogue will wreak havoc . . . upon her reputation and her heart.

The Princess Series

The Runaway Princess

When Miss Evangeline Scoffield comes into her inheritance after a lowly existence as an orphan in England, she's able to live the good life: expensive gowns, glittering jewels, expensive trips abroad. Suddenly sweet Evangeline is a fine lady of indeterminate background. But she finds that acquiring a new identity can lead to trouble when a handsome stranger comes into her life and tells her that not only is he a prince, but they are to be married.

Someday My Prince

Princess Laurentia leads a fairy-tale life, attending lavish balls and wearing beautiful gowns. But after the ball is over, Laurentia finds herself getting into bed . . . alone. She dutifully agrees to choose a husband, but when she casts her eyes over her sea of suitors, she doesn't see a single man worthy enough to claim her—until she is swept off her feet by Dominick, soldier of fortune, black sheep of his family . . . and the man hired to protect her.

The Well Pleasured Series

A Well Pleasured Lady

Prim, plain, desperately virtuous Lady Mary Fairchild stared at the seductive gentleman and wondered—did he remember the particulars of the night they met? Surely not. In the ten years since, she had abandoned her youthful impetuousness and transformed herself into a housekeeper, disguising her beauty beneath a servant's dour clothing and determined to conquer the passions of the past. But Sebastian Durant, Viscount Whitfield, did recognize her as a Fairchild, and when the restraint between them shattered and pleasure became an obsession, Mary had to trust a powerful man who could send her to the gallows . . . or love her through eternity.

A Well Favored Gentleman

For years Ian Fairchild yearned for the cherished estate where he passed his childhood. After being displaced, he can secure his rights to the manor only through marriage with the enigmatic Lady Alanna. But the exquisite hellion has warned him at knifepoint to leave her house. Now with skill and charm, Ian must penetrate the lady's defenses and boldly lay claim to her body and spirit. But first he must prove himself worthy, and he holds the power to enchant and delight, inflame and inspire . . . and to convince this lady her true home is in her lover's heart.

The Knight Series

Once a Knight

Only a threat to her life can make strong-willed Lady Alisoun hire Sir David of Radcliffe to protect her castle. Although he had once been a hero and master swordsman, the good life has been a little too good, and his warrior skills have become as rusty as an old suit of armor. But he needs the money to support his motherless daughter, and Alisoun is in no position to haggle. At Alisoun's grand estate, Sir David does indeed discover mischief-makers afoot. But the danger that surprises him most is how quickly his own well-protected heart is falling to a fiery damsel who brings him to his knees.

A Knight to Remember

Fallen from grace and sheltered in a convent, Lady Edlyn is a skilled herbalist forced to secretly tend the wounds of Hugh de Florisoun. A knight renowned for his prowess on the battlefield and in the bedchamber, Hugh is no stranger to Edlyn's heart. Using the healing magic of herbs and the power of remembered love, Edlyn saves the warrior's life. Now Hugh claims this brazen beauty for his own. But Edlyn, cynical in the ways of men, denies him—even as her flesh burns with unaccustomed fire. Passion becomes their battleground, with no mercy given . . . in a bold age when danger and desire go hand in hand.

cratic Spaniard unleashed a passion the Boston beauty vowed to resist. De la Sola's blood ran hot for the bewitching widow of his most trusted American ally. Consumed by love and honor-bound to protect her, he relentlessly pursued her into the California wilderness. Together, they followed their destinies. From a magnificent hacienda to a glittering cave carved deep in the mountainside, they searched for a golden treasure—and discovered a priceless love.

Move Heaven and Earth

Miss Sylvan Miles dreaded the moment she'd see Lord Rand Malkin again. Once a dashing rogue, he's returned from battle a changed man. Sylvan, too, has suffered. Sharpened by scandal and tragedy, she vows to heal Rand's body and spirit. But when Sylvan arrives at Clairmont Court, the man she encounters is far from the shattered ex-soldier she had expected. But Sylvan isn't fooled by his bravado and sets out to break down his defenses . . . while she fortifies her own against temptation.

Outrageous

Griffith, battle-seasoned warrior and the king's most trusted emissary, expected to find a shallow, vain, frivolous woman at Wenthaven Castle. After all, as lady-in-waiting to the queen, lovely Lady Marian had been in a position of privilege, yet she had been banished from the court. And the rumors were that she had given birth to an illegitimate child.

But when he arrived, Griffith found Lady Marian to be strong, intelligent, and fiercely protective of the young baby in her custody . . . and very suspicious of him. If he were smart, the knight would just deliver the message with which he had been entrusted. Instead, he longs to delve into the mystery that is Marian, to discover what she so desperately fears—and why he so improperly wants her.

The Greatest Lover in All England

Rosie lived a knave's life on the streets of London, singing for her supper with a ragtag band of actors who were always one step ahead of the law. It was a credit to her thespian skills that everyone thought she was a boy. But even Rosie couldn't fool a shrewd observer like Sir Anthony Rycliffe, a dangerous and exciting man with a few secrets of his own.

Now she had to play the most difficult role of her career offstage—as Rycliffe's wife in an arranged marriage. Her only obstacle was the devilish Rycliffe, wreaking havoc with her senses each time he kissed the well-rehearsed smile off her lips.

Priceless

She was one of the celebrated Sirens of Ireland, a captivating creature of fiery spirit. Bronwyn Edana stunned titled society with her courageous exploits and daring adventures. Yet in nobleman Adam Keane, she met her match. From the moment they first clashed, the headstrong Bronwyn was swept away by a breathless desire. Betrothed to Adam, a man branded by his haunted past, Bronwyn soon found herself at the center of a shocking conspiracy that could rock the British realm. From the dangerous streets of London to sweeping Boudasea Manor, she followed her most passionate dreams—and risked everything for the only man she would ever love.

That Scandalous Evening

An innocent English miss conceived of it, her hands gliding across the clay, delineating each smoothly defined muscle and sinew, creating a sculpture of the man she worshipped. When the likeness was exposed, along with Miss Jane Higgenbothem's secret tendre for Lord Blackburn, the *ton*'s gleeful contempt sent the lady back to the country in disgrace. Now, a decade later, she's back in London, as a chaperone to her beautiful niece. But to Blackburn, Jane's unwitting model, the cool, reticent spinster is still a challenge. She once made the arrogant rake a laughingstock: So why is he tempted to revive an affair that almost began so long ago, on one scandalous evening?

Hero, Come Back

Two superstar *New York Times* bestsellers—Stephanie Laurens and Christina Dodd—join forces with one exciting rising star, Elizabeth Boyle, to create this sexy anthology with an exciting new theme. In an innovative twist, each author reintroduces a secondary character from a previous book to star in his own story!

Scottish Brides

A land of legend and wild beauty—of clans, lairds, honor, and passion—Scotland forever stirs the soul of romance. Now, in one incomparable volume, four of Avon Romance's bestselling authors—Christina Dodd, Stephanie Laurens, Julia Quinn, and Karen Ranney—present stirring tales of hearts won and weddings to be, featuring a quartet of unforgettable heroines about to discover the rapture of love in a world as untamed as the men they will one day marry!

New York Times bestselling author

Christina Dodd

THE BAREFOOT PRINCESS
0-06-056117-3/$7.99 US/$10.99 Can

Since the powerful and wickedly handsome marquess of
Northcliff has stolen the people's livelihood, Princess Amy
decides to kidnap him for ransom.

MY FAIR TEMPTRESS
0-06-056112-2/$6.99 US/$9.99 Can

Miss Caroline Ritter, accomplished flirt and ruined gentlewoman, offers lessons to any rich, noble lord too inept to
attract a wife.

SOME ENCHANTED EVENING
0-06-056098-3/$6.99 US/$9.99 Can

Though Robert is wary of the exquisite stranger who rides
into the town he is sworn to defend, Clarice stirs emotions
within him that he buried deeply years before.

ONE KISS FROM YOU
0-06-009266-1/$6.99 US/$9.99 Can

Eleanor de Lacy must have been mad to agree to exchange
identities with her stronger-willed cousin. Worse still, she
finds the man she's to deceive dazzlingly attractive.

SCANDALOUS AGAIN
0-06-009265-3/$6.99 US/$9.99 Can

Madeline de Lacy can't believe that her noble father has lost
his entire estate—*and her!*—in a card game.